DO WE HAVE A PROBLEM?

Imin cut the connection and turned to a nearby junior officer. "Find the Narsima Ettranty. Tell him I'll meet him in his office as soon as possible. I'm on the way right now."

Watching the Guard's commander leave, the com tech commented to the woman running the station on his left, "Looks like things are about to get interesting with the raiders, Marta."

She wasn't a history buff. "What do you mean?"

He grinned at her. "You may not know it, but that old boy on the screen was an Imperial Gladius. The Empire's best soldiers."

The grin turned wolfish. "Say you were rampaging across the galaxy devastating Imperial worlds and killing people. One day you turn around and there's a bunch of those guys standing there giving you a dead cold look. That's the Lord Above's way of letting you know you are about to have a really bad day."

AMAZON KINDLE E-BOOKS BY GEORGE OLNEY

FRENCHY series:

FRENCHY

FRENCHY II: Having a Blast

FRENCHY III: Deathcults and Dancers (Forthcoming)

GLADIUS Series:

Guard at the Gates of Hell

Our Doom and Pride

PRINT VERSIONS

Guard at the Gates of Hell

GUARD AT THE GATES OF HELL

By

George W. Olney

This story, greatly expanded and developed, is based on a novella by the author published in ANALOG YEARBOOK II.

Cover by Acapella Book Cover Design.

With gratitude to the folks on Baen's Bar, especially Edith Maor, for their enthusiastic help.

In the end though, this book is dedicated to all of those that have worn the uniform. Been there too.

Contents

I am a Gladius.
I stand guard at the Gates of Hell.
Nothing will pass and harm
   those I am sworn to protect.
My life is nothing.
My duty and purpose are everything.
If my life is called for,
   it will be given gladly.
I go now to face my enemy.
I have seen him, and I know him.
He will not see the dawn.

  -The Oath of the Gladius

CHAPTER 1

LEGIO XV RHIANNONITHI
(RHIANNON'S OWN)
3224 IMPERIAL COMMON ERA

The greatest political structure in human history was dying... and trying to take all of humanity with it.

The grandly misnamed Empire of Ten Thousand Suns really wasn't an empire and it never had more than three thousand planetary systems under its control. Now, after more than a thousand years, it was rotten and collapsing. The Empire had major internal problems, but protected by the Frontier Fleet and the Corps of Imperial Gladius, it was still safe from external threats.

Shangnaman the Mad wanted both military organizations destroyed.

Emperor Shangnaman XI was a paranoid sociopath, a danger to his Court, his people, and what remained of his fragmenting Empire. In an ironic - but probably inevitable - twist, he focused his fears on the Frontier Fleet and the Corps. Shangnaman felt they were too dangerously independent, which made them a threat. He gave orders to destroy the threat. His staff evolved a plan to set Frontier Fleet against the Corps, hoping to kill both. They succeeded in all too many cases.

A surviving - fleeing - fragment of a devastated legion stumbled on a situation in deep space. When they did, they honored the Oath.

Aboard the nearly empty troop carrier, in Tachyon Field Drive but hidden by its suppresser field, there was agonizing frustration on the control deck as the situation unfolded. Staring intently at the big tactical monitor on his bridge, Fleet Lieutenant Albert Kavasos decided the people on the liner were about to die and there was triple damn all he could do about it. That was a Kayelen destroyer preparing to capture the liner. The destroyer wasn't going to damage the big passenger ship all that much; it was too valuable. On the other hand, he doubted the people on board were worth anything to the Kayelen. He didn't know much about the Kayelen navy, but he was certain that destroyer was packing more firepower than the Fleet troop carrier he was currently "commanding".

"There's nothing we can do?"

The soft feminine voice spoke Unispek in the calm, unemotional tones of a Gladius. Kavasos spared the woman a look, secretly glad to turn his eyes from what was happening on the main monitor. He shook his head. "Nothing."

She stood there in the short sleeved khaki blouse and ankle-length flowing skirt of her uniform, with her flat topped, water drop shaped cap worn over long, straight, pale blonde hair. Her cap was canted slightly to one side to show she was a veteran of low intensity combat. The deadly arm dagger of the female Gladius was clamped to her left forearm. Round faced, short, and curvy like all Gladius women, she had the nearly colorless gray eyes of her people. Her dignified professional manner, underlain with the subtle melancholy and deadly aura of the Gladius, would keep anyone but a total madman from calling her "cute".

The contrast between a short curvaceous Gladius woman and her large, muscular male counterpart was something that long ago ceased to surprise Lieutenant Kavasos. On the other hand, he considered both sexes as unemotional as robots and capable of violence on a scale that still awed him. That dagger of hers was not a decoration.

Her measured, expressionless look seemed to be weighing him. Weighing him and finding him wanting. The strain of the last seventy two hours finally got to him, triggered by that look. "Damn it! What the hell do you want me to do!?! We all got out of that mess on Tombele by the grace of the Lord Above! I have forty-six personnel to run a ship that needs a crew of a hundred and nine! Your people are mostly children! In case you've forgotten, this is a troop carrier, with nothing but some 10 centimeasure guns and no armor worth a triple damn!"

He turned back to the screen. "Which is nothing," he continued softly. "Not compared to a destroyer. All we can do is continue on to Niad and hope the base there hasn't already been trashed. If it has, we're all as dead as those people."

Major Camille Paten made no answer. She was only a Centurion 4 herself, a Major with a responsibility that by rights belonged to the legion's Commander. But Legion Commander Poranis was dead with her husband, and Camille's husband, and the rest of the XV Legion, buying time for them to escape the death trap that was Tombele when the New Fleet ships came and the legion's assigned 15th Fleet Support Group joined them, turning their guns on former comrades. Camille was now in command of what was left of the XV Legion, the *Rhiannonithi*, Rhiannon's Own.

Her mind ticked down the personnel roster, a task that was as automatic as breathing to a female Gladius. There were two hundred and seventy five children and teenagers, a hundred and ninety women, and fifteen men. All that was left. Until the attack, the XV Legion had an operational strength of over twenty thousand.

Now, they were escaping to the 10th Fleet Support Group base on Niad, also the current base of the X Legion, Valeria. The only hope Camille could see for the survival of her little group was to find an intact legion. She said a silent prayer that the madness infecting the Empire hadn't touched Niad. If the Valeria was destroyed, a possibility that frequently kept her sleepless, she had no idea what to do next.

She let none of her worry show. There was a situation in front of her that had to be dealt with immediately. Imperial citizens were being attacked by the Predator and it was the duty of a Gladius to protect citizens. It was the Fleet's duty, too.

With what? Fourteen men and a damaged troop carrier that was no match for a corvette, much less a destroyer, in combat?

She glanced sidelong at Lieutenant Kavasos. The tortured set of his shoulders betrayed the direction of his thoughts as he watched the slow, inevitable, capture of the liner. Those on the troop carrier were invisible, safe behind their suppresser screen, and she knew his ship's safety was another torture to the Lieutenant. He was hiding as he watched innocent people - people he was sworn to defend – condemned to death. The Lieutenant was an honorable man, taking the carrier out when the Commander that was its proper captain was either dead or in a new uniform. He deserved well of her. The Fleet, too, had its honor and its charge.

Camille took a deep breath and straightened her spine. They had First Cohort's *brushara,* the legion's Sunburst, a few of the legion's adults and - miraculously - many of the younger children. The legion still lived. It was time, and past time, to start acting like it.

The Predator was out there and the legion, however reduced, still existed. The Oath still held. Do something, Camille, she thought. Slowly, a plan took shape. Thank the Lord Above this was a troop carrier.

"Lieutenant," she began with a soft voice, one that turned softer still as the man turned to face her and she clearly saw the expression on his face. "I understand what you are saying, and I'm not criticizing you."

"But we can't *do* anything!" he nearly yelled, waving his hand at the screen in a gesture of pure frustration. "We can't fight a destroyer." He said his last sentence in a low defeated voice. "We don't have the weapons."

"Yes, we do." She saw the frustration leach away from his eyes, to be replaced by curiosity and hope. "This is a troop carrier. You forget what our primary weapon really is."

The Narsim Clarine Femiam knew what was happening. As a former political leader of the Empire of Ten Thousand Suns, she knew trouble when she was in the middle of it.

She and her daughter Lana were passengers on this ship to Cauldwell, but passengers with a difference. Of average height, elegantly mature with a not quite slim but still graceful carriage, black haired Clarine was the physical embodiment of the Empire's aristocracy. Her rise to the top was aided when opponents underestimated the intelligence, drive, and ambition hidden behind her beauty. A short fashionable marriage had brought her Lana, a teenage version of her mother, and the entry she schemed to get into the inner circles of Court power. Finely honed political ability and a strong instinct for survival kept her there. Until everything blew up.

That instinct for survival led to this trip. A few rumors and a whispered word were enough to tell her she'd made a fatal misstep in that snake pit of intrigue on Central. Emperor Shangnaman thought she was on the wrong side on the Restructuring Question, but that was enough for that paranoid bastard and his Office of Investigations. Clarine shuddered. When OI got you, nobody ever saw you again, even if you were General Secretary of the Progressive Conservative Party. Clarine and Lana were only one jump ahead of pursuers, but that jump and the ones that followed were enough to make it to this antiquated liner headed for the back of beyond.

Clarine shook her head. General Secretary no longer. She was gone from the halls of power. Gone but alive, thank the Lord Above. She and Lana had little enough luggage, but at least she had a strongbox in secure storage with enough bullion and Imperial securities to live comfortably, thanks to the Prog-Comp treasury. She also had a cousin, Matic Ettranty, highly placed on Cauldwell. Once solidly entrenched on Cauldwell, she could start back upward again far enough away from Central to remain unnoticed by the Emperor. Now it was beginning to look as if money and political contacts were moot. Somehow, they'd been tracked.

The cabin door slid open noiselessly and her teenage daughter entered. A younger version of her mother, her classically beautiful face betrayed a tense urgency under fierce control. "Mother," the girl asked in an only slightly shaky voice, "what's happening? What's that vibration? I know something's wrong. What is it?"

Clarine looked at her, wondering how much to tell Lana. What was happening was obvious enough to her. Unless they were very smart or very lucky, they were going to die soon. She decided on the truth. Let the girl have that. "We're being attacked. That vibration is gunfire on the ship's drive field."

"Gunfire? Why?" Tension made Lana's voice flat and curt.

Clarine shook her head. "Pirates. Or whatever. They're trying to collapse our field and capture the ship intact. If the field gets too weak, the crew will drop us into sub-light drive and whoever's doing the shooting will board us."

Lana looked astounded. "Why go sub-light? That's just giving up!"

Her mother's expression was grim. "If the crew didn't decelerate, a crash translation at this speed would kill everyone aboard."

Clarine's voice became brisk. Survive first, worry about everything else later. "That's irrelevant. What we have to do now is figure out how to get out of this. The escape pods might work, but even if we weren't in TFD, we can't eject while that pirate or whatever can see the pod leaving. I think our best bet is to try for one when they board the ship. They'll be too close to see the pod."

Lana's words betrayed the fact she still hadn't completely accepted the situation. "You really think they're going to do that? Board us?"

"If they weren't going to board us," Clarine replied dryly, "we'd be dead right now."

The Kayelen commander was considering boarding action at that moment. His orders were explicit. There were two human females he had to obtain then that liner was his by right of capture.

He reflected that the Empire was not only turning soft, but corrupt as well. His superiors were arrogantly contemptuous of this particular mission, but pleased with the Imperial bounty offered for the two females. A hint of greater concessions after the successful capture pleased them even more. Someone in the human Empire apparently wanted these two badly.

He spared a moment from monitoring the chase to study the solidioptic of the two females. They looked ugly to him. No proper jaw ridges and they totally lacked the feathery topknots that were a sign of Kayelen beauty. Still, they were valuable for some reason. The boarding party would need this representation to identify their quarry. Humans were too weird looking. Best to ensure the right ones were brought back, more or less alive.

11

He ordered the assault boarding tube readied then fell into a reverie of upcoming wealth. Once all but the two designated humans were out the airlock, the whole lovely ship in his screen was his.

He felt uneasy for a moment. For over a thousand years, what he was about to order was as good as a death sentence and racial memories died hard. Still, there was nothing left in that corrupt, crumbling human sphere to threaten him. He was soon going to be rich.

#####

Camille eyed Lieutenant Sharon Ariel and Sergeant Domnik Passal as they stood at attention in front of her. Ariel was in the same uniform and looked much the same as she herself did. A normal female Gladius. The Sergeant was a typical male Gladius: tall, muscular, with short cropped colorless hair under his flat topped, slightly conical duty cap. He was wearing male duty uniform: short sleeved khaki shirt, khaki kilt, and a weapons belt supported by cross straps with a bolt pistol on the right and his compact battle ax, resembling an ancient "tomahawk", and short sword in a double holster on the left. Both sexes wore tractor-presser bracelets that allowed them to control their thrown blades like live things. Camille said, "That's how we're going to do it. Those hell spawn bastards think they can prey on innocents without risk. They're wrong. Any questions?"

They were speaking Copio, the Corps language, and she was carefully studying Sergeant Passal as she asked. There was a problem with him and Camille could see it. Culture and tradition were at war with necessity behind his pale gray eyes. The decurion was relieved to have an officer in command, but Camille suspected he was bothered because Lieutenant Ariel was a female officer. She supposed it worried the decurion to risk a female officer in combat. A woman personified the future of the legion, never risked in battle after she survived her Virgin Mission. Men did the fighting and dying. Women kept the legion alive. That was Sergeant Passal's world. Risking Lieutenant Athan meant risking the legion's future, what they had left of it, in his eyes.

Camille decided the decurion had best get over it. She was prepared for Passal to protest having a female officer to command the little ad hoc unit and she already had her answer ready. Lieutenant Athan was a fully trained Gladius officer - if a bit rusty in combat operations - and she was needed. She was the last junior officer left. She would command, with or without combat command experience. It was just that simple. Sharon Ariel was needed and she was the best choice from the surviving officers.

Passal, only a Decurion 5, was the senior male Gladius left alive in the legion. As such, he had the duty of providing the experience his lieutenant lacked - something a bit above his pay grade - but he was going to do it to make this mission happen. The XV Legion had a duty to the citizens on that liner.

Camille was surprised at the decurion's reply.

"Major", he began, "Lambro and Kain aren't fit for combat. That leaves me twelve men for the operation. Four teams. I'm short enough as is."

Camille nodded. Sergeant Passal had something in mind. Normally, if there were only twelve, twelve would go.

He took a deep breath. "Major, I know you're not going to like this, but I need another team to do this right. We have three Recruits just about ready for their Virgin Mission. Kardo, Smythe and Chofal. Let me have them."

Camille was shocked for a second. A Gladius normally went on his or her Virgin Mission, the first combat mission of all Gladii, at seventeen. The boys he named were years younger than that. Why, Smythe was only fourteen!

Camille closed her eyes for a moment. The boys were too young, but duty to citizens and the legion took precedence. All three were mostly trained. Not fully trained Gladii, but... well enough trained.

It bothered her. Passal was right. He needed another team. She had to give them the best chance she could, but it hurt.

Triple damn Fate! As much as Lieutenant Ariel, those boys represented the future and survival of the legion. But, if the situation was bad enough for Ariel to go, there was reason enough to send them. She replied in a low voice. "Assemble them with your squad, Sergeant."

He saluted and his eyes showed he knew what he was asking - and its price. "Aye. Assembly will be in thirty minutes."

Lieutenant Ariel also saluted. "We'll be ready, Major."

Camille returned the salutes, then added, "Yes, but we are going to need you in the future. *Come back!*"

Sergeant Passal nodded. "That is also in our mission orders, Major."

Thirty minutes later, Camille impassively stood in front of the small formation, hiding her nervousness at the situation with the ability of lifelong discipline. Every survivor of the legion was there in the massive assembly bay, watching and silently sending their support, but she ignored

13

them. The destroyer was close to locking onto the liner and they needed to be moving. Timing was critical to the success of her plan. She regretted the time needed for the inspection, but it was a vital necessity, not a formality. Every Gladius knew time taken checking now meant less to go wrong later, when mistakes and problems could kill. Besides, she had to give them Release.

Lieutenant Ariel marched forward to position herself in front of her superior and salute. "Assault unit ready for inspection, Major."

Camille returned the salute. "Aye."

Sergeant Passal joined them once they marched to the formation and began to walk down the first rank. The troopers were arrayed in standard formation by three man teams, two teams each in the first two ranks and one in the third. Camille noted the boys made up the rear rank team, as befitted juniors.

Ariel and her troops were in combat armor, fully equipped for the drop including B-42 shoulder fired bolt guns resembling the ancient "bullpup assault rifle", holstered pistols, battle axes and short swords hung from their left hips. Their refractive armor and the equally refractive camouflage woven into the cloth of their kilt covers kept the troopers' outlines shifting and blurred, but inspecting men hard to see was an old task for Camille. Visors were up, so she could clearly see the professionally expressionless faces, even the repressed eagerness of the boys.

It amused Camille slightly that Ariel had to wear the standard combat pants of a Gladius woman, or at least she was supposed to be wearing them. Only women in combat training wore the pants universally detested by every female Gladius. She wore them only until her combat mission, the Virgin Mission, was complete, then the pants were burned with great satisfaction. Camille enjoyed the feel of her full skirt and envied the men the regulations that made their kilts combat as well as garrison uniform.

Camille remembered her Virgin Mission and the way she dodged the requirement to wear pants by wearing complete lower body armor. It hid the fact she'd left her pants in garrison. It amused her to note that, while the men wore full upper body armor with thigh guards and greaves under their kilts, Ariel was in full upper - and lower - body armor. Camille was pretty sure what that meant.

Two sets of practiced eyes scanned every trooper as they stepped in front of each one. Gratifyingly, nothing was out of order. Passal was both competent and thorough, a good decurion. Even the boys were properly kitted out, although their less than full growth meant they were probably wearing some adapted portions of women's armor.

14

Ariel escorted her back to the front of the formation, where the two stopped and exchanged salutes. Ariel returned to her position and Camille faced the formation. "All right," she said. "We haven't got any time for speeches. Current situation is that both the liner and the destroyer are sublight and we'll be in normal space by the time you launch. You've all been briefed and Sergeant Passal has done an outstanding job getting you ready in a hurry. You only need to know one thing: The Predator is out there, attacking those we swore to protect. The Predator thinks we can no longer offer that protection.

"I expect you to show the Predator that it's wrong before it dies. Save those people in that liner, then come back. That is your mission."

Ariel saluted, her right arm across her chest, flat hand palm down. "Aye. We have seen our enemy and we know him." She took a knee.

Camille returned the salute and gave the utterly important traditional reply. "He will not see the dawn."

Airel's soft soprano finished the ritual as she rose. "We have release."

Camille gave her final command. "Lieutenant, load your troops on the shuttle."

The Lieutenant stood and did an about face. "Sergeant Passal."

"Aye." He saluted.

"Board the troops."

"Aye."

Gladio alieyo. The battlecry. The Gladius was again coming to protect the weak.

#####

In the shuttle's troop bay, the squad took its places on the long benches that faced each other along the shuttle's walls. The seating made it easy for Passal to see the faces of his men and keep one diplomatically close eye on his new lieutenant. It was her first drop since training, so it behooved him to pay close attention to that most ancient of all noncom responsibilities, Keeping the Lieutenant from Screwing Up, at least until she got her feet under her and the shit started flying. In Passal's experience, junior officers that didn't get themselves killed in the first few minutes generally settled down to do a creditable job and normally survived the fight.

He wasn't really worried about the rest of the troopers. The men were all veterans and the boys were going to be put where they could hopefully live through this triple damned mess. Still - Lord Above help him - he had a new Lieutenant that required his full attention if he wanted her to live through this mosh fuck, three Recruits on a Virgin Mission, half the men he needed, and an enemy of unknown strength. Shit. Another wonderful day in the Corps.

Sharon was also dismally aware of her lack of combat command experience. She rocked in her seat as the shuttle shifted onto the loading conveyer. Its jerky movements up the loading belt shook all of them as it was shifted up the stages into the launching tube. Why the hell couldn't the Fleet use something that moved a shuttle smoothly?

She began to worry what to do next. She'd done this in training, but that was a long time ago. For that matter, her Virgin Mission was a dismounted raid, bush banging, long marches, and all that sort of thing. Boarding actions weren't her area.

What to do next?

Help came with a gentle nudge in her rib cage from Sergeant Passal, carefully hidden from the rest of the squad. She leaned over and whispered in his ear, "What do I do, now, Sergeant?"

"Not to worry, L.T.", he whispered.

Sharon thrilled for a second to hear herself awarded the ancient title of a Lieutenant commanding a combat unit.

"Just tell me to get us set up. I'll do the rest. Follow my lead."

She nodded and looked at the rest of the troops, seated on a small portion of the jump seats that ran the length of the troop compartment. The experienced men had the expressionless, slightly bored air of veterans about to do something they knew was dangerous and probably stupid. The boys wore expressions that were almost burlesques of those the men wore, but their enthusiasm clearly showed through the facade. For a moment, Sharon was melancholy. Those boys were about to get their first experience at the Gladius hereditary trade - war. She didn't envy their loss of innocence.

"Sergeant Passal, take charge and prepare the troops for the drop."

The sergeant nodded to her. "Aye, Lieutenant."

Quickly turning to the rest, he said, "ALL RIGHT YOU MOTHERLESS BASTARDS, LISTEN UP! Secur-r-r-e..."

Sharon wasn't entirely sure about the phraseology of Passal's commands, but the reaction from the troops was swift. Hurriedly, she grabbed the clasps of her own harness.

"...Harness!" Satisfying collections of clicks answered the command. Everyone, including Sharon and her sergeant, raised their right hands to signify their harness was secured. After a careful scan of each man and a close check of his lieutenant, Passal continued, "Prepare for Launch!"

Passal watched carefully as each trooper hugged his chest and braced his feet on the raised and angled foot plates running along the shuttle's troop bay floor. The low power grab fields in the benches held them securely, but the damn fields weren't strong enough to completely offset the maneuvers of a wild assed pilot. Passal hoped to the Lord Above that their pilot was wild assed. Wild assed kept you alive.

The shuttle made a final lurch upward and a loud tone buzzed raucously in the air, followed immediately by the pilot's voice, "Launch imminent. Is the unit secure?"

Passal made the reply. "Unit secure. Launch at will."

There was a breathless pause, then WHAM! The shuttle was fired from the launch tube and they were on their way to a visit with the Kayelen to discuss Imperial law. Passal settled himself on the bench and spent some time stewing again about taking out that Kayelen destroyer with the pickup crew he had, including three virgin underage troopers and a Lieutenant that might as well be Virgin. He was truly thrilled.

#####

In the cockpit, Warrant Pilot Millen and Fleet Ensign Tobarge swung the shuttle into an approach curve towards the Kayelen ship. The Ensign had experienced the "juice" before, the electronic linkage between himself and the ship's computers that raised his mental speed and physical reactions to a level that matched his equipment, but this was his first time under combat conditions. It was a bit unsettling.

Fleet Ensign Tobarge was acting as the shuttle's Electronic Fields Officer and this was first real assault mission. He'd boarded the escaping transport because he was still young enough to be idealistic about the Fleet. He looked up from his monitors for a moment and saw the Kayelen destroyer had already locked onto the liner, boarding tube extended. "Chief," he said, in a slightly uneven voice, "they've tied onto the liner."

Millen, intently watching his projected approach curve on the forward monitor's tactical display, only grunted. He had well over his thirty combat drops. He was on the carrier and on this flight because he was third generation Fleet and believed in what it stood for, not that he'd ever say so. "Watch your suppresser, Ensign. We don't want those bastards to see us until we're right on them. When we drop those boys in back into the destroyer, I want those assholes to wonder where in hell they came from. Understood?"

Tobarge gulped and nodded. It suddenly dawned on him that the shuttle's protective screens and suppresser field, both under his control, were all that stood between him and death. Then he realized the Gladii in the troop compartment were all that stood between the liner's people and death. People. He was trying to save people. Quietly, the nervousness and fear left him. A calm something else took their place.

Millen glanced at the youngster and saw the change in his expression. He nodded with satisfaction. The kid was settling down. Then he set himself to hit the tightest attack curve he could fly without suppresser field bleed-through. The assault shuttle had an inertial negator the size of a corvette's and any good pilot tried to push its envelope. Millen considered himself a damned good pilot. They were about to hit the machine's limits on this one, he thought, then some. There wasn't time for anything else.

#####

Inside the troop compartment, Sharon gave a quiet order, one she remembered well from her Virgin Mission. "Link up."

One of the secrets of the Gladius was a genetic modification made back when the legions were first being created, an extra lobe of the brain. That lobe existed in most humans today, but it required training and some modification to use completely, one of the more important parts of recruit training. The lobe had many functions, including releasing time dilation hormones into the body that speeded up thought and reactions in the same manner as the electronically induced "juice" used by Fleet command crew.

The lobe had other uses - ESP, for instance. Where other militaries or races used sensors, Gladii just *knew*. Gladius units also worked with a smooth coordinated precision previously unknown in war. The secret was an ability born in this extra lobe. You couldn't actually talk back and forth, but each Gladius still knew where all the rest were in battle and what they were doing, a priceless advantage. Privacy, courtesy, and tradition required the mental linkage be restricted, but it was a part of any combat operation. Like now. Sharon could feel every member of her small strike team fitting into her thoughts like pieces of a well-designed machine. The Link became alive with awareness as each member joined.

Passal checked and they were ready, even the boys and the lieutenant. Passal began the traditional game of all Gladii riding a shuttle on a drop. With a flip of his wrist, his tractor-presser bracelet snatched his ax from its holster and into in his hand. His gesture was immediately matched by the rest of the team, except the lieutenant, who used her arm dagger. Ought to make the game interesting. He banged the butt of the ax on the seat frame next to him and half sang, half chanted the traditional ax game song, "Oh-h-h, my mother was a lady..."

With the last word, he snapped the ax through the air at one of the others, catching a thrown ax in return. Each Gladius did the same, banging the butt on a seat stanchion, and the ax game continued, chanting and throwing.

#####

Ensign Tobarge glanced at the troop compartment monitor and gulped nervously. Those axes they were throwing would cut through the shuttle's heavily armored skin without stopping. There was even a dagger flying around. The edge of every one of those blades was tipped with a monomolecular shear field that would literally slice through anything. The short swords were also enhanced, but he didn't care about them. They weren't being thrown. He knew about the games, but watching made him jumpy.

Millen also glanced at the screen, but didn't worry. He had enough to think about and those robots never missed anyhow.

#####

On the troop carrier's bridge, Camille watched the target in the main screen. A lifetime as a Gladius told her what was happening aboard the liner, but she shut the pictures from her imagination. She could only hope they were in time to save as many as possible. "Lieutenant," she said in Unispek, "prepare to open a com channel to the Kayelen."

He looked at her in shock for a moment and she returned the look calmly. "Don't worry, I haven't lost my mind. But I fully intend to tell them we're here."

She smiled the frightening battle smile of the Gladius. "I will talk to them, but they will *not* enjoy the conversation."

Slowly, Kavasos nodded. "As you say, Major Paten."

Carefully, Camille watched the shuttle's icon on the main screen arc along the plotted attack curve, its end terminating squarely on the destroyer. Timing. Timing was everything. There!

"Lieutenant, open com channel."

Kavasos nodded to a rating that touched a sensor on her board. "Channel open. I have a response. They've accepted communication."

The picture in the main screen faded, replaced by the command deck of the destroyer, the surprised figure of its captain looking back at her.

Behind Camille, Staff Sergeant Tna Elanta had quietly coupled the sole remaining *brushara's* transmitter to the ship's com. The sound from the electronically amplified ram's horn was normally loud enough to injure everyone on the command deck and break everything when it was blown. The coupling would transmit the sound to the destroyer without anyone on the command deck hearing more than a muted tone.

Elanta's parents, husband, and children had paid the Gladius Price on Tombele. Now a Predator was within range. Maybe not the same Predator that took her family, but still the Predator. She was proud to be the here now, preparing to sound the *brushara,* the Battle Shout. Normally, only the *brushara* bearer of a Cohort could perform this honored task, but that young Gladius was dead. His mother would do his duty for him.

Camille looked in to the Kayelen captain's eyes. He tried to match her hard, utterly cold look. He couldn't do it.

"Hellspawn," she said tonelessly into the silence. She spoke Unispek and knew the Kayelen would understand. Every educated being spoke it.

"Hellspawn, look at me. You know who I am."

The captain drew strength from the fact that he was facing a small human female, even if she did wear that damned uniform. "I know who you are, but I also know you're beaten, you and all your kind."

"No," she replied quietly. "Never beaten. We die, but we are never beaten."

The captain gave an elaborate Kayelen shrug. "So you die." He smiled unpleasantly. "I can promise you that if you stay."

"Hellspawn," she replied, her words frighteningly soft and even, "I will stay here and I will come for you. You are attacking Imperial citizens, and the penalty for that is death."

The icon of the shuttle was almost at the point where the destroyer's sensor suite would burn through the shuttle's suppresser field. Now was the time. Just hold the captain's attention a moment longer.

She drew herself up and her chin jutted forward aggressively, the immemorial unconscious gesture of a Gladius about to do battle. "Hellspawn, I see you and I know you. You crawled through the Gates of Hell to threaten citizens. You thought you were free."

The Kayelen stared at her, fascinated, unable to reply.

"But you forgot one thing...

"The Gates of Hell have guardians. The Gladius is coming for you. *Gladio alieyo.*"

The last was said quietly and in Copio, the language of the Corps, but it raised hives on the Kayelen captain's skin. He knew what it meant. The Gladius is here.

Behind the captain, a sensor tech said loudly, "COLLISION ALERT! Incoming vessel at 6-2-4-5 mils relative to course, ascension 0-9-5-0 mils!" The incoming bogey was to their front left and just above them.

He whirled, but before he could shout an order, Camille gave a command she never thought she'd ever give in her lifetime. Only a commander of a cohort or a legion ordering Gladii into battle could order the sounding of the Battle Shout, the brushara. Well, she was now the commander of what was left of a legion, ordering it into battle. So be it. In a firm, steady voice, she gave the ancient order, "*Cattan na brushara.*" Sound the Battle Shout.

Taking a breath, Elanta set the brushara to her lips and blew. The transmitted blast of sound scrambled every electronic device on the destroyer's bridge and stunned the bridge crew as surely as a direct hit from a heavy weapon.

#####

On the shuttle, the air in the troop compartment suddenly glowed red. Drop coming. Close faceplates and prepare. Passal sounded off from deep in his chest, "ON YOUR FE-E-ET!"

The time dilation hormone was already in their systems, so the move was made with speed and precision. Passal continued yelling orders anyhow. "ALL RIGHT, INTO LINE. THE LIEUTENANT FIRST, THEN BY TEAMS, SECURITY TEAM LAST."

All of them lined up on the transport rail that ran down the center of the compartment. Sharon braced herself as the men behind her began to push closely into her back. Passal, taking his place at the rear of the line, shoved the group tighter. A tight group kept a better formation when they landed inside the ship. He was still bellowing. "PUSH IT IN, PUSH IT IN, C'MON YOU PEOPLE, MAKE YOUR BUDDY SMILE."

Sharon was amused at that then realized what the last phrase meant and blushed instead. She heard the hands slap shoulders up the line from the rear as each man signified his readiness for the drop. When she felt the man behind her slap her shoulder, she announced over the shuttle com net, // "Team ready for drop."//

The response was a laconic, //"Drop imminent."//

Sharon felt the lock-down field grab her armor, locking her body and those of her team into position, keeping them immobile and protected for the final frantic seconds of maneuvering. The shuttle was executing a

21

normal combat maneuver, ramming the destroyer to deliver troops. Once the shuttle's nearly solid nose was buried in the target, a drop ramp would be instantly extruded into the body of the ship like a hypodermic, ejecting the Gladii into the lightly armored destroyer's hull. Speed was vital in this operation, to protect the attacking team and - just as important - to place the team into fighting range of the ship's crew before it could react.

Sharon knew all of this. No problem. It was what was going to happen at the instant of impact that she dreaded. The grab field would automatically strengthen and secure the rest of her body to protect her from the shock of impact. She didn't relish having her breathing and heartbeat frozen, even for the seconds between initial impact and drop. That was necessary for her safety, but she still didn't look forward to it.

#####

In the front, Millen had the Kayelen destroyer fully centered on the main screen. "Going in. Prepare for collision."

"Aye." Tobarge looked up at the main screen as he acknowledged. His eyes widened as the destroyer grew explosively to fill it, then the incredible shock of impact rocked him in his command seat even though his seat's grab field had him effectively immobilized. The crash automatically initiated the preprogrammed drop sequence.

The shuttle was buried half up its armored nose in the outer hull of the destroyer and the drop tube immediately injected itself, stopping at an internal passageway. The troop compartment air glowed a bright green, and the team was launched through the drop tube like an old-fashioned missile.

Even with her enhanced reactions and thoughts, the drop was almost instantaneous. Sharon landed ready to fight, her B-42's pistol grip in her right hand, butt braced against her upper arm. She sensed rather than saw the rest of the team drop around her and scatter to their positions with the well drilled precision of veterans. Briefly, she noted that even the boys were properly located. She felt a quick wash of disorientation then she was suddenly part of the thousand year old being that was the Gladius, performing the ancient mission of the Gladius. She no longer was apprehensive, only a part of a greater Whole. "Special weapons deploy!"

Sharon took an instant to orient herself on the destroyer's schematic the transport beamed to her helmet then resumed giving orders. "Control's directly below us. Boarding tube's below that. Sergeant, open a path."

"Aye." Sergeant Passal made a brief check to ensure both special weapons teams were headed to the proper ends of the destroyer then grabbed one of his boarding charges and emplaced it where the Lieutenant pointed.

The boarding charge wasn't an explosive. Instead, it was a product of the Empire's highly developed field technology. It emitted shear fields in a wagon wheel pattern, then immediately bloomed with a presser field that blew the sections back and down, like an opening flower. The one the Passal was using was rated for any material up to two measures in depth. The deck was considerably lighter than that.

When the field bloomed and the deck peeled downward, the effect was like an explosion in the control room. The point man jumped in after a quick check. The rest followed. Within a few frantic seconds, any Kayelen still alive in the compartment died from precisely aimed bolt fire.

Sharon didn't waste time looking at the devastation in the control room... or the messy bodies scattered around it. She ordered over her com, // "Seal the breach."//

On the upper deck, Legionnaire Recruit Kardo took a small field generator from his belt pack and, pressing its adherent surface to the hull next to the breach, activated it to produce yet another energy field acting as an air seal. //"Breach sealed, Lieutenant."//

//"Aye. Now get down here with us."// Sharon switched channels and commed the shuttle commander. //"Breach sealed. Prepare to undock."//

Millen replied, //"Aye. Undocking now. Going to hide position until clear."//

The shuttle withdrew its boarding tube and slid gently to hover near the destroyer's hull. It wouldn't do to move away from the hull and into the reach of its weapons, not while guns were still active. Not too close either, not with what was coming. All they had to do now was wait, but there wouldn't be a long wait.

Sharon switched bands. //"Special weapons. Activate. Advise me when accomplished."//

The two teams with special weapons fired their crumple charges. Launched towards opposite ends of the destroyer, the two crumple charges created ultra-small, precisely calibrated black holes running the length of the destroyer, crushing everything in their path - ship and crew - into a tiny mass before reaching their preset point of dissolution. With that, nothing remained of the destroyer but the small section holding the Gladii, the boarding tube into the liner, and the assault shuttle on the remains of the outer hull. //"Special weapons fired. Results nominal."// Both teams were back with the rest of the squad in moments.

Ariel called the shuttle again. //"Feed me a placement on the passengers and the remaining hostiles, if you can get them."//

Her response was a laconic //"Aye."//, followed by a download from the shuttle's bio sensor suite. The schematic on her helmet visor's HUD wasn't pretty. She saw a clump of human life sources below her in the middle of the liner. Her lips tightened at the low number of those sources, and the random scattering of only a few others aboard the big ship. There were far too few for the size of the liner. It took no imagination to realize what had happened to the rest.

She superimposed a schematic of the liner's decks over her image of the main group's location, oriented herself then passed it over the squad net. "Down we go," she said. "Orient on the central lounge of the liner. We'll have to move fast, so I want to just cut through the decks and go straight in."

//"Security team,"// she said over her communicator, // "down here *now*. Follow us through the destroyer. Set up at the mouth of the boarding tube when we get on the liner. Watch our backs when the rest of us drop in on these bastards. Stay out of trouble and keep our way home open."//

Kardo replied with a crisp, //"Aye!"// He sounded excited, but Ariel didn't feel like telling him to settle down. That was a decurion's job, anyhow. At least those three would be out of most of the trouble.

She expanded on her orders as the boys joined them. "That holding point where the passengers are located is our destination. As soon as we get on the liner, I want to assemble on the deck just above the compartment where they're being held. Point, your job is to get us there, understand?"

The point man replied, "Aye."

"All right, let's do this!"

Passal set off another boarding charge, and the unit dropped down through the resulting hole. When they hit the destroyer's deck below, the point man immediately set off for the boarding tube at a dead run. The rest of the unit followed at a precisely drilled distance, far enough behind to let the point trip any surprises, but close enough to provide support if needed. The point didn't waste any time at the mouth of the Kayelen boarding tube, but dove through it, followed by the rest of the teams. Inside the liner, the men didn't break stride as they ran on towards the designated assembly point. Only the three boys on the security team stopped to secure the tube entrance.

Several times the Gladii encountered startled Kayelen marines. Surprise made the Kayelens a little slow with their weapons. The Gladii weren't.

The point skidded to a halt at the designated spot, above the compartment holding the remaining passengers, but one deck above.

24

There was no break in the unit's speed as Passal slapped his third charge on the deck and the rest formed a quick perimeter to let it blow.

#####

The Kayelen marine lieutenant was disgusted with his assignment, but still following orders. The terrified mob he'd assembled in the compartment didn't seem to contain the two females he was sent to find, so they were just so much useless garbage to him. Those damned females were proving hard to find, and the Captain's last transmission to him was showing the beginnings of irritation. Bad. This assignment was choice, but failure to accomplish it with his customarily smooth efficiency would earn him a large black mark with the ship's commander. Not good for the future of his career. He ground his dental ridges in frustration at the inability of his search teams to find the women.

One of the terrified mob under his men's guns chose that moment to scream something at him. Like every educated being, he was fully conversant with the standard language of the galaxy, Imperial Unispek, and this was not the moment to call him a murderer. As he'd already done several times on this mission, he drew his sidearm and shot the offending human, blowing off the woman's head.

Some of the blood spattered on a female child standing to his front and the accursed little beast began screaming. He was training his pistol on the child when a grown female, evidently the child's dam, snatched her up, followed by a male that tried to hold both of them and place his body between the frustrated lieutenant and his family. With a snarl of rage, the lieutenant crossed swiftly to them and, slamming the male out of the way with the butt of his pistol, cracked its barrel over the female's brow then snatched up the child by its hair.

He had only a vague idea what he was going to do with the noisy little monster, only that his frustration needed an outlet. He'd finally decided to jam his pistol into the open mouth of the screaming brat and pull the trigger when the thin thread holding the Sword of Damocles over his head parted.

#####

As the boarding charge opened up the deck, his lieutenant, to Passal's complete aggravation, immediately jumped into the hole without so much as a look. Damn it! That was how wet-behind-the-ears lieutenants got killed!

25

In the seeming slow fall to the deck below, Sharon had enough time to take in the situation below her. She let her B-42 begin to snap back to her armor as she threw her weight toward the Kayelen and the little girl, thinking out what she was going to do when she landed. She hit the deck in front of him, cushioned by her no-weight belt, and spun to her right, her wrist dagger in her hand. With a smooth backhanded slash, she neatly severed the Kayelen's throat to the spine and grabbed the child with a scooping motion of her left hand before the little girl could fall. Continuing her spin, she pitched the girl to one of her troopers and continued her rotation, turning it into a side hand throw that buried her dagger in the chest of another of the marines. She used the tractor-presser bracelet on her wrist to pull it unerringly back to her hand. The rest of her troops were already on the deck and firing, killing the remaining startled marines before they could return fire.

After a wary survey of the compartment, ensuring no Kayelen remained a threat, Sharon slowly rose from her crouch and raised her helmet visor. "Corps of Imperial Gladius," she shouted in Unispek to the room at large. "Are there any ship's officers here?"

A stocky competent looking man in uniform got slowly up from among the still shocked mob of passengers lying on the deck and made his way to face her. Privately, he was a little dismayed to discover she was a woman, and a small one at that. Then the dead Kayelen, her armor, and the imperturbable Gladius calm registered. Things were going to be all right! The Corps was here! "I'm Esterhazy Line Lieutenant Commander Parcalus, Lieutenant, ship's First Officer" he told her with a relieved grin. "Damn, I'm proud to see you."

"Lieutenant Ariel, Lieutenant Commander. How many more are there?"

"This," he said as he spat on the Kayelen's corpse, "had search teams out looking for somebody. We don't know who. I think most of the teams are still out."

"We'll get them," she said to Parcalus. "Thank you, First Officer." Turning to Sergeant Passal she reverted to Copio as she passed her orders. "Detail a team to guard the passengers in case some of the marines return. The rest of us will run a standard search and destroy pattern on the Kayelen"

Passal nodded and raised his own visor, mildly amazed he still had a lieutenant. "Aye. ...If the Lieutenant will permit?"

"Yes?" Sharon answered curiously, slightly lightheaded and elated at the so-far successful mission. She was now truly a combat commander!

The decurion leaned close and hissed, nose to nose with his officer, "If the Lieutenant lives through another crazy stunt like jumping down a hole without a check, the Sergeant will kick her ass as soon as they are back on the ship, understood, L.T.?"

Sharon gulped, her face beet red. "Understood, Sergeant," she said in a small voice.

Passal straightened, saluted and replied in a loud voice, "They will not see the dawn."

Sharon forced her face into a proper Gladius imperturbability. Passal's little sermon had brought her squarely back to reality with a thud. "Aye. Carry on, Sergeant."

Passal was just turning away when their extended mental linkage brought them the same message. Sharon was a little slow understanding. Passal wasn't. "Lieutenant, it's the boys!"

He spun to the rest of the unit. "Ramas! Your team stays here and protects the citizens! Rest of you, up and haul ass!"

#####

As the unit was leaving to rescue the passengers, the three boys quickly - if a little raggedly - fell into a standard triangular security perimeter. As the oldest, sixteen year old Kardo was by unspoken consent the team leader. He checked the positions of the other two and repositioned Smythe slightly to give him more cover in a recessed hatchway. Kardo really wanted to be where the action was and looked a little wistfully in the direction of the departed troops. On the other hand, he was mature enough to realize securing the way out was vital. With a sigh of resignation, he settled into his own position and began scanning the empty passageway.

It was after his third - or maybe tenth - visual check of his two team members that he heard the scream. It came from far down the passageway opposite where the troops went, but the reason was obvious. A citizen was in danger! Instead of calling in the situation to his commander, the boy made a rookie's mistake. An instant's quick thought and he was up, nervously shouting orders. "Something's wrong down there! Smythe, you stay here and guard our back! Chofal, with me!"

Smythe watched the other two speed off down the passage way with a little resentment then realized he was being left on guard while they settled the problem down the passageway. His chest expanded slightly as he settled his B-42 more comfortably against his shoulder. Whatever happened, nothing was getting past him.

#####

27

One of three Kayelen marines had Lana with one hand in her hair and one arm around her neck. The girl could only struggle helplessly and scream. Clarine, on the other hand, was standing, frozen in shock as her daughter was forced into the stateroom and thrown roughly at her. The two women huddled together as they stared fearfully at their captors. It took Clarine's mind a moment to begin working again and try to think of a way out the situation with a whole skin.

In the corridor outside, the two young Gladii were moving silently towards the open door of the stateroom, following the noise. When it died down, Kardo judged there was nothing happening for the moment. He knew that if the screams began again, it meant something bad. The silence was giving him a few moments for him to set up for their move, whatever it was going to be. He knew the textbook way to enter a hostile room and he saw the other boy remembered his own training. Go in fast, hard, instantly assess the situation and use a maximum of violence. Kardo also remembered the tough old decurion telling him it was also an excellent way to get killed.

Not knowing what was on the other side, he decided to lead with his ax. A wrist flex, and his tractor-presser bracelet snatched the weapon silently into his hand. He raised his ax slightly and Chofal motioned readiness with his B-42. Kardo took a deep breath, nodded at his team mate, then ducked through the open doorway, throwing as soon as he had a clear target.

The problem was there were three marines. Kardo's ax took out the first, returning smoothly to his hand in a perfect throw. Chofal's bolt caught the second marine, but the third had time to raise his weapon and fire. The Kayelen's bolt was a glancing blow, but the breastplate fragmented, knocking Kardo backward with a hole in his side. Chofal's second shot took out the marine.

Chofal immediately knelt and unsnapped the damaged breastplate, ripping off the rest of Kardo's upper body armor and his helmet. Armor could staunch wounds, but not one that big on the torso. Quickly sizing up the wound and noting the armor fragment embedded deeply below his teammate's rib cage, he grabbed the first aid kit from his equipment belt, breaking a treatment capsule in the wound and swiftly bandaging the hole. It looked bad, and there was no telling how close to the heart the long sliver had penetrated. Kardo was already shocking out on him and he didn't know what to do. Plug it and pray to the Lord Above.

Chofal looked at the younger of the two women and snapped, "You! Press this pad down until the bleeding stops!"

Lana fearfully approached the downed Gladius. Her mind still hadn't caught up with the rapid change of situation and the Kayelens were scattered messily around the stateroom. Chofal grabbed her right hand and pressed it roughly on the bandage pad. "Here!" he said. "Hard or he'll bleed to death before the coagulant starts to work. He's in shock now and I have to watch the door. Yell if he starts coming around."

With that, Chofal left the girl with his wounded teammate, moving quickly back to the doorway and scanning the empty passageway. Damn! With Kardo down and two citizens to protect, he couldn't get back to the security position. There had to be more of the Kayelen around and he wasn't going to let them get anyone. Making a decision, he called Smythe.

Smythe was still watching the passageway when he got the call on his helmet com. //"Smythe, Chofal. You have to hold, Kardo's down and I have two citizens here. No telling what else is out there. You have to hold the tube by yourself."//

Smythe gulped slightly, but he had a new mission and he was going to do it. //"Aye. Don't worry, nothing's getting past here. Hold up there. The sergeant and the lieutenant will be back soon."//

//"Aye. Chofal out."//

Smythe didn't have time to worry. He heard sounds from up the passageway and they were headed his way. He should have told his team member, but he was too inexperienced to think of that. Instead, he moved his B-42 into firing position, determined to ensure he'd told Chofal the truth about nothing getting past.

So far, the mission was totally unremarkable to the Kayelen marine squad. The two they sought still were on the ship, somewhere, and their job was to continue looking until the women were found. No danger, just hunt and grab. Killing whoever didn't fit the profile for the two ugly aliens they sought made the job a little easier, but the squad leader was heartily tired of looking under beds and in closets.

Boredom accounted for the reason his first two men died as they came around the bend in the passageway. Falling into positions with veteran speed, the remainder immediately returned fire while the squad leader attempted to make sense of what was happening now. "Fire and movement! Take out that *bishuge* while I get the Lieutenant!"

The marines began darting from cover to cover up the passageway under the fire of their fellows. The return fire and occasional casualty told them clearly that it wasn't a frightened civilian in front of them.

29

Smythe triggered his com. //"Chofal, Smythe. I have enemy coming up the passageway in squad strength. I'm delaying. Can you move up?"//

Chofal suffered a momentary agony of indecision, glancing back at the two women and downed Gladius. No way. //"Smythe, Chofal. No. I have two citizens here, and I don't think Kardo's capable of movement. Can you hold?"//

A veteran would have pulled back and joined his teammate to combine their firepower, then moved to retake the tube. A tense fourteen year old boy made a different decision. //"Aye. Get the Lieutenant."//

Chofal could have kicked himself at that last request. Why in hell hadn't he done that sooner? That he was an inexperienced Recruit didn't enter his head.

Cutting his transmission, Smythe reverted to an age-old Gladius tradition. He drew his short sword and drove it deeply into the deck next to him, something made easy with the blade's molecular shear field. He couldn't go back and the Kayelens weren't going past him. Neither he, nor his enemy was going to pass that blade, even in death. "Thus far and no farther," he muttered and took a fresh sight picture.

Chofal's report wasn't exactly dismaying to Sharon, but she took a small satisfaction in cursing the triple damned fiasco fate handed her. She stopped the squad for a minute. Thankfully, they weren't all that far away. //"Shuttle, Ariel. Get me a life form readout in the vicinity of the boarding tube."//

When the schematic came in, she fed the data to Passal, who'd moved up next to her, meanwhile cursing in a steady monotone. "We can't go up and over the Kayelens," she said, "the service accessways are too small to move in any kind of effective formation. If we jump up to the passageway now, we'll only be about twenty or so measures from the Kayelen rear."

He thought for a moment then grimaced. "OK, L.T., we'll have to do this the hard way, fast and up their ass."

Sharon responded with a wolf's grin. "Right," she said softly. "Let's do it then. OK, everyone, go in loud. Shake these bastards up as much as you can. Get to that tube."

Concentrating on the single defender on his front, the Kayelen squad leader was totally unprepared for the screaming, barely seen hellions that smashed into his rear. The Gladii hit fast, hard, and right into the middle, turning the fight into a confused melee that gave them their greatest advantage. It was where the Gladius always fought best.

Sharon launched herself at one of the marines who was totally unprepared for the screaming devil at his back. For the second time on the mission, her wrist dagger did duty for a boltgun. The men's axes were larger, but the dagger was no less efficient in the close quarters of the passageway.

Passal slashed one of the marines in the neck as he charged, throwing the corpse bodily into a second marine and clearing more space for his ax to go to work. He ignored the snarling tangle at his feet as Sharon drove her dagger repeatedly into the Kayelen wrapped around her.

Sharon pushed the dead marine away and stood up slowly, looking around as the rest of her troops assembled and formed a security perimeter. Not all of the Gladii got up. One of them was down, lying with two of his enemies in a final embrace. Still a bit twitchy from combat reaction, she looked at her sergeant. Passal kneeled next to the dead Gladius then shook his head. His look told Sharon she had her first combat death under her command. She pressed her lips grimly together.

"Sergeant Passal," she said firmly. "There're more of these out there. One team to secure here, one team to collect stray passengers after we find out what in hell Kardo and Chofal have been up to. I'll give you locations then call in the shuttle. The team guarding the passengers can start moving them up here. We'll join up when all citizens are accounted for."

Passal nodded. Looked like he finally had a lieutenant that knew what she was about. "Aye, L. T. We're bringing the citizens with us?" That wasn't really a question. He just wanted clarification.

"We can't leave them on this ship. Her drives have been shot out. We'll have to get them back to the carrier. Besides, there aren't enough of us to totally clear the ship of the Kayelens. We'll just leave those misbegotten bastards the hulk after we collect the citizens. It won't do them any good. Citizens are our first concern, now."

Passal acknowledged. "Aye." Then he turned to his men. "Team two, get locations from the Lieutenant and round up the strays as fast as you can, but get every one of them, no matter what. Three, casualty collection point is the base of the boarding tube. Go get Kardo's team, then bring Samford's body to the point. Everyone call in if you hit trouble. Got it? OK, let's do the mission."

#####

31

On board the shuttle on the way back to the transport, Lana cradled the injured young Gladius's head in her lap. He'd nearly gotten killed saving her life. She never knew there were still men like that in the Empire. He was kind of cute, too. Softly, she stroked the unconscious boy's pale bristle-short hair and thought heavily for the remainder of the trip.

CHAPTER 2

LEGIO IX VICTRIX
CAULDWELL

The Wareegans killed Bluefield. Because of that, Matic Ettranty killed Longcreek.

The Narsima Matic Ettranty shifted his corpulent bulk in his lounger, somewhat uncomfortable as he again meditated on that fact. Occasionally, he rubbed his depilated head with agitation. The Wareegans were being given a hint, at the expense of a small city and - despite hastily constructed civil defense shelters - a goodly number of proles. The Narsima quite wished they'd take it and leave the planet of Cauldwell alone before he had to arrange another hint. There were very, very specific reasons why he wished they'd leave Cauldwell alone.

Pirates, raiders, whatever you wished to call the Wareegans, they landed on a defenseless planet, looted, killed, tortured, and kidnapped. The original raid on Bluefield left behind very disgusting evidence of those facts. The Narsima didn't dwell on that evidence, because circumstance and politics had forced him to see it personally. The conclusions he reached after that visit were dismal, but he was pragmatic and realistic.

The first conclusion was that the Empire wasn't going to give Cauldwell any help. There really wasn't much help available for the Emperor to send, not in these declining days. Besides, any visible Imperial presence might just awaken interest in certain quarters, interest that could prove highly inconvenient. The Emperor wanted Cauldwell to be - and remain - a forgotten backwater. The death toll on that backwater was irrelevant to the Emperor, thus to him.

Second, he decided there was absolutely nothing on Cauldwell that could stop the Wareegans.

Third, historical records said that the Wareegans always came back once they'd decided to raid a planet. They kept coming until stopped. The talking heads on the news networks and faxes all harped on the fact. His orders from the Emperor after his initial report were to stop them, no matter the cost, but without creating a military force that might later prove bothersome. Cauldwell had to be preserved the way it was. A totally devastated planet was of no use to Shangnaman. Neither was he, if he didn't find a way to run off the Wareegans.

To stop them, he needed a way to completely destroy at least one raid, or more if needed. The only thing Cauldwell could produce to do the job was primitive nuclear missiles. One hundred thousand people killed by an old fashioned locally produced nuclear weapon were just as dead as one hundred thousand killed, murdered, or taken away for whatever reason by the Wareegans. That was the equation in the Narsima's mind. The difference, of course, was that the people killed by the missile died quickly. Killing the city also killed the Wareegan raiding force. Kill enough raiding parties and the Wareegans would write off Cauldwell as an effort not worth the cost and go away. Simple.

After Bluefield, he announced a "defensive" program. Cauldwell was going to construct nuclear missiles with sufficient power to destroy the next raid. The citizens would be safe in shelters he also ordered constructed - at irritatingly high, but not damagingly high - cost. He knew perfectly well that the mass shelters constructed for the proles weren't going to be sufficient to protect anyone. There was too much graft and corruption in the government for that to happen. Shelters protecting the upper class, however, would be small and hardened enough to survive, especially since the people in them would be very motivated to keep them that way.

Shelter effectiveness wasn't something Cauldwell's Important People wanted discussed. Ergo, that part was kept quiet.

His solution outraged the citizens of Cauldwell to a degree, but not so things got out of hand. The populace had a high, somewhat decadent, standard of living and was trained to be complacent. What happened to someone else in another place didn't impact their personal world, which was going to keep on exactly the way it was. The Cauldwell government and the Narsima kept hammering that point home by the usual population control methods in the media. The Cauldwell press was relatively independent and quite intrusive, but reporters and editors mostly had the same political leaning: the Narsima's. That made it very easy for him and his party to manipulate the media. The media, in turn, manipulated the proles for him. Talking heads, of course, parroted the government line.

The Planetary Guard couldn't stop the Wareegans, not after catastrophic losses taken in the first futile effort. The Narsima forbade any further attacks on their part, other than to deliver a nuclear weapon to destroy the next raider incursion. Building the Guard back to full strength was expensive and time consuming - another infernally irritating expense. Meanwhile, nuclear missiles, while obsolete, were simple and cheap to produce.

The first trial of his new program had wiped out Longcreek, the people as well as the Wareegans. That was something he'd expected, although the media and public reaction was shock. Talking heads were already hard at work explaining that there had been some sort of malfunction in the warhead that had dramatically increased its yield. Remaining missiles would be carefully inspected and the next one, Lord Above forbid it was ever used, would be less destructive. At least the Wareegans were gone, presumably shocked at their losses.

Narsima Matic Ettranty had no intention of reducing the missile's warhead yield. The raiders had to be killed. He had other small cities.

Now he'd best put on his most reasonable and sympathetic face. The Guard's Commander, Imin Webster, was due in his office shortly to discuss the death of Longcreek. Webster was going to protest the Narsima's decisions and needed to be talked back into compliance. Another disagreeable but necessary task. Besides, he somewhat liked the young man. He suspected Imin was probably going to marry his daughter, so it was simply good practice to maintain equilibrium in the family.

When Commander Webster in the black tunic and light blue trousers of the Planetary Guard he commanded was ushered into his office, Ettranty heaved his bulk from his lounger with a bit of effort, then waved to the office bar. "Have a drink, Imin. You appear to need it."

Imin Webster, still shaken and furious, did need a drink. He'd just finished carrying out the death of a city and everyone in it. His own people. Oh, the Wareegan mother ship was gone from the Cauldwell system, but nobody could be sure if, or when, they'd return. If they did come back, the cost in human lives was going to be horrific, even if a "safer" warhead was used. Imin knew that, but knew better than to bring up the fact. The Narsima wouldn't disagree, but he'd already forbidden further argument. At least Longcreek hadn't died horribly, like Bluefield.

Imin gripped his drink in his left hand, rubbing his light blue uniform trouser leg with his right as he brooded over the situation. He was black haired and medium built, with a normally cheerful face that right now showed nothing but anger under fierce control. "Damn it, Narsima, why won't you and the Council let us go down on the ground after them?" he said tightly.

"Imin," Ettranty's breathy voice was soothing, reasonable as he settled his bulk, swathed in the noble robes of his station, back into his lounge chair, "I've told you many times. The Planetary Guard hasn't the training, manpower, or equipment to conduct any sort of ground warfare. Your force was solely designed to protect against threats from space."

"Which we can't!" Webster shot back. "We've tried! We need a ground force."

"And heavier warships as well," the Narsima replied. "Both of which require time, facilities and experience we don't have. We've never needed them before and they're a major expense that may never be necessary again. Without experienced trainers and equipment we don't have or could manufacture rapidly, throwing ground troops at the Wareegans would only compound the casualties and achieve nothing but additional drains on the population and economy. Cauldwell is less than five hundred years old and was settled on a shoestring. That doesn't even take into account that we're isolated out here. It's simply a problem of economics and starting from a small base."

Other than what he told Imin, the Narsima did not want Cauldwell to have its own navy or army, even its own merchant marine. Again, for very specific reasons.

"No, until the Wareegans came," Ettranty continued, "the Planetary Guard is what we needed and could support. We simply do not have the ability to create a large military force as this planet currently stands.

"Now, my friend, if you were trained and equipped like one of them..." he said, waving his hand at a line of beautifully made statuettes on a shelf next to the wall.

"Your collection," Imin snorted. The Narsima was perfectly aware Webster knew who was controlling the conversation, getting it off track to derail complaints. Narsima Matic Ettranty was very confident of Imin's reaction to the situation. If Imin wanted to continue commanding the Guard - and he did - he'd keep his mouth shut when told to do it.

"My collection," Ettranty agreed. "But don't make light of my admiration for those men."

He got up and walked to the shelf, becoming more animated and enthusiastic. "These were all among the best soldiers of their day. Any of them, from this Napoleonic lancer to that Vegan space marine could be at least an even match for the Wareegans, but not your men. It's a matter of the purpose for which they were intended.

"In fact," he said, picking up a statuette from the end of the line, "here is the very individual we need."

Webster glanced idly at the form in Ettranty's hand. "An Imperial Gladius. So what? We haven't seen an Imperial warship here for nearly a century, much less Imperial troops. Everything we hear out of the Empire says they can't help us anyhow."

That resigned statement was music to the Narsima's ears.

The Narsima hid his satisfaction as he studied the lifelike statuette in his hand. The figure was a muscular man with a short beard, wearing a khaki shirt and kilt, boots and a tapering short cylindrical cap. His chest was crisscrossed by support straps for a belt carrying a short sword and small battle-ax on his left hip and a pistol on the other. The total effect was vaguely like an ancient Assyrian warrior. "An Imperial Gladius.

36

Yes," Ettranty nodded his head, "they are exactly what we need. They were the supreme warriors, the ultimate soldiers, and I wish we had them now."

The Narsima was soon to get his wish, though he would come to regret it.

#####

Commander Imin Webster was immediately notified when the ship came into detection range. He was mildly irritated at the interruption because he'd been trying, for the hundredth time, to find a way around the Narsima's nuclear missile option. Dropping the frustrating exercise, he ordered up his air car and driver. Once he got to the PCC, he was both relieved and puzzled. It wasn't the Wareegan coming back. So who was it?

A scanner tech settled the question. "Command, tentative ID. Probable Imperial troop carrier. Identification correspondence 78%. Combat damage showing."

Imin concentrated intently as visual details began to flow onto the main screen in the PCC. It did look a little like one of the old Impy ships. About 780,000 tonnes. With damage, too. A trained eye told him the ship was running on temporary patches, evidence of being a target sometime in the not-too-distant past.

Signals were coming in on an Imperial standard com band, and he nodded to the com tech, "Open communications."

The man that appeared on the communications screen was wearing a blue Imperial Fleet uniform with a pilot's badge. What caught Imin's eye was the heavy bandage that covered part of his head. "Imperial Troop Carrier ITC 901 requesting permission to land and coordinates of your port."

Imin moved into the pickup field for the communicator. "I am Commander Imin Webster, commander of the Planetary Guard. We will clear you for the port, once you state your mission and landing is approved by the Guidance Council. You are the first Imperial military ship in this area in many years, so what are you doing here?"

"We are-" the pilot began then he stopped, glanced over his shoulder at someone out of pickup range and turned back to the screen. "Commander, please wait while I shift you to another com."

Before Imin could say anything, the communications screen momentarily blanked. The figure that suddenly appeared was older than the pilot by a good number of years, but vigorous and powerful. His lined and scarred face was partially hidden by a full, heavy beard, shot through with strands of gray. He wore a tapering khaki cylindrical cap tilted forward above steel gray eyes that were burning with the pure power of the smoldering will behind them. The chest of his khaki uniform was crossed by leather belts that obviously supported equipment, or sidearms, outside the range of the screen pickup. Imin wasn't sure, but he thought the insignia on the man's collar designated him as a legionary Legate in the Corps of Imperial Gladius.

"We are here, Commander," the man rumbled in a bass voice as rough as the scars on his face, "simply because we have nowhere else to go."

Imin gaped for a moment then touched the scramble sensor that launched his backup fighter squadron. With the alert over the unknown ship, one squadron was already up and the backup squadron was on five minute standby. Both squadrons would be taking positions before this conversation, wherever it went, was over. His composure back in place, Imin looked the soldier in the eye and said, "I will require a little more information - Legate - before allowing a shipload of Imperial troops to land here."

The Gladius solemnly nodded his head. "Caution is a commendable trait in a young officer. I like to see that, Commander. Very well, I'll be more than happy to provide you with some answers.

"Simply put, I am Legate Abedu Corona, combat commander of the IX Legion, the Victrix. You are exactly right in your fears about the Empire, because the Empire you once knew is now collapsing, some of it sundered in civil wars and revolts, the rest changed. Very changed.

"Our base was destroyed. I led a fighting retreat that salvaged three full cohorts and attachments, the bulk of the legion's combat strength. We took this troop carrier in an attempt to find a world on the frontier that would allow us free settlement and a return to our original purpose, the protection of humanity. We found Cauldwell by following an old route chip and I now ask the privilege of speaking with your government about a peaceful landing."

His eyes blazed briefly with the fire that was forever banked behind them. "Commander, I believe negotiations are the best thing we can do for the moment. It will prevent my crew from having to carry out the distasteful chore of firing on those fighters we are now tracking."

Imin thought hard for a few frantic seconds. "Legate, I understand your situation," he said, more to buy time than anything else.

There was no need to fight as yet. The Legate appeared to be telling the truth and the pilot's wounds, not to mention those of the ship, backed up his story. They were Imperial troops and Cauldwell was still, however slightly, an Imperial planet. Still... "Answer me one thing,

Legate, if you will. I know the history of the Corps and you have never run from a fight. Why didn't you fall back on the Empire's center? Get reinforcements?"

The grim face glared at him. "The Victrix didn't run from a fight, as you put it. We fought to the end and came out with our wounded when the result became inevitable."

The legate turned even grimmer. "Our base - and everything that made it - was destroyed, even though the enemy paid heavily for that destruction.

"But," he smiled ironically, "as to falling back on the Empire's center? The attackers that destroyed Victrix Base, Commander, were *Imperial* forces."

Imin looked at the fiery Gladius officer for a few more moments, digesting the way the galaxy was turning upside down so suddenly then replied, "I'll get the Narsima Matic Ettranty to speak with you. He's the head of the Guidance Council."

ITC 901

On board the Troop Carrier, Legion Sergeant Major Vladmir Olmeg leaned over to speak quietly to Legate Corona. "Does OCS teach centurions to be so much better than a decurion at spouting official bullshit, Legate?"

Legate Corona twitched a smile. "You have to admit most of what I told that young man was true, Sergeant Major."

"True enough, if limited," Sergeant Major Olmeg replied with his own slight smile. Then he made a small change of subject. "I wonder if the Commander of the Planetary Guard knows what we suspect."

"I doubt it," Legate Corona replied. "I doubt if anyone but this Matic Ettranty and whoever is the Emperor's direct liaison actually knows what Cauldwell really is. If it really is a refuge, that is.

"Here's one thing that's not bullshit, Sergeant Major," he continued with a grim expression. "If Intelligence isn't right about Cauldwell, everything we're planning will be worthless. I don't know where we'll go if they're wrong."

A grim fire flared behind his constantly smoldering eyes. "What I do know is that we're going to do something, whatever Cauldwell turns out to be. Emperor Shangnaman will pay for what he's done!"

CAULDWELL PCC

Imin cut the connection and turned to a nearby junior officer. "Find the Narsima Ettranty. Tell him I'll meet him in his office as soon as possible. I'm on the way right now."

Watching the Guard's commander leave, the com tech commented to the woman running the station on his left, "Looks like things are about to get interesting with the raiders, Marta."

She wasn't a history buff. "What do you mean?"

He grinned at her. "You may not know it, but that old boy was an Imperial Gladius. The Empire's best soldiers."

The grin turned wolfish. "Say you were rampaging across the galaxy devastating Imperial worlds and killing people. One day you turn around and there's a bunch of those guys standing there giving you a dead cold look. That's the Lord Above's way of letting you know you are about to have a really bad day."

CITY PORT
BEAUREGARD,
CAULDWELL

After a period of further negotiation between the Legate and the Narsima, the troopship was allowed to land. Although the negotiations were off the record, the landing was not. Given Cauldwell's highly active press, the Narsima simply resigned himself to their participation. He had control to a degree, but that control had its limits. Besides, they already knew about the troopship - leaks had occurred immediately - and he had no idea what his daughter would do if he didn't publicize the landing. Throw the press - and her - a bone to keep them docile. Soon enough, he'd need their silence on something else much easier to hide.

Cauldwell World News Network's star reporter, Shana Ettranty, was the Narsima's daughter and only child. Shana's appealing - if not quite tridio star beautiful - face, shoulder length brown hair, and athletic figure were perfect for a tridio personality that inspired trust and showed earnest dedication to her profession while being very easy on the male eye. Her beauty, as much as her connection to the Narsima, were what got her started in her tridio news career. Her intelligence, initiative, and a practical nature that overlaid a well-hidden inner core of steel took her to the top of a highly competitive profession. She always studied her subject in depth, something too many of her colleagues and competitors didn't do, a major reason she was usually first with a scoop.

She was also discreet. Along with a very few others, she knew the actual story behind the legion's damage and arrival here on Cauldwell but held it to herself. The Narsima had suggested - and Legate Corona had agreed - that a cover story was necessary. The idea the Empire was collapsing might unsettle the populace. The ship's damage and the legion's casualties were attributed to the actions of an unspecified "rebellious warlord". The rest of the story could be safely left to the contradictory speculation of talking heads to confuse and cloud.

The landing was unspectacular. The troopship settled softly into position as Shana's tridio crew got some great shots of combat damage and she speculated into her mike about the how and why of it. Cargo came out and was loaded into carriers. The offloading of the troops was also routine, simply men in khaki kilts unloading gear, then assembling into units. Some carriers left as soon as they were loaded, headed for the location the Narsima had ceded to the legion in the undeveloped area near Beauregard.

Shana's father was present at the Port in his official capacity and he was a natural for her to interview. He became very warmly paternal as the tridio cams focused on him. "The Legate said he wanted his men to march to their new base," the Narsima told Shana and her audience as the legion completed forming.

"Humph," he snorted. "The base is thirty kilomeasures away. That's quite a bit of marching in my book, but that was their standard daily distance, when the Corps chose to march. Goes back to the ancient Romans, I understand. Tradition is important to a Gladius."

Shana gave her sound man a look that ensured he was editing the Narsima's remarks before broadcast. The man just grinned back. He was an old hand at making sure politicians didn't embarrass themselves on the air.

Shana turned back to the troop assembly when she heard the legion band strike up. The beginning was almost ghostly, ethereal. Then, as commands - audible at even this distance - were given, the music began to take on a slow rhythmic pulsing beat. The formation began to flow forward with a ponderous marching stride.

Shana couldn't understand what the unit commanders were saying. The words weren't in Unispek. The Narsima supplied the answer. "The Corps of Imperial Gladius has its own language, Copio."

"Each legion has its own band," the Narsima continued to explain. "Music like that hasn't been heard in Cauldwell for several centuries, and I've never even seen recordings of a marching legion."

As the legion slowly came abreast of the spot where Shana and her crew were interviewing the Narsima, she got a better look. Their slow marching pace wasn't awkwardly ponderous when seen close up. Instead, it spoke of massively irresistible grinding power, the force of Empire that controlled thousands of suns and glacially sintered any resistance to dust.

This was the ultimate power of the Emperor on the move. The formation was led by the legion's Sunburst, fixed on a staff carried by a Gladius wearing some kind of animal skin draped across his head and shoulders. Shana noted the grim, bearded commander behind the Sunburst, marching at the head of his troops.

The faces struck Shana next. They had no expression. They weren't quite immobile, but, in some way she couldn't define, projected the emotionless facade of a formidable machine, totally uncaring and always utterly dangerous. The troops seemed oblivious to the crowds, but Shana could sense that each Gladius was totally aware of his surroundings and assessing everything in it. They marched in immaculate formation, each legionary cohort led by a commander and a boy in his mid-teens bearing what looked like a ram's horn, followed by armored carryalls for crew served weapons and battlefield equipment.

The ram's horns sparked Shana's interest, but now wasn't the time to launch her father into a long winded explanation. The rows of khaki clad grim men in their blouses, kilts and carrying personal weapons were a powerful visual image and she wanted as much of it going out as possible. Elaboration would come in the studio. Help had come to Cauldwell, but it was a little frightening. Maybe it was what they needed, she thought.

"No women, no children," the Narsima muttered. "A full legion is the entirety of a very strange people and the women march in the Legion Support Group, but all I see is the fighting strength, and not all of that. Less than three thousand. I wonder what happened to them. Just how bad was that fight they escaped?"

Before Shana could ask the Narsima for an explanation, he said something chilling. Narsima Ettranty scowled at the passing men, marching at a pace that proclaimed their power. "Those men terrify me," he muttered softly.

That remark wasn't broadcast.

#####

Later Shana Ettranty was in her father's apartment as a member of a small select gathering featuring Imin Webster, her father, and the man she most wanted to get in front of a tridio lens, Legate Corona. Shana sipped her drink and stayed in the background. She wanted to avoid calling attention to herself while she studied the soldier. He was her objective, the subject for her next major story, and she was as careful as any hunter on a stalk. She was willing to admit the man fascinated her. That he also frightened her was something she was not prepared to admit, even to herself.

Everyone in the room knew the real story of the legion and the Empire, but they also knew it wasn't a topic of conversation for this meeting. Or anywhere else except in the most secure circumstances. The cover story was working, aided by plenty of smoke and mirrors in the public information nets. That didn't bother her. She'd hidden things before when politics required it. Her interest in the Gladii was from a human angle anyway.

She glanced at the Legate's aide, standing with all of the animation of a statue in the corner, and felt again a little thrill of fear. He was the one that answered the door on her arrival and she found herself in her first face to face meeting with a Gladius. Her immediate impression was of a clean-cut fair young man in a strange uniform, his dark bronze skin contrasting with his very pale blonde hair and eyebrows.

Then she saw the eyes. They were an indeterminate shade of light blue, but terribly emotionless, simply assessing her. Shana felt he would think less of killing her than she would of swatting a fly. If it was called for, her death would be ordained for objective reasons and carried out with a maximum of professional skill. From that moment, she fully understood the mystique - and the fear - of the Gladius.

The Legate was a different story. She thought he seemed to be smoldering with suppressed fanaticism. If his men were ice, he was fire. With his beard, he reminded her of one of the prophets from the Old Christian Bible. On the other hand, he seemed to have a speck of humanity in him. At least he could laugh. Maybe that was why he fascinated her.

Truthfully, the whole legion fascinated her. She felt the urge to dig deeper, learn all she could about them. Shana interpreted her feelings as the professional instincts of Cauldwell's premiere newswoman. She had high hopes of parlaying this little cocktail party into an in-depth study of the entire unit. Adam, her editor, was practically salivating at the idea.

The Narsima was carefully pouring quantities of Cauldwell brandy into everyone's glass, except for the aide, who would take nothing. Once finished he offered the toast, "To the future!"

The Legate responded, "May your harness never fail."

The Narsima explained with the air of a well-prepared student giving a favorite presentation. "Gladii ride into battle on six man antigrav sleds. When they reach their objective, they release themselves and drop to the ground using no-weight belts. The sled continues on, becoming an explosive missile to disrupt the enemy. If a man's harness fails him, he is condemned to ride the sled on until it blows up."

The Legate nodded. "Exactly right, Narsima."

Ettranty's beefy face beamed, betraying his pride in his ability to show off in his hobby.

Shana decided to pounce on the opening. She asked interestedly, "That sounds like a horrible fate! Has it ever happened, Legate?"

He looked at her with what she guessed was the Gladius version of a mildly amiable expression. "Occasionally, Sim. In fact, it happened to me once."

Shana, for her part, was thinking about the formal way the Legate used Unispek like it was a foreign language he'd learned from a book. Did they all speak that way? Enough woolgathering. Get the story. She leaned further forward in her chair. "Please go on," she said. "Tell us how you got away."

The Legate took a sip of his drink, secure in the knowledge he had the full attention of his audience. Away from everyone's attention, a tiny smile played around the corners of his aide's mouth. "Well," he replied in deadpan tones, "I didn't. I was killed."

"But you're here, now!" Shana dithered.

The rest were silent for a moment, then the fact that they were the butt of a rather strange joke registered. The Narsima snorted and Shana blushed a fiery red.

Legate Corona smiled as he took another sip of his drink. "I apologize, Sim Ettranty," he said. "Simply my little attempt at humor."

The Narsima took a look at the expression on Shana's embarrassed face and chuckled. "I credit you with a score on us, Legate, especially my daughter. You turned the tables as neatly as I've seen it done. You are to be congratulated, Corona.

"But," he waved a lordly finger at the room, "enough of this. Commander Webster has a small presentation to make."

He made a grand gesture at Imin, theatrically turning over center stage to him. Imin nodded in acknowledgment, "Yes, thank you, Narsima."

Imin leaned forward in his chair and fumbled with some hard copy in his hand before arranging it to his satisfaction on the low table he'd placed in front of him. He placed a small tridio projector next to the papers then looked at the Legate. "Legate, have you ever heard of the Wareegan Raiders? I'm not sure if that's your name for them. We discovered it in some old records."

Corona's face took on the intent, deadly look of a ferocious predator hearing the distant hunting cry of a natural enemy. Shana noticed his left hand stole to the holstered ax at his side. "The name is correct, Commander," he replied in a grim, deadpan voice. "They once were a pest in our sector until we cleaned them out. If you are suffering from Wareegan raids, it is a problem we can permanently solve."

Shana was taken aback by the simple deadly bloodthirstiness of the declaration. Then she realized her assessment was wrong. Legate Corona wasn't a predator. He was the anti-predator, a guard dog marking a threat to the flock. He didn't regard the Wareegans as enemies; he regarded them as the reason he existed. She shivered slightly at that mindset.

Imin also looked slightly shaken. He was a career military man, but the natural killer in front of him was far outside his experience. He looked away from the older Gladius as he continued. "Ah, yes, ahh… at any rate, we have a shot of the only body we've been able to salvage. This will tell you if it's the same species you earlier encountered."

He activated the projector and an image appeared in the air between the four. It showed an insectoid alien around three measures tall, covered with thick leathery skin and colored a dark green. The creature had two arms, two legs, and a bulbous head on a short neck. The limp body was dangling like it was suspended from invisible wires. To Shana, the grisly thing reminded her of a carcass dangling in a slaughterhouse. Knowing what the creature was capable of doing, she shuddered slightly. The triple-damed things were a living nightmare!

His voice now calm, Imin continued in an unemotional tone. "We strung this one up to get a better three dimensional representation. An interesting point is that it is actually hemoglobin based and mammalian. Apparently, this specimen was artificially neutered."

"They bleed red," Corona said in a flat voice. In more conversational tones, he added, "That is one of their warrior caste. All are apparently neutered. Where was this slide taken?"

"At Bluefield," the Narsima injected, "where they first hit. The devastation was terrible. Also, we aren't exactly sure what happened to the bulk of the population. We didn't find as many bodies as we expected. Normal things - manufactured items, raw materials - were taken, but why they took the people we don't know."

"I do," Corona's voice was flat. "They have compatible metabolisms with humans. They can digest the same foods, if properly treated for such things as trace elements. We found when we were cleaning them out of the sector that they tended to take all of the organic matter they could grab to process in their protein tanks. That includes the residents of wherever they raid."

Shana gulped, fighting a sudden surge of nausea. From the looks on the other two Cauldwell faces, she wasn't alone. "That's ghastly!"

"Not to them, Sim Ettranty," Corona replied, turning his fierce glare at her. "May they be damned to everlasting hells throughout time for

45

it, but it is still their way of life. They ceased all production of their own needs millennia ago and converted totally to a raiding economy, living on their mother ships. The pattern isn't unusual in humanity, either."

He broke off, looking at the two men. "In the past, they exhibited wanton cruelty where they hit. Examples were usually left to intimidate survivors and future victims. What happened at Bluefield?"

Imin's voice was now the flat tones of a man under tight control. "We have several slides of the human remains we did find at the scene. I'll run through them."

Shana didn't watch. As one of the first reporters on the scene after the raid, she still had nightmares about that.

Corona sat quietly. The only reaction he betrayed at the distorted horrors in the projections was a tight grip on his ax. When Imin finished, he asked baldly, "I'm aware there was another raid. What did you do?"

Imin was embarrassed and defensive. "The Planetary Guard was no match for their ships. The only thing we could do is let them land and nuke the site with a missile."

"WHAT?"

The Legate came half out of his chair in outrage. "You wear that uniform to protect your people, boy," he roared, "not kill them! Don't ever forget that!"

Narsima Ettranty leaned in to pour oil on troubled waters. "Restrain yourself, Corona. I understand your outrage, but it wasn't this man's fault. He was under orders."

The Legate glared at the corpulent Narsima. "Whose? Yours?"

The Narsima nodded then held up a restraining hand to ask for silence. Legate Corona - reluctantly - settled back, clearly holding his anger in check. "Thank you," the Narsima said after the Legate appeared to be back under tight control. "Please, hear me out and consider our options. I assure you, we are talking about a last resort in this case. His men did their best, Legate. Half of our Planetary Guard was lost in our first attempt to attack Wareegan assault craft before I forbade any further action. We have nothing that can fight them on the ground and we're totally outmatched in space. We tried to protect the people of Longcreek with shelters, but the warhead malfunctioned and proved too powerful. Our other shelters should prove safe with smaller warheads. I intend to continue missile attacks if there are any other raids. Our only hope is to destroy enough of their raiding parties that they will cease their attacks and go elsewhere."

"Only to do the same thing over again," Corona replied with dangerous intensity. He obviously had his doubts that the warhead "malfunctioned".

46

The Narsima shrugged. "That is not our problem. Hopefully, wherever it is will have more and better armaments than we."

The Legate glared back. "Enough!

"There will be no further missile attacks, and the Wareegans will not be allowed to complete another raid. My men and I will see to the next one ourselves." He looked piercingly at the thoroughly cowed Imin. "Possibly you cannot protect your people, Commander. We will. It is our pledge."

The Narsima settled back in his chair, pleased. He had the aid he wanted against the Wareegans. Better yet, they were completely expendable, since they had no ties to Cauldwell. With any luck, these problematical visitors would totally spend themselves in battle, neatly taking care of the future troubles they represented. Excellent. If they didn't, well, other measures could be taken.

"I believe, then," the Narsima continued, "that we may ignore further pleasantries and begin discussing the hard details of how we can work together to rid ourselves of our disagreeable visitors."

The Legate grunted. "My Operations Officer will be over in the morning to begin work with your staff and that of the Planetary Guard. We have a few tricks for the Guard as well."

The Legate looked at Imin. "Judging by the way you came at our troop carrier, your formations and tactics are very poor, young man. We'll show you how to fix that and win next time."

Imin bridled, but kept his mouth shut. To the Narsima, the reason for Imin's reaction was obvious. If they could teach him how to beat the Wareegans, it was worth the harassment. He hated the loss of his people and hated the nuclear option worse.

"Legate."

The word was rather hesitantly spoken in a soft, feminine voice. The Legate turned to look at Shana. "Yes?"

She continued, "I'm a newswoman with a job to do. Cauldwell needs to know more about you. Will you allow me to visit your compound? Perhaps do a story?"

The Narsima's face pursed with disapproval. The last thing he needed in his relations with the legion were more complications, something the newsies were excellent in providing. "Shana, I'm afraid the Corps never admits journalists to their compounds."

Corona waved the Narsima down absently as he intently studied Shana. After a few seconds, he appeared satisfied with what he found. "Never in the past, perhaps, Sim Ettranty, but I think it's now time for a change. Your people must know us. You have my permission to begin shortly. We will contact you when it is proper for you to visit our base. I will assign an officer to act as your guide."

#####

Later, as they were leaving the Narsima's apartment, Shana felt Imin's hand steal around her waist. She smiled up at him as he asked, "I was wondering, Sim Ettranty, if there was any possibility of asking for a date with you tonight?"

She pursed her lips and assumed a mock-serious expression. "I'm sure there isn't, Sima. I am afraid I have a prior engagement to make dinner at the Commander's apartment tonight. Perhaps another time?"

Imin frowned back and said in mock pompous tones, "I know the Commander, Sim, and I fear his no doubt romantic intentions where you are concerned. I'm sure he will preoccupy you to the point any further social congress between us will be fruitless. If I must yield this truly beauteous prize to him, may he know its worth."

Shana laughed. "I've told that fool I don't know how many times that he has a treasure in his arms. Knucklehead never seems to listen."

Imin laughed. "Tell him again tonight. I bet he'll pay attention."

His expression changed. "Shana, I wish you wouldn't go out to the legion base. We don't know enough about them. Anything could happen."

"Imin," she replied firmly, "it's my job. I have to go there if I'm going to get any kind of story."

"I've said it before," he continued gruffly, hugging her, "you don't need this job. You could marry me like I have been asking you to do for the last year."

"No," she shook her head. "Not yet. I, mmph..." The kiss stilled all conversation.

After she and Imin had gone their separate ways, her mind went back to the Legate's last comments. Assign an officer as a "guide"? The last thing she wanted was some official stooge hiding the things she most wanted to see. She and that officer were going to miss connections. That was certain.   ·

#####

In his office, the Narsima was also thinking about his conversation with the Legate. The man was simple but thoroughly irritating. He and his people needed to be dealt with, but not yet. Not while the Wareegans were around. Later though, when they were weakened by battle. Then…

48

Outside, the Legate and his aide were met by Legion Sergeant Major Olmeg and the command driver. Piling into the grav carryall, the weathered, scarred old Sergeant Major leaned forward to talk to the Legate in the front passenger seat while the carryall lifted and headed towards the compound. "Did they buy it, Legate?"

Legate Corona snorted a laugh. "Bought it? Completely, Sergeant Major. That fat corrupt fool is fully convinced he's in total control of a mob of slightly stupid barbarian warriors. I imagine wheels are spinning in what passes for his mind right now, planning our removal once we've gotten rid of the Wareegans for him."

The Sergeant Major grinned. "Told the harness story, did you, Legate?"

Corona smiled back. "It served its purpose."

Corona's face grew thoughtful. "There was a young woman there, too. Ettranty's daughter. From what I could sense of her, she may well be what we're looking for."

Now it was the Sergeant Major's turn to grow thoughtful. "Lord Above knows we need one. You think she might do?"

"That's why I invited her out to the base, so we could see," Corona replied. "If so, she's someone for you to work with."

The Sergeant Major grew pensive. "Well, Cauldwell might have everything else, but it's nothing without the one we need. Colonel Athan's already got scouts out looking for caches, just to see if we were right. All we need now is her or someone like her. I hope and pray you're right, Legate, and she's the one. I hope and pray you're right."

"So do I, Sergeant Major," Corona said quietly.

CHAPTER 3

LEGIO IX VICTRIX
CAULDWELL

The steady deep hum of the velotrike's motor provided a monotonous background to Shana's thoughts on the trip out to the legion compound. It was a wonderful morning and she was perfectly happy to use her velotrike instead of a grav cab. More fun, too, she thought as she shifted in the saddle and hugged the trike's body with her legs, expertly controlling a turn with a body lean. Her father disliked the trike and claimed it wasn't suitable for a woman of her station and status, meaning he thought it reflected on his station and status. Shana didn't care. This wasn't the first difference she had with her father over lifestyle.

The trike was fun and a way to leave newscasting behind for a while. Especially Adam, her editor. The man was going practically nuts with all the possibilities of the Gladius story, flip flopping from one direction to the next, first declaring them rescuing heroes, then an insidious danger to the stability of Cauldwell. For her part, Shana decided to ignore Adam, especially since he was giving the legion to her as an exclusive assignment. Negative or sensational reports made money and got ratings which made more money, the purpose of any news network, but that sort of thing could wait until the Wareegans were defeated. Shana sometimes wondered if the Wareegans were real to Adam. They were real enough to her and she welcomed any help Cauldwell could get.

It had taken almost a month for the Legate's formal invitation to materialize. The reason given for the delay was the legion was still in the process of getting settled, without the time to give her the stories she wanted. That was a reasonable excuse, except Shana wondered what was being hidden during that month's time. It would take a while, but she was going to find out.

Cruising smoothly up the country road from Beauregard to the legion base, Shana carefully studied what she could see of the camp's layout as she headed for the main gate. Overhead imagery of the base showed it laid out in a hexagonal pattern with a systematic military precision using four standard sizes of domes. Just what could be expected, she mentally sniffed.

She noticed the huge troop ship was grounded on a new landing field established to one side of the compound and that was a bit of a surprise. She didn't know it was already out of the repair yards. Interesting.

Things were happening fast. A refugee troopship lands, requests aid, is welcomed as a new defensive partner against the Wareegans, and a month later all of the Imperial forces appear to be distancing themselves from the rest of Cauldwell. Also interesting.

Approaching the gate, a Gladius in duty uniform suddenly appeared and signaled her to halt. His conversation with her was polite to an almost artificial degree, like he was repeating lessons learned in a classroom. It was funny, she thought, Gladii used Unispek with an almost archaic cant and courteous precision that tended to emphasize their differences from normal people. With the formal courtesy of someone speaking a second language in diplomatic relations, he directed her to the legion's headquarters in the center of the base. She cheerily thanked him before leaving, knowing full well that was the last place she wanted to go.

Other eyes watched her as she left, just as they'd watched her come up the road. The watchers didn't move from their hidden places surrounding the base, simply reported. There were devices watching as well. The base was secured by far more than a fence and the sentry, but none of that was intended to be seen by an observer.

Shana deliberately kept the speed of her trike to a slow walk, to give her time to find a place that looked worth investigating. The sameness of the domes was depressing. They varied only in size, giving no hint of their purpose. When she heard music coming from one of the larger domes, she pulled into the street in front of it and parked the trike, taking off her leather jacket and helmet to stow in the trike's cargo compartment.

The guard at the gate was quietly following her progress on a remote monitor. When she stopped, he commed in a supplemental report. The Tactical Operations Center also had her on screen. The TOC watch officer called HQ and someone was sent to gather up the wayward visitor before she could get into trouble.

Standing in the dome's entrance, Shana listened to the music and cheering as the studied the dome's layout. The interior was a small amphitheater with tables on various levels surrounding a raised stage and large open space in the center. The place was dimly lit except for the stage where four Gladii were engaged in a highly athletic dance. The tables on the surrounding levels were full of drinking, cheering troopers, happily enjoying the show and singing. The music was provided by a small group, with Gladii playing several guitars, battle flutes, and brass wind instruments. As the tune picked up speed, the crowd began to chant in time to the music, "*Yawm, yawm, yawm dan schici, schici ya, schici ya!*"

The words made no sense to her. Apparently, they were in the Corps' private language. She was fascinated by the dancers, until a hand touched her arm. Facing her was a young Gladius who had walked unnoticed next to her. She found herself looking up into colorless, emotionless eyes. In his turn, he looked her over like some kind of strange animal. His imposing size and expressionless face scared her slightly.

He smiled minimally and asked her a question in the Gladius language. Another little surprise. Now what? When she shook her head in incomprehension, he repeated it in almost artificially formal Unispek. "You are local? Unattached?"

"Yes," Shana said, trying to figure out what the young man had in mind.

"Good," he nodded. "Then, will you come and sit with me?"

Oh, Lord Above, how did she get herself into this? The youngster was apparently trying to pick her up! Clumsy, to be sure, but the intent was obvious. Now what was she going to do?

"*Antak.*"

The word came from the open doorway behind her. Although it was spoken in a conversational tone, the voice drilled through the background furor with perfect legibility. The trooper backed away from her instantly and snapped into a position of attention, not even an eyelid quivering. She turned and saw a Gladius officer, apparently somewhat older than her, standing in the doorway.

He strode up to the unfortunate youngster and spoke to him for a moment, his clipped phrases coming in low, even tones that wouldn't let her make out the words, only that they weren't Unispek. The man saluted the officer with a straight right arm across his breast, flat hand palm down, then trotted to his table for his cap and out the door, never breaking his pace or further acknowledging her presence.

Shana blinked at the little drama then told her more-or-less rescuer, "Thank you, I think, but I could have handled him. Where is he going?"

The officer nodded with a quick, slight motion. "I apologize for him and for the Victrix. I am Colonel Athan, commander of First Cohort, Ninth Legion Victrix. That man is on his way to the Duty Sergeant for punishment tours."

"Oh." She was flustered. "I'm sure that wasn't necessary. Really. He probably just made a mistake... or something."

"He was being forward and a bit impetuous. He was also somewhat drunk, or he wouldn't have bothered you. The troops have been told we will be interacting with the local population, but not when that interaction would take place. He knew you were a local and, as I assume

52

you guessed, was trying to pick you up. He was being entirely too forward. The punishment is necessary because he overstepped his bounds.

"We have yet to be allowed open contact with local civilians, something unprecedented in any case. The Victrix cannot casually treat visitors with anything but the utmost courtesy, especially on a world on which we are guests. You are an important visitor from the local population. He will have time to meditate on those facts and will not forget them once he is finished."

In spite of herself, she was curious. "What are punishment tours?"

He replied calmly, "A punishment tour is a twenty-four-hour route march with full kit. He will be finished day after tomorrow at this time."

She was aghast. "But-!"

He ignored her outburst. "The Legate has ordered you be given full freedom of the compound and I am to answer any question you may have." He turned away from her and faced the stage. "Right now, for instance, we are in the Legionnaires Club and the men generally put on a good show to entertain themselves. I recommend we watch, if only out of courtesy."

The cool rebuff irritated her and she got a little hotter at the thought of what this martinet had done to the unfortunate young soldier. All the guy thought he was doing was making a pass at a pretty girl. Older woman, sure, but still a pretty girl in his eyes. She tried to ignore the fact that his clumsy approach rattled her for a moment. Then she got a grip on her emotions. Anger - and a bit of fear - weren't going to get her what she wanted. Settle down, girl, she told herself. You're a professional. Act like one.

The dance was over, and a clear pleasant voice was now beginning a bouncy, merry song from somewhere in the crowd.

"Eyn mol, eyn mol, eyn mol,
        eyn mol tu ikh zikh banayen:
A gantse vokh horevet men dokh,
Af shabes darf men layen..."

The song was lively, sung to a beat that was clapped or stamped out by the grinning men in the audience. In each verse, the singer sang point, and counterpoint was sung by the rest of the troopers in the room. Even without knowing the song's language, Shana could tell it was a happy-go-lucky sort of tune. But there was something else these men were reading into it, something a bit more ominous.

It was funny, but she could close her eyes and almost get a picture, something like a massive armed aircraft (?) racing low over a rough landscape. There were other aircraft in formation with the first. What was that all about?

Athan was watching her. "That's a very old drinking song, thousands of years old, like much of our music. It belonged to a fierce warrior race. They were scattered once, dispersed for over a millennium, but they never forgot. Even scattered, they were feared when they put down their books and turned their hands to war. That song was written during the period they were dispersed. Whatever its original purpose, it is part of our heritage and now it's often sung when we're going in for a jump into hostile territory."

He looked out at the room and showed a flash of teeth that wasn't friendly or humorous. "The beat, the music, the joy... all get you in the mood to be ejected out twenty measures over beings that don't like you very much."

Shana saw his eyes and shivered slightly. Then she realized Athan had made a joke. A grim one, but a joke. About fighting and killing. What sort of mentality did these men actually have? Once she got over her distaste, the question began to intrigue her.

Now there were men in a circle on the stage, dancing to different music with high kicking steps and arms crossed across their chests. One fell and Shana realized they were trying to trip each other as they danced. It wasn't just a dance, but a game as well. Axes began to fly through the air, spinning in wide ovals and flying back to their owners.

"How do they do that?" She asked Athan, indicating the axes.

For answer, he pointed to a metal bracelet on his wrist, the twin to another worn on his other wrist. "These. They are tractor-presser units, controlled by wrist movement. The range is about twenty measures. Every trained Gladius wears them. The men use them for their axes and short swords; women use them for their daggers. It's big day in the life of a young Gladius when they are awarded their blades and bracelets. It means they are now no longer Recruits, but fully trained members of the legion."

That sparked another question, but Shana had no time to ask. A 45 centimeasure long battleax flashed through the air, stopping centimeasures from her face. It hung in the air for a few seconds then spun back to its owner. Shana froze with shock, but Athan simply considered the whole incident with benign calm. "That was a bit of a test and a welcome to the club. No harm was intended. The men enjoy hazing a newcomer. You were right to show no reaction. They respect that."

Getting a firm grip on her still shaky stomach, Shana decided to continue with her questions as though nothing had happened. The first rule here appeared to show no reaction to any provocation. Okay, she repeated to herself, she was a reporter with a story to get. Keep that in mind, girl.

Drawing a deep and shaky breath, she asked, "You mentioned female Gladii, but I've never seen one. What happened to the female members of your legion?"

Athan gave her a piercing look and the unemotional robot persona clamped back into place again. "That question isn't for me. Come, you need to talk to the Legate."

As they waked away, Shana was irritated with herself. Athan was starting to open up in his own strange way before her unguarded question shut him down like a bolted steel box. Damn! He was some sort of underling, and probably an easier nut to crack than the Legate. Damn, again.

She decided to take a more harmless tack. Maybe he'd relax again - as much as any of these emotionless robots did. "You said that was the Legionnaires Club. Do you have others?"

Athan nodded without looking at her. He seemed intent on getting to the Legate as fast as possible. "The centurions - the officers - have one and the decurions - the sergeants - have one."

He gave her a minimal smile. "That last is far the most decorous of the three."

A boy in full uniform, somewhere in his late teens, walked past them, giving the officer the Gladius palm down, across-the-chest salute. He had a ram's horn carried by a strap across his front and was one of those she'd seen marching next to the cohort commanders when the legion disembarked.

Shana gave the boy a searching glance as Athan returned the salute. Apparently the officer knew the question she was about to ask, because he explained without prompting. "That was Legionnaire Third Class Kamal Mako, the Second Cohort's *brushara* bearer. A *brushara* is a ram's horn, blown to lead a cohort into battle. Legionnaire Third Mako accompanies his commander into the fight. The *brushara* is electronically augmented to vastly increase its volume, with tones in both the supersonic and subsonic. It will shatter plass at a kilomeasure and is as much a weapon of war as a signaling device. It's the soul of the Cohort, a rallying point, and proclaims the continued existence of the unit, no matter the casualties."

Shana couldn't help but comment. "It seems cruel to send a boy that young into battle."

Athan's expression was tight. "Possibly, but that is the life we're born into. Mako is already a trained soldier and was the best of his recruit class. Because he's a Bearer, he's constantly under the commander's eye in action, and one of the most protected men in the Cohort. Still, some of

55

them pay the Gladius Price from time to time. Regrettable, but a fact of life and chance."

Athan's reaction interested Shana. Gladii were the ultimate soldiers, bred for war. It sounded as though they didn't particularly care for the fact, but were resigned to it. That was something nobody had mentioned in the resource material she'd previously scanned.

Shana wasn't sure what to expect when she walked into the dome housing the legion's headquarters. What she found was a large outer room that looked like any other office, except it was staffed exclusively by men in Corps uniform. Men in kilts were still a strange sight to Shana and it was a bit disorienting to see obviously tough, physically imposing soldiers engaged in prosaic administrative tasks. Everything was spartan, plain and economical, with none of the disordered little clutter of individual items that marked human personalization.

Even the Legate's office, when Athan finally walked her inside, was plain and unadorned, geared towards a machinelike efficiency with a lack of personalization and decoration. Correction, she thought, there were several personal touches of a sort. The Legate's armor, hard to see due to its refractive camouflage, was on a stand in the corner. Nearby, a short efficiently ugly bolt gun hung on the wall, magazine in place behind the handgrip/trigger arrangement halfway up its length. From her research, Shana knew it was called a B-42. With weapon and armor at hand, the owner of this office was ready to respond to a threat in a matter of moments.

The Legate sat behind a small well organized desk, with another Gladius sitting in one of the office's low chairs not far away. The other Gladius was older, with a scarred face, a leg stretched in front of him, and the no-nonsense expression of someone that had seen it all.

"Please sit down, Sim Ettranty. You too, Karl," Legate Corona said. "Welcome to the Ninth Legion Victrix, Sim Ettranty. This is Decurion Tenth Vladmir Olmeg, Legion Sergeant Major. There will be... yes, here they are."

A young Gladius entered the room, bearing hot drinks for all. Shana guessed it was coffee, but was surprised to be given her favorite type of herbal tea. She was about to comment, then realized that the chamomile tea showed how much the legion already knew about her.

Shana thought furiously for a second or two, taking a sip of her tea to cover her thinking, and decided to say nothing. Wait and see how the Legate was going to direct the conversation. This was another test, more sophisticated than the ax, but still a test. After a few moments of silence, the Legate turned and looked at the Sergeant Major, and Shana got the distinct impression of an unspoken comment and reply being passed back and forth.

The Legate looked at her calmly and opened the conversation. "You have questions, Sim Ettranty. We are here to hopefully arrange or give the answers."

Putting down her mug, Shana said, "Thank you for the tea, Legate, but I'm interested in why I was invited to this base. In the last few weeks, I've done my research in Father's collection and every other reference I could find - all of which were limited - and I've never found a time when the Corps willingly hosted a reporter."

Corona nodded. "Nor will you. You are the first, as far as I know, so we are a bit into unknown territory here. I have my reasons and I'll explain them."

"Please do."

"It's obvious to all of us, Sim Ettranty, that the legion is here under extraordinary circumstances."

"Shana, please."

Corona nodded and continued. "Shana, then. We feel your people need to know more about us. As I said, we are here under extraordinary circumstances and Cauldwell has been uninvolved with the Empire for some time, although your rulers have more contact with the Empire than I suspect you know."

"Contact?" Shana interrupted. She was flabbergasted for a moment. He'd tossed the last sentence out casually, but it was a blockbuster. Wait. Was it really so casual? She began to suspect that the Legate never said anything casually. She also began to reevaluate the Gladius "barbarian warrior" image that was current among tridio talking heads. "That's impossible Legate," she finally said. "There's been no communication with the Empire for more than twenty years, other than occasional liners and tramp freighters."

Something occurred to her in a flash of inspiration. "They leave us alone and we don't care."

Corona looked grim. "I'll explain in due time. Meanwhile, your father and the Guidance Council know exactly what's been going on in Empire politics. They are players, trust me."

Her father? Mixed up in Imperial politics? More important *was* he really in contact with the Empire? For some unaccountable reason, she didn't doubt the Legate. Her newswoman's instincts said everything he was saying was true. She thought furiously for a moment, then little bits and pieces, remarks made in unguarded moments, started to connect. "You know, Legate, you have given me no proof of your statement and I'm inclined to take it with a heavy dose of salt, but I'm not discounting it. If what you say is true, *that's* the biggest story of the decade, not your arrival."

Corona smiled grimly, which was the way all of these people seemed to do anything. "I'm sure it would be if you published it, but you won't, not yet. You'll keep what I just said to yourself until you get supporting evidence. That's your habit, Sim, and it's a good habit.

"In any case, if you submit the story, it will never be let out to your viewers. Put what I said in the category for later discussion and let's move on with our conversation. I have other things to tell you. However, I ask that you take the time to contemplate why we ended up at Cauldwell out of any other possible destination."

She nodded cautiously. All these frustratingly vague hints were irritating, but she could live with them for now. Her work was just beginning. He wasn't telling her everything, and he wouldn't, but that was perfectly all right with Shana. Nobody ever told her everything. She found it out anyhow.

"I've issued orders you be given the freedom of the base. We won't censor your reports either. Just try not to interfere with our duties and I ask that you respect the privacy of the men if that becomes an issue. I'd originally planned to have Colonel Athan be your guide, but he commands nearly a thousand men in his Cohort and many are orphans from destroyed units that need integrating. He has his hands full.

"Therefore," Corona said with a sly glance at the Sergeant Major, "I've decide to use someone that hasn't got any pressing responsibilities, Sergeant Major Olmeg."

The Sergeant Major shot the Legate an irritated glance, then turned a gimlet eye to Shana. "You can ignore any irrelevant comments from the Legate, girl. I'll show you what you want and provide the explanations."

Shana suppressed irritation at the "girl" remark then nodded at Olmeg. At least he'd be good for background information before she brought in the tridio crew. Besides, he was the first one besides the Legate that spoke Unispek with something approaching a normal speech pattern.

Corona was still smiling, more at Olmeg than her. Sparring between the two seemed an old game. "You have complete freedom to tell our story, Shana. I also have a great deal of confidence you'll get it right. You seem to do that more often than your colleagues."

This time Shana had to react. "You apparently know quite a bit about us for being here such a short time, Legate."

Corona nodded. The grim look was back. "We are the most capable soldiers in human history, Sim Ettranty. People forget warfare takes many forms. It is not solely a matter of gunbolts and axes, but sometimes a matter of economics, other times a matter of public emotions, other times... well, many things. Information - and how you use it - is also a form of warfare and we have become very, very good at warfare during our existence."

He took a chip folder from is desktop and handed it to her. "Here. This contains Copio, our language. I suggest you take the hypnocourse on those chips as soon as possible. You'll need it. You'll also find selected images of us and our lifestyle that you won't get in open sources. Consider them background.

"Now, I have some things to accomplish this morning."

With that, the Legate nodded, turned to a data terminal, and the interview was abruptly over. Colonel Athan simply got up and walked out while the Sergeant Major heaved himself to his feet with a slight awkwardness Shana was unaccustomed to seeing in that uniform. Olmeg's somewhat stiff left leg looked like the reason. "Come on, girl," he growled as he took his cap from its nearby peg and planted it firmly on his head, cocked slightly forward. "I'm supposed to teach you about the Victrix. Well, let's go do it."

Shana found herself swept up behind the Sergeant Major's irresistible force without a chance, or the inclination, to argue.

Her paralysis lasted until they were outside the headquarters. She stopped dead and kept her voice level, although she felt like screaming at this ignorant uniformed robot and his disgusting mannerisms. "Wait right there, Sergeant Major! I'd like a little explanation as to what in the hell is going on here!"

The Sergeant Major favored her with a grin. "Mad, eh? That's good. I thought you had enough in you to not take anything lying down. All right, girl, I'll tell you what's happening."

"And while you're at it, you can stop calling me 'girl'!"

The growl was back. "I'll call you what I call you until you earn a different name for yourself. Nothing you've done so far means a shit to me, girl. Where we start is right here where we are now. Where we go is up to you.

"Now, do you want to know what's happening or not?"

Shana bit her lip to keep from telling this damned old relic to stuff it where the sun didn't shine. Settle down, girl, she told herself. Getting mad won't do any good. Control yourself. Then she blushed uncontrollably when she realized what she'd called herself. Okay, so the Sergeant Major was a bastard and a son of a bitch, but he was a bastard and a son of a bitch she was going to have to work with to get what she wanted. One of these days, though...

Once she got control of herself and took a deep breath (to the Sergeant Major's amusement), Shana said, "Okay, I'll put up with you for now, but I have limits, do you understand that?"

The Sergeant Major nodded. "I do, girl, but I'll bet you're going to find out more about them than you ever knew if you continue to hang around the Corps. We tend to do that to folks."

Chuckling, he turned and pointed at a unit marching in from the badlands on the far side of the base. "That's Third Century, First Battalion, Second Cohort, coming in from a forced march. If you can shut up about being pissed at me for a while, you'll hear them when they sound off."

Curious, Shana temporarily set aside her irritation and listened. The men were singing to the slow pace of their march. Strangely, the song felt as though it should be sung at a faster rhythm. The words were unfamiliar, nothing like the legion's language. "What are they singing?"

"Le Boudin. It's damned old, girl, and the Corps inherited it from another Legion. Took their marching pace, too. They took it from what was supposed to be the marching pace of another Legion, a good two thousand years older than them."

Shana could follow a lead in when she got one. "Is that why you march so slowly, tradition?"

Sergeant Major Olmeg looked at her and smiled slightly again. "We march at 88 paces per minute and most militaries march at 110. You'd be surprised how fast you can move troops across bad terrain at that pace and have them pretty fresh at the end. Fresh enough to fight, anyhow. The first Legion that used it walked across the known world. The second crossed deserts. We took it to the stars. The cadence works and I've walked many a weary kilomeasure to that beat.

"Now," he continued, "I'm going to show you around today so you won't get lost." He gave her an ironic look. "Again."

They covered the base over several hours time and Shana found herself fascinated, even if she didn't understand half of what she was being shown. By midafternoon, she voiced just that complaint to the Sergeant Major.

His response was characteristic. His minimal smile wasn't. "You'll get an interview with the Legate every morning you come here, girl, and he's the man for the tough questions, so hold them for him. Me, I'm detailed to play tour guide for my sins and show you around. If you want to know what something is or what someone is doing, ask. If you want to know *why*, you ask the Legate. That okay with you, girl?"

Despite her irritation, she found herself warming to the old fart for some reason and smiled back. "Okay, What for you and why for him. Sounds like a deal."

The next morning, Shana was sipping her tea in the Legate's office while he drank his coffee. This looked like it was going to be a regular ritual. It was a nice enough one, Shana decided.

"You've seen the compound, Shana," the Legate said. "What did you think?"

Shana studied the Legate. "You were run out of your old base with just a damaged troop ship. Where did all of this come from?"

The Legate gave a small grimace. "That's a good question. There are several kits to construct a base like this and a complete heavy equipment issue on every Imperial troopship as standard equipment. I ask you to consider the implications of that for the Gladius. When we set down on a world for even a short time, this is our home, the only one we have. All of our equipment, uniforms, weapons, even our field rations, are packed in duplicate sets on the ship. Our normal garrison rations come from food synthesizers. We can also fabricate replacements for anything that isn't alive, so those sets are constantly being regenerated as they are used.

"In other words, a Gladius is simply the human part of a superbly efficient mechanism for transferring military power wherever it's needed in a minimum of time. A man's personal belongings can usually be put into a small pouch. A Gladius, Shana, has no clothing other than his uniform. Everything is replaceable by an identical duplicate. The Gladius is the most highly refined soldier in history and the system under which he lives is the ultimate refinement of the way military forces have been treated for millennia. In our case, however, we don't live that way for the course of an enlistment or a career like other military forces, we live like this for generations, and know no other way of life. To Imperial planners, Sim Ettranty, we are not people, we are a weapon. A most complex and dangerous weapon, but a weapon. *Ultima Ratio Regis...* the last argument of kings. We are treated as such."

Shana shuddered slightly. The idea of a life lived like that was so alien it was almost repellent. She couldn't live that way. "That seems like a cold impersonal existence."

The Legate nodded. "It seems so... and civilians, even other militaries, feel that way."

He looked down and started to take a sip of his coffee. "As do you."

Shana started to hotly deny the accusation, then shut up. He was right. "Okay, you caught me. But you aren't that way among yourselves, are you?"

Corona shook his head. "Far from it. We place no value on possessions. We look inward instead of out. That's why we value music so highly. We say the ax is the soul of the Gladius and the *brushara* is the soul of the Cohort. Both are true, but the soul of the Corps is our music."

Shana thought about yesterday in the Legionnaires' Club. "Come to think of it, I've seen men singing as they marched and heard others doing it just for fun. I begin to get the idea of what you're saying."

She mulled that over and decided it was time to ask a hard question, one that had punched a button every time so far. "What happened to your women? Your families? All I see here are men, and every open source record I've viewed only shows male combatants. Why did you restrict combat to your men? Weren't your women capable?"

Briefly, Shana thought of several pictures she'd viewed in the Legate's briefing chips. In sharp contrast to the big muscular kilted male Gladius, a woman was much shorter - a good bit shorter than Shana, in fact. Gladius women also shared several other characteristics. Long straight colorless hair where the men wore only stubble and a body that was very curvy, nearly stocky. The briefing had also included material on Gladius rank insignia and Shana was intrigued to discover many of the women in the pictures were very highly ranked.

Women wore the same khaki shirts as the men, but without the weapons belt. Instead, they had some sort of dagger fixed to their left forearms. They didn't wear kilts, but long flowing skirts instead. Shana usually wore pants or short tight skirts occasionally and wondered how a long flowing skirt felt. A female Gladius's appearance and uniform was in sharp contrast to her male counterpart, but there was a feeling of rightness about it. Still, she wondered about the surprising difference. Maybe the Legate would explain it.

Legate Corona snorted. "At the time of her death, my wife was several times your age and could probably break you in half. She was also the legion's Commander. Every legion is commanded by a woman. Still, she hadn't fought since her Virgin Mission in her teens. Female command was by our own design, not the idea of our creators."

Shana was silent, simply waiting while he explained. The Legate appeared slightly sad. "Legio I Primus established, or more properly broke, the pattern intended by our creators. After a number of small wars and other conflicts, it became obvious that our life was to be one of constant warfare. Legate Batiste made the decision that not every Gladius would be condemned to that future, and established the idea of the Exempt. Every Gladius must first prove themselves on a Virgin Mission involving combat, but we deliberately exempt our women from fighting after that mission. Your ideas of sexual equality have nothing to do with it. To us, our women have a greater responsibility. They keep the Corps whole for the future, no matter what happens to the men. They also form our leadership because of the stability of their lives, hence the fact that my wife, not I, was the legion's Commander. It only makes sense to us to keep our heritage and leadership for as long as possible. Men fight the battles and, because of that, normally have much shorter life spans than women.

"A Legion Support Command is staffed by our women and they drop onto a hostile planet behind the fighting Cohorts. That still puts them in danger, but they no longer have a duty to kill, only the right, and that's good. We deliberately genetically modified ourselves and bred for physical differences to make our men larger for physical combat while our women are smaller. A female Gladius is normally much shorter than you."

Corona's face took on a sardonic expression. "The Empire's leadership regarded that as an unforeseen side effect of their own genetic meddling and eventually stopped bothering us about it. The men were getting the job done and seemed more suitable to the task, so the Empire was happy. Besides, only a portion of any military force is involved with personal combat. The remainder keeps the fighters supported. Our women performed that task superbly. The Empire didn't realize we'd deliberately exempted part of our population from killing and pain, as much as we could."

Shana took a chance and decided to reveal her own brand new ability in Copio. "It sounds to me like you don't like your lives very much."

The Legate smiled at her language shift and continued in Copio. "Would any rational civilized being want to live with generations of killing and war, Sim Ettranty? However, it's a task that needs doing to protect the Empire. The Gladius does it better than anyone ever has before and we're proud of the fact. We're satisfied that some of us, supposedly born to a life of constant battle, do not have to fulfill that destiny. The rest of us uphold our pledge, and people sleep safe because of that. Do we like our lives? To a degree. There are some things we wish we didn't have to do, but we do them well and that's enough."

Still. "Legate, I know this must be painful, but I have to ask again. What happened to the women and children?"

His answer was curt, harsh. "The Empire turned on us. They are turning on all of the Gladius units and many of the Fleet units."

He sat back in his chair and inhaled a deep breath through dilated nostrils. "The Empire has hit hard times. They do not produce many new combat ships for a number of reasons, but they can muster ground forces. The tactics forced by that problem are simple enough. I saw them in action. Imperial representatives suborn the leadership of the Fleet Support Group and turn their guns on the legion based with them. Defecting forces are supplied with special ground troops brought in for the strike. They know you can't suborn a Gladius. Only a fool would accept such a declaration if it was made, since it would just be a tactic to gain time to strike back. No, they kill the entire legion.

"In our case, they made a miscalculation. Several, actually. I had the Victrix out for an exercise when they struck." Corona grinned evilly. "As it happened, it was a live fire exercise, so we were fully combat loaded with live ammunition. We made it back under fire from Fleet defectors while the new Imperial troops were still overly preoccupied with destruction of the base. Our casualties were heavy since we lacked air support."

The Legate suddenly looked like an old man. "The Imperial ground troops hit our quarters, the Support Area, and the schools first. They killed our women and children, the legion's future, deliberately. They paid heavily doing it, but they did it."

Shana gasped. "That's horrible!"

He looked her dead in the eye. "Sim Ettranty, they wanted us destroyed and killing our future was the fastest and most inevitable way to do it.

"However..." he continued, his voice shaking with emotion, "we came back right through those miserable black uniformed bastards the Imperials thought were ground troops. Once we got our crew served weapons deployed, we were able to clear the skies for a space. We gathered the legion's survivors and enough Fleet personnel to man our ship and took off. There were very heavy casualties in the process.

"In that attack, Sim Ettranty, I lost my wife and children. Every man you see on this compound lost a wife, children, a mother, a sister. Someone dear. They killed our women and children. THEY KILLED OUR FUTURE!" His fist crashed on his desk.

After a moment, he was back in control and speaking in calm tones. "However, they didn't manage to totally suborn the entire Fleet Support Group. One of the reasons we escaped was that a good bit of the Group was still loyal and already up or managed to lift with us. They didn't accompany us here because of the second miscalculation the Empire agents made.

"The Fleet has its own honor, Sim Ettranty. The men in those ships held to it. They were locked in combat with the defecting ships as we went into tachyon field drive. I have no idea how the battle ended, but I have to think the defecting force was destroyed. I personally saw a collier ram a defecting cruiser. The Fleet Support Group, I believe, went down taking its traitors with it."

The idea of such an orgy of mutual destruction made Shana shudder. Lord Above grant nothing like that came here! She noted the

Legate made no mention of civilians around the base, and she decided she didn't want an answer.

It was a relief a few silent moments later when the Sergeant Major came into the office to pick her up. "Well, girl, want to see some more, today?"

Shana was glad of the chance to escape the doom filled scenario she'd just had described. "Of course, Sergeant Major. Legate, if you will excuse us?"

The Legate nodded absently, his eyes distantly focused on something Shana had no desire to see.

Outside, Shana tried hard to think of a distraction. Anything other than the horror she'd just discovered in the Legate's office. The Sergeant Major looked at her with a cool assessment and said, "There's a combat football game going on right now. Want to watch? You can even play if you want, although I don't recommend it. You aren't in shape for that kind of thing."

That stung her pride. She ran a minimum of ten kilomeasures a day whenever her schedule permitted, and usually did weights and aerobics, too. "I'm in better shape than you think, Sergeant Major. I want to play, not watch. I have my stuff in the trike. Where can I change?"

The Sergeant Major grinned. "I admire your spirit, girl, even if you've bitten off a little more than you think. We have an unused set of officer's quarters erected and you can change there."

Inside the dome the Sergeant Major pointed out, Shana took a quick look around before changing. It was two stories inside, with two bedrooms and a bath upstairs. There wasn't a single personal element in the entire dome, probably normal, especially for unused quarters. Opening the closet in one of the bedrooms, she was surprised to find a full set of uniforms for a woman. There weren't any in the legion, and the Legate had just explained why. Why did they stock the closets? A quick check of built in drawers showed undergarments for a woman also? Why these?

Out of curiosity, she measured one of the soft flowing skirts against herself, and found it too short, and a little bigger in the hips. That figured. Female Gladii she'd seen in some of the material she'd gotten from the Legate showed a woman both shorter and a little curvier than she was. So this was all standard issue. Is that why the clothing was here? It simply came with the quarters? They just put it up out of habit? The concept was so impersonal it bothered her.

Changing into athletic shorts, sports bra, a pullover shirt, and her running shoes, Shana braided her hair then trotted back out to the Sergeant Major. "I'm ready."

He nodded at her attire, although he showed no real interest at her as a woman, which left her slightly miffed. She knew she had good legs, damn it! "All right, girl," he growled, "let's get you in the game."

As they walked over to the playing field, he explained combat football. "It's simple, you see. There are few rules, but four referees help keep down broken bones and such. There are two balls, two goalies at each goal, and you can move the ball by kicking, throwing, or running with it. The teams can be any size but they should be about equal. Usually have about twenty men on a side."

"Do women play?"

"Oh, our women play along with the men. And they take their lumps along with the men, too. You won't be out of place to the Gladii on the field, except that you're weaker and slower than they are. It isn't a matter of your conditioning, girl, but the fact that we're stronger, faster and longer lived than you."

Shana gave him an interested glance. "Genetic traits?"

The Sergeant Major replied, "Some, but we use nannie mods for most of that. We can duplicate those mods in a normal person if we want to do it. We do it when we take in recruits from local populations if they pass our tests. We could do it to you, too."

"Me?"

The Sergeant major nodded. "Not a problem. Two days in the hospital on the troop ship."

He gave her another searching glance. "If you're so keen on studying us, girl, you might consider an abbreviated recruit course. That goes with the mods. Get to know us from the real inside out."

He gave her an evil grin. "If you survive this damn fool notion of playing combat football, that is."

Shana turned her face forward and walked in an irritated silence, but her brain was busy with what the Sergeant Major had said. Live longer? Be faster and stronger? What woman who cared for her body wouldn't want that? She even considered the recruit training and immediately rejected it, but the vagrant little thought kept coming back. Why not?

As they approached what looked like a riot between two soccer goals, Shana started to have second thoughts. As she watched, one of the Gladii body checked another, sending the man flying and grabbed one of the balls, heading for a goal, only to go down in a mob tackle. When the Sergeant Major waved to one of the officials, whistles blew and everyone took a break, heading for the water bottles laid out on nearby tables.

The Sergeant Major turned to her and pointed out onto the field. "Just get on out there. There aren't any positions except the goalie. Just move the ball to the opposing goal. The boys without shirts are one team, the ones wearing shirts are the others. Team numbers are close enough, so adding you won't make any difference.

"Given Cauldwell's ideas on the female body, I'd imagine you'd want to be on the shirts' team," he finished dryly, "not the skins."

Shana walked out on the field, self-conscious and a bit intimidated from the looks she was getting. By now all of the men knew who she was, but it was obvious they were a little surprised at her presence on the field.

One of the younger Gladii, a member of the shirts team, walked up to her and said in Copio. "Glad to have you, Sim Ettranty. You won't get much contact if you stay on the fringe. Just keep your eye on the balls and try to move one into that net whenever you get the chance," he said pointing to one of the goals. She'd never seen the man before, but he knew who she was. Hmmm.

With that, he was off and the game resumed. Shana found herself running up and down the field at a speed that was quickly becoming tiring, even in the shape she was in. Suddenly, a ball shot out of the melee and towards her. She stopped it and got ready to kick it back towards the opposing goal, but a flying body check knocked her several measures and left her dizzy on the ground.

Two strong hands lifted her to her feet. It was a member of the skins team and he was grinning. "Good stop, but keep moving next time. The boys have accepted you, so there'll be little mercy. They won't be as gentle as I was."

Shana realized the bare chested giant that had picked her up was Colonel Athan. He was also the one that had knocked her on her ass. He nodded to her with another minimal Gladius grin and returned to the swirling mass of yelling men. Shana shook her head to clear the cobwebs and also ran back into the game.

She finished with a case of total fatigue, bruises and scrapes all over her body, and the satisfaction of actually haven gotten the ball to a teammate who managed to score. The shirts won by one goal, so she figured she'd given a worthwhile performance. Given her limits. The number of teammates that told her she'd done a good job made her feel good, too. When her team mobbed in celebration with yells and high hand slaps, she was yelling and slapping right along with them. The slaps hurt her palm, too. She ignored the pain as insignificant.

Colonel Athan walked up to her. His comment was interesting, if a bit of a backhanded compliment. "You're slow and a little out of shape, but you have heart, Sim Ettranty. We appreciate that. You went a long way towards being accepted today. You're welcome back on the playing field."

Slow and a little out of shape! She was in better condition than ninety five percent of the population of Cauldwell. She began to think about the nannie treatments again, while she showered in the quarters. She tried to ignore the idea, but it was insidiously seductive. Live longer and be stronger, for nothing more than two days treatment. She wasn't the kind to make impulsive decisions on important subjects, but she could feel herself leaning towards acceptance.

The recruit training idea was getting to her, too. She'd really see the Gladius as he was, because she was being trained to be one. She was a reporter and had no desire to be a soldier, especially the way the Legate told her they lived. Still, it would be a challenging project, and she didn't back off from challenges. Maybe if they'd let her do segments about her training. She already had a couple of stories in mind, but nothing with real meat. Putting her into the life of the legion would have tremendous human interest. She decided to ask Adam and see what he said.

Outside, she faced the Sergeant Major. As usual, he wasn't at a loss for words. "You did well, girl, considering you started far behind our standards. Want to see some more now?"

Shana shook her head. "All I want is a good meal and a chance to treat these bruises before bed tonight. I think I've had it."

The Sergeant Major laughed, took her over to the Decurions Club, and fed her a dinner that would have passed muster at any expensive restaurant on Cauldwell. On her trike headed back to Beauregard she was still mulling the nannie treatment and the recruit training offer. If she accepted the course, she was going to have to accept the nannies. Nobody said so, but she'd be far below par unless she did. Another reason for the treatment. A little voice told her she wanted to live longer and be stronger and she was simply justifying the decision she already knew she'd make.

#####

Back in her apartment, she called Adam. When his chubby, balding figure materialized above the holophone, he was monitoring the rival tridio networks on several split screen monitors, tossing hardcopy and chips from one pile to another in a frenetic search for something he found right in front of him, meanwhile shouting contradictory orders off screen. In other words, he was his usual self. "Can't talk much, Shana," he began abruptly. "The Times is playing up that bribery scandal and we've got to show the Federal Populists are at the bottom of it." Two days ago, the Beauregard Times, Cauldwell's largest newsfax, had broken a story about three members of parliament taking bribes and kickbacks totaling nearly two million Marks. The MPs, however, were from the rival Progressive Statists.

Shana didn't blink at Adam's statement. Federal Populists were generally in opposition to the Guidance Council, and a frequent subject of condemnation at Council meetings, so CWNN had to somehow get them into the picture. Out of curiosity, Shana asked, "Suppose they aren't involved?"

"Oh, they will be," Adam breathlessly shot out as he scrabbled through piles of fax. "I'm sure of it. If we can't get anything, we'll let the Times play their games and move on. Your story will grab viewers anyhow, so it's a good thing you're out there with those Gumbys, or whatever. I have Roberto on the FP story, anyhow. How are you doing?"

Shana sniffed. Roberto was way behind her in the ratings and she was sure she was going to grab more airtime with the stories already in her head. "Good. Send a crew out tomorrow and I'll shoot some reports."

"They killed anybody or blown up anything yet?"

That was an ordinary question from Adam, but one that somehow irritated her. The Gladii were simply setting up and preparing for the Wareegans. That was where her story arc was headed, towards the confrontation, although Adam didn't seem interested in the survival – or lack of it – of Cauldwell. "Send a crew out tomorrow. I'll put two stories in the can then. Look, let me tell you about an offer they made..."

When he heard about the idea of Shana undergoing recruit training, Adam nearly jumped out of his chair. "Lord Above, yes! Go for it! Viewers will love shots of you being abused. Talk about viewer identification and human interest! This'll be big! How soon can you do it?"

"I'll find out tomorrow," Shana replied. They talked some more, then Shana broke the connection with a feeling of dissatisfaction. She had a great story, the editor was happy, so why was she getting a bad taste in her mouth?

#####

The next day, the Legate listened to her ideas about stories calmly and only commented on her plans to take the nannie treatment and undergo recruit training. "Are you absolutely sure you want this, Shana? Not the treatment, although that is usually only given to recruits since we have to be judicious as to who has it. I have no problems in your case, by the way, but recruit training is grueling. We are now going to start it again for the four young men we managed to bring out with us. They are years ahead of you in the basics, so we'll give them a break for a few weeks so you can at least learn a little of what they already know. They have the necessary ground work already and you will be far behind them. Are you sure you can handle that?"

Shana nodded emphatically. "I can. Sure I'm a woman, but I'm in good shape."

The Legate leaned back and gave her another of those searching looks she was becoming accustomed to from the Gladii. "Being a woman doesn't matter. Every Gladius takes recruit training. Sex is irrelevant to us for training purposes and you're about to become acquainted with the unpleasant aspects of that attitude. Still, if you think you're ready, you have my approval. We will continue our discussions again when things settle down for you. In fact, I look forward to them. I think you have a lot to learn."

This returned Shana to a subject that had been bothering her. "You're talking about my father and the Empire? Is that it?"

"In due time," the Legate said. "That is a complex subject and one for the future. For when you get to know us better. As of now, I've been notified your tridio crew has arrived at the gate. You need to meet them. You will start your treatment tomorrow, and recruit training two days after that. Prepare yourself."

After she left, the Sergeant Major walked in through the private door from his adjoining office. "She's going for it?"

The Legate nodded. "All the way, Lord Above bless her and keep her. We'll schedule the integration formation soon, as soon as she's ready. I have complete confidence that young woman will pass the training satisfactorily. I just wonder what it will do to her."

#####

Shana had experienced nannie work before, so she was prepared for injections and therapy, but the ship's hospital was more advanced than any she'd ever seen on Cauldwell. "Just relax, Sim Ettranty," a very pleasant ship's doctor said. He was short, somewhat overweight, and had a mild fatherly air. "We usually work with the Corps so we have a lot of experience in putting people back together who are missing a few things here and there. Since you have all your body parts, including, I might add, a very necessary additional lobe to your brain, this will be much easier. That lobe is present in many people, but they don't know how to use it. You'll be able to use yours when we finish. As to the nannie work, you'll experience the usual degree of aching, because these are some very serious mods we'll be doing to your body. Nothing that hasn't been done millions of times and the mods don't take long. Every Gladius undergoes them

70

before taking recruit training, so I'm sure we've got the bugs worked out by now."

It wasn't until later that Shana realized her mild, fatherly doctor was one of the Fleet contingent from the original Victrix Base. That mean he'd gone through heavy fire to board an escaping troop carrier and become part of a desperate hope for survival, simply because he had an oath to honor. The guy didn't look like the do-or-die type. More like a pleasant shop keeper. There was obviously much more depth to these people than she was seeing. Another reason for Recruit training. She wanted to get inside their heads.

The fact they might get inside hers didn't occur to her.

She spent the second day in the physical therapy box and was on her feet and ready to leave the hospital the following morning. And why, she thought to herself, couldn't Cauldwell do that?

The Sergeant Major showed up leading a bulky, tough looking decurion. "This is Drill Sergeant Howard," the Sergeant Major told her. "You are his personal project for five hours a day. That's a normal training day and you get special time for your stories and other requirements."

Well, that was a relief! Shana was wondering how her training was going to impact her job. She immediately forgot that little problem.

Howard shoved his face into hers. She recoiled in wide eyed shock. "The Sergeant Major just said you belong to me. Pity it isn't all twenty six hours a day, Ettranty, 'cause I could use a hobby.

"Now," he growled, "we'll learn to use that new body of yours. How about a brisk little trot to the supply shack for your uniforms then we'll really start to get you into decent shape."

Howard's idea of a "brisk little trot to the supply shack" differed from hers. By Shana's (aching) estimation they circled the base twice before being presented to a supply clerk, who shoved a khaki coverall and a pair of boots at her. "Put that on in there," he said, pointing to an empty room. "We'll put your clothes in your quarters."

After her first training day, Shana wasn't exactly surprised to be shown back to the same dome she'd used before the game. She wasn't really surprised, either, when the closets now contained multiple sets of the same shapeless khaki coveralls she now wore, except they were clean - not grimy and sweat stained from more forms of physical exercise, jumping, crawling, and climbing than she knew existed. She was now also familiar with standing at attention, facing movements, and saluting. Other, more arcane, mysteries would follow. "I'll teach you to march," Howard declared with exasperation, "when I'm sure you can walk in a straight line for more than two steps."

Shana was nursing a real desire to prove the bastard wrong. She also wanted to kill him, except he scared her too much.

#####

Several weeks later, Shana was coming to terms with the increased abilities of her modified body, no longer quite as exhausted when she stumbled back to her quarters to clean up. Her grinning tridio crew had more than a few shots of her doing exercises, climbing various obstacles and ropes, and jumping in and out of pits. Shana was particularly proud of one report she'd filed after completing an obstacle course, her words coming in gasps as she recovered. She no longer rode home at night. She was losing too much time on the road.

There were advantages to being out at the base, too. Adam was, as usual, all over the place whenever she talked to him and it was beginning to get on her nerves. Imin was becoming a problem too, urging her to drop the story and get back to where they could resume their relationship. Her father was his usual disapproving self.

When she had time to think about it, she wondered why she was letting Adam bother her. He never had before now. Was she changing her perspective on things? Certainly, the Sergeant Major was taking time each day to tell her as much as he could about the Gladius and what it meant to be one, and that was interesting. More interesting than crooked politicians, certainly. Imin... well, that was another situation - and one she didn't want to examine yet. Maybe it was time to cool him off and look elsewhere.

When Shana reported for training the next day, she got a surprise. Howard trotted her (directly, for a change) back to the supply office. There she was issued a Gladius uniform of khaki blouse, the first pants she'd seen on the compound besides her own, a belt, and a cap. The cap was about fifteen centimeasures high, flat on top with smooth tapered sides. Seen from above, it looked something like a water drop with the rounded front over her brow and the point over the braid she now habitually wore. Howard told her to change.

When she was again outside, Howard looked her over and then, with the usual growls, straightened what he called a "gig line" as she stood to attention for his inspection, lining up the front seams of blouse and pants with the edge of her belt buckle. "There - you have your recruit training uniform, Ettranty. If you disgrace it more than I expect you to, I'll make you regret the fact. Come on."

Off they went at the usual trot, to join a group of four boys in their early teens at a training area across the base. "Recruits," Howard said laconically, "all we have left, Ettranty. You are now twenty percent of our

72

recruit strength and the last member of this squad. The fun begins for certain, now."

He raised his voice to snarl at the whole squad. "All right, idiots, remember this! You are all worms beneath my feet. You know nothing. You can do nothing right. All I can hope for is that you learn to be a Gladius one of these days in the far future. Right now all you have is your squad, nothing else. You are in this together and you have to take care of each other. Remember that! Watch your buddy's back. Nobody else is going to do it for you."

They were trotted over to a level grassy area and issued plastic dummy weapons, short belt axes resembling the ancient "tomahawk" for the boys and a 25 centimeasure long straight double edged dagger for her. "This is where you begin to learn your basic weapon," a craggy faced instructor told them. "These are soft plastic so you won't cut yourselves. Whenever the distant time comes I hope you can be trusted with a live weapon, you'll get one. Right now, you are here to learn the basic moves of defense and attack, both with the blade and without one."

Howard, to Shana's mild surprise, took her to one side and began drilling her with the dagger. "Drill Sergeant," she asked during a short pause, "how do you know a woman's weapon?"

To her greater surprise, he didn't growl back. He even seemed human as he corrected her posture before answering. "A weapon is a weapon, Ettranty, and you learn 'em all as you grow up. Those lads in your squad have been around these things since they got out of diapers. You haven't and I don't expect you to become an instant expert. For one thing, issue blades have monomolecular shear fields along their edges. A live blade will cut anything, including you. You'll spend some time with a dagger every day from now on. I want to make sure you cut only what you're supposed to cut before you handle a live blade. You'll get a real one of these when you graduate from Recruit Training and I want to make sure you know how to use it safely. Now, show me that underhand slash again."

Shana was left to exercise on her own for a few moments, earning a bark from Howard when she just stopped, staring. What he'd said had just sunk in and left her a bit stunned. These people were actually planning to give her one of their weapons to keep!

She lost that thread of thought when a Legionnaire Fourth Class came trotting up and spoke quietly to Howard. "Ettranty!" he yelled. "Shag ass over to the Legate's office. He wants to see you."

Shana was amused at the wide eyed looks on her young squad mates as she left, double timing, for what she hoped would be another interview. The Legate was a distant god to these boys and this old woman

73

in their midst actually talked to him! She wondered what the boys would say the first time they were all alone.

As she started to walk into the Legate's office, the Sergeant Major, standing just outside, growled, "Report properly, Recruit."

"Aye!" She whipped off her cap, snapped to attention, and blurted out in what was now an involuntary reaction. "Legate, Recruit Ettranty reports."

As impossible as it seemed, the Legate's eyes were twinkling as he looked at her. "At ease, Sim Ettranty. Sit down. You didn't think we'd go this far, did you?"

Shana was slightly stunned at her reaction to the Sergeant Major's command, but she sat, still without thinking as she followed the order. "I didn't know how well you condition people!" she said, shaken. "Or how fast!"

Then she started to get irritated. "You had no right to do that to me, damn it! You got into my head! I'm still going to be a civilian when I leave here!"

"If you say so," the Legate returned imperturbably, "but you will carry something of us forever, even after you leave. You will also have the right to wear that uniform, and I will not allow you to devalue it. Besides, you wanted to know how a Gladius thinks, not to mention getting some juicy tridio stories. You are accomplishing both of your aims."

She had the grace to blush. "Yes, Legate. All right, I suppose you have me. Will I be fit for polite company after you finish?"

"Very fit, Shana," he replied. "But you *will* take something of us away with you. That's not why I asked you here this afternoon."

"Ordered."

That produced a slight smile. "Ordered. I wanted to talk politics with you. Some things will be a bit clearer to you after we talk, I hope."

The recruit was gone and the reporter back, now. "I'm waiting."

The Legate leaned forward and put his elbows on his desk, clasping his hands. "Sim Ettranty, I will be blunt. I've never seen a planetary culture so corrupt as Cauldwell."

She was wide eyed at that, but before she could gasp out her outrage, he bored mercilessly on, his voice flat. "You have a Planetary Guidance Council that exists only to serve itself and the plans of the Empire, a Parliament that only does housekeeping and remains perfectly docile otherwise, a military that kills citizens in wholesale lots when ordered, and a general population that couldn't care less."

She opened her mouth to hotly deny it, then stopped, putting together some of the things her father had said, Adam's attitudes, the Legate's unfortunately accurate description of Parliament, and some well-hidden thoughts about the Guard. She also remembered her blasé attitude about all of that from only a few weeks earlier. Instead, she thought hard for a few silent moments and commented, "I'm not sure Imin had an alternative, Legate."

The Legate looked her dead in the eye. "He might not have thought he did, but the Council gave orders and he followed them. The Wareegans aren't all that difficult to kill, Shana, even with the Guard's equipment. We've been teaching them how to do it for some time now."

Somehow that didn't surprise her.

"The Council knows nothing about our training program, simply because they don't care," he said. "And Imin Webster hasn't seen fit to tell them."

That didn't surprise her either.

After a moment, she realized her father and his cronies were beginning to leave a bad taste in her mouth. That couldn't be right, she thought to herself. He was her *father!* A merciless little voice of honesty took that moment to remind her of all of the growing differences she was having with him. That gave rise to a number of unpleasant thoughts.

She decided to change the subject a little. "That's twice you've said my father was in touch with the Empire."

The Legate nodded. "And he is. Regularly. Enough that Corps Intelligence knows all about Cauldwell. We didn't come here by accident. We knew all about this planet and it seemed like the best refuge."

He snorted. "Refuge! Do you know what Cauldwell is, Sim Ettranty? Cauldwell has tremendous unused and undeveloped resources. All it ostensibly lacks is the up to date mining and manufacturing equipment to exploit those resources, not to mention up to date shipping. Shipping and equipment, including modern warships, such as are hidden in camouflaged depots all over this planet. That equipment and those ships aren't touched, Sim Ettranty, because they are for a very specific purpose, as are the population of human cattle that are kept docile and decadent for the same reason."

"Cauldwell," he finished, "is the Emperor's designated refuge in case of overthrow, and has been for well over two centuries. The only reason you've never seen any of this is the previous five Emperors either died naturally or were killed before they could get here. Shangnaman hopes to break that trend. I doubt if he will."

He looked at her amazed face for a few seconds. "It really won't matter to the population of Cauldwell, Sim Ettranty, whatever happens. Unless someone changes the situation."

Shana wasn't a political innocent, not in her job. She was also a good judge of truth when she heard it. She was hearing it now and, Lord

Above triple damn him, the Legate was saying something that made horrible sense. "You know this? And you are the ones that will change our lives? The saviors?"

The Legate snorted. "Saviors? Hardly, not in today's Empire. All anyone can do is hold on to any stability possible because the Empire is falling apart at the seams. We'd best hope the Emperor never does show up here, because a hostile battle fleet will probably be right behind him.

"Corps Intelligence had full information on Cauldwell fifty years ago. We knew everything about a number of situations, it seems, except the Emperor's plans for us. Purblind to that, many of us died. Others may still die. I have no idea what is happening to other legions, because I've had no contact for months, except for a tachyon data packet from a surviving scout of the IIX Legion, literally just before things blew up for us. I was on that exercise I told you about when I got it. He told me what had happened to his legion. I assume he died shortly after he launched his warning.

"It was addressed to every Commander and Legate in the Corps," Corona added dryly. "I can only hope the others got their notifications in time. Given the fact the man was in the middle of combat at the time, I'm not sure how many he was able to send out and I'm also unsure how many actually were received. I only know I got his warning barely in time to save what I did.

"This particular plot of Shangnaman's seems to be working, Shana. We may be the only legion left in the Corps... And we aren't whole.

"In any case," he said, leaning back in his chair, "the question becomes what you - and I - are going to do about Cauldwell's situation. Frankly, I intend to do nothing until the Wareegans are dealt with, and I suggest you keep your mouth shut until then also."

She gave him a piercing look. "You must be very sure of me," she said coldly.

The Legate nodded. "You would be surprised to know what we found out about you. You are independent, intelligent, and used to moving in the highest circles. You are also unusually trustworthy for a citizen of Cauldwell as well as a realist. I don't expect you to be on my side, but I know you'll keep your mouth shut until you deem it the right time, and I trust your judgment about that time. In any case, my invitation to you would have been different if our background investigation had turned out negative."

There was more to the conversation, but the Legate's thermonuclear bomb preoccupied her thinking. She decided to take a meal in the Legionnaire Mess and sleep over in her quarters, as she normally did now. She had no desire to meet her father or Imin until she could digest what she'd been told.

She caught herself at the mental plans she was making. Mess and quarters? She was thinking like a member of the Corps. She suspected that was another reason Legate Corona trusted her with his information about Cauldwell. Maybe the primary one.

#####

The next morning was more weapons drill. After learning a few moves, the recruits were introduced to sparring, which was more fun. After working with each other for a while, they were taken to the training pit.

Their opponents for the next stage were manlike robots covered in a doughy flesh-like substance for some reason. Dull steel bladed axes were given to the boys and Shana had a steel training dagger, while the robots were using wooden short swords. "The golems are standard drill equipment," the instructor told them, "Everyone uses them, but we've stepped down their reactions and speed for you. Remember, the object here is for you to learn, and a blow from a wooden weapon is a pretty good teacher. You'll each take on a golem down in the training pit. Each recruit will be given a realistic training situation to solve on their own.

"Remember this: YOU MUST SOLVE IT BY YOURSELF! NO HELP! I've got punishment tours waiting for anyone that disobeys.

"Ready? Novak, you first. Get down there!"

The training pit was actually a miniature version of an old Roman stadium, with a sunken sand floor beneath surrounding stands and a raised wall about two measures high circling the floor. The other four recruits stood in the stands and cheered on their squad mate while Novak, who looked to be about fourteen to Shana's estimation, jumped down to circle and spar with the golem. He had more ease and grace with his weapon than Shana was sure she was going to show. Still, she was excited about getting her chance. Hm, she thought, this would make a good segment for a report. Maybe she could get a crew here another time and get footage of herself fighting a golem.

Her newly informed self brought that idea to a screeching halt. Until she knew what was actually happening on Cauldwell - and what the Legate was actually trying to do - revealing anything about her own abilities was not a good thing. Better innocent shots of Gladii on training exercises and such. Right now, nobody needed to know what she was really learning or about her own rapidly developing abilities. And a careful eye had to be kept on Corona.

She was brought out of her brown study as three more golems came trundling out from a door in the pit's side wall. Novak was suddenly one against four.

She didn't think. She jumped into the pit and her squad mates were right behind her. She landed just behind one of the golems. The spurting blood and high squeal of pain when she drove her dagger into its back, right in the spot she'd been drilled to use, threw her off for a second, the horror of what she'd done hitting her. A swipe from a wooden sword that just missed her head brought her back with a rush and she helped kill the other robots, full of an adrenaline rush at her victory over the first one.

After a few seconds, the recruits were standing in the pits, the golems realistically dead at their feet. All of them were in a daze and a bit shaken, experiencing a mixture of elation at their victory - and nausea. Every golem had bled and made dying noises. Shana looked at Novak and could see the shocked expression of a boy that felt he'd killed someone, no matter what his mind told him. She suspected her face looked the same. Same queasy stomach, too.

"Attention!" All five snapped to.

"Good work, recruits." Howard dropped down into the pit with them. "You've learned an important lesson, all of you. Never abandon a mate in trouble, no matter what. No matter what anyone says, no matter what happens, you don't abandon a mate."

His voice grew softer. "Also... welcome to the world of the Gladius. Killing. And it isn't pretty. It's messy, bloody and damned disgusting. A golem is set up to emphasize reality, recruits. On purpose. Killing is our ancestral trade and we're good at it. Better than anyone else. Why? Because we were born to the job and it's a job needs doing. Always remember you're fighting and killing because someone else is in danger. That's why we exist - to protect citizens. Citizens may never know it. They may never care. They may be scared shitless of you or stupid enough to hate you. But we do it. We do it because if we didn't, some poor bastard would be looking at a damned bad day. We pay the Gladius Price because innocent people shouldn't. More to the point, you're being trained so that you *won't* pay the Gladius Price the first time you face some asshole that thinks it's *fun* to kill people."

His voice grew softer. "We're the Guards at the Gates of Hell. That's in the oath you'll swear when you join the Victrix as a trained Gladius. We mean that... and we've meant it for a thousand years."

He kicked a downed golem, lying in a pool of blood at his feet, and grinned a vicious wolfish grin at them. "That's why the bastards this thing represents shit their pants or whatever they're wearing when they see us coming, recruits. And you're going to be just as scary, trust me.

"The Predator can come after us, people, if he's stupid or ignorant or determined enough. We'll be happy to take him on, every time. And we'll win. *That's* what it means to be a Gladius. We're the best soldiers in history. The best soldiers in the Universe. We're the Lord Above's and humankind's answer to the Predator.

"Okay, get out of the pit and form up outside. I've got something else to say."

Outside the wall, Howard faced a line of recruits as rigid as statues. "There's a formation in two hours. You're dismissed to quarters to clean up and put on a fresh uniform. Novak, Callen, Legnt, and Bratz, return to your units after changing. Ettranty, you report to the Sergeant Major. Dismissed."

Trotting back to her quarters, Shana thought about Howard and what he said in the pit. The mask was off. What she'd sensed the first time she'd seen a Gladius was now suddenly bare for the world to see. Yet... Yet, she was now a part of it. She'd killed an enemy - just a golem, but an enemy - to protect a comrade she didn't really know. This was stupid! She wasn't a killer! She wasn't a soldier! She was a reporter working on a story, for Lord Above's sake!

Yet... Yet, she was now a part of it. Something strange had happened to her. Something she didn't plan on when she decided to undergo recruit training on a lark. She'd passed another test today, of some kind. Gladii talked about not wanting to kill, but would jump on an enemy they regarded as the Predator with professional expertise and complete willingness. Lord Above help her, she was beginning to understand that! She was thinking like a Gladius, and that was more than a bit frightening.

So what did that make her and where was she headed? Was she going to be the same person after she finished training? Somehow, she didn't think so, but the Victrix had changed her enough that she was going to finish training. Her fear of Gladii was gone, too, now that she was on the inside. Their grim and unemotional facade was just that, a facade. Once she got to know the troopers, they were simply men, with joys, sorrows, and a real sense of humor. She hadn't spoken anything inside the compound but Copio for weeks, and the troopers around her spoke it just as informally as she normally spoke Unispek. They were simply less outwardly expressive than the normal run of humanity, but emotions were there to see once she got accustomed to the lack of major cues.

The Gladius love of music and dance intrigued her. Singing and music were everywhere in camp and the number of hardened troopers that played instruments surprised her once she started noticing. Dancing wasn't the type she was familiar with, either. Single men and groups in the various clubs often danced to pickup bands, dances like she used to see on the stage, but very different in style and content. Gladius male dances were very masculine, especially the one that consisted of military formations from the ancient past. Good material for one of her stories.

What she didn't show in the story was the impression she'd gotten that the men's dancing was a counterpart to women's dancing and the sadness because the legion thought it would never see women dance again. Certainly, she couldn't sing or dance! Not like the dances she saw in the Legionnaires Club! More food for thought.

She regarded Gladii as pretty good people, all in all. Good to be with.

Her friends wouldn't understand. Her father wouldn't understand either. Screw them and especially him! She was becoming a part of something that protected people, something that made a difference. That was a pretty good calling. She wanted more than a taste of it. The calling came with a price, and she decided it was one worth paying. Good enough. Time to get changed.

The Sergeant Major looked her over carefully when she found him near the parade ground. She wasn't worried at the inspection. She was wearing a new, freshly pressed uniform from her closet and her gig line was straight.

He nodded with seeming reluctance at her appearance, then commented, "Good enough, I suppose. Girl, you're about to witness an integration formation. It's something we do to rebuild a shattered unit, and it's not often done. All you have to do is stand where I tell you and bear witness. Salute the legion's Sunburst when it passes, other than that, watch and do nothing. I'll be nearby, but keep silent until it's over. Understand?"

Shana took the position she was shown. She was fairly bursting with reporter's curiosity, but kept patiently silent. She would find out in time what was happening.

The band started playing music with the slow heavy marching beat of the Corps and the legion marched onto the field, each man holding his ax with its head cradled on his right shoulder, edge to the right. Shana stared, because the formations weren't compact. There were gaps in the first three cohorts and behind those scattered men marched out, so separated from the rest they were almost totally by themselves. The band continued to play marching music long after the men were on the field, but the rest stood in formation on the far side of the field, facing where she was standing, with the Legate and his staff (some of them, there were gaps there too) in the very center of the field halfway between her and the troop units. The formation was unbalanced because there were plenty of men to the Legate's right, but the field to his left had only oddly placed Gladii and nobody at all in a large area on his extreme left.

When she saw the Sunburst fall in directly behind the Legate, she wondered if she ought to salute. She must have made some kind of motion, because the Sergeant Major growled softly, "Not yet, girl. I'll tell you when."

The Legate did an about face, scanned the troop line, and commanded, "GIVE your commands parade res-s-s-t-t-t-t... Ho!"

He faced each cohort in turn as their commanders echoed his order. Shana got a spooky feeling as he looked past the units with commanders to those sparsely placed men, who responded as though a commander had given the order, then did the same at specific locations on the empty portion of the field.

Marching music began as a carryall was driven in front of Legate Corona and he got in, standing in front of his seat as the carryall started to drive along the troop line. They started at the band on the formation's far left, then progressed slowly towards the right. Commands of "Attention-n-n-n-n... Ho!" then "PRESENT Arms-s-s-s... Ho!" followed his progress and the Legate saluted each cohort, each man at attention with his ax head, blade outward, in front of his face, with his own ax as he passed. When he got to the widely separated men, they reacted as though the orders had been given and their weapon salute was returned. As he rode down the empty stretch of the parade field, he did the same, as though there were units present.

Shana suddenly found a lump in her throat as she realized what was happening. Each of those Gladii on the field was in their assigned place on the day before the attack, the attack that gutted the Victrix. Those empty spaces were empty because the men assigned them were now dead. The bare space on the parade ground was where the women of the Legion's Support Command once stood in the formation and they, too, were getting a salute. The remaining legion was arrayed on the field as it was when it was intact.

Her eyes were misty with unshed tears, but now she thought she could see shadowy figures mixed with the real ones out there on the field. Somehow, she was seeing the Victrix at full strength.

The Legate returned to his position and left the carryall. He spun on his heel to face the troop line and commanded, "PASS in review-w-w-w-w... Ho!"

The music began again as the commands echoed down the line, heavy with a steady drumbeat, and she could swear she heard more repetitions now than the first time she'd heard commands echo down the field. Now it was "COHORT, attention... Ho! Right turn... March!" running in sequence down the line. All the way down the field. *All* the way down the field. The cohorts began to coil out into a marching formation that turned left in front of the band and left again to march down the line in front of the reviewing stand, one battalion behind another, feet steadily stepping in time to the band's 88 beats per minute.

The music began to swell and dominate her surroundings. She began to feel a part of the music as well as a part of the parade. There was something happening here, she wasn't sure what, but she could feel whatever it was, deep in her mind, deep in her being. She didn't know how, but she felt as though she was becoming part of Something, greater than just one person, greater than her, greater than everyone here, yet part of everyone on the field.

Shana got the feeling she wasn't alone. She didn't turn her head, but it seemed like there was someone standing next to her. A woman, older, shorter, and stockier than she was, in the flowing skirt of a Gladius woman's uniform. The Legion Commander, taking the Review. Corona's wife.

As the Legate marched in front of her, he commanded, "MARK tim-m-m-me... Ho!" His head snapped to face her and she could see the set, sad, grim expression on his bearded face. His ax snapped up from its carry position against his arm to be held rigidly upright in front of his face in salute. Shana knew the salute wasn't for her, but for someone else, someone not here in body. She wasn't supposed to salute, but she did, holding it as other officers marched forward to fill the holes in the staff formation. When it was full, the staff moved on, followed by the Sunburst, then the rest of the units.

As each battalion paused, marking time in front of her, men closed holes in the formation or came up from the destroyed units. She held her salute. By now, she knew why she was here. She represented all of the women that were half of the Victrix, half of the Whole. She was standing formation for their real commander and each woman that had died. The Victrix couldn't have reintegrated before now, because it didn't have a woman in it, but her recruit status meant she was officially a part of the Victrix. Now she was here, a living representative for all these men had lost. She stood straighter and held her aching right arm rigid across her chest in a perfect salute, tears streaming as each battered unit passed at eyes right with its commander rendering an ax salute, its shadowy dead vanishing as a man moved up to fill a hole left by death. Some holes remained unfilled because there weren't enough extras from the destroyed cohorts, but the men closed up to make full lines and the shadows of the dead vanished.

The music soared to a crescendo as the last manned unit passed, but there were still shadowy figures marching in review, the women of the Support Command. And still she held her salute, her head high. Shana felt approval from the misty figure by her side, now flanked by the very real Legate, who was also holding a salute with his ax.

As she, a reporter and a recruit by casual decision, stood there, she knew the Victrix was intact again.

It was because of her.

CHAPTER 4

LEGIO IX VICTRIX
CAULDWELL

Shana tossed and turned through an almost sleepless night in her quarters. There were so many new questions rolling over and over in her mind, questions it seemed nobody wanted to answer. Neither the Legate nor the Sergeant Major had spoken to her after the formation and none of the rest of the legion's men were talkative either. The legionnaire mess hall was normally loud and active whenever she ate there, but the young troopers around her were quiet and thoughtful that night.

Come morning, she resolved to get some answers. Probably the Sergeant Major. The Legate was as human as a moving statue the last she'd seen of him, with an invisible wall between himself and others. It had to be the Sergeant Major.

At the first break in her day's training, Shana walked up to Sergeant Howard. "Drill Sergeant, I need to see the Sergeant Major."

Howard gave her one of those piercing Gladius looks that seemed to totally assess her. "Not surprising. Report to his office now."

Inside the headquarters, Shana marched up to the Sergeant Major's open door and knocked. "Sergeant Major, Recruit Ettranty reports," she announced to the man behind the desk.

He looked up. "Come in, girl, at ease and have a seat. Close the door behind you."

Once seated, Shana studied the Sergeant Major, turning the usual tables. "I need to know this, and you're the only one I can think to ask. Were those figures - the dead members of the Victrix - real?"

Sergeant Major Olmeg looked at her calmly. "As real as you and I. Just away Somewhere Else. The Corps isn't just the people here, Recruit, it's everyone that ever made it up, and we join with Those Now Gone when things warrant. The ceremony brought them back because it was needful."

He settled back in his chair. "There's a lot in our makeup that isn't obvious, girl. Some of that shows up in the general population from time to time. Mutations, I suppose. It's something we look for when we accept a recruit from outside the Corps. Whatever it is, you have it, or you wouldn't have seen Those Now Gone. You wouldn't be here in this office, either."

Shana took a deep breath, mildly surprised at the matter of fact answer, but just as surprised to find she wasn't *very* surprised. Not even about herself. "That's why you asked me out to the camp?"

The Sergeant Major nodded. "That, plus you're intelligent, resourceful and have initiative. You are also here because you're a woman."

Things started falling into place. "You needed a woman in the Victrix because all of your own women were dead. What am I supposed to be, breeding stock?"

The Sergeant Major glared at her for a moment. "Say that again, girl, and you're out on your ass! People aren't animals! They aren't, or they aren't worth dying for!"

Shana, blood up, bored in. "So why am I here? You needed a woman, didn't you?"

The Sergeant Major looked uncomfortable for a moment. "This isn't my area, but you deserve an answer. You ought to be talking to the Legate."

"I'm asking you!"

The Sergeant Major nodded after a moment's silence. Then he gave her a slight smile. "You get mad and you fight, but you fight intelligently. That's what I like.

"You're right, girl. We deliberately looked for a woman, and you filled our bill. The women of the Corps are essential to what we are. We couldn't have done that integration parade yesterday without a woman member in attendance. You were a recruit, but close enough to Gladius status to stand for every woman that was killed."

He broke off and looked at her shrewdly. "But you figured that out, didn't you?" She looked at him silently, but didn't dispute what he said.

The Sergeant Major nodded again. "Good. You appealed to us because you were a woman and the Victrix isn't complete without its female members. But we also wanted you because of *you.* Who you are and what you are inside. We were looking for a *person*, girl. The fact that you're a woman meant we could make a start at becoming whole again, but it's the person, not the plumbing, that matters."

He looked at the wall with a thoughtful expression. "As Sergeant Major, I'm a keeper of the legion's tradition, but it's our women that really do that. They tend the legion as a body, a living, breathing organism. I'm not supposed to do that, but I have to try until the day comes when we can recruit women to take up the job again. Part of why you're here is to record who we are so that we won't be lost. That all those Gladii you saw won't be lost and gone. That's why your tridio crews are welcome."

85

He turned to her again and waved his hand outward. "Out there, some of those boys are going to die when the Wareegans come back. Maybe most of them. It happens and it's the Gladius Price. But we were able to at least integrate and bring every man back to belonging in a unit because you were here. You may go back to being a reporter after your training, girl, but you'll be someone that understands us, a part of us will be inside you, and you'll have a record of the Victrix. Our spirits and Those Now Gone will still have an existence.

"That's a soldier's greatest fear, did you know that? To die alone and forgotten, to do your duty but be lost forever. That's why you're here, Recruit Shana Ettranty," he said intensely, using her name for the first time, "to capture the memory. To hold it so no matter what happens we won't be forgotten."

Shana had to swallow a lump. Suddenly, she was responsible for the continuing memory of a legion, this legion. Her legion... and she finally admitted it. The weight of what they wanted felt crushing for a second then she squared her shoulders, taking up the challenge. It was her responsibility as a person, as a Gladius. "The Victrix won't be forgotten, Sergeant Major," she said softly. "No matter what I do, I won't let that happen." He nodded at her, satisfied.

#####

For Shana, time began to flow. Her twice weekly stories led the broadcast ratings, to Adam's frenetic and slightly puzzled glee. She blandly ignored his repeated requests for shots showing her abused or anything involving blood. Instead, lifestyle and action stories brought in the viewers. She also made it a point to never show her own steadily improving physical capabilities.

She had good reason. The political pot was now boiling in Beauregard and she knew the Legate was deep into the mix. How deep, she didn't know, but she was determined to find out. Low profile and keep her eyes open.

Between stories, she concentrated on the ever expanding subjects handed her. The Sergeant Major began teaching her many of the Corps songs, some of them thousands of years old and all part of their heritage. She learned something of the history of the Corps, but it wasn't the usual names and dates. Her training was strictly about tactical lessons that could be learned from various engagements, most nameless, that stretched back over a millennium. The Corps didn't seem to care much about its history as a history, but every trooper seemed to know it very well. She also took hypnotraining on the makeup and capabilities of the Corps, tactics,

86

weapons use, and - her favorite - the tractor presser bracelets that allowed a Gladius to control his or her blades.

The live portion of the bracelet training began, as usual, with Drill Sergeant Howard. "All right, people, see these?" He held up his wrist, pointing to his bracelet. "They control your blades. Look at what happens when you don't have them."

He took several throwing knives from a small stand next to him, then turned and threw the first one at a target a short way down range. It bounced ignominiously. The next one stuck at an angle, then fell to the ground. Only the last stayed buried in the target. "I let up on the force I used so I could get accuracy," he said. "Not too much penetration, huh?"

Then his short sword snapped into in his hand. It flew straight as an arrow down range, burying itself up to the hilt in the target, quivered for an instant, and then flew back to his grasp. "I've got it back to use again, people. I haven't thrown away my weapon. A knife or throwing weapon spins, and hitting your target with the point depends on distance, force, and knowing the spinning radius. Good to know, but we don't need that. Your bracelets control the speed of the flight and keep your weapon pointed straight. When you throw, your weapon doesn't spin. It's deadly all along the flight path, people, and that's handy in a fight. You have a hard time judging ranges in combat, recruits. There's usually too much confusion and most of what you do will be by reaction until you have some experience. Remember that and use your training. We're giving you the reactions and they'll appear when you need them. Now fall out and pick up the bracelets and blades on the stands in front of you. When you throw, DON'T try to bring the blade back unless you want to duck it and look like an ass. You aren't good enough the first time."

The results of their first throws, as could be expected, varied, but Shana's dagger flew a reasonably straight, if somewhat wobbly path and embedded itself in the target, slightly cocked. At Howard's nod, Shana couldn't help feeling pleased. The hypnotraining seemed to have taken well in her case.

BEAUREGARD

The pool party, in Shana's experienced opinion, sucked. It was one of the political things the network did, and Adam had brought her back from the Victrix camp to be a network representative, much against her better judgment. Several higher ranking Progressive Statists and business leaders were going to be there, expecting the usual fawning veneration they got from the Cauldwell media. Ergo, CWNN was going to make sure they were got it. The party at someone's expensive mansion was political stroking, pure and simple, and the most popular news woman currently on the air was ordered by her boss to go stroke, so she went.

Shana was reclining in a lounger near the water, deep in a brown study. Her bathing costume was tiny in the current Cauldwell fashion, but the twenty or so square centimeasures of cloth and string that made it up was far more than some of the women were wearing. She cast a jaundiced eye on several adorned solely in waterproof body paint and sniffed. Show offs.

Her innate honesty compelled her to remember she'd have worn the same paint six or seven weeks ago, and thought nothing of it, or the flirting and sexual innuendoes the paint brought. Remarkable how her outlook was changing, she thought. Becoming more prudish?

Or just seeing some things more clearly, she mused, watching attendees in various stages of undress buzzing around the floating trays of alcohol, canapés and recreational drugs. She and Imin used to do synthetic endorphins at parties like this, she remembered. Seemed like a vapid waste of time now.

"I have to say, Shana, you're looking more toned than I've ever seen you," Imin said as he came up to her. He handed her a drink and sat on the lounger next to hers.

"Been working out." She sipped the drink and regarded Imin steadily over its rim. Just like everything else, she was beginning to see Imin in a new light. Not necessarily a favorable one.

He squirmed slightly under her emotionless look. "Hey, I'm glad you're back in town. Why don't we go over and have a quiet dinner at Barceiv's after this thing is over?"

"I'll think about it, Imin," she said calmly. "We'll see."

Imin flushed and started again, "Look, I - -" He glanced up behind her, picked up his drink and left. That warned Shana that some kind of VIP was coming over. More bother. She stood up and turned to see who she'd been left to face.

The man strolling confidently up to her was tall and wearing a brief pair of swim trunks that showed off his well-shaped body, perfectly biosculpted face, and wavy brown hair streaked with gray. It was Kantanzakis Theodore, one of the Parliament Members and a power on the Appropriations Committee. He was showing signs of enough alcohol and other substances that his natural arrogance was coming to the fore. Theodore was also widely, if quietly, known as a compulsive womanizer, and it looked like Shana was his target of the moment.

"Ah, Sim Ettranty! I thought I'd tell you that I'm one of your biggest fans."

Like hell, you bastard. You're a fan all right. That's why your eyes are roaming all over my body and your tongue is practically hanging out. "Thank you, Member. It's always nice to meet a fan."

"I'd like to introduce you to our little group over by the bar, if you would permit." That was a command, not a request, and Shana felt pushed just about as far as she was going to be pushed. Two months ago, she'd have gone with him and been excited to do it. No longer.

"I think I'll pass on that one, Member," Shana said. "I'd rather stay here and catch some sun."

A brief scowl flitted across Theodore's face. Nobody turned him down. "Perhaps you didn't understand me Shana, if I may call you that. I'd very much like to have you in my group."

You'd like to have me in your bed, asshole, Shana thought. "I understood you perfectly, Member. I'm simply not up for company at the moment."

The scowl was back, now, in full force. "Listen, you little plebeian. Nobody refuses me..." He reached for her arm to pull her forcefully with him, enraged that one of the masses could actually refuse his order.

Member Theodore's next sensation was of flying through the air and impacting in the pool. Unarmed combat training at work, here.

Shana didn't even bother looking at the gasping, splashing man in the water. She snarled, grabbed her towel and headed to change.

Adam intercepted her on the way out the mansion's front door. "Shana! What in hell do you think you were doing!?"

"Missing," she snarled. "I wanted to put him on the plascrete. It hurts more."

Adam recoiled slightly at Shana's fury, but started up again in a panic. "For Lord Above's sake, Shana, Theodore is a Power! We have to keep him satisfied! So you might have to sleep with him, so what?"

"I'm not a whore!" She shot back.

Adam took a deep breath and told himself to relax and get Shana to do it too. He was close to losing his top reporter, but what Theodore could do scared him. "Okay, so you don't sleep with him. Look, I've already calmed the guy down. No sex, but you have to do something. The Bayview power station is opening next week. That's a big thing in his district and I've told him you'll cover it. Interview him, too."

"WHAT?"

Shana was shocked as well as mad. Covering a routine utility opening wasn't something for a premier reporter. That was beginner stuff and way below her level. Not to mention the interview was a way for Theodore to rub her face in the dirt. "Power station! You're handing me to that piece of shit, Adam! The bastard will revel in grinding me into the dirt on camera."

Adam looked rueful. "Yeah, I know. But just do it. Try to keep in mind it's for the good of the network. And both our jobs. We have to keep the guy happy, at least until we catch him doing something we can use. That won't be hard, and he'll see reason after that. Meanwhile, just do the story, do the interview, and everyone goes away happy, okay?"

Shana wasn't going away happy and she was sure Theodore wasn't going to forget his wetting either. But he was egotistical enough that he might let up on the network if he made her feel punished. She'd have to handle the rest as it happened. And try to keep her job. "Okay, Adam, I'll do it. But anything he does goes on feed, got it?"

Adam wasn't happy with that, but a tridio lens had a way of controlling politicians. He secretly sympathized with Shana, but this was disaster recovery for the network. And his job. Still, Theodore might control himself on a live broadcast. "Yeah, I understand. Just go out there and do the story. Theodore'll behave."

Shana nodded grimly. "I'll eat crow for you, Adam, but I won't put up with that pig if he tries something."

BAYVIEW

The interview looked like it was going to be as bad as Shana expected. She gave the usual fluff stuff about the power station and its economic impact on the local economy. She could do that in her sleep. The bad part was putting up with Theodore's childishly vindictive ego as she prepared to smile through the interview. "Member, you have certainly scored a coup in bringing this economic boon to your district. How do you feel about that?"

Theodore was on his best on-camera behavior. He smiled brightly into the tridiocam clipped to her left ear, well aware that her support crew was doing detailed shots for later editing with their own more capable equipment. Be nice, he told himself, this bitch was shooting live. That was a nasty surprise. Nobody had told him and his makeup wasn't in place. Well, the lower resolution cam on the bitch's ear wouldn't catch enough for him to worry about. He chalked up the live cam trick as something else she'd regret later. His time was coming. "Well, Shana, I work long and hard for my people, and I'm glad you recognize the fact." The superior smile said she'd better grovel some more.

90

Shana took a deep mental breath and prepared to grovel. "It's certainly a sign of your dedication Member -"

That's when the raid alarm broadcast started.

PLANETARY COMMAND CENTER

PCC personnel were some of the best in the Guard's ground component, priding themselves on stoic professionalism. They also had more experience than they wanted dealing with Wareegan raids.

The tech on the outer system scan was tense, but didn't let it show. Her voice was the professionally approved level monotone made traditional over the millennia. "I have tachyon drive field collapse at twenty-two light minutes, 3-2-4-5 mils relative, 1-2-2-9 mils ascention. Time, one three oh seven oh three zulu... mark. Configuration and mass consistent with Wareegan mother ship."

"Mils", known as "milliradians" on formal occasions, were the Imperial measurement of arc, with 6400 of them in a circle. "True" directions were based on a line from the star to galactic center. A "relative" direction in this case was based on a line from the planet to the star. Aboard a ship, "relative" was always based on the ship's current course. All of that meant that the Wareegans were coming in from a direction that was roughly four o'clock to the planet's relationship to the star and about two o'clock above the ecliptic.

"Condition Red. Drones, get a scanner on that bogie now. I want details." The shift supervisor was equally tense, equally professional. "Fighter command, alert the ready squadrons on Luna and Lunetta. Commo, inform the Commander and start the call-in list."

The next command took a second's thought. It was a new procedure. "Contact the legion commo center and get the Legate up on conference holo."

"Looks like we have another one, boys and girls," he continued grimly. "Time to go to work."

#####

Less than ten minutes later, The Planetary Guard Commander and the Narsima Matic Ettranty were standing next to the holo image of Legate Corona. All three were watching the approach of the mother ship's symbol on the Big Board's screen. "They always launch a flight of landing beacons at thirty light seconds from Cauldwell," Imin said. "With luck, they won't modify their routine when they launch their assault shuttles. They'll get inside Lunetta's orbit before they drop shuttles if nothing's

91

changed and I'm betting it hasn't. I've already ordered Defcon Four and Op Plan Delta One."

The Narsima had only yesterday been briefed on the new defensive plans worked out between the Guard and the Victrix. The briefing did not make him happy. "I still say this is a waste of valuable defensive firepower, Corona," the Legate rumbled. "The Guard would be better used closer to Cauldwell."

You mean over Beauregard and your fat priceless self, the Legate thought but didn't say. He and the Narsima maintained, at best, an armed truce in their dealings. "As I told you, Narsima," he said instead, "hitting them in near-Cauldwell space will protect the entire planet to the extent of the Guard's ability. They cannot hurt that mother ship, but they can kill assault shuttles and now know how to do it. We can handle the Wareegans on the ground, but every one they kill during the drop is one less for us to deal with."

The Narsima wasn't necessarily adverse to Gladius casualties, but he was realistic enough to know his survival depended on the two men with him. Using that hidden Imperial courier boat to extract him and his Imperial liaison from the situation was out of the question as long as the mother ship was not engaged in combat. The courier boat would be run down and caught before it could engage tachyon field drive and the probable results of capture produced images the Narsima shuddered to contemplate. Well enough. Hopefully the Guard and the legion would fight back this incursion. Then other courses of action could be contemplated.

He favored the Legate's holo image with a glare. "For all our sakes, Corona, I hope you know what we're doing."

The Legate returned the glare with emotionless imperturbability. "It will work. The only question is casualties, and we hope to keep them to a minimum, if your shelters work." Both knew a great deal of the appropriated money had been skimmed off at various political levels, so the shelters weren't deep or hardened enough for good protection. Still, they were better than nothing.

The Legate hoped that those shelters would keep collateral civilian deaths to a minimum, but he didn't nurse high expectations. There were going to be dead citizens. That was certain. Again, he mentally damned the Narsima and all the other types that were concerned with nothing but their own enrichment and perks of power. Dying in one of these raids wasn't real enough to them and the average citizen didn't matter. Then again, if his own plans worked out, that situation would change.

BAYVIEW

Member Theodore was sipping a cool drink, but was anything but calm as he surveyed the feed from the PCC's screen. The beautifully paneled walls and the quiet background music were all part of the VIP bunker, much more strongly built and far more deeply buried than the one built for the proles, designed to withstand the ten kiloton blast of the missile intended to obliterate a Wareegan raid. The public shelters weren't built to that standard, but it wasn't necessary in their case. They could always spare some of the underclass, Theodore sniffed to himself, so skimming some of the public shelter money to build the power station was only logical. Besides, saving him and his fellows was simply necessary to the continuation of civilization. He'd felt no remorse as his bodyguards and handlers shoved people out of the way in their mad dash for the shelter. Saving him was only proper and they were sure to survive. So why was he nervous?

######

Shana was already heartily sick of Adam yelling frenetic instructions through her broadcast headset. "Get panic shots! Crowd movement! Confusion! That's what grabs the viewer! Get it!"

She was sending out live feed from her ear cam and Adam was getting his money's worth from the frantic flow of the crowd. The police were doing their best to keep things orderly, but trouble had started early when Theodore and his group had started a panic by barging off in a dead run for someplace, knocking men and women down, nearly trampling a child. She had shots of that, but she was pretty sure Adam had blocked them. Now she was getting the jostling crowds headed for the shelter. The sickening thought in the back of her mind was this wasn't the bad part. The public shelters were too small to hold everyone. The real panic would start once the blast doors were closed and people were locked out. She put that worry aside and prayed to the Lord Above Bayview wasn't the target.

PLANETARY COMMAND CENTER

Imin sat in his command chair in the PCC, watching the mother ship's symbol creep ever closer to Cauldwell. Everything was set and all he could do was wait. In a way, he wished the Legate hadn't given him those chips on fighter tactics. The Guard used to fly in beautiful formations, vics of three, with him up there leading them as he should be.

93

The first time they'd fought Wareegan assault shuttles, Imin thought, they'd come in fat and happy, with big beautiful formations and no idea what they were really doing. Lord Above, but they were dumb! They'd lost half their strength for their trouble, not to mention a whole city. He resolutely didn't think about the second one.

Now things were different. The Legate's chips were standard Impy training manuals, showing the way real combat pilots did it. That was enough for him to radically shift the Guard's tactics and operating procedures. Imin planned to win the next battle. This battle. Now they knew how.

Imperial tactics dictated two ship flights, lead and wing man, moving in an interlaced pattern to make them harder to hit. Squadron direction under the new procedures came from the squadron commanders and they in turn got direction from an overwatch bird loaded with scanners and space control personnel. Entirely different, but everything worked. Very well, in fact. They'd practiced hard enough over the last weeks enough to know that. Now he was down in the PCC, ready to pass operational decisions to the controllers who, in turn, would tactically direct the squadrons. And maybe, just maybe, if the Guard and the Victrix did their part, they wouldn't lose another city.

So far, the Wareegans were following the script. The Guard had drilled against an opposing force simulating the Wareegans' tactics and come out ahead nearly every time. After action reviews identified and corrected tactical faults. Imin wasn't worried if the damned raiders followed the doctrine they'd showed so far. If they changed, he had the flexibility to adapt, but it would create some temporary confusion and reduce the number of kills. He just wanted those bastards to come in like always.

There! They'd launched a beacon flight. Ground defense would let the beacons through so he knew where to send the Victrix. The beacons were inbound and they'd get a course track in just a few... The course track blinked into being on the screen as the computers analyzed the data.

Oh, Lord Above!

He opened his personal communications channel to the Legate. //"We've got a landing site."//

Imin had to swallow the nervous lump in his throat. //"It's Bayview."// He paused for a second. It seemed silly to talk about a single person, but they both knew her well. //"That's where Shana is right now."//

The Legate was silent for a moment. //"Understood. And noted about Sim Ettranty. We're already formed and will be loading as soon as possible, but I estimate at least four hours before we can hit them. How long before you expect landings?"//

Imin looked at his tactical screen. //"Less than that,"// he said flatly. //"Call it around three. They're launching now. We'll be hitting them as soon as they clear the mother ship's defensive fire envelope. After that, it depends on the Lord Above. All I can say is hurry."//

The Legate's voice was grim. //"We will."//

A red light began blinking urgently on Imin's control board. //"Legate, wait. Something important."//

His face developed a sickly hue as he got the Analysis Section's report. //"Legate, they're doing something different. They've only launched twenty or thirty assault shuttles in the past, but Tracking says they've launched about a hundred. That might be their full complement. Analysis says this is no longer a raid."//

//"They're coming to stay this time,"// the Legate finished the report for him. //"I was wondering what they'd do about your nuclear strike. Now we know. They'll take Bayview for a beachhead, set up antimissile defenses, and fan out from there under a defensive umbrella. They want to clean off the planet."//

The Legate's voice was now flat and unemotional with the notorious Gladius calm. //"Commander, that is their plan, but it's not going to work. We'll get there in time to stop the anti-air defenses from being emplaced then it's our turn. Your job is to stop as many of those assault shuttles as you can, any way you can."//

//"Legate,"// Imin said quietly, //"each of those shuttles carries around a hundred aliens. That means they've launched nearly ten thousand raiders. If we kill half of them, you're still outnumbered by sixty percent."//

//"Commander,"// the Legate continued in tones that were just as quiet but far more relaxed, //"they are the Predator. They are what we hunt and kill. They will not see the dawn. Out."//

"May the Lord Above be with you, Legate," Imin said softly to himself. "And with us." Then he looked at the tactical screen. The assault shuttles were just about in the right place. Time to start the party.

He switched channels and spoke. //"Execute Delta One."//

LUNA

Fighter pilots were by definition aggressive and arrogant, and they reveled in it. Possibly it was reaction to being considered expendable. That at least was Squadron Commander Taduz "Bat" Berkowicz's considered opinion on the matter as he watched the feed on his fighter cockpit's small tactical screen. The feed was coming from the observation station on Jack Luna's Moon.

For a second, the irrepressibly whimsical portion of his brain wondered how in hell Cauldwell had gotten two moons named after First Ship's most notorious bootlegger and his daughter Lunetta, thinking of several hilariously wild scenarios. Bat quit woolgathering as the controller's voice came over his headset. //"All Zulu formations, command imminent. Zulu Two, execute on my command. Stand by."//

Bat didn't reply. Com silence and all that. He knew everyone in his Second Squadron, Planetary Guard, AKA Jawbreakers, AKA Zulu Two, had lifted from their forward base on the moon and was ready. Directional transmissions had confirmed readiness ten minutes ago, after they'd settled into their hide in Luna's airless valleys. Zulu Three was here somewhere and Five would be coming off Lunetta. One and Four had the hard part, coming off the planet's surface. They'd be at a disadvantage because of the gravity well, but they just had to get in front of the assault shuttles. Six was in the middle, swinging around from the planet's shadow as a reserve. Thank the Lord Above this happened in the middle of a duty day so all pilots and crew were already available to scramble!

They'd practiced this in simulators and in space, with live opposition and in drills. It ought to work. Getting retrained because of information from the ground pounders was irritating, but the wonderful tactics they'd been given soothed bruised egos. Besides, the Gladii weren't really doing the training. All they did was tell them there was a better way and give them the materials on how to go about it. Every pilot in the Guard had undergone a religious experience when the new tactics were explained. Bat, the Commander, and the rest of the Guard leadership took it from there for five or six frantic weeks. Now they were about to test the result in the only examination that counted. And it was pass - fail. Bat intended to pass with flying colors.

//"All Zulu formations,"// came the dispassionate voice, //"be advised Zulu One and Four have lifted."//

Okay, Bat thought, looking at his tac screen, those assholes ought to be reacting soon. There were a hell of a lot of them. Lots more than previously. No matter. It was a classic target rich environment, as the ancient phrase went.

Bat had only flown combat once in his career - the first raid - and had gotten his squadron's ass handed to him. So, okay, now they knew how the game was played by the big boys and they intended to play the same way.

There they went, he thought, as the Wareegans spread out into a mutually defensive linear formation. One and Four were coming up and they were showing the old dumb tactics of going straight for the assault shuttles. Uh-uh, baby, not this time. Just stay in that wonderful line, waving your big fat asses at us. We've got a surprise for you.

//"Zulu Two, Zulu Three, Zulu Five, execute."//   This time the controller's voice was showing a little suppressed excitement.

No response. Still commo silence. The movement of his fighter as it slowly lifted up where the rest of the squadron could see him was enough. As soon as he came out of his terrain blind, Luna base would report execution via secure transmission.

Sure enough, his tac screen showed the other five fighters in the squadron rising and falling into formation with him. Further out, Three was popping into view also. Time to go. //"Zulu Two,"// he said, coming up on the squadron net for the first time, //"go, go, go. Go, go, go. Go, go, go."//

He got five triple tones in response as he applied full military power. Zulu Two and Three shot out from behind Luna to join Zulu Five in the first fully coordinated space attack in the Guard's history. They had a blood debt to settle.

ITC 901

The Legate was in full armor with his B-42 slung across his chest, helmet in hand, and his armor's refractive camouflage fully active as he jumped off the carryall, running up the nose ramp of the troop carrier and onto the bridge. He racked his helmet next to his seat and picked up his headset. He came up on the all hands channel. //"Victrix,"// he said, //"the Predator's coming."//

The Legate could sense the grim anticipation his men radiated at that phrase. //"We're probably looking at five K plus, gentlemen, but we have a little advantage. They don't know we're here... and that fact will come as a most unpleasant surprise. Make the best use of it. As soon as you're seated, check your tactical downloads. I expect the raiders to be on the ground when we get there, so we'll go with Op Plan Hotel. I'll pass on which variant when we see what the raiders are doing.

//"Recruit Ettranty is down there, people. Anyone who can, get her out. That's a priority, but your main priority is the Predator. We've been hurt, but the Lord Above gave us this gift to soothe our souls. The Predator is coming to Bayview. We see him and we know him. He will not see the dawn.

//"*Gladio alieyo.*"//

Gladio alieyo. The battlecry of the Corps and the most feared words in the galaxy, more often spoken softly than yelled. It was translated a variety of ways, but the most chilling was the simplest: The Gladius is here.

The three thousand or so men on the landing deck, weirdly hard to see because of the refractive capabilities of their combat armor, showed no reaction, but none was expected. Instead, there was a feeling of vast grim anticipation. The Predator was coming. So was the Victrix.

VICTRIX BASE

A young Captain and his intelligence section were also loading out on a cutter, one with a high powered suppresser field and other devices to make it nearly undetectable. He, his men, and the legion's four recruits weren't going on the operation. They were heading for a wasteland on the other side of the planet. The legion was going to survive and it needed a place to return to after the battle.

ITC 901

On benches near their sleds, men stoically sat with their thoughts then a clear strong voice started a song.

"Aaaaay, Eyn mol, eyn mol, eyn mol,
        eyn mol tu ikh zikh banayen:"

"Eyn mol tu ikh zikh banayen," three thousand voices replied, stamping the time with booted feet.

"A gantse vokh horevet men dokh,
Af shabes darf men layen-n-n..."

"A gantse vokh horevet men dokh,
Af shabes darf men layen..." came back with a roar and a stomp. The singing - and the heavy stamping of boots - continued as the troop carrier swung out over the water headed for Bayview. The ship was low, suppressed, and totally off any sensors looking down from the assault shuttles.

The Victrix was coming, Predator.

CAULDWELL NEAR SPACE

Wareegans were straight ahead. Two, Three, and Five were slashing into the classic position dead astern of their targets - targets preoccupied with One and Four. Datalink assigned individual targets within squadron sectors of fire, and Bat made a quick check of his targeting solution before he pressed the gun button on his control stick. A burst of two centimeasure bolts streamed into the engine compartment of an assault shuttle.

As his target vomited explosive glare and disintegrated, Bat calmly reacquired another shuttle. These were the easy kills before these bastards woke up, but he'd take every one he could get. It wasn't like they could turn around and engage him. They had to go down to the planet. Well, he thought as his second target blew apart, they were going down - in pieces.

The Wareegan formation shifted to a shallow vee and began returning fire, reorienting shields to protect against fighter attack to the rear, but it didn't make any difference to the squadrons corkscrewing from the back. It just meant targeting an assault shuttle with two or more fighters. It also meant more of the fighters would die. It didn't mean they were going to stop killing Wareegans.

A flash out of the corner of his eye and a red dot on his tactical screen told Bat he no longer had a wingman. He hard rolled, spiraling around a short stream of bolts from an assault shuttle in a maneuver that simultaneously avoided return fire, edged him closer to the dancing pair of fighters on his left, and kept his targeting systems locked on the assault shuttles. Tone and fire. Score one more.

One and Four, now in a *real* combat formation, kept boring into the front of the Wareegan formation, keeping up the pressure. By now, Six had come around the planet's edge and were in the fight, attacking the flank of the Wareegan formation. It wasn't a melee - the formations were too widely separated for that - but it was a killing ground. The Wareegans wanted down and the Guard was going to make sure the raiders had to come through them to do it.

PLANETARY CONTROL CENTER

In the PCC, Imin was carefully watching the Big Board, judging the battle. They were getting kills. The new tactics were working, but it was a mathematical equation. The raiders had started with over a hundred shuttles and he only had thirty six fighters. No, twenty eight... twenty seven, he thought as he checked fighter status. They had over thirty kills and the total was steadily climbing, but they weren't going to be able to stop them. He opened his channel to the Legate. //"Legate, they're going to make it. Analysis says about fifty plus will land. About what we figured. Be ready."//

//"We are,"// came the reply in even tones. //"Thanks for thinning them down. We can't make it in time to catch the landings, not and remain undetected. They won't be down long, though, before they have other problems. Let's see what ground defense can do."//

Anti-air, remotely controlled robotic guns, won't do much before they were eliminated by the assault shuttles, Imin thought, but maybe something could be done. //"We'll keep 'em busy, just get there and finish the bastards off."//

//"Victrix will do that, Commander,"// the Legate said with calm certainty. //"We've done this before. One zero mikes to drop point."//

BAYVIEW

By now, Shana knew they were in real trouble. The guns outside the city were firing. Worse, there were explosions from Wareegan return fire and the ground fire was thinning out. The Wareegans were coming to Bayview. Shana prayed to the Lord Above that some jackass wouldn't nuke the landing then wondered if it might not be better if he did.

No, the Victrix was coming.

She and her crew huddled under a building arch as the explosions grew deafening. Debris was flying in all directions. Looking up, she saw the assault shuttles screaming into a landing just outside of town, one exploding from a shot by a lucky anti-air gun. The rest were down.

She turned down the audio on her headset. Adam was screaming, "Great! Fantastic! Get civilian casualties! Viewers will love it! Get as much of those Gumbies firing as you can! We'll run 'em together!"

The Victrix wasn't here yet, asshole, Shana thought, ducking as a fragment ricocheted past. How about you wait until they were before demanding pictures?

BEAUREGARD

In the studio, one of the producers looked at Adam with surprise. "Why those two shots? Besides, they aren't there yet."

"Not there? Then we'll punch that up! They ought to be there!" Adam yelled back excitedly. "Good call!"

"Adam," the producer said with growing exasperation. "What the hell are you trying to do? Those guys are going in to defend us. They may not live through this. Hell, WE may not live through this!"

"Oh, they'll win," Adam waved such a silly concern away. "I just want to make sure they don't get any political capital out if it."

The producer stared at Adam with open mouthed amazement.

#####

100

The Narsima Matic Ettranty was thinking along Adam's lines as he sat watching the tridio in his underground bunker. A shame about Shana and all those proles, but some things were more important. If everything went well, Corona and his men would be a spent force after the battle. If things fell apart, the escape craft was on five minute notice. If he had a little luck during the takeoff, he was perfectly safe.

BAYVIEW

Shana wasn't safe, and neither was her crew. The two men with her were as scared as she was, but just as determined to cover the battle. Shana wondered for a second how many were seeing the coverage. Then all those concerns became silly as she looked down the street and saw the large lanky insectoid figures dashing from cover to cover. Her recruit education told her what they were. Wareegan scouts!

She swallowed her nausea as one of the Wareegans reached into a building entrance one handed and casually held a struggling human high off the ground. They were too far away for her to see if it was a man or a woman, but the sounds of the screaming came to her faintly. She wrenched her head around to the men behind her. "Out of here, now! They're coming and we're too exposed."

The other two didn't question her, just followed as she ran crouched along the front of another building. There was a bank further up the street. Maybe there. The THWACK of a bolt and a chopped off squeal told her they were targeted, but she didn't stop to see who was dead. She couldn't do anything. Just run.

Inside the bank, she looked around, to discover Samma Cosma, her sound man, wasn't there. Jhom, her tridio technician, stared back into the street through a window, white faced and shaking, but seemingly in control of himself. "Dead," he muttered to her, meaning Samma.

"We will be too if we can't find someplace to hide until the Victrix comes," she shot back. "I'll keep watch. You check the offices and try to find something."

As Jhom scrambled off to look for a better hiding place, a heavy bolt hit shook the building, dropping pieces of the ceiling, debris and dust around them. From where she'd ducked behind a counter, Shana stared at the debris for a moment then something registered. There was a thin metal tube, less than two measures long, lying with the rest of the rubble. It was only slightly bent and the end was broken jaggedly. A weapon?

Howard's voice came to her. "There are no dangerous weapons, recruits, only dangerous people." She darted over to pick up the tube, holding it tightly as she scuttled back to her temporary shelter.

101

She was breathing more slowly now, and her thoughts were running into unaccustomed channels. Shana suddenly realized she was no longer thinking of flight, or hiding, as anything more than an expedient. For some reason, time was slowing. The time dilation hormone her extra lobe produced - and she didn't know she had - was starting to enter her system. One of the results of her medical treatments before becoming a recruit. Fear was gone and something else had taken its place. Her body was ready to fight and, as yet unknown to her, her mind was starting to work in the channels her Gladius training had created. The Predator was here and she was developing the urge to hunt him. Hunt him, but be smart about it. Was this from her Gladius training? Whatever it was, she no longer saw herself as helpless prey. She was the hunter, concealed and waiting. Shana eyed the street outside through the plass front windows with a different attitude.

She slipped further back around the corner of the counter, only an eye watching the street outside as the tall horror cautiously strode into view, weapon held across its chest in ready position. Wareegan. Could she get the alien's bolt gun? No, let it pass if it was going to, time and patience were on her side. The Victrix was coming. Stay alive and protect Jhom. Shana slipped off the camera headset. It was no longer a part of what she had to do and Adam's frenetic directions were irrelevant.

She was calm as she watched the scout walk alertly into full view. Something in her reached out and melded with something else. She could feel it. She was no longer alone. She was part of a Whole, a Whole that had made hunting the Predator its coldly professional avocation for a thousand years.

For the first time, she could repeat the age old words, words she never before felt she could say. Now, as part of the Whole, she knew she had a perfect right to them. She was part of something that included Those Now Gone, and others that were here. Others that watched with cold, cold eyes and waited until the right moment.

"I stand guard at the Gates of Hell," she said softly to herself, but she was saying it with others, the ones with the cold, cold eyes.

"Nothing will pass and harm
            those I am sworn to protect."

The Oath came easily and she understood its true meaning.

"My life is nothing." Howard was saying it with her. His eyes were cold, cold as he watched through his combat visor.

"My duty and purpose are everything." Her words were softly murmured, but said at the same time by three thousand grim, deadly men.

"If my life is called for,
            it will be given gladly."

102

The volume of the Oath grew louder from the watching men. She said the words with soft tones, but with just as much deadly finality.

"I go now to face my enemy." There were many eyes watching, many voices speaking. Men in harness in the sleds, heavy gun crews, scouts already in Bayview, the Legate with terrible fire in his eyes. Her. All were One now.

"I have seen him, and I know him." She knew they were here waiting, waiting with terrible patience for the right moment.

"He will not see the dawn." The Victrix was here. Her legion was here.

The Gladius was here. Outside Bayview watching with cold, cold eyes. Inside Bayview quietly developing the situation and killing Wareegan scouts. Crouched in this bank and no longer afraid. The Gladius was here.

Gladio alieyo.

As the Wareegan scout drew cautiously even with the bank's entrance, Jhom came out of the back. "Shana, the vault was left open. We can..."

The alien saw Jhom's movement and heard his voice. Instead of firing, it started into the bank, lured by the urge for more pain and fear. It was going to have fun with this food grub, then kill it and go back to its mission. There was nothing to stop it. This place was safe. Jhom froze in terror as he helplessly stared at the steadily approaching Wareegan.

Shana waited with frightening patience and just as frightening purpose as she watched the alien pass in front of her position, then darted out, full of the soul-deep urge to kill the Predator. With the force of her charge and thrust of her newly trained strength, she drove the rod's jagged point into the Wareegan's back, filling the air with her war scream. The jagged point burst out the front of the insectoid's leathery carapace and the alien fell, dropping its weapon. In one smooth move, Shana scooped up the fallen bolt gun and pointed it at the flopping alien on the floor. She fumbled with the unfamiliar weapon for a second then found the firing button. One shot, and the alien had no head.

BEAUREGARD

Adam and the crew at the network had been watching and listening. They couldn't see much once the camera had tumbled to the floor, tilting the picture to a crazy angle. The pickup volume was down, so they could hear Shana speaking softly to herself, but not make out the words. They could see the Wareegan's legs as it passed through the field of view and an indistinct portion of Shana as she made her rush. The scream came through clearly.

"FANTASTIC!!!" Adam screamed. "Did you hear that death cry? Punch it up! I want a quick piece about Shana getting killed because of her devotion to duty! Get me a talking head to say it was because the Gumbys weren't there! Work up--"

"Adam," the producer interrupted, "I don't think that was a death scream."

"WHO CARES?!!" Adam yelled back. "THIS IS GREAT STUFF!! We'll do a big welcome home if Shana turns up alive, but we've got the viewers hooked!"

The producer stared at Adam. "What happens if WE don't live through this, you idiot?"

Adam gave him a look of total incomprehension.

BAYVIEW

Shana turned to a stunned Jhom. "Head for the back," she said calmly, an icy coolness running through her, her mind calculating the situation and assessing chances. Through her Link, she felt the Victrix already had men in the city, but she wasn't experienced enough to know exactly where or what they were doing. "I'll cover. The Victrix is here. We just have to survive for a while."

"Your survival is my job now, recruit," a youthful tenor voice said behind her. "You did damn good."

Shana spun, looking for the disembodied voice. A visor came up to reveal a face and she recognized the young trooper she'd met that first day in the Legionnaires Club. He was smiling. "Legionnaire Kamikal. Scout. I started looking for you the moment you joined the Whole, Recruit. We all have been. We don't abandon our own, and you're one of ours now. I've reported and the Legate knows you're safe. Street's clear now, so let's get the hell out of here."

Jhom looked at the frightening disembodied face of the young Gladius, then at Shana standing calmly holding a strange gun, frightening in a different way. She was no longer the person he'd known for years. Something inside her was changed and she was different, deadly, focused. Then he looked at the headless body of the alien on the floor. If these two were what was coming, he thought, remembering his terror as the Wareegan approached him, that was good. Time to scare *those* bastards shitless for a change.

The scouts had ridden into the city on small one man sleds, little more than a seat, an engine and a small suppresser field. Even without the sleds' suppresser fields they were nearly impossible to see due to the reflective camouflage of their armor. A cloud of bird-shot sized recon nannies had preceded them, both the scouts and the legion getting their take.

The scouts had the dual mission of defining the situation and eliminating enemy reconnaissance. The legion's eyes, the scouts were slowly, inevitably, blinding the alien force.

Behind a low ridge just outside Bayview's landward side, a long line of assault sleds hovered, the men on them professionally calm as they watched the situation on their visors' Heads Up Display. Far out on the flanks and dispersed from their crews, the legion's 16 CM heavy guns were already targeted for preplanned fires. Terminal guidance of the rounds would come from recon nannies.

//"We're about ready,"// the Legate sent to the Cohort Commanders. //"They're boarding their armored personnel carriers now. We'll let the situation develop until they're out of the assault shuttles, then it will be our time. Fire Support, target the shuttles first, then the APCs."//

The fire support officer sent an acknowledgment tone, with no further comment.

The Legate gave a slight smile. He knew he was being redundant. The FSO was highly capable and didn't need his reminders, but he was the Legate. He could do what he wanted and if he was translating his nervous anticipation into redundancy, he had the privilege.

And he wanted this battle, like no other he'd ever fought. The Predator was down there. A man who'd lost his family to a Predator, the Legate wanted to come to grips with this one with an almost sensual passion. He knew his men were feeling the same way, but his desire was more intense. He'd always been more emotional than everyone else, something his wife had forever teased him about, but there it was. Now, as he watched the reconnaissance battle on his visor screen with eyes that promised the fury of the Lord Above's own lightning, that same vital energy was about to be loosed. Three thousand of history's greatest killers were about to be launched - guided and directed by a man that had no mercy within him.

The Legate watched the green icons of his scouts as they slid through the town, silently stalking Wareegans that had no idea the scouts were there. Every so often, a green icon would meet a yellow Wareegan icon, and the yellow icon would vanish with deadly finality. Rarely, the

105

yellow icon would vanish and the green icon would turn red, indicating a scout's death. The Wareegans were being blinded and the Legate was sure they knew it, but not how it was happening. With any luck, the Wareegan commander would hurry his main force into Bayview to attempt to fix the problem. Fine. That was exactly what the Legate wanted. Urban areas were the most difficult and confusing terrain in which to fight. Confusion was where the Gladius fought best.

The wind ruffled his beard beneath his helmet visor as the Legate stood next to his command sled, and waited with inbred frightening patience for just the right moment as the time dilation hormone produced by the extra lobe in his brain began to take effect. Things began to slow down, as his mental processes speeded up, one of the secrets that made the Gladius so deadly in combat.

The last APCs were loaded and moving away from the assault shuttles. Now.

Legate Corona came up on the all hands net. //"9-6, assault power."//

All down the line, the eerily blank faces of helmet visors carefully watched power indicators climb as the sled drivers inched their throttles towards maximum, still holding their quivering sleds in check. Strapped in behind their drivers, grim faced men, expressions hidden by their own visors, tightened harnesses and settled themselves for the charge. Next to the three Cohort Commanders, fully trained Gladii that happened to be teenage boys opened their own visors and placed their *brusharas* to their lips. The coming of those that hunted the demons of Hell itself would be well and truly announced.

The Legate was aboard the command sled, strapped securely in place when three triple tones sounded in his helmet. All three Cohorts were ready to go. He raised his right arm, hand open as though clawing at the sky. He could feel the energy of the Victrix, straining at the leash. His lower jaw jutting forward in the unconscious gesture of a Gladius about to attack, he closed his hand as though grasping the power of a sun to throw at his enemies and brought it down with a snap as he gave the old, old order.

//"*CATTAN NA BRUSHARA*!"// Sound the battle shout.

Two of the firing battery's six guns went into rapid fire mode with ten 16cm guided bolts on the way in less than a minute. The gun mounts used directed grab fields directed by recon nannies to bend the paths of the bolts to the desired impact point, the Wareegan landing zone. Assault shuttles, defensive screens down, started to erupt in explosions from the bolts' plasma fields. It took the standby crews on the shuttles precious seconds, seconds they didn't have, to get their own guns and defensive screens ready. By the time turrets were targeting the two legion guns, over thirty of the shuttles were destroyed. As return fire blew away the first two guns, the second pair of guns in the firing battery erupted, continuing the fire mission. Again, Wareegan assault shuttles fireballed. The third pair of guns started firing bolts on the traffic flow of Wareegan APCs. Raiders tumbled out, getting away from their now dangerous vehicles.

Aboard the racing, jinking, bobbing sleds the *brushara* bearers sounded their horns, announcing the coming of the Victrix with a solid wall of sound. The electronically amplified blast of the horns was as much a weapon as a summoning of the Gladius to battle, and a Gladius always made best use of any weapon. Window plass was shattering in Bayview.

#####

The Wareegans flinched from the horns, loud enough even at this distance to be painful, and knew the return of an ancestral nightmare, a horror mentioned only softly at rare times. The Wareegans thought the Gladii were gone away, leaving the outer worlds of humanity defenseless and vulnerable. They weren't. The Gladii were here and they were coming. Run, hide, tremble, or fight. It was all the same to the coldly professional, terrible, terrible, kilted hunters with their axes.

The Wareegan commander also heard the horns and everything that had happened on this raid suddenly fell into perspective. This planet was already proving expensive, but now it was going to be catastrophic. They were in the killing ground of an ambush such as they'd never known.

He was an experienced veteran of profitable attacks on many worlds, seeking food and goods. Now he had to salvage as much as possible from this situation. His heavy weapons were back on the mother ship, left because they were unnecessary. Nothing on this planet was supposed to be well defended. Now that he needed his heavy firepower, he was forced back on individual and light crew served weapons.

So be it. In clicks and hisses, his orders went out, changing deployments and fire plans. Once in the city, they stood a chance against the oncoming avengers. The remaining assault shuttles retargeted their guns, turning from counterbattery fire to attack the sleds. But the sleds weren't easy targets.

A combat sled was mostly a motor, controls, a warhead, and passenger platform, but it did contain defensive screen and moved with incredible agility. The sleds were hard to hit, but, here and there, the Wareegan gunners were lucky.

#####

The Legate's visor HUD showed the position of his sleds and the losses he was taking on the charge into Bayview. He felt the loss of every man he'd taken out of the deadly confusion of Victrix Base, but the cold, professional part of his brain assessed his losses as minimal for an attack. They were taking hits, but the turn of the Gladius was coming.

The yellow icons of the Wareegans were flowing into Bayview, and that was what he wanted. The strobing lights of the beacons deployed by the scouts were clear, marking essential objectives. First Cohort had the responsibility for protecting the shelters. A battalion of Third would continue on to the Wareegan landing zone, tasked to capture four carefully preserved assault shuttles. The Legate wanted the mother ship, and those shuttles were key to his plan. He wanted the Wareegan force away from the assault shuttles.

Second and most of Third would be delivered in key positions among the raiders. Unlike earlier military forces, the Corps didn't seek linear battle. With their inbred coordination ability and psychic link, the Gladii knew where they were and what they were doing within the wholesale confusion of a melee. They made full use of it. The Corps came, not to oppose an enemy frontally, but to get among him, to kill from within his formations.

//"Beacon minus fifteen,"// the driver's flat voice came over the com. Fifteen seconds.

Drop.

Like the other five men on his sled, the Legate hit his harness release and fell free on his no-weight belt. The sled continued on to explode in the Wareegan landing zone. Other sleds, now free of their passengers, rained down on the remaining shuttles, destroying almost the last vehicle mounted weapons supporting the Wareegan advance.

The Legate expertly landed with a springy bounce at a street intersection, quickly joined by his staff and security guards. The Predator's eyes were gone, as well as his fire support. Now it was time to start fighting the battle. There were still far too many Wareegans left, but that was irrelevant. The Gladius was here to kill the Predator and protect citizens. That would be done.

The Wareegans were veterans, experienced raiders. That meant they were accustomed to the fire and crashing confusion of combat, but only with forces less capable than theirs. They were predators who sought out the weak and took what they wanted, including helpless victims for food. Now, hearing the sound of the horns, they were confronted with an ancestral nightmare. They were predators, but those that hunted predators were here. Fear coiled through the confusion in their forces wreaked by constant bolt fire, a fear out of their darkest dreams, now made real.

Creatures over three measures tall, insectoid horrors to much of the galaxy, now clicked dry maniples in nervous fear and clutched weapons tighter in their long gangly arms as they loped to defensive positions. They were afraid. Afraid of barely seen deadly killers out of nightmare.

#####

Over eighteen hundred men of the Second and Third Cohorts hit the Wareegan formations like the pellets of an ancient shotgun blast. Hitting dirt in three man teams, the Gladii immediately started moving in a carefully drilled interlaced weave with speed and perfect coordination, killing as they went, cutting holes and furrows in Wareegan positions. The Gladius wasn't a linear fighter unless he had to be one. Instead, every legion tried to insert itself into the middle of an enemy then chew its way out through their guts. In Bayview, they succeeded.

The Wareegans tried to form, tried to create lines and positions out of the howling chaos caused by the deadly hunters in their midst, but it wasn't working. The raiders were responding like the veterans they were, but they were shooting their own more often than they hit the indistinct figures forming the murderous teeth of the buzzsaws tearing away at them. Most of their fire was wasted. The Gladii teams flowed in and out, killing and vanishing, hitting who knew where next. Gradually, the Wareegans were being pushed back, broken up, herded into groups that had no ability to support each other. Once that happened, they were dead.

Improvised command posts were thrown together by frantic effort and as quickly destroyed by whichever Gladius team was closest. A team would hit a Wareegan CP, only to vanish back into the howling chaos after seconds of high intensity firepower destroyed everything. Groups of Wareegans fell into positions with no time to set up lanes of fire or any kind of mutual support. Sometimes they would survive for minutes, pouring out bolt fire at fleeting targets, then the demon hunters would find a weakness and suddenly be down in those positions with them. Close engagement with a Gladius in full combat mode wasn't survivable by anyone or anything. Axes and short swords did for bolt guns in close, or plasma grenades would wipe a few more Wareegans from the face of Cauldwell. Battle dissolved into total confusion, confusion that was the home of the Gladius. The Wareegans were veterans, but not from this kind of battle. None of the Empire's enemies were. None that fought the Gladius were left alive.

Each of the public shelters were surrounded with legion perimeters, small fixed nodes of a single three man team each, with other teams in constant motion on the outer edge of the shelter's defensive perimeter. Colonel Athan's command team was also moving fast, checking positions, marking approach areas, moving between shelter perimeters, killing the odd Wareegan, but still taking contact reports and coordinating actions.

Colonel Karl Athan had his cohort well in hand, as much as Protac and Evns smoothly controlled their own cohorts in the chaos of the main battle. That meant Karl was aware of the incoming scout and his companions when they entered a shelter perimeter and was on the scene to meet them shortly thereafter.

"Good work, Kamikal," he said at the general location of where he knew the scout was. He opened his visor for a few moments to look at the two refugees. One was a male citizen, but the other was the legion's newest recruit. He looked at the Wareegan bolt gun in Shana's hands.

"Got it off a dead Wareegan she killed," Legionnaire Kamikal supplied. "Shana did good, Colonel." Athan nodded.

"Well done, Recruit," he told Shana. "I thought you were coming along properly. Glad to see I was right."

He started issuing orders. "Legionnaire, take the citizen to the shelter then get back out there where you belong. Ettranty, you may join the citizen or take up a guard position with the final security teams. Unless it all goes to shit, you've done your fighting but we take no chances with citizens' lives. Which is it?"

Shana took a tighter grip on her weapon. "The Victrix is here, and I'm part of the Victrix." Jhom looked at her with wide eyes, seeing something he'd never imagined.

Athan smiled. "Good enough. Move."

Jhom was escorted down the long zig-zag passage below a large building and inside the shelter's heavy blast door, while Shana was given a combat headset for communications purposes and assigned an overwatch position at one of the building's upstairs windows. As she looked out the window, she settled herself and realized she was feeling contentment. She was a part of the Whole.

The battalion detailed to capture four Wareegan assault shuttles already had three of them. The fourth blew when a crew member induced an engine overload, destroying the shuttle and the attackers on board. Spoof and implosion packages were quickly but carefully installed aboard the other three, then the teams got off fast. In the past, Wareegan ships quickly recovered a shuttle when its crew died, preventing its use by enemies. The spoof packages were to keep the mother ship from knowing what was on board and the implosion packages were the reason. The powerful black hole generators in the implosion packages would put paid to the mother ship if the plan worked.

The assault shuttles lifted under data link control and soared skyward. As soon as their departure was reported to the Legate, he acknowledged, and turned his attention to controlling the overall battle. Third and Second were close to meshing. When that happened, the Wareegans were finished.

PLANETARY CONTROL CENTER

The mother ship was bringing back the surviving shuttles, but it also launched more help for the beleaguered force on the planet. Imin watched carefully as the icons of fighters and several more assault shuttles separated from the mother ship.

"Force detached from the mother ship," the tracking rating announced. "Five assault shuttles and fifteen, say again one-five, fighters escorting. They're on track for Bayview."

Imin nodded. Reinforcements or aerial support. It made no difference. Warning orders and deployment vectors went out to the depleted Guard squadrons between the Wareegans and the planet. No ambush this time. This one was going to be a straight up knife fight. He opened his channel to the Legate. //"They're bringing in air support. Fifteen fighters and five assault shuttles. We'll cut them down, but I'm not sure we can take them all. You're going to get leakers. Our fighters will follow them down into atmosphere, so be careful who you shoot."//

//"Understood,"// Corona responded. //"My anti-air teams have your IFF. Wareegan assault shuttles are configured for air to ground, but not their fighters. I suggest you make shuttles the primary targets. If the mother ship takes in those implosion packages, the Wareegan fighters will be orphans. Good hunting."//

//"Good hunting."// Imin passed on his targeting orders as he watched his squadrons orient to hit the Wareegans.

CAULDWELL NEAR SPACE

The remaining fighters in the six Guard squadrons outnumbered the Wareegans, but they had to get through the alien fighter screen to get to the assault shuttles. This was going to be an old fashioned fighter-to-fighter furball. That was perfectly all right with Bat. The Guard was ready. Bat already had six confirmed kills and he wanted more. So did his pilots.

//"All squadrons,"// came the flat voice in his headset, //"this is Control. Designate hostile approach vector as zero incoming. Zulu One, Zulu Five, vector 4-0-0-0 mils relative to hostile approach. Zulu One at five o clock, Zulu Five at eleven o'clock. Zulu Four, Zulu Six, vector 2-8-0-0 mils. Zulu Four at eleven o'clock and Zulu Six at five o'clock. Zulu Two, Zulu Three, vector zero reciprocal with Zulu Two at eleven o'clock. Primary target is the assault shuttles. Good hunting, out."//

Bat nodded. Okay, the Jawbreakers were hey-diddle-diddle, right up the middle. Fun. The Wareegan formation was in range and gunfire began crossing. No pretty formations this time, assholes, Bat thought. His people were weaving and dancing, defensive shields maxed forward, grabbing snap shots when they could. Bat skidded to his right, depending on his new wingman to handle fighter interference, then targeted an assault shuttle and fired. The Wareegan blossomed with a momentary brilliance then Bat was locked on another. Third squadron nailed another, but two of the shuttles were past him, streaking for Bayview. Cursing, he hauled around to dive after them, calling for assistance.

Behind him, the recovered assault shuttles docked on automatic and the mother ship suddenly became a gravity crumpled piece of space debris.

BAYVIEW

In Bayview, fleeing Wareegans blew their way into a chance-found shelter that wasn't on any of the Legate's maps. The raiders took a few moments to kill the screaming, terrified occupants - including MP Theodore - then turned to form a defense at the entrance. They were too late.

The Gladii team closely following them went in at top speed behind the fire of their bolt guns then finished the job with axes. The team leader took a few seconds to survey the luxury of the shelter and the scattered bloody pieces of human bodies. Dead citizens. What he was here to prevent. Report it and move on. There were more raiders out there, if fewer and fewer. The Predator was dying hard, but dying. The Victrix was winning this one.

#####

Wareegan assault shuttles cut into the air above Bayview, marked by the flare of burning atmosphere on their shields and announced by the crash of sonic booms. Right behind them came Guard fighters, sideslipping and banking as they frantically tried to force an attack curve out of unforgiving physics. The Wareegan pilots only could only make one firing run before the fighters were on them and they knew it. All thought of careful targeting and the heavy weapons that were their cargo went out the airlock. There was no contact with forces on the ground. Do something else. They programmed maximum effect firing passes. Whatever they hit might be an enemy, after all. They were going to die and this was their only chance to kill the nightmare hunters described in choppy, frantic transmissions from the ground.

The two shuttles blasted many of their own, but they also killed Gladii before an anti-air team smacked one from the sky and Bat personally fireballed the other. Among the Victrix dead was Legate Corona, killed by mere chance and the laws of Murphy.

CHAPTER 5

LEGIO XV RHIANNONITHI
NIAD

When the troop carrier holding the survivors of the liner and the surviving fragment of the Rhiannonithi arrived at 10TH FSG Base on Niad, it was mostly empty. Not abandoned, Major Camille Paten told herself as she made her way to Base Headquarters to turn in her after action report. Unit signs were still up and the base was still functioning, but the Fleet Support Group and the Tenth Valeria were both gone somewhere. Correction, she thought as she saw several Gladius children on a nearby playground, they were on a mission. Non-combat personnel and nondeployables were still here.

Inside the headquarters, the Naval Intelligence section was still fully staffed and a Fleet Lieutenant, no name mentioned, escorted her into a private office for her debriefing. He took the chip with her report and put it into the office terminal, then said nothing more while he read. Looking up at her after the report, he said, "Good report, Major, unfortunately, I don't think it's unique. From what we found out last month, I suspect things like the destruction of the Rhiannonithi and the attack on that liner are happening all over the Empire."

The Lieutenant was conversant enough with Gladius expressions to see her amazement and distress. He shook his head with a grim smile. "I think I can say it's official. The Empire is collapsing."

"Most of the reason is the Empire's been in decline for the last couple of centuries," he continued. "The rest of it is Emperor Shangnaman is bat-shit crazy, a paranoid sociopath to a degree that would have him committed if he wasn't running things."

"Attacks like this are happening all over?" Camille asked, knowing better but hoping he'd deny it.

He didn't. "Yes. They tried a takeover on us a month ago. It failed because one of the two Imperial operatives involved, Major Claude Ancel, went over to our side and blew the thing wide open in time for us to stop it. He also said the Empire is doing a major smash and grab on Tactine right now. Tactine's not too far from here and it's also the strategic, commercial, and economic center of this cluster. If it's devastated, most of the surrounding worlds - including Niad - will be left without the resources, manufacturing and shipping capability to keep running. Tactine has to be preserved for everything out here to keep functioning. That's where the FSG and the Tenth Valeria have gone - to stop the Empire from ruining the entire cluster."

Camille's shock got deeper. "But, for Lord Above's sake, why raid?"

The intelligence officer smiled grimly. "Ancel filled us in. It's as hard for me to believe as it is for you, trust me. Shangnaman's faced with an Empire that's slowly being starved for resources because whole sectors are breaking away while other worlds, such as those in this cluster, are simply drifting out of contact with the central government. The Emperor has ordered raids by new military forces he's created to hit the breakaways and outworlds for everything Middle Empire needs. He doesn't care that they're leaving devastation behind them."

Camille thought fast and hard. "Shangnaman is killing off the most viable worlds to preserve the declining center of the Empire. If he keeps it up, he's going to destroy civilization if Middle Empire collapses like you say."

"And leave whatever's left vulnerable to conquest by half a dozen alien governments we could both name," he replied grimly. "You've got the problem in a nutshell."

His face got hard. "But there's more to it.

"The people of Middle Empire are so sheltered and out of touch with what's happening to outlying Empire sectors that they have no idea the crash is coming. They aren't ignoring or in denial about things like breakaways or a failing government. They simply don't know. When the collapse hits them, it's going to be tragic. What's even more tragic is that there's nothing we can do about it. Billions, trillions of people will suffer and many will die. Possibly all of them if – when - those alien governments I mentioned attack.

"Like I said, Shangnaman's a paranoid, and one of the things he fears most is us: the old line military, Corps and Frontier Fleet, even though we're the ones keeping Imperial borders intact. He knows perfectly well we won't support the Imperial See's pillaging human worlds, so he's trying to eliminate us and doesn't care about the consequences.

"According to Major Ancel, the plan works like this: the government sends in agents such as him to suborn key members of an FSG then uses the FSG to destroy the legion based with it. What's left becomes a part of the new forces."

Camille slowly nodded. "That's what happened to us, I think. In all of the confusion of the attack, I wasn't really sure. Are there any more of these operations? How much of the Corps has been attacked?"

"We don't know," the Lieutenant replied. "Your attack and the failed attack on us are the only two we have any information about, but it's reasonable to assume it's happening all over the Empire. We've had no contact with other Corps units or FSGs for a while, even Fleet and Corps Headquarters. Once Legion Commander Garua and Admiral Mackinnie return, we're going to try to find anyone that's left and gather them here. If we can create an area strong enough to keep the Empire off, we might be able to save human civilization, at least in this cluster. The rest of the Empire is on its own."

After the debriefing, Camille walked slowly back to their temporary quarters, deep in thought. The pending catastrophe for billions was so horrific she couldn't grasp it, not yet. The second part of the news, Empire attacking human populated worlds, the very worlds she and the Corps were sworn to protect, was something she could understand very well, if not the reasons. Those attacks made the Empire the Predator, she thought, the worst one in human history. The Empire - the bedrock of human civilization - was the enemy, an enemy the Corps had to defeat to save this cluster. As Camille thought about what that meant for the future, she found her thoughts even more frightening than the Rhiannonithi's destruction.

#####

In another part of the base the Narsim Clarine Femiam and her daughter Lana were having it out in their own quarters. They'd been informed a chartered tramp freighter was going to take the liner's survivors to Cauldwell and there was a major disagreement between them. The argument wasn't a quiet one.

"I don't want to leave!" Lana shouted.

"And I say no!" Clarine replied just as hotly. "I'm not leaving you here in the back of beyond with nothing but these uniformed barbarians just because you've got the hots for some boy. There are plenty more on Cauldwell. You'll find someone there to pass the time."

"Suppose I don't want to just pass the time," Lana said grimly, her hands clenched into fists. "I suppose you don't know - or care - that I'm sick of the way you live."

Clarine glared. "The way I live has gotten us where we are."

"Yeah, refugees and broke."

"No, once we get to Cauldwell, my cousin will get us set up again," Clarine said with grim determination. "I refuse to yield to this setback. Yes, our money disappeared on that liner, but I still have connections. We won't be destitute long. Now forget that boy!"

"That boy, as you put it, Mother, risked his life to save ours. If I recall correctly, there is absolutely nobody on Central that would do that!"

Lana took a deep breath. "I got to know him in the ship's hospital. He's a decent person, and I didn't know any of those. You don't know any of those either! I didn't know they still existed!"

"He's a Gladius," Clarine snarled. "They aren't anything but robots. They have no emotions and no purpose except to kill. You're nothing to him but a concept. Once you were safe, he couldn't care less what you did. He's forgotten you. Now, we're going to Cauldwell - together!"

Both did go to Cauldwell together. All of the survivors did. It really wasn't noticeable to anyone on the ship, but several members of 10th FSG's Intelligence section went with them. Cauldwell was another key world in the cluster. Now that the Empire was truly collapsing, Intelligence wanted to know about the situation on the planet.

#####

Legionnaire First Jamie Kardo hadn't forgotten Lana. Right now, he was on heavy equipment maintenance detail but it gave him time to think. Supervising the mindless mechs that serviced the Fifteenth Legion's remaining heavy weapons wasn't hard and gave him time to consider Lana. He'd never known a citizen before and wondered if they were all like her. There was a shell of cynical hardness around her, but he thought there was someone underneath he'd like to know better. Besides, there were only a few girls his age in the legion after the base destruction. Lana was different, and that intrigued him. Oh well, there were girls in the Valeria and he wasn't a Recruit any longer. He could date now. Still... Lana. He could daydream a little, couldn't he?

BEAUREGARD

The Narsima Matic Ettranty was in an elemental rage, but maintained enough control that it didn't show... very much. Sitting at his desk, he fumed silently, glad that nobody was in his office to see his anger. Revealing feelings was dangerous. The entire Lord Above triple damned legion was gone - just gone. The men, their casualties, their equipment, even the bodies of their dead, were all gone. Their base was just an empty shell, completely abandoned. The troop carrier was gone too, and that was even more worrying. Were they off planet or in hiding somewhere in the wilderness? On an off chance, he'd even had his Imperial liaison check the surveillance monitors in the hidden depots, but none of them showed any sign of activity. So where were they? Webster was no help. He'd denied any sign of them after what he said was a thorough search - if it was one and he wasn't in collusion with those damned Gladii. He couldn't arrange such a thing as a thorough search in the hours after the Wareegan battle anyhow.

Ettranty shook his head, annoyed with himself. Webster was totally reliable. Ettranty told himself to stop looking for shadows. Webster promised another search as soon as his force could reorganize. It had to be done soon. That legion was dangerous, and he had to know where they were. He'd messaged the Emperor with the situation long ago and his orders were to keep the legion under close surveillance, to be disposed of once the Wareegan pests were gone.

Now the legion was also gone - to who knew where - and he wasn't about to tell the Emperor *that* little fact just yet. No matter what his liaison said. Not until he had control of the situation again. He simply had to find them, and soon.

Momentarily, he wondered about what happened to his daughter during the attack, but shrugged the distraction away. She was certainly among those killed, although they didn't have her body. Jhom, her tridio technician, said she was dead. The network had even announced her death while the battle was still in progress, of all silly things! The memorial service for her and the other casualties was tomorrow afternoon. He had to go to it, of course, and put on a properly grieving and sympathetic air. The sheep loved melodrama and Shana's death would increase his popularity ratings by a solid ten percent. At least she'd done some good dying.

CAULDWELL, 48 HOURS EARLIER

Shana was very much alive. After the battle, she and the rest of the legion were hastily boarded on the troop carrier and now they were heading for what she heard was some sort of huge underground depot. She gathered the thing was under one of the larger mountains in the Atlas range, clear across the planet from Bayview. One of the secret depots the Legate told her about.

That thought brought a quick flash of grief. She'd been told he was dead and it surprised her how much that hurt. Well, she still had her legion, and it was hers completely now. She'd fought as part of it, even without a uniform or orders. She was a Gladius in the Ninth Legion now.

Jhom, who knew her as well as anyone, could see something different in her, something scary. Something Gladius? She imagined that was one reason he'd readily agreed to her request to keep her survival a secret. When she'd asked him to let her drop out of sight, he'd said plainly she wasn't the same anymore. Then he'd hugged her and told her to follow whatever path was opening in front of her.

For some reason, following that path and accepting whatever changes it brought just felt right to her. Recruit training? Whatever had started it, she was beginning a new life.

Just how far she was down that path to a new life was shown to her a few minutes later by Staff Sergeant Howard. They were all crowded into a large - huge - deck, but decurions were sounding off and the men on the deck were rapidly draining into passageways as the ship went somewhere in a hell of a hurry. She was trying to figure out what she was supposed to do when Howard appeared before her, an unaccustomed smile splitting his unlovely face. "You did well, Recruit," he growled.

Shana wondered if the man knew how to speak in any other tones, but the thought vanished at his next words. "So well you're no longer a Recruit. That little fracas qualifies as your Virgin Mission, Ettranty, and you did real well on it. You're a Recruit until your Virgin Mission, and you've just had yours, so now you're a Legionnaire. Just don't think you're a fully trained Legionnaire."

He slapped her shoulder. "Okay. I admit it. You survived, but not only survived. You were unarmed, but you took an enemy weapon and saved a citizen's life with it. That's good work. Colonel Athan has okayed your promotion to Legionnaire Second."

So now she was not only a real Gladius, she was one step above dirt. Actually, that felt pretty good now that she thought about it. "Uh... what now, Sergeant?"

Howard laughed. "Well, you're not all alone in the great big wild galaxy, Ettranty. First thing, you need to get into a real uniform. No more pants, either. You've earned your skirt, Legionnaire, and something else. First, these."

He put two metal things in her left hand and she looked down at them. Insignia. One was the crossed ax and short sword on a sunburst that was the Gladius emblem. There was a big IX overlaying the insignia. No, it wasn't an IX. It was the numeral nine in the ancient Roman numbers. The crest of a member of the Victrix. Her legion. The other was a number two, her new rank. As she closed her hand on the two insignia, she realized they meant more to her than any jewelry she'd ever owned.

Then he topped the award of her insignia. Strangely, he blushed a little as he reached behind his back and pulled something from of his belt. "The Commander should give you this when you get your rank, but she's not with us anymore. I gotta do it. Put it on with your uniform."

It was a Gladius woman's arm dagger with the tractor - presser bracelets hung around the handle. She was truly a female Gladius now. "Now," Howard said uncomfortably, "you don't go thinking you really know how to use that little toy. Like I said, you need a lot more training

119

and you're going to get it, but you're a full Gladius and not a Recruit any more.

"Normally," Howard continued, in a *soft* growl this time, "you'd get all this in formation. We don't have time for that right now, so get to your berth and get squared away. Then you report to the Sergeant Major. Here's a locator card. Follow it to your berth. It'll take you to the Sergeant Major when you're ready, too."

Numbly, she took the card in her right hand, her left still clutching the precious bits of metal and her dagger, and put her thumb on the activation spot. She'd used cards like this dozens of times in the past, so she knew to follow the little shining ball that appeared. Berth? She had a berth on this huge ship? Apparently so. She looked up into Howard's eyes and tried to say something, but he shook his head, still smiling.

"Don't bother, Ettranty. You did us proud today, Legionnaire, so go get into uniform." He slapped her shoulder again. "Then go find the Sergeant Major before he has my ass.

"Dismissed." The growl was louder this time. "And for Lord Above's sake, wear everything *right!*"

Automatically, she moved off, following the glowing ball. It led her down several passageways into an elevator that started as soon as she was inside. Once out of the elevator, she found herself on a deck that seemed strangely deserted. She pondered that feeling of emptiness as she followed the ball down the passage, then she noticed a sign. Female Legionnaire Quarters. Oh. It was empty because there were no women left in the Victrix. She was the only one.

The thought didn't really hit her until she was inside the tiny compartment. There was a set of bunk beds, two sets of lockers, empty bookshelves, a tiny desk with a terminal, and not much else. One set of lockers was empty. The second set had uniforms in one locker and combat gear in the other. There were khaki blouses, long flowing skirts, coveralls, but no pants. Knowing the Gladius attention to detail, they were certainly her size. Automatically, she sat down on the lower bunk and began to remove her shoes.

Then she froze. She was alone in this section because it was for the legion's junior women and she was the only one. There were no senior ranked women, either. No women at all. She was the only person in this whole empty section, the only woman left in the Victrix. The only one left - and she was recruited on Cauldwell. None of the others had survived to come to Cauldwell. She was the legion's only woman. Dead, all the rest of them, dead.

Some of it was combat reaction, some of it was the situation, and some of it was grief. She'd seen the shadows on the parade ground during the integration formation. They were the women of the legion, her legion, and they were dead. Now she was a woman of the Victrix. The only one left.

She never knew how long she just sat there, staring into space, tears trickling down her face. Mourning for those she could never know. Then she felt a gentle presence, something she couldn't see but knew was there. She wasn't alone. She was a Gladius, and a Gladius was part of a Whole, part of generations before, part of those now here. She was being welcomed by those women gone before her. She was a Gladius woman... and there were others with her.

Time to act like it. She stood up and noticed something she'd missed. In the corner behind the door was a small sink with a mirror, a shelf, and a cabinet. There was even a box of tissues on the shelf. Beyond a doubt, this was women's quarters. Let's get cleaned up and squared away, Ettranty. You have to report to the Sergeant Major.

And for Lord Above's sake, wear your uniform *right*! You represent every woman in the legion. Be proud.

She was a little uneasy as she stepped back into the passageway and followed the little ball to wherever the Sergeant Major was located. She thought everything on her uniform was right, but she wasn't sure. She dreaded appearing in front of the Sergeant Major with even the littlest thing wrong. She was in a larger passageway when she started to walk past four young Legionnaires headed the other way.

One of them stopped her. "Hold it, mate."

She stopped. What now?

One of them, a boy almost ten years her junior, said, "You're Ettranty."

Shana nodded, still nervous.

Another said, "It's good to see that uniform again, but you're not quite right. First decurion that sees you will have your ass.

"Here," he said, as he started to adjust the position of her insignia, "this is how they go. Better never forget that."

Another one told her, "Cock your cap a bit forward. You can do it now. You're veteran of a real battle, not just a little fire fight." She tipped her cap forward slightly, to general approval. After all, she was a veteran Gladius, no matter how she got that way. "Only newbies and pricks wear their caps straight up," the young Legionnaire finished, producing some laughter.

A third said, "Arm dagger's off, too. I'll bet that's uncomfortable. Let me fix it for you."

He unclasped the dagger and reattached the mounting band in a little different position. She flexed her arm. I did feel better. "Thanks,

121

guys," she replied with a smile. "That does feel right. And thanks for helping me with the insignia. I've got to see the Legion Sergeant Major and I want everything to be correct."

"If you're on your way to see Olmeg, you'd better get your ass in gear," one of them said. "Least we can do for a new mate." The group looked her over carefully and pronounced her ready to face the Sergeant Major.

She didn't think. The question just tumbled out. Looking at the young Legionnaire that had adjusted her dagger, she asked, "How did you know how a woman's dagger should be worn?"

She wanted to pull the question back as soon as it was spoken. The youngster's eyes darkened for a moment. "Mother and two sisters, mate. Grew up with it."

"Sorry." It was all she could say.

He shook his head and his smile returned. It was cold, cold. "They paid the Gladius Price, Ettranty. So did everyone else's mothers, or sisters, or daughters in the Victrix. We all do, sooner or later. But the Predator paid way more. And I took some of it."

His smile grew warmer. "You took some, too, I heard. Good. Now get on. Olmeg will crawl all over you if you're overdue."

She started to walk away when one of the young Legionnaires broke the somber mood. "Great ass, Ettranty," he called, "but you're a bit too tall and way too old for me."

Shana spun to look at them in something akin to shock that anyone would say such a thing. Then she suddenly realized they were young soldiers. Soldiers were like that. And she was a soldier too. "When I want to play with children," she called back, "I'll look you boys up."

She put her hand on her hip and gave them all a brazen grin. "It'll probably take all of you if I do."

They were still laughing as she walked away. She was, too.

As she walked the passageways, Shana became aware of a peculiar phenomenon. Every Gladius she saw was smiling. Even crusty and grizzled decurions. Even the officers, in a little more restrained fashion. At her. Not a "guy-looking-at-a-pretty-girl" smile. Well, not most of it. There was friendship there, too. She was a member of the Victrix, after all. But members of the same legion didn't go around smiling at each other all of the time.

Then she realized. It was the uniform. Oh, they all knew about her, but it was the uniform, the skirt and what it represented, that made the difference. She was a Gladius woman in duty khakis, something these men had seen all their lives. Something they thought gone and lost forever. It was that simple. Before her, they had no future. Now, she and her

122

uniform symbolized a future. Up to her to justify that, and there was still a little something in the background of her mind that said she wasn't alone. Those Now Gone were with her and approved.

Her carriage got a little more erect and she stepped out with self-confidence. If being a living symbol was her duty, well she could damn well do it. She was a Gladius now. She knew about duty.

She found the Sergeant Major, standing with several other decurions on an immense balcony over that huge empty deck, talking and watching various Gladii crossing the deck on unnamed errands. He looked over her figure, rigid at attention, with a hard eye that missed nothing. "All good, Ettranty," he pronounced his verdict. He had to know she'd had help with the uniform, but didn't ask from who or why. It was unimportant. Gladii helped Gladii.

"Stand easy." Even he smiled. "It's good to see that uniform again. The Victrix is going to be right, one of these days.

"Ettranty, you would normally be in Support Command, but there isn't one at the moment." A shadow crossed his face. "There will be again. But for now, there's the little question of where to assign you."

Shana debated a reply, but decided the time wasn't right.

"The Victrix is about to pick up a whole new mission. The Colonel will brief us on it once we're on the ground. Because of your civilian experience, he wants you assigned to Corps Intelligence Section.

"That's Sergeant First Class Span. Intelligence. He'll be your boss." He indicated a senior decurion a couple of measures away where the other two sergeants had retired so the Sergeant Major could conduct his interview. Then he pointed to the other one. "That's Sergeant First Class Steel. He'll take you to where you're going to stand in the formation. You'll form with First Cohort today. You were with them on your Virgin Mission, even if you didn't know it. You stand with them."

He leaned over and whispered in her ear. "Do you remember the song I taught you? The Gladio?"

She nodded. "Yes, Sergeant Major. I still say I can't sing."

The Sergeant Major smiled. "No one will care, Ettranty. They need to hear a woman's voice today. That's enough. Just sing it when you're told to do it. That's all they care about."

He stepped back. "Good enough."

The Sergeant Major looked at Span and Steel. "She's all yours. Dismissed, Ettranty."

Now here she was, part of a small sea of khaki uniforms. Just kilts and her skirt, and not a pair of pants in sight. The odd thought almost made her giggle. Stop it, she told herself. You're too damned old to giggle like a school girl. A school girl in the middle of a bunch of hairy soldiers that had just fought a major battle, too.

Besides, she liked the flowing feel of her long skirt. It felt graceful and more comfortable than the pants from her civilian past. She also liked what it symbolized. It made her feel proud, just like the insignia and her arm dagger. She was a full-fledged female Gladius. The only one in the Victrix.

For that matter, certainly the only one in Fourth Platoon, Second Century, First Battalion, First Cohort. Sergeant First Class Steel's platoon. Lieutenant Tremp, the platoon leader, seemed a little nonplused when he showed up to collect his charges, but adapted gamely to the discovery one member of his command was just a bit different from the rest. Like any good decurion, Sergeant First Class Steel helped the young L.T. adjust and all was once again well. So Shana was at the end of the last row in the platoon formation when they assembled to disembark.

There was a good bit of standing around waiting in formation, left foot in place, leavened by various wisecracks. None of them were hostile and a few were actually funny. Shana tried to give as good as she got. She didn't feel uncomfortable. The men seemed to be perfectly relaxed with her presence, woman or not. There weren't even any questions about why she was here. They all knew her and seemed happy she was in their platoon, at least for the moment. She was simply another Gladius trooper and that was all there was to it.

She was learning about troops. She was also learning these men were as tired as she was. They were all in splendid condition, but no amount of conditioning would prevent the emotional and physical aftereffects of major combat. In her mind, Shana judged the entire legion as just about ready for a day in the bunk. However, they had things to do before they could rest, a good many things, and the Colonel was about to tell them what they were. Then they would do them. Maybe afterward, they could just collapse somewhere. Shana was also learning that this sort of thing was perfectly typical of a soldier's existence.

Just take it and get on with the job, Ettranty.

The move off the ship looked confused and her ant's eye view showed no organization, but there were decurions loudly, profanely, and - usually - vulgarly giving orders everywhere. One thing that struck her was the vulgarity dried up when she was around, but the orders were just as loud and profane. It seemed the troops were just a little different around a woman.

In almost no time, the platoon was at its designated location in the formation in the middle of some huge floor. Probably a landing area because there were other immense ships, types she'd never seen, parked just a short way from the troop carrier. Stealing a glance around, she realized the cavern they were in had to be nearly as large as a small city. Amazing. And amazing it was all here and there was never a hint it existed.

"Eyes front! You characters aren't tourists and I know damned well you aren't buying any real estate today!" The bark of her squad sergeant brought her back to reality with a crashing thud and she settled at a parade rest like everyone else, philosophically resigned to standing there until someone would do something sensible.

"Settle down, people," Steel's voice growled from somewhere behind her and the platoon got very, very quiet.

Suddenly, "Cohorts!" "Battalions!" "Centuries!"

"Attention-n-n-n, ho!" The crash of nearly three thousand sets of boots echoed through the cavern as their heels came together in precise time.

"Stand easy, Victrix, and listen up." It was Colonel Athan, standing on a balcony overlooking the landing area, speaking over a PA system. They were about to find out what was happening.

"Okay, people, we were run off our last base. We took some of them, but we were still run off. We came here and they had problems with a Predator."

He paused for a second, looking around. Shana, from her position in the formation, strained to look at Athan. She knew him reasonably well, but now she was seeing him from a legionnaire's perspective. He started to speak again. "They no longer have that problem."

The cavern filled with a low growl in an incoherent noise like thunder flowing from the sky. Athan let it run its course, just standing there. The men deserved to make that growl. It was an affirmation of a needed task well done. They'd once again destroyed the Predator. It was in their blood to hunt and kill the Predator, as it was in Athan's. Had he been in that formation, he'd have joined the sound.

Finally, it was quiet. "That's a task well done, men." He stopped for a second and smiled wryly. "And woman.

"But it's not the final task. We all know who ordered the destruction of Victrix Base... the Emperor. One day, he and his will regret that. So now we have a new mission, to bring about that day of regret, sometime in the future. This legion will undertake that mission. Legate Corona had a plan, and it involves Cauldwell. He and his staff are dead. But I'm alive and we're going to carry that plan out."

Shana suddenly began to worry. As a former reporter (*former* reporter?) she was a political sophisticate. Was the Victrix planning to take over the government? Was she going to be a part of a military dictatorship? The thought made her stomach turn sour. That was the Gladius in her reacting. Risking a few glances around, she noticed the expressions around her and it looked like the men were all thinking like she was and the thought was just as upsetting to them.

Athan seemed to read the mind of his legion. "No, we aren't going to take over the government. I'm a Gladius, just like you, and just like Corona. He wouldn't do it. I won't do it. And you won't do it. We're going to do something different. We're going to make something that will be new and lasting, but we can't do it by becoming military dictators.

"No, we're not going to take over the government, but it's still going to fall. We know how to do that, people, and we're just as good at that kind of warfare as any other. It's what comes after the fall we have to worry about, which is why we're going to do this slowly, carefully, and above all, right.

"Because after we take out the government of Cauldwell, we have to take out the Empire." That bombshell produced total silence.

He gestured at the immense surrounding cavern. "See this nice little hole we've dived into and pulled in after ourselves? It's an equipment depot, created by the Empire, and there's ten more like it... right here on this planet."

Shana was shocked. *Eleven* of these huge depots? On Cauldwell?

Athan was speaking again. "The EW section detected signal emitters all over the planet, where there weren't supposed to be any. Several of you scouts went and did a little looking and found them. The Empire got too smart, folks. All of them were electronically monitored. All of the monitors except the ones here show the condition of the depot. We fixed these a while back. The Empire doesn't know that. Those dumb sons of bitches don't know we're here."

Cheers and laughter.

"We're right under their noses and they don't know where the Victrix is. Good thing, too. We're too dangerous for them to allow us to exist." Another growl. "You're in your new home for a while, at least until we can succeed on Cauldwell.

"Our new operations plan is long and complicated. The Legate and your senior officers have been preparing this one for a while, people, and it'll work. The Victrix is good enough to make it work.

"But I'll give you the short form. The people of Cauldwell are going to wake up and learn to take care of themselves. And we're going to help. Meanwhile, we'll be looking for others like us. I'm sure there are more legions and Fleet units out there. We're going to find them. Once all of that is done, we're going to smash that whole rotten mess back on Central. Then we're going to buckle down and help build something new.

126

What it will be yet, I can't tell you. That's a job for some other unlucky bastards. All I can tell you is that they will be civilians. We want no part of a military takeover, for any reason, people, so we'll find some other poor assholes to do the rebuilding. It just won't be us doing it. We'll help, but we have enough problems of our own."

Cheers.

Athan wasn't through. "You'll learn more in the days to come, but we have things to do right here and now and we'll get to them. This is our new home, people, and we need to settle in. We have to work on this cavern and expand it until we have a real base for the Victrix. I know you will all work cheerfully." Laughter.

"First, though... We fought a battle and saved a world. Again. We need to remember who we are, people. We are the Corps of Gladius. I say we are no longer the Corps of Imperial Gladius, but we are still the Corps of Gladius. And we are the Victrix. There's something we can do right now, something we never thought we could do again.

"Legionnaire Second Class Ettranty."

Shana couldn't help herself. She already had the gut reactions of a Gladius trooper. She popped to attention and yelled, "Aye!"

Athan smiled again, a small movement of his lips. "Legionnaire Second, you've been taught to sing by the Sergeant Major. I'm sure none of us want to hear him, so you have to do it. Sing, Legionnaire."

To save her life, Shana could never have sung in front of a group, let alone thousands of men she barely knew. But it was an order, and she could follow an order. "Aye!"

Despite her overly critical personal opinion about her singing, to the men her voice was high and sweet, oh so sweet to the Victrix, as she began a well-loved piece of music.

"Gladio, Gladio alieyo, tu Bestiaeo
et dai ne admanda conamor."

There was a soft shuffle like a wind in the trees as the entire cavern came to attention without orders.

The men of her platoon started singing with her, singing the chorus. Then she sang the verse and every man in the cavern joined in on the next chorus. She was singing the *Gladio*, the anthem of the Corps, always sung at attention, and traditionally sung by male and female. The women sang the verse and the men sang the chorus. Without a woman, it couldn't be sung, and the men never expected to hear it again. Shana sang and she put her heart into it. She was allowing the Victrix to once again sing about what they were, the Gladius, the Protector, the ones who hunted That Which Stalked From Hell. They protected people, just people, who wanted to live their lives without threats or fear.

127

Shana began the song a second time, as the massed male voices crashed about the cavern, thundering counterpoint to her own high sweet tones. They were affirming themselves as Gladii, and making a promise.

The Empire was dying, but humanity wasn't, and the Gladius was now the protector of humanity, not the Empire. They were going to kill something and build something new in its place. The Gladius was no longer a simple destroyer of enemies. The Victrix was going to build something new in the universe. That was different and it felt good. Shana held up her head as she sang the old, old words proudly.

The Empire was now the Predator. For over a thousand years, the Gladius stood charge to hunt down and destroy the Predator.

Here, in this cavern, a pledge was being made. The Gladius was hunting the Empire.

CHAPTER 6

LEGIO IX VICTRIX
CAULDWELL

The two Naval Intelligence operatives on Cauldwell established themselves quietly and quickly then went about the business of finding out things. What they found once they started looking was very interesting. According to news broadcasts, a portion of a Gladius legion had shown up not too long ago, stopped (read: destroyed) a Wareegan attack, then vanished. It was all very sensational and mysterious. The tridio networks were full of it.

The operatives, who currently resembled someone's aging aunt and uncle, also found it mysterious and wanted to know more. One monitored the sensationalist tridio "investigations" while another began to run a very circumspect signal search with some highly classified equipment. She was both passively looking and occasionally pinging on a very obscure and specific band in the communications spectrum. It took no more than a day for the ping to be answered.

An aging couple, who were certainly not Naval Intelligence, went out for their daily walk in White Point Gardens. They happened to see two young men, who certainly looked nothing like Gladii except for their height and built, jogging their way along the seawall bordering the park. One stopped and adjusted his shoe then both went back to running. Just as they passed the aging couple, the woman stumbled slightly, to be caught gently by one of the young men. She patted him on his upper arm with a smile of thanks and squeezed his hand with obvious gratitude then both pairs went on their way.

As the man and woman passed the point where one of the young men had adjusted his shoe, the woman chanced to look down and stopped, peering at an object on the seawall walkway. "Is that a coin?" she asked the man.

He reached down and picked it up. "No," he said, examining the object, "just a washer." He tossed the washer over the seawall in a horribly normal pollution of the local waters. The data chip, originally secured in the hole in the center of the washer, eventually ended up in his pocket.

Sometime thereafter, the generally unremarkable and little noticed couple purchased an old skimmer from a private seller, commenting they wanted to look at prospective property in Bayview. The government was

129

offering financial bounties to new residents there and they were very interested. For some reason, however, they never arrived in the city. That was a pity, since the real estate opportunities in Bayview were excellent.

Several days later, a tachyon data packet, a TDP, protected by an equally small suppresser field, wended its way slowly out of the atmosphere from nowhere near the hidden location of the Victrix. Then its tiny drive field activated and the robin's egg sized drone headed for Tactine. The news it contained was going to set events in motion that would affect the history of the human occupied galaxy.

#####

Colonel Karl Athan sat back in his office chair and thoughtfully examined the chip he'd just finished viewing. It was brought by one of the Naval Intel people. Legion Intelligence was still debriefing the agents, but Karl was perfectly capable of making his own conclusions on the encrypted information the chip contained.

It looked to him like Corona's plan for the Empire was about to be modified - rather heavily modified - and he was now in a position he really didn't want. He'd had his eye on the Legate's job eventually, but it wasn't an all-consuming ambition. He liked commanding First Cohort. Unfortunately, he was senior officer now that Corona was dead. That meant he was the unfortunate bastard that had to take the worry seat. And that worry seat was about to have a few more worries added to it. Grand strategy wasn't his thing. He was much happier with his Cohort and operational level maneuvers.

He grimaced at the thought. Grand strategy was now his job, want it or not. Just another wonderful day in the Corps.

The chip contained some major news. There was actually another legion out there, intact by the Lord Above's grace. It also confirmed the Empire was trying to destroy the Corps and Frontier Fleet. Karl had suspected that, but having it confirmed was a punch in the gut.

The X Legion Valeria, commanded by Legion Commander Shyranne Garua and her husband, Legate Khev Garua, was on Tactine. Before things started coming apart, the Valeria was based on Niad. The Empire had tried a raid in force - more like out and out pillage - on Tactine using a division of those black uniformed bastards of New Troops and a part of their New Fleet. The Valeria and the 10th FSG arrived, and the aforesaid raid turned into a resounding disaster for the Empire. The Imperial forces no longer existed. Karl closed his eyes, knowing what the Garuas and the FSG commander, Admiral Lane Mackinnie, felt when it was over. The Empire always fought an enemy to total destruction.

Always. Karl understood the policy, but the ones that paid the price for that in their souls wore his uniform and the Fleet's.

Now Legion Commander Garua and Admiral Mackinnie were working with the government of Tactine to protect the local stellar cluster - which just happened to contain Cauldwell - from the Empire's collapse. The ships and equipment in the hidden caches on Cauldwell were going to be very important in that effort. That part was a relief to Karl because he didn't have trained crews for those ships. The Corona plan was a little too optimistic there.

Karl wondered if the Garuas and Mackinnie had followed the logic chain to its inevitable conclusion, like Legate Corona had. The Empire was already fragmenting. Over the last fifty years, whole sectors had declared independence or simply been abandoned. Take away the Corps and the Fleet, let the Empire collapse, and the Kayelen and half a dozen others were going to move in on what was left. The whole of humanity was about to enter a period much like the Dark Age before the Empire, but the external threat was different now, more aggressive. Unless somebody did something, chances were good that humanity wouldn't survive the Dark Age this time. Even if the race survived, hundreds of billions of people would die and human interstellar civilization would collapse.

Corona had decided the only way for humanity to survive the crash already underway was to accelerate the destruction of the Empire. Take it down before everything totally collapsed, then salvage key worlds that could best preserve human civilization. The Corps and the Fleet couldn't save everything. The best they could do was pick what they *could* save, and do anything they could. That was a grim, ruthless plan because it simply abandoned whatever parts of the Empire that couldn't be salvaged. Like the idea or not, it was probably the highest probability chance to keep the race going. Karl tried to avoid thinking about what Corona's plan meant for the innocent people that didn't happen to live on those key worlds. He knew too much about what an uncaring galaxy could inflict. A legion and a half and one FSG couldn't save the whole Empire. Concentrate on saving what could be saved and hope the nightmares went away.

He was going to have to meet the Garuas and Mackinnie and integrate Corona's plan with whatever they were thinking. The Empire, what was left of it, was going to have to die and they were going to decide how to kill it.

Maybe, while they were at it, they could figure out how to solve a problem that had nagged at generations of the Corps. They were hereditary soldiers, but who in his right mind would want to raise children that had no other future but fighting and dying? It looked like Shyranne Garua was, by default, the senior officer. Maybe she could figure out how to break the cycle. He hoped so. He didn't want to see another generation with no other option but the Corps.

THE NARAKA
TACTINE NEAR SPACE

The *Naraka* was a Hell Ship, the ultimate in space going brute force. It was over a century old, but carefully maintained and updated. It was the ultimate warship, and there were only ten ever built. Several were assigned to Frontier Fleet, which was how the *Naraka* ended up with 10th FSG. In Middle Empire, the remainder had been scrapped and Central thought none were left. The *Naraka* had been a nasty surprise for the Imperials when 10th FSG hit them during the Tactine battle. It was also Admiral Lane Mackinnie's flagship.

"I've got some news for you two," Lane told Shyranne and Khev when they arrived aboard. Lane was a big man, slow moving, thought slothful and slightly stupid by those that didn't know him. The two Gladius senior officers knew him very well. "I should have told you earlier, but we needed to be here on my ship. This is important information and that bunch down on Tactine doesn't need to know about it until we decide they do."

"Snoopers?" Khev asked.

"Intelligence is still assessing what capabilities are left on Tactine, but I don't want any surprises," Lane replied. "Granted, Speaker Turner seems to have the situation under control in their government, but I still prefer that we decide what to do before it becomes general knowledge, and nothing is surer than a leak as soon as a politician gets into the loop."

Shyranne made a face. "Granted. Still, those people are the best hope of building a cluster wide government, Lane, and we must be an arm of that government, not its masters, if everything is to work."

Lane nodded. "I agree in principle, but we keep family business in the family for a while. At least until those people down there grow up."

"Family business?" Khev asked. Lane had the full attention of both Gladius officers.

Lane nodded. "The short form is that fragments of two legions have appeared in this cluster: the Victrix on Cauldwell... and what little's left of the Rhiannonithi just came into Niad on a carrier with a skeleton crew. The Rhiannonithi personnel are almost all women and children, and not that many of either. The Empire's plans worked there."

He looked at the bleak faces of the other two. His own was equally bleak. If the Empire had succeeded, that meant a Fleet Support

Group had defected to the New Fleet. The thought left a sour taste in Lane's mouth.

After a second, he continued, "The Victrix is entirely combat formations. Three full cohorts. According to my information, the Imperial plans misfired somewhere along the way and everything dissolved into a general fight. Those cohorts got away while the Fleet and New Fleet units were hammering it out, but the legion base got wiped out early on. There are no women and children with the cohorts, just fighting men."

Shyranne sucked in her breath in shock. The loss of a Legion's women and children was a nightmare. The Victrix was completely crippled. Khev's face got bleaker.

Lane looked at the two then said, "Things aren't entirely bad on Cauldwell, and the survivors of the Rhiannonithi managed to stop a case of Empire sanctioned piracy. We need to talk about the implications of that too, but not now."

He slid a data chip into a reader and all three turned to the terminal screen. After it darkened, Khev nodded and let out a deep breath. "Given what they were handed, both legions did well. I knew Corona, and he was always a deep thinker. I'm sorry he's dead, but Athan's a good man, too. It looks like Corona set them up with a reasonable plan. I'm beginning to think we can integrate it into what we want to do. The leadership needs to meet as soon as possible."

Khev looked at Shyranne. "You go? Or me?"

She thought for a second. "Ordinarily, I'd say you ought to go. Jon Kandal can handle the legion for a while. The Rhiannonithi complicate the situation, however, and the Victrix has lost all of its women. This Legionnaire Ettranty they've recruited and what they say about her is interesting, too. I think they need to see me, a woman, especially since I'm the senior officer we have left in the three legions. I think the Rhiannonithi orphans will end up with the Victrix, but both units need to be prepared. I'll send Camille Paten a warning order then move her people once we figure out what we want to do."

The Admiral nodded. "Most of that bunch down on the planet would just as soon they didn't see either of you, but Narsima Randl Turner can deal with Khev and the problem children will duck any meeting with him in it."

Lane's mouth twitched in what for him was a smile. "We're lucky the most powerful politician in the Tactinese government is former Fleet, so he's on our side. That will make it easier, especially since things are starting to gel there. I'm fully capable of keeping them headed that way and Turner would probably prefer that I be the sole representative, anyhow. Just the sight of a Gladius uniform sends a few of their more excitable politicians into a whirl. I'll loan you a pocket battleship that's set up as a flagship so you have space on board and I'll add someone that might help, that ex-Imperial Intelligence man, Ancel."

The defection of Major Claude Ancel, Imperial Intelligence, was the prime reason the attempt to destroy the Valeria failed. He'd warned them of what was happening and helped defeat the attempt. Major Claude Ancel was now Lieutenant Commander Claude Ancel, 10th FSG, by his own request. Mackinnie and the Garuas considered him a good man.

Shyranne nodded acceptance. "Good enough. Tomorrow?" At Lane's nod, she got up to leave. There were things to do if she was going to be gone for a while.

CAULDWELL

The little battlewagon came into Cauldwell's system under a heavy suppresser field, translated from TFD with infinite slowness to hide its signature, then drifted ever so carefully onto the planetary surface. From the screens on the staff deck, Lieutenant Commander Claude Ancel saw what looked like almost half a mountain open before them as they gently slipped up to it, then inside. The pilot was an expert and the landing was feather light. What surprised Claude was the sight of other ships in the cavern. There were a variety of types, but Claude was sure he saw at least one modern cruiser in the background alongside a battered troop carrier. What the hell?

The faces on the welcoming committee were professionally immobile as they stood in a small formation with a century sized honor guard, but Claude could see the joy on the face of the Fleet Lieutenant in the formation. Command of a troop carrier was usually a Fleet Commander's slot, but the Lieutenant had apparently done the job. Things had gotten rough.

A Gladius Colonel saluted once they exited and formed up. "Welcome to Cauldwell, Legion Commander," he said, his voice leaking carefully hidden relief. "Very welcome."

"Colonel," Shyranne returned the salute. Then she stopped in a second of surprise, as the Colonel gave the traditional welcome from one legion to another legion's commander.

"The Valeria!" he shouted in a command voice. From somewhere in the background, a small military band struck up the *Gladio*. Every man in the cavern started singing the opening chorus, followed by a lone female voice singing the lead verse. The visiting party came to attention with the rest of the personnel in the cavern. Shyranne joined the unseen woman in the second verse, singing the *Gladio* as it should be sung.

134

The message was simple. The Victrix had been shot to hell. They were understrength and improvising like mad, but they still considered themselves a viable force - and they were Whole.

#####

Shyranne took her seat at the conference table in the small briefing room and put her cap on the table next to her. She waited for everyone else to be seated then asked, "Who was that singing?"

The Sergeant Major answered her, his raspy voice showing just a tiny bit of pride. "Legionnaire Second Ettranty, Commander."

Shyranne nodded. She knew about Legionnaire Ettranty, and the way the Victrix felt about her. "Well, she's still the only woman here and needs a good bit more training."

The Sergeant Major spoke up again. His position gave him the right to converse with a Legion Commander informally and Shyranne had never known one that didn't use it, right to an exquisitely defined line - defined by the Sergeant Major in question, that is. "We're giving her training, Commander. One of these days, the girl will make a good officer, too."

Shyranne had an idea what officer grade the Sergeant Major had in mind. "She still needs training, Sergeant Major, training in being a female Gladius and you can't give her that. I'm going to help you there," she said in friendly tones.

Karl Athan looked a bit worried, Sergeant Major Olmeg pugnacious. "Here," Shyranne continued and smiled slightly at their relief. "In fact, the Victrix is about to become a growing concern again."

Athan's face changed from worry to surprise. "Grow?"

Shyranne lost her good humor. "The Rhiannonithi were hit just like you were. Some of the women and most of the younger children made it to a carrier with a few of the men. They're all that's left and they need a home. I'm going to send them to you. Major Camille Paten has acting command at the moment. She'll reform your Support Command, but you'll command the Victrix, Karl, on my authority as surviving senior officer. Paten's too junior for the position and doesn't know the Victrix anyhow. I'm also going to send you some of our excess women and any more we can find when we finally - Lord Above help us in that - contact other surviving legions. I'm sure there are some out there. It's only a question of making contact. One of these days, the Victrix will be back to normal."

Karl Athan, felt relief at first. Reinforcements! Female reinforcements! Then a feeling of grief overcame it. A legion, the XV Rhiannonithi, had died.

After a second, he put both feelings in another compartment and moved on. There were problems to solve and the Victrix was officially his, now. "We'll give them that home, Commander. Now, since you're senior Corps officer, we need to know what's happening elsewhere and you need to know what's happening here. You read what we have planned for Cauldwell?"

Shyranne nodded as Athan spoke. Then he continued. "You know the bare bones, but we have a detailed briefing prepared about the situation here. Legionnaire Ettranty will be giving it. She's assigned to the Intel Section because of several important points. First, she's a former news person." He looked Shyranne in the eye. "Second, she's the daughter of the head of the Planetary Guidance Council. She knows a lot, and she has a perspective we can't get from any other source."

Normally, someone so junior wouldn't even be in the room, but Shyranne had to agree Ettranty was important in this case. She began to look forward to what a Legionnaire Second could tell her about the political situation.

The briefing made Shana a bit nervous. Oh, she was used to talking to people in a public forum, and her audiences used to total in the millions of viewers, but this presentation was a little different. Now she wasn't just a talking head. She was representing the women of the Victrix. She'd never seen any of them in the flesh, but she still thought of herself as their representative. Then there was also the little fact that she was a Legionnaire Second in front of a Legion Commander. That was enough to make any trooper nervous.

Legion Commander Garua was fascinating to Shana. She was the first Gladius woman she'd ever seen in person and reminded her of pics she'd seen of Legion Commander Corona, the last commander of the Victrix. That alone gave her kind of a mystic aura. Then there was the fact that the Commander was a woman born into a life she had only recently adopted herself. There were also physical differences between herself and a real female Gladius. Real? Get a hold of yourself, Shana. You *are* a real female Gladius. You're just a bit different than the others.

Physical differences also interested Shyranne. Oh, Legionnaire Ettranty's uniform was immaculate, and worn with precise exactness, but you could tell indefinable little things that said she was still becoming accustomed to it. Ettranty was taller than the norm, more slender, and wore her softly waved brown hair cut just at neck level with a flip under at

136

the end. Shyranne enjoyed the luxurious length of her own straight pale hair, but Ettranty couldn't manage hair that length, not and look regulation.

Shyranne snorted mentally. Here she was, getting an excellent background brief on Cauldwell and she was judging another woman, a junior Legionnaire at that, by her hair style. Go back to being a Commander, Shyranne. You can be a woman later.

When Legionnaire Ettranty finished, Shyranne nodded, "Good brief, Legionnaire. Hold yourself ready in the outer office. I need to speak to you."

She could see the Legionnaire swallow a gulp, and knew what she was thinking. What now? The only possible reply, "Aye."

Once Shana was gone, Shyranne leaned forward over the conference table and spoke to Athan. "Karl, you and your command group got the message about Tactine. We're trying, along with Lane Mackinnie, to save this cluster from the crash as the Empire goes down. I'm reasonably conversant with what you have in mind here and I think we can integrate both plans without too much change. I want to think it over some, but I'm beginning to get the basics of a real strategic scheme. We'll discuss it privately and begin to put some flesh on it."

Athan nodded. "I and my senior commanders have been gaming some ideas. Now that you're here, Commander, I think we can really get something going. It's nice to know we aren't alone. It gives me hope for the future."

"We'll talk about that future over dinner tonight, Karl," Shyranne said easily, "then finalize things tomorrow. I think I'll be able to get you some more help, too.

She sat up straight. "Now that I know what's happening here, I need to take care of some other business. If you gentlemen will excuse me, I need to meet with Legionnaire Ettranty."

Amid a few casual comments, the meeting broke up. As Sergeant Major Olmeg heaved himself out of his chair, he gave Shyranne a piercing scowl. She smiled back at him with real humor. She knew what he was saying. She was a Legion Commander, but she wasn't *his* Legion Commander. Don't mess with his troops! Her smile was broader as she said, "Aye, Sergeant Major."

A snort was his only answer as he left.

Out in the outer office, Shana was sitting very erect and nervous in a chair, waiting. She had no reason to be nervous, she kept telling herself. She was an educated, sophisticated woman, a major success in a highly competitive planetary media. In her old life, a call from *her* would make someone like the Commander nervous, not the other way around. So why was she acting like a schoolgirl caught in the act?

One of the troopers on clerk duty looked over at her and asked, "How'd it go in there?"

"Well enough, mate," she replied. "For some reason the Valeria Commander wants to speak to me alone. So here I sit."

"Better you than me, mate," he replied then busied himself in his work as the conference room door opened.

As the Sergeant Major stumped by, he glared at Shana and waved a hand vaguely at the door. "Go report, Legionnaire."

"Aye." Shana was up and standing to attention in the open doorway in less time than it took to think about it. She raised her hand gave the customary two raps on the door frame, the door being open at the time.

"Come."

Shyranne had turned her chair away from the table so it faced the door. Shana paced forward steadily until she was about two measures away then came to attention. "Legion Commander, Legionnaire Second Class Ettranty reports."

Shyranne pointed at a nearby chair. "Go close the door then sit down, Legionnaire. I want to talk to you."

As she touched the door switch Shana's mind was consumed with a question as old as the military, what the shit have I done now?

Once Shana was seated, the Commander looked at her calmly, her pale eyes taking in every detail. Shana once again had that feeling she had in her first days with the legion, the feeling that she was being studied inside and out.

For her part, Shyranne was thinking about the young woman in front of her, someone totally alien to the Corps, except for two key attributes: the willingness to become a Gladius and the ability to do it. Those were very rare outside the Corps. Toss in her background in the highest levels of Cauldwell society. Then add the minor fact her father was one of their bigger problems, a problem that had to be had to be solved, one way or another. Legionnaire Ettranty had come a long way, and had another, far more bitter, road to travel. But not yet. No, not yet.

"Do you feel alone, Legionnaire?"

The soft question caught Shana by surprise. It also surprised her how much she wanted to hear another female voice. "No, Commander."

Shyranne smiled softly. "You can say what you are really feeling, Legionnaire Second Class Ettranty. I won't get upset and I won't bite you if you tell the truth.

"Besides," she continued with a quick grin, "Sergeant Major Olmeg would have my hide if I did bite you, and I have a deep respect - read fear - of any Legion Sergeant Major."

Olmeg? He was looking out for her? For whatever reason he was doing it - and Shana had her suspicions - it was comforting. She let out a deep mental breath and relaxed slightly. She didn't realize it but her old sophisticated powerful self was long gone in her mind, replaced by a junior Legionnaire. Still... Shana looked down for a moment, then back up at the Commander. "I miss having another woman around, but I'm not lonely, Commander. The men missed not having women around, too. In a way, they were the lonely ones until I joined the Legion. I feel like they care about me, because I'm a woman - and because I'm a Gladius, now. That means a lot to me, too.

"And..."

Shyranne gave her a warm smile. "Go ahead. And what?"

Shana was a little uncertain of what she was going to say. Then she decided the Commander would understand. She was a female Gladius. Shana took a deep breath and jumped in. "And I know I'm not alone. I feel them. I feel all the other women that were part of the legion. Those Now Gone. When things are quiet, I can feel them and they are with me. Supporting me. I feel like they are part of me." She paused for a second, trying to put into words what was just a feeling. "...Am I making sense?"

Shyranne leaned back and pinched her chin between thumb and forefinger, looking at the trooper in the seat in front of her, a Gladius despite her physical appearance. The big question settled. "Yes, Legionnaire, I understand fully. You are a Gladius. Whatever has happened to you before this, I want you to understand you will one day walk through hell because you have joined the Corps. Sooner or later, we all do. But when you walk, you will not walk alone. No Gladius does. Ever. Welcome to the Corps, may the Lord Above bless and keep you."

Shana felt tears starting, but fought them down. She was a female Gladius. She wasn't going to cry. The Commander could have told her differently. "I've been welcomed, Commander," she said, "by Those Now Gone and by the Victrix, but thanks for that. More than you know."

Shana looked the Commander steadily in the eye. Her chin jutted forward and she didn't know that was the unconscious gesture of a Gladius ready to do battle. It was something she'd absorbed, like much else, in her training and association with the Corps. She was ready to do battle, but her battle was moral, not physical. "I have a duty to the Victrix, and I intend to do it."

Shyranne knew what the Legionnaire was feeling, and she noted the expression. Good. Now on to something else. "Legionnaire Ettranty, you are not going to be the sole female in the Victrix for very long. I'm transferring the personnel from a devastated legion, the Rhiannonithi, to the Victrix. They total thirteen men, one hundred and ninety women, and two hundred and seventy five children. That's all that's left. Learn those numbers, and the numbers of the Victrix. Any female Gladius can quote strength figures in her sleep. I'm also transferring female personnel from my own legion, the Valeria. Major Camille Paten will be the senior female officer, but she will be subordinate to the Legate, and I'm approving Colonel Athan's field promotion to Legate as well as Commander of the Victrix. Both are extraordinary circumstances, but necessary in this mess in which we find ourselves. I've also decided something else about you."

Shana held her breath again. What was the Commander about to do? Even if the Commander gave her an order, she wasn't about to leave her legion. Not even for a little while.

Shyranne continued in the same calm, soft voice. "You need a great deal more training than you are getting, or will get from the Victrix as it's now constituted, Legionnaire. You are going to get it." Shyranne gave another small smile. "Men do a good job training us for combat, but our real training has to come from a woman. You'll begin training once the transferred personnel are settled. Wait until you meet your first female decurion, Legionnaire. That's an experience right up there with your first drill sergeant. Trust me on that one. I once sat where you are sitting."

Shyranne sat up straighter. "In any case, I'm satisfied with this interview. I'm sure you recognize that I was looking for more than just answers. I like what I found. Once the Victrix has been reinforced and the reinforcements fully integrated, it will be conducting an Officer Candidate School. You will be in that class. I expect you to excel. You may go."

Shyranne stifled a smile as Ettranty snapped to attention in a daze, saluted, did an about face by reflex alone, and managed not to hit the door frame on the way out. The shock of finding out she was going to officer school appeared to hit her hard. Right between the eyes.

Shyranne looked at the young woman leave, smiling a bit more broadly now that Legionnaire Ettranty couldn't see her. She remembered her own Commander telling her once in the long ago that she was going to OCS. Legionnaire Ettranty was older than most of her peers, more educated and very sophisticated. She'd make a good junior officer. The rest would take care of itself in the Lord Above's good time. Shyranne was now certain of that.

LEGIO XV RHIANNONITHI
NIAD

On Niad, the Fifteenth Legion, Rhiannonithi, was having a formation. Orders had arrived, and everyone was worried. Camille took her position facing the tiny remnant of her once formidable legion. There weren't many out there, Camille thought to herself as she faced her little command. But they still had their pride and their duty. Oh, yes, she thought, remembering a dead Kayelen destroyer and citizens saved, the Rhiannonithi could still perform their duty.

"Attention to orders," she said. "The following orders have been received from Commander, Tenth Legion Valeria."

She took out a printout and began reading the key passages. "Fifteenth Legion, Rhiannonithi, will stand ready to embark to Cauldwell on order. Once on Cauldwell, the following personnel will be transferred to Ninth Legion, Victrix, exact assignment of transferred personnel to be determined by Legate, Ninth Legion, and acting Commander, Fifteenth Legion. Transferred personnel are as follows..."

The survivors in the formation held their breath. Without the remainder of the Corps to replenish their personnel, they knew there was realistically no way they could hope to keep the Rhiannonithi in existence, but it hurt. How it hurt. The Rhiannonithi was their millennia old tradition, their family, the bedrock of their lives. Transferring to another legion wasn't bad. It happened. What hurt was the dissolution of the Rhiannonithi.

Every Gladius at parade rest in the small formation listened carefully as the names were read, noting their own as it was spoken, and dreading as Camille got further down the alphabetical list. By tradition, the men were read first, then the women, then the children that would accompany their mothers or a guardian.

Then Camille stopped reading. The list of children wasn't complete. There were two names missing.

Camille spoke again. "The following personnel will be attached to the Ninth Legion, but retain original unit of assignment." She read the names of the youngest boy and the youngest girl among the children, babies really. Suddenly, there was a feeling of relief. By keeping the youngest male and the youngest female as part of the Rhiannonithi, it still existed. The Sunburst and the surviving brushara would be reverently stored, kept in trust until the day they could come forth again, because the Rhiannonithi was still alive, waiting until the day that it could be built back to strength. The Rhiannonithi wasn't dead because it still had members, members raised to keep a trust and over a thousand years of memory intact.

The former members of the Fifteenth Legion, Rhiannonithi, were content. All but two of their number were going to a new Legion and a new life. Those two would remain, keeping the Rhiannonithi alive. The former members of the Fifteenth Legion, Rhiannonithi, were very content.

LEGIO IX VICTRIX
CAULDWELL

The group wandering among the ships in the Cavern was composed entirely of Fleet officers. It was led by Lieutenant Albert Kavasos, defacto commander of Fleet personnel here on Cauldwell. "Commander," he said, waving his hand at a light cruiser in front of them, "there are two of these here. Given that there are ten more depots like this on Cauldwell, I'm guessing at least twenty two overall."

Claude already knew about the number of the depots, and that Cauldwell's real reason for existence was as an Imperial refuge. Ship strength like this was only to be expected. Still, as a former Imperial Intelligence officer and someone that was once part of the Court, the implications of that refuge were very interesting. "Have you checked any of the other depots?"

Kavasos shook his head. "Only scanned. Getting into this one was chancy and complicated enough while they weren't looking for us. They've been turning over every rock since we vanished and there's no sense in taking any more chances."

Claude nodded. Then Kavasos motioned him around the side of the cruiser. "There's something back here that you need to see. Ensign Ellis here found it first. Ensign? You tell him."

"It's a new class, Lieutenant Commander," the Ensign said, then pointed. "Look."

The ship the Ensign was pointing out was smaller than a normal destroyer, and sleeker, with strange lines. "That's a frigate!" Claude said in surprise. "It's supposed to be almost as powerful as a cruiser, faster, and a whole lot more maneuverable. But those things are only in prototype right now!"

It was Kavasos's turn to be surprised. In answer to his look, Claude explained. "I was Imperial Intelligence in another life. I had access to military R&D. As part of the mission the Emperor assigned us, we kept a very close eye on naval officers and what they could do. The

Emperor ordered this design suppressed because it gave a lower ranking naval officer too much power.

"Apparently," he continued in a dry voice, "The Emperor had plans for the design he didn't tell us about."

"I'm glad you know what it is," Kavasos said. "We sure as hell didn't until we found the technical library." The Ensign opened a panel on the ship's side, touched a sensor, and the personnel lock swung open with a boarding ramp extruding to the floor of the cavern. As they entered, Kavasos continued, "It has a crew of five - less than a corvette - cruiser size guns, and stuff we still aren't sure about. One other thing. This bird is *fast*. The usual Maximum Military Speed is 3500 lights, as I'm sure you know."

Claude nodded with a bit of irritation. He was, after all, Fleet.

Kavasos took a deep breath. "Well, Commander, tech data says this ship is rated for 4500 lights MMS."

Claude winced. He wasn't exactly surprised. The documents he'd seen of the prototype had hinted as much. Having it so baldly confirmed was still a little unnerving. This ship was very bad news.

"Did you try to test anything?" he asked, looking around at a bridge that was a generation ahead of current design. Looking at the stations, he wasn't even sure what several of them were for.

"My people are all ship's crew," Kavasos said. "We didn't want to trip any alarms by accident. In addition, the manuals imply the ship's AI is way ahead of current Fleet AIs. I'd rate this frigate every bit as capable in combat as a heavy cruiser, not to mention way faster, with a much higher acceleration in normal space. Frankly, that was scary. We had no intention of messing around with anything. Real investigation will take some of the technical support folks from your FSG, now that you're here."

Claude nodded. Despite Corona's overly optimistic belief they could use the ships in the cache, the troop carrier they'd arrived on simply didn't have enough technical support, let alone crew, to operate them. The intelligence officer in him made him wonder where the support and crew would come from if the Emperor had to dive into the hole that Cauldwell represented and pull it in behind him. That was an important question, and it needed an answer.

Shangnaman had a paranoid's mania for hiding things, best done in totally closed compartments. Corps Intelligence had found out about Cauldwell, but obviously, there were compartments that had yet to be discovered, let alone opened. He needed to talk about this with Legion Commander Garua. The FSG had found these frigates, but what else had Shangnaman hidden?

The lights were low and the background music was pleasant but unobtrusive in the Senior Officers' Mess. Because of the subject matter to be discussed, the diners were from a very exclusive list. The Cohort Commanders from the Victrix were present with their new Legate, as was Legion Commander Garua as guest of honor. That was it.

The meal was over and Shyranne pensively fingered her wine glass, staring into the clear liquid as though searching for images from the future. The discussion had begun during dinner and was still in full swing. A great many things were coming together at this table, and she was thinking hard. "I believe," she said, "that we have the beginnings of a working plan, here. We're all in agreement what to do about our future operations... and about Central."

"The Empire has to fall," Karl replied. "It's become dangerous to the Frontier worlds, and, by extension, to humanity. If it's left to die naturally, it could well take human interstellar civilization with it. That would open the door for other races. If those races get the chance, I don't think you'll see a human controlled planet in this galaxy ever again. They've been waiting a long time and Shangnaman is stupidly willing to hand them the chance. That sanctioned piracy the Rhiannonithi stopped is a symptom of the rot. So is the Tactine attack."

"True. However, Tactine's something else," Shyranne replied. "It's an almost perfect basis to begin building a new human civilization. It has strategic location, a healthy growing economy, and people that aren't afraid to look forward. That politician I mentioned earlier? The Narsima Randl Turner? Once we talked with him, he bought into the idea of growing a new star nation out here, one that not only expands its own economy, but looks for new worlds. We have to grow if we're going to survive, gentlemen. It's not enough to just take down the Empire. That will bring some degree of security, but we also have to expand if we are to have any kind of future for the race. Like any organism, once the race stops growing, it will start dying. If we stagnate out here, everything we are planning will come to nothing in the end. I want what we are doing to be the first step toward a renaissance for mankind, not just an act of vengeance for what Shangnaman has done to the Corps."

Karl's voice was hard and grim. "Central and that fool Shangnaman owe us a blood debt. I intend for the Victrix to collect it."

Shyranne nodded. "With the Valeria and any other Legion we can find.

"Lane Mackinnie will be overjoyed once he discovers what ships are here in the Cauldwell depots. With what we already have and what we

144

can cobble together, that makes a pretty good sized force, available without much effort. If we can get the Tactinese to build more ships - we're working hard on that - Lane will have a fleet big enough to go back into Middle Empire and take out anything they have. Then it will be the turn of the Corps."

Karl smiled grimly. "The Corps could probably do it alone, but I don't want to. We need to create a military force for the cluster and they'll go in with us on the day we clean out Central. Corona's plan was always to somehow do that, once Cauldwell has become something other than decadent. We can make his plan dovetail with what you and Khev want to do, but Corona was always looking at Central."

He took a sip of wine. "Personally, I see our plans as complimentary. You concentrate on looking outward, exploring, building up Tactine and the rest of the cluster while seeing what else is out there. The job of the Victrix is changing the Cauldwell government and waking up its people. Then we can start preparing the way inward to Central."

Shyranne said, "That's pretty much the way I see it. You take care of Cauldwell and we'll look outward. I'm sure that there are other legions out there that either escaped Imperial plots or haven't been attacked yet. Once they are gathered into our forces, we can begin moving inward towards Central, politically subverting sectors or other worlds we need to have out of our way."

Karl remarked, "We both agree the cluster needs its own armed forces, new and without ties to us other than a few traditions. There's a lot of raw material right here on Cauldwell for those forces. I'm sure you can provide more from Tactine. Every world we bring into a new political structure in the cluster will add more. One of these days, humanity will be responsible for itself again."

"Given that," Shyranne again said something everyone at that table knew was true, "killing the Empire has to be our job. The Fleet and the Corps sustained the Empire."

Her face was set as she looked at the others around the table. "Finally killing it is our responsibility."

Colonel Paolo Evns nodded then spoke up. "So much for light preliminary work."

His comment sparked chuckles and broke the grim mood around the table. "Actually," he continued, "I'm encouraged about your plan for the Corps, Legion Commander."

"Not just my plan," Shyranne answered. "My husband, Khev, actually came up with the basic idea. We both refined it. There're some advantages to having a husband and wife team as Legion Commander and Legate."

"Well," Karl said, "I've got no problem with providing you some volunteers for your exploration program. That might be a future that won't mean being soldiers for eternity. Most of us, though, are going to be tied down on Cauldwell, taking down the government. That's going to be a very slow and delicate process, given that Narsima Matic Ettranty is in regular communication with Central, possibly the Emperor himself. We don't want him - and Shangnaman - to know anything about us until the bad news arrives at his front door." His grin was wolfish at that last sentence.

Paolo shook his head. "The Emperor again," he remarked woefully, again to chuckles. "Leaving aside that crazy bastard, I'm glad to see someone is giving some thought to the future of the Corps. I like the idea of making it voluntary."

Shyranne smiled at him. "It will be, too, if I have anything to say about it. Khev once said the idea of a race of hereditary soldiers is obsolete. I firmly agree with that. We can take specially screened volunteers and give them our body mods and proper training. The result will be very much like our own capabilities if we do it right. No more requirement for a child to become a soldier by accident of birth."

She looked at the expressions around the table. "I see you all agree with me."

"Gentlemen," she continued, "right now the Gladius is condemned to war and the human race as a whole is condemned to collapse.

"We will change both of those things."

CHAPTER 7
LEGIO IX VICTRIX
CAULDWELL
3226 I.C.E.

The Narsima Matic Ettranty entered his outer office and paced ponderously past his receptionist, a waiting appointment or two, and several subsidiary clerks with the smooth massive implacability of a huge liner approaching a docking bay. He took note of the individuals in his waiting area and mentally dismissed them. There was nobody of importance to see him this morning. He had something to do before he began his daily business.

That missing legion - and the Emperor's reaction to its disappearance - was his current headache. Not only was the legion gone, it was nowhere to be found on Cauldwell. A repeated series of extended searches over the last two years had confirmed the fact. His Imperial liaison had even gone so far as to make a very discreet visual examination of the cache points, done at very widely spaced and irregular times so as not to call attention to the fact. No disturbance was discovered. Legate Corona and his men were obviously elsewhere and no longer his problem. It was up to the Narsima to draft a carefully worded message that would state his first conclusion with exquisite documentation, and just as carefully ignore the second. Hopefully, that would stem the increasingly shrill messages he was getting from the Imperial staff.

The Narsima was never given more than that task - to discover the whereabouts of the Victrix. However, he was fully capable of deduction from the tone of the messages and what was said between the lines. He strongly suspected there were other legions and renegade Fleet forces missing. Those were hostile forces the Emperor couldn't ignore, but they certainly weren't his problem. Neither was the Emperor's fear of them.

No, he thought as he glanced at the row of beautifully crafted figurines that was his collection of model soldiers then fastened his gaze on one in particular, the Gladius was gone from Cauldwell.

#####

Well, no.

Inside what was once an extremely secret cache of warships, logistical support, and heavy equipment of varying types and purposes, the

147

Victrix went about its current mission: to bring down the corrupt government of Cauldwell. They were making good progress.

After completing their base and integrating reinforcements, the Victrix had begun infiltrating personnel into the general population. The start was slightly ragged, but the process was now well underway. So was the establishment of a political movement to overthrow the current government by peaceful means.

Legate Karl Athan left the conference room after the staff meeting feeling reasonably good about things. Infiltration school was proving to be the solution to many small problems. Corporal Ettranty, despite her junior rank, was a major reason for that. As a former top reporter on Cauldwell's premier broadcast news channel and a member of upper level society on the planet, she was a sophisticated observer and was quite able to use those observations to train others. She did it very well. So well, in fact, Intelligence Section regarded her as essential. Needless to say, they weren't very happy after this meeting, but they were going to live with that unhappiness. Especially since he'd just put his foot down about sending her to the next OCS class. Corporal Ettranty was an outstanding trooper in a staff intelligence slot, but now it was time for her to move on and up. She was certainly officer material.

Once in his office and seated at his desk, Karl spent a few moments thinking about her. She was a woman full grown, he thought, years older than her peers, more mature, and a good soldier. Very interesting person, too. They hadn't had more than formal contact since going under cover, but she was someone he thought he'd like to know better. Fine looking woman too, he finally admitted.

Now that was an interesting thought, he told himself. For a moment, he visualized Shana. Taller than normal, with a figure appearing a bit more slender because of her height, but there was intelligence, capability, and depth of personality inside the bodily shell. Very interesting.

#####

Shana was in her quarters at that moment, reclining on her bunk in a T shirt and shorts and at peace with the world. She had the rest of the day off. What to do with it? Sleep? Always an excellent option. Go look for a game somewhere? No, everyone else was pretty well occupied at the moment. Go over to the gym and work out, then? Maybe. She wanted some more blade work. She was learning the ax and short sword, and that was fun.

Maybe she'd go over to the Legionnaires Club and see what was happening. One interesting difference she'd noticed between herself and the female Gladii transferred into the legion was her association with the male troopers and their activities. Oh, after her initial grounding in the Victrix she'd missed female companionship, but she enjoyed what the guys did a little more for some reason. They seemed to like having her around, in sort of a brother - sister way, too.

The fact that she was living underground and had lived that way for two years didn't enter her head. A Gladius did whatever was necessary to make a plan succeed, even living in a glorified hole for years. She knew the general plan, knew what she had to do, ergo... adapt and move on. Think about that or not - the reporter that she once was would have but the Corporal she was now didn't bother her head - she was still at loose ends.

The door opened and her roommate, Karyn Docket, strode in. Karyn was a typical Gladius female in the usual physical mold, short, solid, and curvy with long pale hair. Shana's opposite, in other words. She was also a good bit younger, which befit a normal Legionnaire Third Class. "Hi, sis," she said.

Shana remembered the first time she'd called a female Gladius "mate", like the male legionnaires called each other. The subsequent correction was firm and to the point. Only men were "mate". Women were "sister" or "sis". On the other hand, the young troopers of the Victrix still called her "mate".

Female decurions were a grim discovery. A female sergeant was as hardnosed as her male counterpart, if not more so. Shana quickly learned to mind her step around such creatures, even more than she did around male sergeants. A revolting situation, but simply a condition of life as a legionnaire, to be absorbed and then move on. At least she was a Corporal now, worthy of a minor degree of respect from grumpy and abrasive female beasts with more stripes.

"What's up, Karyn?"

"Well," she replied, "some of us have to work while you're playing lady of leisure, but mine is done for the while. Want to hit the pool?"

Shana swung out of her bunk. "You know, I was just wondering what I wanted to do and you've solved the problem."

Karyn laughed as she started to change. "Only on condition you don't start playing with the boys. I'm trying to find myself a good one and you distract the whole bunch, you know. You get around the guys and they stop thinking about sex and start acting like you're one of them."

Shana laughed with her. "I don't see you having any problems, sis. If anything, that's my trouble. I could be bareassed in the pool and they'd still treat me like another guy."

149

Karen started removing her uniform to put on her swimsuit. "If it was anyone else, I'd probably doubt that statement, but not you. Let's face it, sis, you're way too tall, skinny, and flat as a board to boot."

"I'll boot you, short and wide legionnaire," Shana laughed again, then threw her T shirt at Karyn as she began to change.

Both women were nearly into the Corps issue one piece swimsuits when there was a loud knock at the door. "Hold on," Shana called, as she pulled her swimsuit the rest of the way up and hurriedly adjusted the straps. After a quick glance to see if Karyn was fully into her own suit and a look at the mirror, she headed for the door, pulling here and tugging there to get the suit completely adjusted. For a woman accustomed to body paint or a wisp or two of cloth at the pool, Shana decided, she was actually getting to like the Corps suits. Different, like the skirts, but they showed her figure to nice advantage.

That thought train was derailed as she opened the old fashioned door and found herself facing Sergeant First Class Homs, her section chief. "Uh, what's up, Sarge," she said, slightly flustered. Then an awful thought bloomed. "I'm not back on duty am I?"

The fact that Homs had to look up at Shana was mildly irritating to the sergeant. A female Gladius shouldn't be that tall, dammit! On the other hand, Corporal Ettranty was a good trooper. Best junior noncom she had in her section. If what Homs guessed was right, she was about to be losing her. "Lieutenant Colonel Paten wants to see you, Corporal."

She glanced at Shana's well filled swimsuit. "I don't think that's the right uniform to go visiting a colonel, either. You'd better do a quick change and scoot."

"I had the day off!" Shana said woefully.

"And still will, but you gotta see the Colonel first," Homs replied firmly. "Now change, then shag ass. She wants to see you now."

"Now" translated into about ten minutes before Shana was knocking at the open door frame to the Colonel's office. "Come."

Shana marched in and came to a position of attention. "Lieutenant Colonel Paten, Corporal Ettranty reports."

Camille Paten was looking over some hard copy on her desk. "Close the door, Corporal, and have a seat."

Shana closed the door as instructed and seated herself with proper military decorum, meanwhile mentally running down a list of her possible sins, wondering which one had caught up with her.

Camille glanced up, took note of the Legionnaire's body language, and stifled a chuckle. "No, Corporal, you aren't in trouble. I want to tell you that you're finally going to OCS. Your recent work has made you too valuable to give up until now, but we managed to stifle the screams over at

Intel and you've been cut loose. You report day after tomorrow. Make you feel better?"

Shana let out a mental deep breath and then it hit her. She was finally going to OCS! The first delays were a bit discouraging, but everyone said she was going to get there. Now it looked like they were right. "A good bit, Colonel," she replied carefully, trying not to show her relief. "I have to say I'm happy to get the chance."

"I expect you to graduate high in the standings, too, Corporal," Camille said dryly. "I've been looking over your record and it's exemplary. I'm sorry that duty kept you from going before now. The fact is I need good female junior officers. I expect you to justify that confidence.

"Now," she continued, "you've got today and tomorrow off. You're free until you report, so make sure you've got your gear and yourself ready when you report."

"Aye." That was all Shana could say. She was already thinking about OCS. It was supposed to be rough, but she was looking forward to the challenge.

Then Camille leaned back in her chair and fingered the hardcopy again. Looking up at the Gladius on the chair across from her desk, she asked, "Corporal, I know about your father. Tell me, did you ever know your mother?"

That brought Shana to earth with a crash. She had to think for a moment. "No, Colonel," she finally got out, "I really don't. Father always told me she died just after I was born, but she's never been a part of my life. All I've ever seen of her were old solidiopics he gave me."

"Did your father ever talk about her?"

Shana thought hard, suddenly realizing she'd never really had much, if any, interest in the phantom that was her mother. In fact, she actually knew nothing about her. "Colonel," she said thoughtfully, "he never spoke about her and it's just now hit me that I've never been interested in her."

Shana's eyes narrowed. She was smart enough to suspect she'd been conditioned not to show any of that interest. Looking back, it became obvious. She looked Lieutenant Colonel Paten in the eyes, and her expression wasn't that of a junior Legionnaire. "I don't think he ever wanted me to ask about her. Frankly, it never occurred to me to ask, and I'm beginning to think that was intentional on someone's part. Now I'm curious why *you* are asking."

Camille nodded. Ettranty was sometimes too sharp for comfort, but Camille didn't know if she was ready for this yet. Camille wasn't even sure what "this" was. "As to what or why your father didn't want you to know about her, I can't say, Corporal. Maybe one day we'll know. What counts now is you're a Gladius. You have another family and they all wear this uniform."

Shana the reporter recognized an "official explanation" when she heard one. On the other hand, the Gladius in her trusted the Colonel to fill her in when the time was right. Lieutenant Colonel Paten appeared as uneasy as she was. Patience, girl, she decided. Whatever was bothering the Colonel was going to come out. If not, she was perfectly capable of digging on her own once the legion was out in the open and Cauldwell was free.

"The reason I asked is because I've also been reviewing your medical records," Camille said, leaning over the desk and clasping her hands. "You have an unusual genome. From what we've been able to sample from the Cauldwell population, it doesn't match the planetary standard and I was curious."

She leaned back in her chair and looked at Shana a moment longer. "I assumed that was from your mother, but there's no way for us to tell at this time. Right now that's an intellectual puzzle, Corporal. Once we get this political mess cleared up on Cauldwell, though, I'll do everything I can to help you solve it. You have a right to know. Will that suit you?"

Shana nodded, still wondering what Pandora's Box had just opened. "Aye. I appreciate that, Colonel, but now I'm starting to think about my mother. I know I'm a local recruit, but I've got this urge to know about my family, just like any other Gladius."

Camille sat up, her usual businesslike attitude returning. "Agreed. As I said, I'll do what I can to help you. Meanwhile, you've got two days off, then OCS. I suggest you use your off time wisely then be ready for the shock when you report."

She smiled wryly. "I certainly remember that shock from my own OCS days. Dismissed, Corporal."

"Aye." Shana popped to attention, spun in an about face, then marched out. As she left the office, she was thinking hard. Her lack of curiosity about her mother wasn't natural. What in the hell had her father done to her? And what in the hell was the real story? Shana felt confident the Corps would help her find out. Best forget the problem for now. She had two days off then OCS in front of her. That was enough to worry about. But she couldn't stop thinking.

Inside the office, Camille was looking over Shana's medical records again. How in the hell had the doctors missed this one when Ettranty was given her recruit treatments? It didn't matter, she decided. The fact was they had. She wasn't happy about not giving a fellow Gladius the full truth, but she wasn't exactly sure what the full truth was. Whatever it was, it was now her responsibility to get to the bottom of it. She'd told Ettranty she was going to do it and that was a pledge graven in stone within the Corps.

She wasn't a geneticist, but she'd started in Medical Support and she could still read records with the best of them. No wonder Ettranty was seen as a desirable recruit. She had almost a full Gladius genome! There were unusual differences, but the statistical similarities were too high to be simple chance. Time to talk to the medics. There was something very strange here.

In the hall outside the Colonel's office, Karyn was waiting for Shana, a small haversack with towels, accessories, and underwear for them both hanging from her shoulder. Karyn was in full uniform, although, like Shana, she was wearing her swimsuit underneath. Barring a disaster in the Colonel's office - not really expected - both women planned on hitting the pool after this detour was over. Karyn started to tease her roommate about woolgathering then noticed Shana's expression. "Hey, sis," she asked, "what happened? She's not moving you out to another legion or something, is she?"

That was the most ghastly fate Karyn could imagine, even though she'd done it herself. Nice crop of boys here, she thought to herself, so there were compensations.

Absently, Shana shook her head. She was still mulling over the suddenly revealed problem of her mother. And her father. "Um... no. The Colonel asked me a question I couldn't answer and now it's bugging me.

"Oh, and I report to OCS day after tomorrow."

As they started to walk off, Karyn gave her a wide eyed look. "Wow! OCS? That's great! That means I'll have to break in a new roommate, but I'm really happy for you, sis."

Karyn stared ahead for a minute, meditating. "That means I'll finally have a roommate I can swap clothes with. That custom tailoring your skinny frame requires can be a pain, you know?"

That took Shana out of her mood and she whacked her grinning roommate on her shoulder as they both left the office section of the cavern and headed on out into the main tunnel. The tunnel was over forty measures wide and twenty high, sufficient to move any of the Legion's equipment, and counted as "outdoors". Therefore, both women donned their caps. Shana tilted hers a little forward as befitted a veteran of a major battle. Karyn, whose Virgin Mission had been of the ambush/raid variety, followed the custom of tilting hers to one side slightly to show she was a veteran, but not of the kind of battle Shana had seen. They walked happily down the main tunnel, headed for the pool area.

Not too far ahead of them, the Legate and the Sergeant Major were standing in an alcove just across from the Legionnaires Club entrance, discussing how to add more tunnel space to the cavern. The discussion was interrupted when the noise inside the Club got even more raucous and a young legionnaire flew through the open doors to land in an untidy heap in the middle of the main tunnel. It sounded like a brawl was in full swing, not an unusual occurrence. The Sergeant Major scowled and started forward, but the Legate held him back with a hand on his arm. "Just wait a minute, Sergeant Major," Legate Athan said with a grin. "The boys need to work off a little steam first. Besides, I see something interesting and I want to watch where it goes."

What the Legate saw were Shana and Karyn, stopped short and staring at the crumpled trooper at their feet. Shana took two steps forward and stood over the trooper, fists on her hips and looking down, her expression one of military displeasure. The trooper started to gather himself and get up then noticed the female boots and skirt at eye level. Looking up, he saw Shana glaring down at him. "Oh, hi, mate," he said with a sheepish grin.

"Mate my ass," Shana growled. "It's Corporal to you, trooper."

Uh-oh.

"Up!" Shana snapped. "Attention and remain there until I get this sorted out. Understand?"

Jumping into a rigid position of attention, the young Gladius popped off his answer. "Aye!"

Squaring her shoulders, Shana marched into the Club with its crashes, bangs, and other sounds of a building riot. The sounds ceased abruptly, shortly after she disappeared inside. Some moments afterward came a loud and aggravated female voice. And shortly thereafter, "One, *hup*. One, *hup*."

Out the open double doors came a double line of young Gladii, Corporal Shana Ettranty on the left in the leadership position counting cadence. "Section, hal-l-l-lt, ho! Left *face!*"

Shana glared at the fifteen or so troopers now facing her, uniforms disheveled and most carrying rather than wearing their caps. The glare was supplemented by a few minutes of ass chewing that would have done credit to Drill Sergeant Howard. Finally, "You yard birds will now fall out and reenter the Club. You will then clean it for inspection. Upon being inspected and released by the Club manager, you will report to your

154

quarters and remain there and sober up until mess. AM I UNDERSTOOD?"

The reply was a shouted chorus. "AYE!"

"Fall out!"

The young men tumbled back into the Club to get to work while the pair of women resumed their progress down the tunnel. Unseen in their alcove, the Sergeant Major was beaming with paternal pride. Legate Athan was grinning. "It seems that our former recruit makes a good decurion, Sergeant Major."

The Sergeant Major nodded judiciously. "Aye. She'll make a good officer too, Legate." The Sergeant Major took note of the way the Legate's look followed Corporal Ettranty as she walked off. Diplomatically, he said nothing. He simply nodded in satisfaction.

#####

Revolutions run on money, reflected Commander Claude Ancel as he studied the figures on his terminal, and they were getting a touch short. Oh, nothing serious, but they could certainly use some more. Perhaps they ought to open another cache. The gold they'd found in this one had gone a long way towards setting up their current operation on Cauldwell. So had the various anonymous numbered accounts in a variety of Cauldwell banks, all of which were accessible from certain terminals found in the cache after Combat Information Technology had very carefully entered the banking computer network and deactivated the tags and alerts placed on those accounts. It took a while to do it, but the money was a big help

They should have suspected such things existed, Claude reflected. If this was going to be part of an Imperial hideout, the Emperor's staff had to hide enough money to keep things going. That brought up the thought - again - that there ought to be more money in other locations. He needed to talk to Captain Folsom about it. Conditions might just be right for them to open another cache.

Commander Claude Ancel, once a fighter pilot in the Fleet, then an agent of Imperial Intelligence, then an assault shuttle Electronic Fields Officer in the Valeria's FSG, now deputy head of the Frontier Fleet Intelligence office here supporting the Victrix, got up and headed for his boss's office. Frankly, Claude told himself once again, he preferred being on a fighting craft, not behind a desk. He still wore his flight suit as a duty uniform, his right as flight crew, but he wasn't getting much in the way of space time, and especially not for the last year and a half. The Admiral promised him a return to space after things cleared up here. Maybe.

Meanwhile, there were compensations. Like that date tonight with Gladius Lieutenant Carlita Yarrow, now a member of the Victrix. An unusual match, if one wanted to be objective and Claude didn't. He had to secretly admit that her transfer from the Valeria to the Victrix was the deciding point in his accepting the Cauldwell job.

Fleet Captain Folsom's door was open, so Claude strolled in. "Boss," he began once Folsom looked up, "we need to look at opening another cache. By my reckoning, we're at fifty five percent of funds and that's a bit low for comfort. We're on budget, but that's still a bit tight."

Folsom nodded as he thought for a moment. "Let's see where we are as far as an informal risk assessment goes," he finally said. He waved a finger over one of the sensors on the console next to his desk. "Passant will be here in a minute," he said, looking at the console as a light came on over the sensor. "Time we three had a chat about this."

It was only a moment before a Gladius major walked into the office, his bearded face showing mild curiosity at the unexpected call. He was the commander of the Victrix tactical intelligence unit and defacto commander of the infiltrators being inserted into the Cauldwell population. "Have a seat, Thomas," Folsom said. "Claude here has brought up a situation with funding we need to look at. We might just have to recommend opening another cache to get at whatever money it might be hiding. What are you getting from Ettranty's office?" They'd managed to bug it almost ten months ago.

Passant humphed a laugh and nodded. He was proud of that little operation. "Pretty much the same. Ettranty's bothered, but not too bothered anymore. He's certain that the Victrix is gone and he's said so to Femiam several times. We still haven't got a handle on what he's messaged to Central, but there hasn't been anything resembling a search for the last six months or so."

"What about his Imperial liaison?" Claude asked. They'd pinpointed Narsima Antony Andews a year back. As Recording Secretary for the Guidance Council, he wasn't exactly inconspicuous, but he was a good example of hiding in plain sight.

Passant shook his head. "Andews is a perfect Imperial functionary. He does whatever the Emperor's staff tells him and nothing else. My guess is that he passes on whatever Ettranty says with no comment either way. Any comment would smack of having an opinion and that could be dangerous, even out here. In any case, none of our sources say he's done anything about pushing for more searches. My take from both Andews and Ettranty suggests that the heat is off and we might be able to get into another cache with a reasonable degree of safety."

Folsom nodded. "Okay. I'll see if the Legate is willing to take a chance and put some scouts on the other ten caches. Let's see if we can pick a good candidate to open."

"Aye."

In another part of Cauldwell, another conversation was taking place. "Matic, this Popular Movement for Good Government is starting to make me nervous."

Sitting at his desk, Ettranty shrugged massively at his Assistant Council Secretary and - merely a coincidence - his cousin, who was seated before him. "They're harmless, Clarine. The usual sort of minor organization that emerges from time to time among the proles. We've had them before and they've all come to nothing. All they do is allow the underclass let off a little steam."

The Narsim Clarine Femiam shook her head. "Maybe you have. I don't know about that, but this one is starting to bother me. They're getting money from somewhere, and they're mounting candidates for the Parliament, even here in Beauregard. If they win enough seats, we might start having problems."

Ettranty put down his water plass and looked at her. For a moment, his expression was frightening. "We won't have problems. If these candidates of theirs do cause difficulties, there are ways we can deal with them. I regret they are unpleasant ways, but those candidates will regret them more."

Clarine looked at him, her expression unreadable.

That night, while cleaning Narsima Ettranty's office, a man slightly past middle age with long gray hair gathered in a ponytail quietly tucked Ettranty's water plass into the utility bag attached to his work cart. He was on the tallish and heavyset side, but obviously the type of person that would still be working for a janitorial service at his time in life.

For some reason, they wanted the Narsima's DNA back at base.

In a desert area of Cauldwell, a scout was on a mission to survey one of the hidden caches. In point of fact, his sled was nowhere near any of them, or anywhere near Victrix base, but that was intentional. Scouts were always given plenty of time when stealth was important, and they were prone to use all of it. Low, slow, indirect, and a damn good

157

suppresser field were more than techniques and tools of the scout's trade, they were survival.

Low at this particular moment meant down in a desert wadi, creeping along its length until he could rise gently and find another masking feature that would take him in the general direction he wanted to go. As the wadi started a turn to the right, the scout was alerted by his Terrain Penetrating Radar. He stopped his sled for a moment to analyze the reading. The results were very vague, but he was willing to bet there was something manmade in the wall of the wadi. He grounded and took a more powerful TPR from his equipment case, along with a Mass Anomaly Detector. Both pieces of equipment said there was something in the wadi's wall, and now that he was able to get better readings, under the floor of the wadi as well. He spent a full day carefully and stealthily mapping whatever it was, finally concluding he'd found a twelfth cache. Interestingly enough, this one had no electronic signature of any kind. It was also far better hidden than any of the others. He finally got back on his sled and meandered carefully on his way. Several days from his discovery, he dropped a burst emitter then continued on his original mission. Twenty four hours after it was dropped, the emitter transmitted a highly secure microsecond long directional transmission that sounded like cosmic ray static unless a receiver had the proper code. Then it self-destructed leaving almost no trace. The encoded report started wheels rolling in Victrix Base.

#####

Captain Folsom pointed to the briefing hologram in Legate Athan's office. "Legate, you know about the other ten caches." A bright dot appeared in some desert area, just like the dot that marked the other ten caches, but larger. "It looks like we've found another one. This one's interesting, because it appears larger and better hidden than the others, and those are damned well hidden."

Major Passant took up the briefing. "I've ordered a full scout sweep of the find. Given the way scouts do things, I don't expect a better picture for several days. By then, we ought to have the entrance pinpointed. Breaking in may be a different story. Those boys will take plenty of time to clear any booby traps or alarms and I'm in full support of that."

Folsom nodded to the third man he'd brought to the meeting. "Once we have good information and can get in safely, Commander Ancel will move in with the exploratory team."

Legate Athan thought for a moment. "Any idea why this one is different?"

Claude spoke up. "This is a wild assed guess, Legate, but I think it's a good one. All eleven we've identified until now are pretty much the same, and far less hidden than this new one. That tells me this one is different - and different because it's important. I'm guessing this new one is the command center for the other eleven."

"That means it's probably also the Emperor's personal hiding hole," Karl commented. "I'd expect that one to be better hidden than the rest."

Folsom nodded. "Our thought, too. I'd also expect that it has some surprises."

Claude was silent, thinking about a subject he'd had on his mind since the twelfth cache was found. He'd always wondered about the crew for all of these ships the Empire had hidden. Were they there?

#####

It took a good bit of time, but finally Claude and his team were given the all clear. A young scout approached Claude, his visor up. With the reactive camouflage of his armor, it looked to Claude like a disembodied face moving across the dusty wadi. When he arrived, he came to attention and saluted. Or at least Claude thought so. Formalities out of the way, he explained, "There were a few traps, Commander, but nothing electronic or any kind of powered field. All the triggers, even the door locks, were entirely mechanical. There was nothing that would show up on detectors. We might have tripped something without using TPR and MAD."

"Chemical or nuclear explosives?"

The scout shook his head. "No, Commander. We found and deactivated a booby trapped control console just outside the door that was set up to use nonemitting fiberoptic transmission. If you used the wrong deactivation code, it released tachyon data packets. How many and from where, we still aren't sure, but without the console, the signal can't be sent. We did find a few of the TDPs. We're guessing the destination was Central."

Claude nodded. "Probably. Good work. Are you our guide?"

"Aye. Security will pick us up at the door."

Claude motioned to the rest of his team to follow and trailed the young Gladius to a huge gaping door in the wadi wall. Looking at the door, Claude judged it was smaller than the doors to the other caches. It wasn't large enough to take anything larger than a corvette, or maybe an armed yacht if his guess about the Emperor was right. He looked back for a moment and noticed that the two Gladii on his intelligence team, male and female, had their B-42s at combat present. That looked like a good idea to him and he drew his handgun, motioning to the Fleet members to do the same. The Gladii were in regular combat armor, but the four Fleet personnel just wore Corps issue helmets for communications capability.

And something else, Claude remembered. //"Scout leader, do we have a schematic of this place yet?"//

//"Aye. Here you are, Commander."//

A wire diagram of the cache suddenly appeared on Claude's HUD. He studied it for a moment then made a decision. //"All team members. I see two large chambers below this tunnel. If this place is like the other cache, the rooms at this level are offices and quarters. Be advised, I expect at least one set of quarters will be very large and luxurious, probably with automated guards, so be careful. In fact, let's stay away from them for the moment. I want to know what's in those two big chambers."//

//"Commander, scout leader."//

//"Go."//

//"Commo's probably on the first level and probably the computer center too. Request permission to send two teams to look."//

//"Granted, but keep in mind what I said. This place may have been intended to house the Emperor. If it was, you can expect very good AIs and automated weapons traps in real depth. The AIs are probably on standby and just your presence would activate them."//

//"Understood, Commander. Been there. There were a few when we opened up Victrix base the first time. If we run into anything, we'll pull back and let CIT technicians handle that."//

//"Good luck."// Claude smiled to himself. Clearing the cache that was now home to Victrix base probably took weeks. It was amazing what Corona had managed to do right under the noses of Ettranty and his people. However, he now had a cache of his own, one he was sure was far more heavily guarded. Wake up and remember that.

Claude's eyes were constantly scanning as they combat-walked carefully down the tunnel. The dark-penetrating ability of his visor gave everything an eerie greenish cast. At least it let him see something of the scouts ahead of him, moving with even more care, their heads and weapons constantly turning as they moved. True to their nature, the scouts were slow, but that was all right with Claude. A fast and bold scout was a dead scout and he heartily approved of everyone taking their time and staying alive.

They found an elevator, but it was inactive and would stay that way until it was safe to turn on the cavern's power. The emergency stairs were next to it. The slow creep down the stairs in total darkness was, frankly, scary. The Gladii were, true to their nature in uncertain terrain, nearly soundless. His own people weren't anywhere near that, but they were also trying their best to keep quiet. It really ought not to matter, Claude thought, since there wasn't supposed to be anyone here to hear them, but he was also trying not to make any noise. A human reaction against the unknown.

They reached the bottom and Claude saw two large metal doors that looked like they belonged on bank vaults. One of the scouts held up his hand and the entire party froze in place. The scout took a device from his belt and, with the greatest of care, began scanning the walls. Another joined him and began doing the same with another device. Then they scanned the floors and the low ceiling of the stair landing. One of them took a marker from his belt and put an X on four widely spaced spots on the walls. The other motioned for two other scouts to join them. Once in place, all four drew their axes. At a signal Claude couldn't hear, the axes slammed as one into each of the spots, cutting deeply into the wall. After that, all four relaxed. //"Automated guns, Commander."//

Claude let out the breath he was holding. Automated guns. The scouts' suppressed armor kept them from being detected, but not his people. That would have triggered the guns. Then the intelligence officer in him woke up. Why were guns here? //"Understood. Can you get the doors open?"//

//"Aye. Pick one."//

Claude pointed to the one on the left. He expected more special equipment, but the scout simply sheared his way through the armored door lock with his ax. As he casually pushed it open, he asked, //"Do the other one, Commander?"//

//"Aye, smart ass,"// Claude snarled.

He could hear the chuckle as the scout answered. //"Aye, Commander. A moment."//

Claude carefully moved forward and looked through the first open door while the scout cut the other open. The chamber inside was big, so big that he couldn't see the end of it. What he could see was row upon row of large cabinets, with forty millimeasure sized disks evenly spaced across the front of each. If the whole place was like this, there could be thousands of disks. Claude tuned up his visor's magnification and saw a code number on every one within range.

One of Claude's Fleet technicians came forward with more sophisticated equipment. //"Commander, there is a heavily suppressed low level power field in this chamber. Not dangerous. It seems to be powering these banks of whatever they are. I'm also getting readings consistent with stasis fields. The suppresser is to keep the power emanations from being detected outside the cache."//

Claude began to get a very bad feeling. //"All personnel, out of here. We need to check the next chamber. NOW!"//

He didn't even need to step into the chamber or have his tech tell him there were active stasis fields. This chamber was also immense and just as full as the other. As far as Claude could see, there they were, in row upon row of blank metal coffin shapes. Thousands of them. Stasis chambers. They'd found the crews.

//"Scout leader, Commander Ancel."//

//"Aye."//

//"Pull all of your personnel out of here. Very carefully. We've found what we came for. We need full scale tech teams from Niad here for this one, not us."//

The scout leader didn't argue. //"Aye. Disengaging now."//

Claude was shaking a little as they backed carefully from the chamber and worked their way back up the stairs. Lord Above, he kept thinking to himself, just what had they found?

CHAPTER 8

LEGIO IX VICTRIX
CAULDWELL

The destroyer headed for Cauldwell at 3500 lights MMS. Admiral Lane Mackinnie, now Chief of Naval Operations for the Frontier Fleet, was aboard along with SOC Shyranne Garua, Senior Officer of the Corps of Gladius.

Neither of these were hollow titles either, Lane mused as Shyranne placed her tray on the dining table across from him. He was still vastly amused that a flag officer shuffled off to a dead end command under one Fleet could find himself CNO in another, very real, one. The now officially constituted Frontier Fleet consisted of four formerly Imperial FSGs - Lane's and the other three they'd been able to find. Even now he had ships combing the old Empire, trying to find others. That brought refugees straggling in constantly to supplement the small number of ships carefully recovered from Victrix base. With the growing flow of pocket battleships finally coming from Tactinese yards, the Frontier Fleet was going to be formidable.

With cross assignments to the Victrix, the addition of the Third Augusta, the Seventh Rapax, and the Twelfth Ferrata, not to mention orphans from other legions that kept turning up, Shyranne Garua was SOC of five nearly full legions. That was a positively scary fighting force in anyone's book. Lane couldn't recall when more than two legions had ever been used at any time in the Empire's history. All five were going back when the time came to clean out Central. Impressive, he thought with dry understatement.

Lane was Chief of Naval Operations - and Commander, First Frontier Fleet - because of the happy circumstance of seniority. However, the plan he and the Garuas had developed offered the best chance for survival and the other senior officers knew it. It was agreed he was going to be the CNO whenever the current Frontier Fleet became the Cluster Fleet. Forming a Cluster government to own that Fleet was the business of the politicians. Lane's business was to ensure every spacer under his command knew there was a big difference between themselves and the old Imperial Fleet. For one thing, he'd already changed Fleet uniform colors to gray. Other changes to follow.

Lane wasn't sure what mechanism the Gladii used to select the SOC, but he suspected the same type of common sense. In any case, Shyranne was his counterpart.

The news of the Emperor's last ditch sanctuary, and suspicions about its contents, were enough to bring both of them to Cauldwell. They were about a month behind the technical team clearing the cache, so there should be some solid information available by now. Both Frontier Fleet and Corps Intelligence had done a good bit of informed speculation. If even half of it was correct, someone was going to have to make an important decision very quickly. Lane and Shyranne were that someone.

Shyranne looked up at him with a small smile while she unclipped her fork and knife from the serving tray. "Well, Lane, any new ideas about those people in the cache?"

Lane looked at her in silent accusation. Her question was, of course, was what passed for Gladius humor outside of a legion. They'd done nothing else but endlessly discuss the cache. Stasis banks in one cavern had turned out to contain thousands of embryos. Fortunately, there were access points for standard medical diagnostic equipment on the bottom of each embryo tube so they knew a good bit about the babies inside; including the fact their DNA was different from the normal genome of the current population. Oh, they were still human, but with differences. What those differences were and why, nobody yet had a clue. The only thing they knew for sure was the embryos weren't clones.

"A fetus is a fetus," he rumbled. "No matter the differences, we can work with them when it comes time for the children to be raised. It's the adults in the stasis cabinets that bother me. We can't get any sort of medical readings from them except the standard life signs on the cabinet instruments. I suspect they are adult versions of the embryos and I'm going to order the revival of one once we get there."

Shyranne looked at him. There was a bit of unease under her Gladius calm, if one knew her. Lane Mackinnie knew her very well. "Something tells me we need to be very careful with that experiment, Lane. What kind of Fleet crewman would let himself be put in stasis for an indefinite length of time merely as a precaution? Those caches are over a decade old."

Lane snorted. "I suspect that's when the people in those chambers were emplaced. I agree, no normal Fleet crewman would volunteer for that. Oh, a few would, I suppose. There are always some individuals that would do something, for whatever reason, the rest find reprehensible or frightening, but there are five thousand stasis cabinets. I don't think you could find that many volunteers in the Fleet, and conscripts would be useless once awakened to find themselves in the final bastion of a hunted

164

Emperor. You can't conscript reliable warship crews, especially in circumstances like a last ditch situation."

Shyranne took a bite of her food and thought as she chewed, looking off into the distance. "That speaks to me of fanaticism," she said finally. "Fanatic devotion to the Emperor, not the Empire. Did you see any trend in that direction before things started falling apart?"

Lane shook his head in a slow, massive motion. "The opposite in fact. Witness how many Fleet units are now backing various rebellions - or revolutions - against the Empire.

"Including ours.

"No," he rumbled, his voice low, "this is something different from the Fleet. What it is, I don't know, but it's bothering me."

VICTRIX BASE
CAULDWELL

"We're about ready to move some more of the standard ships out to you," Claude commented as he and the Admiral walked down the tunnel to Victrix Base hospital. "We still haven't got a good handle on those frigates, though, so they'll stay here for a while."

Admiral Mackinnie asked, "What seems to be the problem?"

Claude grimaced. "We're not sure about the AI. There're attachments on the AI housing that look like they ought to fit a governor or supplemental device, and the controls on the boards aren't complete. There's some kind of interface missing between the ship and the crew. Those are features I didn't see on the original plans back when I was Imperial Intelligence. Someone added some things when they built the production models we found. The rated speed is a good indicator of that. Right now, nobody can say how those ships would do in combat, but I suspect they'd be damned good."

Lane grunted. "Whatever it is, we have to find out before we meet those frigates in Middle Empire. I'm not happy with the Empire having that big a technological jump on our ships."

Claude nodded agreement as they arrived at the hospital door. In one of the examining rooms, they joined a group standing around a naked muscular man lying on a hospital bed. There were several doctors in the group, along with Shyranne and Major Passant. Four young legionnaires stood, quietly watchful, in the background. Shyranne was uneasy about the man on the bed, the first they'd removed from a stasis chamber. The guards were evidence of the fact.

The supervising physician, Lieutenant Commander Jandrews, welcomed the Admiral, and began explaining. "Since we got him out of the cabinet, we've been bringing his vitals up slowly in a standard curve, just like the cabinet would do if left to a normal revival sequence, but we've also got him in an anesthesia field until we want him to wake up. Right now, the field's the only thing keeping him inactive."

Lane nodded and the doctor continued. "We've done a medical work-up and now have a pretty good picture of his body. First of all, he has a very well developed musculature, almost as well developed as a Gladius, but with some differences. Again, his genome is remarkably similar to that of a Gladius, but missing some of the features in the current type."

Jandrews walked over to the bed. "He's heavily augmented, with what appear to be subcutaneous drug reservoirs and various electronic devices." He pointed to the man's wrists. "There are tractor presser devices embedded in his wrists, and, here in his chest, what looks like communications equipment. We've got jammers already working in case he tries to send some sort of message. His head also contains receptors of some kind, but I can't guess at the purpose right now."

"You're describing someone surgically enhanced to be one of us," Shyranne commented.

Jandrews nodded. "I think that may be a very accurate guess. I'd also suspect other more subtle mental modifications, but I'm not prepared to say what their purpose might be."

Lane looked at Shyranne. "Are we ready to wake him up?"

Shyranne looked around at her guards and nodded. Quietly, Passant put his hand on his ax. "Yes, go ahead."

Jandrews looked at his monitors and brushed a sensor on a small control in his hand. "Anesthesia dropping," he said in an abstracted voice that showed his concentration on the monitor screen. "Vitals coming up. Approaching nominal. Nominal.

"He's awake," the doctor said in a quiet monotone. The man on the bed hadn't moved a muscle.

Suddenly, his eyes flew open and flipped back and forth as he rapidly scanned the room, then he leaped like an attacking tiger, straight at one of the guards. A straight arm to the chest walloped the Gladius back as the other hand dipped and came up with his short sword. The man continued on without breaking stride, headed for the door. A thrown ax smacked his legs and felled him.

The man was back up on his feet in an instant, but Passant's ax was back in his hand by that time. Action slowed as the two squared off, every muscle tense with explosive power held in check. They crouched and began a slow sideways movement, the man trying to get a clear path to the door and Passant moving to block him.

166

"Gladio alieyo," Passant said softly, his unfocused eyes watching every aspect of his opponent as the two carefully stepped sideways in the deadly dance.

"Ave Keesar." The man spoke his first words in a mellow baritone. What he said caused Shyranne to suddenly frown in concentration.

While the two squared off, the three remaining guards had immediately taken blocking positions in front of the door, axes out. The fourth trooper was still down, although moving. One of the doctors was out of his shocked paralysis and starting to kneel next to him. The naked man slowly shifted back into the room to a position that gave him a view of the door and the guards blocking it. He smiled slightly. "Prodator. Prodator et..."

Then he leaped towards Passant, sword blade flashing in a killing stroke.

When someone speaks, most people will listen politely until he is finished. That's an old mistake in a knife fight. Passant didn't make it. As the sword blade shot forward, he leaped up and sideways, his body curved to give his right arm power as he swung his ax in a flashing downward arc completely cleaving the man's neck. As he swung, Passant turned his blade slightly to sever the man's arm in the middle of his forearm. If he hadn't, the twist the man gave his body would have kept the sword moving upward. Both had the reflexes to correct in mid strike and the naked man's blade would have slashed Passant across the torso even after death. As it was, blood from the severed arm flew in an arc across Passant's chest, showing where the sword blade would have slashed - and killed - him.

For a few seconds, everyone stared at the naked body bleeding out on the floor. Then Shyranne knelt down and picked up the man's head, looking carefully at his face. "Oh... Lord... Above," she breathed quietly.

"What is it, Shyranne?" Lane rumbled.

She was still staring at the severed head in her hands. "I thought they were legend," she said. "They're real. I'm holding the head of one."

As she carefully put the head down and stood up, Lane asked. "*What* legend? What are you talking about?"

She looked at him grimly. "There were always stories in the Corps about the lost legion, the Hispania. The Hispania was an unlucky legion in the old Roman army, supposed to be cursed. In our stories, the Corps Hispania went to serve the Emperor as an Emperor's Guard then vanished. The name was retired. That's why there isn't a Hispania today, or so the story goes.

"Nobody now knows if it was true," she continued. "That happened just after the Corps was originally formed. Nobody has seen a

Hispania trooper, or any sort of Emperor's Guard, in over a thousand years. Now it appears they are real. Shangnaman had them brought back from wherever they were. Major Passant just killed one."

Jandrews gave her a piercing stare. "Are you sure?"

Shyranne turned her calm, grim gaze at him. "Our language, doctor, is a highly modified version of Old Latin with a great many invented and borrowed words because of our military life. Probably only twenty percent is still from Old Latin, but we can still recognize and understand it. What he was speaking was a much earlier version of the Corps language than ours, but with some differences. I could still understand him. His battlecry translated as, 'Hail the Emperor.' Also, I can recognize racial kin now that I'm looking for it."

Lane commented. "It sounded as though he was calling you the Predator in Unispek, Major."

Passant was cleaning the blood off his ax with one of the room's towels and still looking at the man's body. "He wasn't, Admiral. 'Prodator' is from Old Latin. The word means traitor. He saw your gray uniforms and our khaki ones. Gray meant a different Fleet, thus an enemy. Gladius khaki also meant an enemy to be eliminated. That man knew the political situation when he went into stasis ten years ago, and the destruction of the Corps and 'disloyal' Fleet units was probably already in the planning stage. To him, any military not part of the Imperial structure - and the Emperor specifically excluded the Corps from that structure - was classed as an enemy and a traitor by definition. He knew exactly where he was and who we were as soon as he opened his eyes. We're lucky he attacked first, instead of playing us as a member of the Corps would do."

"As soon as you analyze his genome, doctor," Shyranne said, "I think you'll find he's the original type of the Gladius, before we modified ourselves and other differences grew up. That man is our basic stock, the original genetic modification that produced the Corps."

Lane spoke decisively. "Shyranne, we have to discuss this. Ancel, Passant, you too. Let's get back to my office."

Jandrews leaned over and picked up the severed head. "Meanwhile," he said with grim satisfaction, "I intend to dissect our friend here until I know everything about him." He didn't like having patients attack him or his people.

"Be very careful, doctor," Shyranne said. "I expect everything in his body that might be some form of secret has already self-destructed. Even then, there are probably booby traps, concealed weapons, and anti-capture devices. We have them. Do your dissection via remotes and under a heavy suppression field. There will be surprises."

"Oh, yes," the doctor said abstractedly, still examining the head, "I will be most careful. He won't be allowed to kill anyone."

#####

In the event, the discussion was delayed to allow the doctor time to finish his dissection, giving everyone time to change into uniforms without blood spatters. There was also time for other senior Legion and Frontier Fleet officers to be gathered.

Doctor Jandrews made his presentation first, detailing what he'd found as the body was reduced to components. "We destroyed the remains after extensive recordings," he finished up. "As you said, Legion Commander, he was full of little items that were reduced to lumps, but we could mostly deduce what they were for by placement, if nothing else. I ordered the body destroyed in case there was something we missed, but also because a capsule we hit released some form of nannies as soon as it was touched by a scalpel. They were contained, but I saw no reason to take any more chances."

Lieutenant Colonel Camille Paten was in the meeting as Support Group Commander, and she was still thinking about the genome chart on one of the doctor's displays. She'd seen it before, somewhere. It would come to her, she knew, but the thought bothered her.

Lane spoke. "Thank you, doctor. Good brief."

He looked at the people seated around the table. "We've all had a little time to digest this. Thoughts, anyone?"

Major Passant spoke up. "Admiral, Commander Ancel and I have been brainstorming, trying to fit this man into various scenarios and we think we've got something plausible. With your permission?"

Lane settled back into his chair and nodded. "Continue."

"Aye," Passant answered. "Briefly, it appears the Emperor possesses a military force of these people. How large it is, we aren't prepared to state, but the thousands of embryos in stasis, much less the adults, are very indicative. We have to assume there are many more embryos and adults, possibly children, on Central than there are here. We also know conclusively they are the ancestor type of the current Gladius. These people were the soldiers that founded the Corps and we should treat them with a great deal of caution. Their counterparts in the early legions were extremely capable and created our traditions.

"However there is a critical difference. While the Corps is dedicated to the protection and preservation of the Empire - now humanity as a whole since the Empire has rejected us - these people are devoted to the protection and preservation of the *Emperor,* in all probability

169

fanatically devoted. You will see evidence in a few minutes that will back up that conclusion.

"Looking at the situation objectively, I can't see Shangnaman having more than a legion's active strength on Central and being able to keep it hidden. If he had them, my guess is we would have seen them on Tactine. Possibly, he's still growing the bulk of his Guard from embryos raised normally while the ones we've found were force-grown. Certainly, the ones in the cache appear about twenty standard years in age, none older, and, judging from the one we woke, fully trained. We also assume they're trained as ship crews as well as ground forces, given that the ship crews had to come from somewhere. We doubt Shangnaman expected to bring many New Fleet spacers if he was making an escape.

"Forced growing has very severe limitations," he continued. "It limits the life experience of the subject, reduces life span, and reduces mental capacity by a measurable fraction. To have the best soldiers, Shangnaman would have to let them mature naturally. That tells us that the Guard on Central has a generation naturally maturing while the bulk of his current fighting force is force grown. Today's Gladius is fully trained and capable at seventeen, so the younger generation may be coming into the Guard force structure soon. How soon, we can't tell since we don't know when this program was started. There's a good probability, looking at the time the stasis chambers were emplaced and the age of the occupants, that naturally grown soldiers are already in the pipeline. In essence, the Emperor's Guard probably consists of older soldiers with slightly lesser ability and younger troops with little to no experience but more capabilities."

Shyranne asked, "Major, under your scenario, how would you match the fighting ability of their younger troops - I will *not* call them Gladii, no matter their genetic makeup - against our young legionnaires?"

"About on a par, Senior Officer, with an edge to our youngsters since they've been trained by combat veterans and have a millennium's Darwinian selection behind them. However, I have to emphasize that the Emperor's Guard is the most capable force we've ever faced. We have to look at them as an even match."

Passant looked around, but the table was silent, digesting his last statement. "Now Commander Ancel has more to tell you." His expression said they weren't going to like it.

"We went back and found another little room off the main chamber," Claude spoke up, his face carefully expressionless, "and we've solved the mystery of how the frigates are intended to be run. I suspected as soon as those receptors were found in the subject's head that the ships were designed for a mental tie-in by the crew but there were fittings for additional augmentation for the AI. We went looking for the reason for the augmentation and we found it."

He leaned forward and looked at each person at the table in turn. "That room contained half measure sized cubes with attachment points for the AI. When we scanned the cubes, we got human life signs. The cubes are just the right size to hold an immature human brain, probably from a child. Those ships are cyborgs, designed to use a programmed human brain. That accounts for their small crews."

Shyranne sucked in her breath in horror. It took a lot to shake a Gladius, but she was shaken. "That's a violation of every ethical code in the Empire! To intentionally do that to children! Shangnaman is a monster."

Claude nodded. "Monster, yes, but a monster with a highly effective military force that's fanatically loyal to him."

One of the cohort commanders spoke up. "Where in hell did he get the genetic material for all of this? None of those embryos are clones."

Claude picked up the display control. He started running through a series of tridio stills as he spoke. "Remember we told you the lost legion became something dedicated to the preservation of the Emperor. Once we digested that, we found them. We got these from the carrier's library and from the Information Net on Cauldwell. As you all see, they're public shots of past Emperors, and they all contain one major indicator, no matter how old they are."

He stopped at one. "Here's a good example. This is Claudius XII." Suddenly, there were individual yellow circles around faces surrounding the Emperor. "Look closely at the Emperor's security people."

"That was over five hundred years ago," Lane rumbled.

"And those look remarkably like our friend, Admiral," Passant said dryly. "It appears the lost legion was never lost, simply transformed and kept very, very secret. We told you of their dedication to the Emperor's person, and now we know how they were used - for an utterly reliable security force. Used that way, and in small numbers, they were under everyone's radar. Nobody has ever asked how Imperial Personal Protection was staffed. IPP was simply there. They were completely separate from any other Imperial entity. They spoke to no one but the Emperor, interacted with no one. Now we know why.

"Apparently, Shangnaman hit on the idea of expanding their mission. They were devoted enough to the Emperor's person to go ahead with his plan to the fullest degree. Commander Ancel and I now believe the original security force is the source material for what appears to be a totally new factor in the Imperial equation. Sperm from the men and ova from the women, in vitro fertilization, and you have what we have in those

171

caches in the Emperor's hideout. The initial generation was force-grown to hurry things up and make the plan practical. All very technical and unhuman. The Corps now has more against Shangnaman than pillage, rape, and murder of his own citizens. We can also assume he has a highly capable force nearly the equal of our own, a deadly enemy to the Corps, the Frontier Fleet, and all we represent."

"This makes our planned attack on Central extremely problematical," Lane told the group. "We have to do a lot of work to decide how to handle the possible capabilities of this Emperor's Guard."

"They are dangerous," Passant spoke up, "highly capable, but inexperienced. The man I fought knew what he was doing, but it was obvious to me that he'd never been in a real fight with a live blade. We have centuries of combat experience to draw upon. They don't."

"Possibly something we can play on," Lane said, "but we need to wargame this carefully, and train with these people in mind. Those frigates, for instance, are far more dangerous for their size than any ship type we have. Our pocket battleships might be able to take one out, but not on a one-on-one basis."

He sat forward and said decisively, "Shangnaman is widely known to be brilliant, ruthless, and paranoid. Given that paranoia, it's natural for him to keep the Guard close to him, for protection if nothing else. I don't think he'd want them out from under his personal control. He wouldn't use them for anything else unless he had a great many of them and a very important reason. That, by the way, speaks against their use on Tactine."

"So now we have something very important to train towards," Shyranne mused aloud. "We didn't know about them, but they knew about us. Now we know about them also, but we have combat experience they lack. They're new at the Gladius ancestral trade."

She looked pensively down at the table for a moment. "There's a full legion's combat strength in the cache. I wonder just how many more of them are out there."

Camille's eyes suddenly shot wide and she gasped. The action was so totally uncharacteristic of a Gladius that everyone stared at her. "I think I can tell you," she finally said. "I've seen that genome before, in one of our troops. We have one of the adults here at the base with us.

"Cadet Shana Ettranty."

#####

Shana raised her hand and knocked on the OCS Commandant's door. She knew perfectly well she was standing near the top of her class and hadn't screwed up anything lately, so the summons was a mystery. A voice came from inside, "Come."

Shana marched in and started to report, but it wasn't Major Bellows behind the desk, it was Lieutenant Colonel Paten, and sitting next to her was Sergeant Major Olmeg. Correcting herself with only an instant's hesitation, she snapped out, "Lieutenant Colonel, Cadet Ettranty reports."

Camille looked up at the legionnaire at attention in front of her. OCS apparently agreed with her. Her uniform was its usual immaculate self, with a senior cadet's blue tab in place of her rank badge and a cadet rank brassard on her left sleeve showing a Captain's three pips. She was the designated class leader. Camille now had a good idea why. She also felt slightly sick at what she was about to order. Thank the Lord Above the Sergeant Major was here to take over this triple damned duty. "Cadet Ettranty, I told you once we would look into the matter of your mother. We've done so, but that raised a number of urgent questions that now need to be answered. I'm ordering a full medical and psych examination of you. The results will answer those questions. Legion Sergeant Major Olmeg will take you to the hospital for that examination. After it is over, you will be brought here and all of your questions, including the need for this examination, will be answered. Is that clear?"

It wasn't clear to Shana, and her expression made that plain, but an order was an order. "Aye," she said.

"Move out with the Sergeant Major, Cadet, the doctors are waiting."

"Aye." Shana spun on her heel, waited for the Sergeant Major to heave himself out of his chair then followed him out of the office.

After Shana left, Camille crossed her arms on her desk, put her head on them, and fought the nausea down. Ettranty was a good trooper, one of the best. And this whole triple damned situation forced her to lie to her. That lie went directly against everything in her nature as a Gladius. Thank the Lord Above the girl was following orders. If the examination turned up nothing, Camille owed Ettranty a full explanation.

If the wrong things turned up, Second Lieutenant Ettranty's body would be burned with honors.

#####

"What's this all about, Sergeant Major?" Shana asked as they left the office.

The Sergeant Major looked at her as they walked. He finally admitted to himself she was the daughter he'd always wanted. His wife and both his sons were dead in the battle to get them to Cauldwell. Now he had her - and she was doing well. He was proud of Shana, damned proud, but he'd also been in the meeting on the Emperor's Guard. This girl could be one of the best officers in the Victrix one day or a deadly threat right now. They were on their way to find out which. "I can't tell you, Cadet. It's classified. Big stuff. Let's get this poking and prodding out of the way and get back so Lieutenant Colonel Paten can tell you. I can't."

That was all he'd say until they got to the examination room. Once a very puzzled Shana was lying on the pad, he leaned over as she started to lose consciousness. "You've done me proud, girl," he said in a husky growl.

He went stumping back into the control room where various doctors and technicians sat looking at monitors and took a seat where he could see through the window to where she lay. He hated misleading her, but he was pragmatic and experienced enough to know it was necessary. Olmeg was perfectly certain there wasn't a disloyal thought in Shana's head, but there was no telling what was buried in her subconscious, or what would trigger something that might be buried. There was certainly no device in her body that the Victrix hadn't put there. The operations that gave her Gladius physical capabilities would have revealed anything.

Likewise, when they'd tweaked her mind to improve her natural mental sensitivity, nothing was out of the ordinary. In fact, she was more sensitive than normal to begin with and possessed other mental capabilities the Corps wanted. He and the Legate had felt them when they met her, and that was why Corona chose her. Now the Sergeant Major knew why she had those capabilities. She was from ancestral stock. The question was what had been done to her by the Empire and this examination was looking for the answer. Another question was why Ettranty had the girl as a daughter, but that could wait. There was a reason, of that he was sure.

Sergeant Major Olmeg wasn't a deep thinker. He left that to the officers while he and the rest of the decurions got on with the business of running the Corps. Shana, from her first day with the Victrix, was the responsibility of the decurions. She still was, as far as he was concerned, especially once she finished OCS and mounted that pip on her collar pronouncing her a Second Lieutenant. Then she became a decurion's responsibility to continue training until she grew up eventually and became a good officer. If this examination turned out right, Olmeg had no worries on that score.

If it didn't, well, she was still his responsibility. He'd already told the doctor to keep his hand off the kill switch. He'd do it himself with his short sword. If Shana had to pay the Gladius Price through no fault of her own, she wouldn't be the first in the history of the Corps. At least he could make sure she went out like a Gladius should go.

As for the contents of those chambers, Olmeg had already made the common sense recommendation for the embryos. Get some incubators. The embryos were too undeveloped for the Empire to have done anything to them yet. Some of those embryos would be born as children in the Legion and others would find civilian parents. New blood and the Corps could always use it. The civilian community could also use the capabilities those children represented. The plan was for the Corps to eventually return to humanity as a whole, anyhow. May as well get a start now.

Meanwhile, that left them with five thousand adults, totally unrecoverable and highly dangerous if revived. A full legion's fighting strength. The decision there was obvious, too, but Olmeg shied away from it. Killing people, even an enemy, while they were helpless was one of those decisions that stained the soul. Every soldier had decisions, made in seconds during the heat of combat, that had no right answer, just made so the unit could survive or accomplish the mission. He had a few on his conscience that returned to haunt his dreams from time to time. He was glad this one was above his pay grade.

Olmeg's head snapped to one side as Doctor Jandrews made a sound then said, "Ah. Found it." The doctor's hands got busy on his control panel.

Olmeg stared at the doctor until the man finished and turned to look at him. Jandrews smiled. "No problem now, Sergeant Major," he said. Olmeg sighed deeply, then turned back to watch Shana.

Shana opened her eyes to a familiar sight: Sergeant Major Olmeg was scowling at her. "Hope you had a nice sleep, Cadet," he growled. "Let's go see the Colonel." Shana got the distinct sensing that the Sergeant Major was relieved. For some reason, that made her feel better.

Even for a man with a game leg, the Sergeant Major could set a pretty good pace. It was a fast trot, but Shana could keep up easily and try to ask a few questions about what the hell was happening to her. He made it impossible. Every time she opened her mouth, he spit out a question about something in one of her classes, all of which he'd apparently memorized, and she shot the reply back. A correct answer simply prompted another question while a hesitation or wrong answer received a minor butt chewing and a textbook solution.

Shana's reporter's sense was fully awake now. She was being played and she knew it, but the Sergeant Major wasn't giving her an opening. She was going to get answers as soon as she saw Colonel Paten.

In the event, she did get answers. As soon as she was back in front of the Colonel, Paten handed her a reader and told her to sit down and review the information on the chip in it. What she saw left her speechless.

"That's the full history, so far as we know it, of the lost legion and the Emperor's Guard," Lieutenant Colonel Paten said after Shana finished, "along with everything we've been able to deduce."

"As you saw, it includes you," she added dryly.

She gave Shana one of those piercing looks. "To recap, your father's DNA shows no family relationship to you. In fact, your DNA shows you're not from the Cauldwell general population. What it does show is that you're one of the ancestral versions of the Gladius, the same as the people we found in the cache. Since you're one of the ancestral types, we had to assume you were one of the Guard embryos. It's interesting that Ettranty got you from Nero V, the Emperor that Shangnaman replaced, because it tells us the embryo program goes pretty far back. It also makes us wonder how many more like you there are in the Cauldwell general population, given its purpose as an Imperial refuge."

Shana was still in mild shock. She was one of the original Gladius gene types? Then her eyes narrowed. "That's why all of this running and bustling to doctors?"

Paten didn't reply immediately. Instead she touched a sensor and a hologram of Doctor Jandrews appeared, apparently sitting comfortably in a chair next to the desk. He smiled smugly at her. "I hate to run so I took the easy way," he said pleasantly.

"Cadet Ettranty, until proven otherwise, we had to assume you were a major danger," Paten said evenly. "It's been proven otherwise."

"And if I was a danger?" Shana said in grim tones.

"We'd have had to kill you, Cadet," the Sergeant Major said in an iron voice. "I would have done it myself. You deserve a proper death from the Victrix." He looked her firmly in the face as he spoke.

Shana returned the look as she thought hard. The Gladius in her fully understood what he was saying. They were here on Cauldwell secretly and survival depended on that secrecy until they could bring down the government. Her Gladius outlook said if she was a danger to the legion, she had to die. "Thank you, Sergeant Major," she said softly. He humphed softly then settled back in his chair, looking at the floor for a few seconds with an expressionless face.

"So you found nothing?" Shana asked the doctor.

"Oh yes we did," Jandrews said with the same cheerful expression. "A beautiful compulsion buried deep in your psyche. In fact it was a little obvious and I'm naturally suspicious, so I kept looking and found the one it was supposed to hide. I've reduced both so that you will feel them if they activate, but they will be no more than a slight inclination to you. You can override them at will."

"What was I supposed to do?"

Jandrews crossed his legs and cradled one knee with his interlocked hands. "Well, let's see. They were both pretty much the same, to tell the truth. Basically, when given a certain order you would repeat everything you saw or heard at a time you were given - dandy compulsion for a spy by the way. The hidden compulsion was a bit more ominous. It would cause you to do *anything* you were told by the person giving the order. I expect the person with the key words was your father."

"Or his Imperial liaison," Paten added. "Cadet, you were intended to be used as a spy - or a possible assassin - by your father. The doctor went deep into your mind and instances started to surface when you were used as just that by him - a spy, anyhow - as a child. Those episodes continued into adulthood. The last one was just before you underwent Gladius modification. Apparently, he felt it might be too dangerous to 'turn on your playback' after that. He had no idea what we'd implanted."

Shana looked sharply at the Sergeant Major. "And did you implant anything?"

He scowled and answered. "No, girl, we did not. That's against our beliefs.

"You were so important to us," he continued uncomfortably, "that I'm not going to say we wouldn't put in a suggestion or two, but that's as far as we were willing to take it. Even that wasn't needed because you turned out to be a perfect recruit. You took to the Corps naturally... like it was your real home. Like one of us."

"I understand why, now," Shana said thoughtfully. "I am one of you. I always was. I'm a Gladius. You know, everything felt so right once I began to relax and get into the training. Ideas and feelings began to float up from nowhere. I can see and feel Those Now Gone like any Gladius."

She looked down at her uniform and touched her arm dagger. "I'm comfortable now. I like what I am. Looking back, I feel that way for the first time in my life."

"Still..." Now the reporter was looking at the Colonel.

"My *father*," the word was an epithet, "was given me to use, as a spy if nothing else. Easy to do, since I was his possession, not his child. People will say and do things around children they won't do or say around adults. Is that why he got me?"

Lieutenant Colonel Paten looked at her with sympathy. "Cadet, I can't speak for the man, so I can't say what that was in his mind then, or now. All I can tell you is that he seemed to do a good job of raising you until we came along and grabbed your life. You were a pretty good person before you became a Gladius."

"I always was a Gladius," Shana said grimly. "Thank Teenie, my nurse, for the rest. She raised me. My so-called father wasn't around all that much."

Shana could feel the anger building in her, like an impending explosion. Her fury at her father, at an uncaring Emperor, at the Victrix that had used her in its own way, was snowballing, piling anger on frustration on pure fury at being lied to and used. Even this whole business of resolving her past was based around a deception.

Sergeant Major Olmeg took a hard look at her face and reached a conclusion. Decurions ran the Corps and this particular decurion was going to salvage what would one day be an excellent officer if things didn't get out of hand. "Attention, Cadet!"

Reflexes took over and Shana snapped out of her chair into rigid attention.

He walked over and growled in her face. "Cadet Ettranty, you are carrying a bit too much steam and I am going to do something about that. You will accompany me to the gym, where we will do three rounds of full contact. You will make the attempt to kick my ass. You will fail, because I will kick your ass instead, but you will make your best attempt. Am I understood?"

"Aye!" Shana popped off. Her military reflexes in full control now.

"After that, Cadet, you will accompany me to the Decurions Club. There you will proceed to get stinking drunk. I am awarding you a twenty four hour pass from OCS to sleep it off after we finish. Any questions?"

"No, Sergeant Major!"

"Very good, Cadet Ettranty. Follow me. Forward at a trot... ho!"

As the pair took off out of the office, Doctor Jandrews grinned then looked at Camille. "Can he do that?"

She smiled. "Olmeg's a Legion Sergeant Major. The Sergeant Major of this legion, in fact. *I'm* certainly not going to stand in his way. That's not the way I'd do it, but she's not a normal female Gladius. I suspect his way will work better than mine would."

#####

Sometime later, two Legionnaire Thirds acting as Club orderlies were watching a packed table with a group of very senior male decurions and a solitary brown haired female Gladius with the collar flash of an OCS cadet. War stories and liquor circulated around the table in abundance.

The rest of the Decurions Club was bustling, too. Over on the dance floor a female decurion was gracefully dancing to the music of a small band, including a deep toned hand beaten drum that had materialized from somewhere, her body sinuously swaying to the heavy beat.

"You know," one said judiciously to the other as they looked at the table loaded with senior decurions and a cadet, "Shana's going to end up blasted before this is over. I've never seen her like this."

The other one shrugged. "You going to argue with them?" He jerked a thumb at the number of stripes and grizzled heads around the table.

The first one grinned. "That's how I ended up with this detail, mate, and clean up duty to boot." He smiled tolerantly at the group. "I expect we'll be carrying Shana back to her quarters, or someone will."

He watched as she finished off one drink, only to have another put in front of her. She waved away the drink, then got up and headed purposefully for the dance floor, empty now that the woman had finished her dance. It was plain that Shana was planning on doing the next one. That was an event, since nobody in the legion had ever seen her dance.

The band started, a slow sway of sound supplemented by an exotic beat at the chorus. Shana picked up the beat with her body, swaying, her hands holding her skirt outward from her sides, each side of the skirt swaying in turn as she paced gracefully forward in time to the music. The chorus started and she released her skirt then kicked forward just enough to make it flow around her outstretched leg. At that point, she extended her arms to one side and began to sway, turn, and whirl with unexpected grace to the flow of the song. It was plain to everyone in the Club that Shana wasn't an experienced dancer, but just as plain that she shared the Gladius love of dancing and music, and - inexperienced or not - she was reading the music with her body with the natural ease of any Gladius. Her improvised movements interpreted the music as joyful and, just as important, as a release. Her dance was a perfect match for the song.

"I've never seen Shana dance before," the first young trooper remarked. "She's pretty damned good, if you ask me. Those moves she makes are a little different from most of the girls I've seen, but I kind of like them."

"Well," his partner said, "what do you expect? She was a recruit. She wasn't born to this like the rest of us goons."

The first one waved the comment away as irrelevant. "Hey," he said, "she's a Gladius, just like we are."

Shana, dance finished, was now back at the table, blushing to the riotous applause from the entire Club, led by the crusty decurions at her table. This time she took the drink and slugged it down.

"Yep," the first trooper said, "she's definitely letting her hair down and getting tanked."

"Well," he continued magnanimously, "she's entitled to have a blow off I suppose, for whatever reason. Does a man good, every once in a while."

"She's not a man," the other said.

"Like any careful observer," the first young trooper answered in a superior manner, "I'd noticed. Of course, I'm not sure a regular girl would go on a bender in the Club with a bunch of senior noncoms. My girlfriend wouldn't. But Shana's different."

"Of course she's different," his friend topped him. "She's our Shana."

CHAPTER 9

LEGIO IX VICTRIX
CAULDWELL

An OCS graduation was usually a somewhat sedate affair. Friends and family normally made up a small audience to watch the cadets receive their pips and become newly minted Second Lieutenants. This one was a little different. One cadet had no family in the audience, but over three thousand members of the Victrix thought it fit that they see her graduate. A number of those brought girlfriends. A smaller number brought wives. Several married couples brought new babies, forcing the ceremony to be held in one of the largest chambers of Victrix base.

In the clear area between the audience and the stage, all twelve members of the graduating class stood in formation. Centered and two paces to the front of the formation was their leader, Cadet Captain Shana Ettranty, standing at perfect attention and wishing the itching under her skirt's waistband and the butterflies in her stomach would go away. She couldn't do anything about the butterflies, but it would have been wonderful to be back in the ranks where she could discreetly scratch without anyone knowing. No such luck. Sometimes rank sucked, thought former Corporal and current Cadet Captain Ettranty. Even in formation, she realized, scratching was out. She was being watched by most of a legion. Sometimes notoriety sucked.

She had been astounded and flattered on being told the graduation was being shifted to the Main Hall because the surviving members of all three original cohorts wanted to see her cross the stage. It was a tiny bit embarrassing, truth be known. Deal with it, girl, she told herself, the guys were family. That's why they were here. Put up with the damned itch.

Shana stared straight ahead like a proper little Cadet but seated in those rows behind her were the members of the Victrix still alive from the day she'd joined. The thought gave her a lump in her throat and that lump only got bigger when she realized she was sensing the original women of the Victrix. She was still their embodiment and they were still with her. Stand proud, girl. Her impish side made her add that soon enough this formation would be over and she could scratch.

Legion Sergeant Major Olmeg stumped to the center of the stage and looked down on the class, favoring each individual with a gimlet eye that promised dire consequences for past sins. More than one individual,

Shana included, ran through a catalog of such past sins at that look. "Cadet Captain," the Sergeant Major growled as he gave her the last order he'd ever be legally entitled to give her, "bring your class to attention and present arms."

Shana did a crisp about face. "Class, Attention-n-n-n... Ho!" she sang out in a parade ground voice. "Present Arm-m-m-m-ms... Ho!"

She spun on her heel to face the stage and her right arm snapped level with her breast, hand flat and palm down, in a salute. She and her class held the salute as the Legate replaced the Sergeant Major.

Legate Athan commanded, "Give your class order arms and parade rest." Then he watched as Shana went through the commands and the formation responded with precision. He smiled to himself. He knew what they were dreading. Well, he had a surprise for them.

"I'm not going to make a long speech, people," he said conversationally, and the smile he was hiding almost broke free as he could see the subtle shifting that showed relief in the class ranks. "I'm just going to tell you a few things you ought to know by now. You are about to be commissioned Second Lieutenants. That means as soon as you attach that pip you will suffer an immediate brain drain and become a danger to all about you."

He noticed Shana wince and decided that little bit of humor was ill chosen. Oops. Well, it wasn't the first mistake he'd made in his life. She'd live. "You men will be assigned troop units where your immediate subordinate will be a decurion. You women have all done your Virgin Mission so you are Exempts. As Exempts, you will be assigned sections within Legion Support Command. Your immediate subordinate in that section will also be a decurion. In some cases, those decurions will have more service time than you have time on two feet. Listen to them, people. A Second Lieutenant is given that rank so he or she can learn by doing. The person teaching you will be your decurion.

"Some of you were pretty good legionnaires." He looked around. "A couple of you were decurions with a little time under your belt. You may think that makes a difference and you won't make the mistakes you all saw Lieutenants make. It won't. You'll make mistakes all your own and your commanders will make you aware of them. Some of those mistakes will be real beauts and will live on in song and story for decades. Your decurion will help you keep from making the worst of them, and if not, try to keep you from making them more than once. That decurion runs your unit or section for you."

He continued, "However, there is one fundamental difference between that decurion, or the decurion that you were, and the centurion

182

that you are about to become. Responsibility. Decurions have authority, people. Centurions have responsibility. You are responsible for the mission, the troopers under you, and for yourself, in that order. As a commissioned officer, you have the power of life and death. And the responsibility. Never forget that."

His lips quirked. The smile was about to break through again. "Now that I've scared hell out of you, we're going to set about making you officers. Cadet Captain, bring your formation to attention. Weapons salute."

Shana gave the commands for weapons salute then joined the class with her arm dagger held point up in front of her face. Instead of returning the salute, the Legate slowly pronounced the commissioning oath, pausing at the end of each line to allow them to echo his words. As she kissed the flat of her dagger blade at the conclusion of her oath, Shana felt a thrill. That was it! She was now an officer! And she knew damn well she wasn't going to screw up like the Legate predicted. She gave the commands to return weapons and parade rest then settled in to wait as names were called and the class crossed the stage one at a time to have their pips attached to their collars. She had a fair wait because the commander was always last to be commissioned. Sometimes rank sucked, she thought, and she still had that itch. The butterflies were gone, though.

When her name was called, she marched up the steps and crossed the stage to halt in the middle and salute the Legate. Normally, a family member or former commander would affix the pip to her collar. She expected to see Captain Lathik, her former commander, because she had no family in the Legion. To her surprise, the Sergeant Major stumped forward to take the pip from the Legate and attach it. "You're doing good, girl," he growled, softly this time. "Don't screw up. I'll be watching." As he did so, the Victrix started cheering. Shana found herself blushing so hard it was difficult for her to maintain her bearing as she saluted the Legate and marched off the stage.

When she reached her position in the formation again, the Legate looked at her - a bit strangely, she thought - and said, "Dismiss the class, Lieutenant."

She spun on her heel and commanded, "Class Dismis-s-s-sed... Ho!"

After that, a somewhat embarrassed Shana found herself receiving congratulations from thousands of men. Truthfully, she didn't mind the crowd. They were her guys, her Legion. The Legion she'd joined as a recruit. The original Victrix.

Up on the stage, the Legate and the Sergeant Major watched as newly minted Second Lieutenant Ettranty was being mobbed. The Sergeant Major turned and this time fixed his gimlet glare on the Legate. "So when are you going to ask her out?" he growled.

The Legate shot Olmeg a deadly look. "Sergeant Major..."

The Sergeant Major broke in. "Bullshit, Legate! I'm shot up. I ain't blind. I see the way you've been looking at her, and I don't blame you. Now that she's commissioned, you've got a chance. Not so much distance between the two of you now and that girl was born to be an officer anyway. I will say you've got a ways to go, because with all Shana's been through, she's kind of forgotten you exist as a man. You need to remind her you're not just a Legate."

Karl Athan looked back at Shana in the center of her mob and stroked his chin. For some odd reason, she was scratching a spot on her waistband. "You have a point, Top. You do have a point. Let's go back to my quarters and have a beer over it."

"Makes sense to me," Sergeant Major Olmeg huffed. "Lead on, Legate."

#####

"Lieutenant Colonel Paten, Lieutenant Ettranty reports." Now that she was commissioned, Shana's next big step was to find out what she was going to be doing. Getting her assignment, in other words. Like everyone else, she'd filled out a dream sheet. Of course, hers was a little different from that of a normal female Gladius. She snorted mentally. Well, she was a little bit different from the normal female Gladius.

Colonel Paten looked up from the hardcopy in her hands, took note of the insignificant being occupying a spot in front of her desk, then went back to something more important. "Have a seat, Lieutenant," she said in conversational tones, still reading. Then she looked up at Shana and asked in those same conversational tones, "Were you drunk when you filled this thing out, or just temporarily insane?"

Shana sat precisely erect, her hands carefully holding her cap in her lap, the cap with its precious new pip instead of a legion crest. "Neither one, Colonel," she said in even, reasonable tones. So far this interview was living up - or down - to expectations. "I was asked to state where I would like to be assigned and I did so."

Camille leaned back in her chair and fixed the very junior single pip Lieutenant in front of her with a searching look. "Every assignment on your list is a combat assignment. Even a Strike platoon, for Lord Above's sake! You have to have a line unit assignment before you can even be considered for Strike. Did you know that?"

"Aye," Shana said with a nod. "I was aware of that. I'm also different from a normal female Gladius and we both know why, Colonel. I like Intelligence, I like being with troops, and I'm very comfortable with the men. I think they're comfortable with me as well and a good decurion will help me there. I want to be out on the cutting edge. I know I have to have a unit first, but Strike's where I want to end up."

"You know you're Exempt," Camille said softly.

Shana nodded again, with a little less military precision. "Aye, but I don't want to be Exempt. If I have to have a desk job, I'll do it, but I'm more at home with the guys and always have been. Even as a reporter, I liked to be out in the field and the rougher the assignment, the better. Maybe my heredity is why, but that's who I am."

She took a deep breath. "Colonel, I feel like I still have a job to do for the Victrix and I'd do it better in the field with troops. I'm grown up enough to understand that means fighting, killing, dying, but I'm not a child. I'm ready for that. I've seen it. I was in civilian clothes for my first battle. I want to be in uniform for my next one."

Camille gave her a very long study. "You come from our ancestral stock, Lieutenant. Back then both sexes fought. I came along after the Corps intentionally changed itself so that some of us wouldn't have to kill. Personally, I think that was a good move. However..."

She made a show of looking at her terminal. "As it happens, I've discussed your request with Colonel Protac, and he tells me First Cohort is willing to give you a try. After I talked to him, he discussed you with his battalion commanders and I understand the meeting was very interesting. It seems they all wanted you. However, I've been told you once stood with Fourth Platoon, Second Century, First Battalion on a very significant day for the Victrix. They appear to remember it and they currently need a Platoon Leader. Fourth Platoon is yours if you want it."

Shana's eyes widened. Did she want it? Did she want it! Lieutenant Colonel Paten was handing her a dream. She was a Gladius woman. An ancestral type of Gladius woman, but still a Gladius woman, just taller, brown haired and a little slimmer. Despite the Corps culture as it was now, she felt that a troop unit was where she fit. "Aye Colonel!" she blurted out. This was more exciting than the day SOC Garua told her she was going to OCS! "I'm ready for my platoon!"

"I wonder if they are ready for you," Camille said in dry tones. "At any rate, Sergeant First Class Steel is in the outer office. You're his child to raise now."

185

Camille touched a sensor. A few seconds later the door opened and a well remembered grizzled decurion entered. The last time Shana saw him, he was drinking her under the table during her alcohol therapy session with the Sergeant Major. He came to precise attention in front of Camille's desk. "Aye, Colonel."

Camille waved her hand. "Sergeant First Class Steel, Lieutenant Ettranty. She's your new platoon leader, Sergeant. Kindly keep her from getting killed or killing someone we don't want dead. Oh, and keep catastrophes to a minimum will you?"

The husky decurion turned as Shana rose and shook the hand she extended. A twinkle in his eye told Shana he also remembered their last meeting. "Nice to see you again, Sergeant Steel," she said.

"And you, Lieutenant," he replied. "Glad to see the pip. The boys are happy to have you, too."

"Wonderfully heartwarming," Camille broke in dryly. "Now out of here, you two. I have a lot of work to try and undo the damage I've just done to the Victrix. I need to get back to it. Dismissed."

In the outer office, Steel told her, "I said the boys are happy to have you, Lieutenant, and I meant it. They're kind of proud, actually. They're waiting for you in the platoon CP. It's not procedure, but the Colonel told me we could meet them first. After that, we have to go meet your commanders from Colonel Protac on down."

He gave her skirt a quizzical look. "Then we draw your equipment. I'm afraid, Lieutenant, you're going to have to draw pants, too. I'm sorry about that, but those will work better than your skirt for our usual duties."

Shana smiled at him. "I wore pants for the first twenty six years of my life, Sergeant. I don't look at them the way another Gladius would. I'll also draw an ax, but I intend to keep my dagger. Lead on."

The Narsim Clarine Femiam was working late, not an uncommon circumstance. The returns from the outlying towns were bothersome. This new Popular Movement for Good Government was going to have more Members in Parliament after the election. They were still a small group, but steadily growing stronger. The most bothersome thing about them was they just weren't susceptible to the usual tactics. So far, money or women or men hadn't been able to buy or suborn one. That was acceptable for a small fringe party, but her projections showed real growth. If things kept up, the PMGG would be a major force inside of a year. They could conceivably control Parliament after the next elections. Absurd, but true.

Clarine sat back away from the light on her desk and rubbed her eyes. Too many late nights. Matic told her time and time again the Movement was simply a small splinter group that could be safely ignored. If they got to be too much trouble, he had ways of handling them. Maybe he did. She wasn't sure she really wanted to know those ways. Put that sort of thing out of her mind. That was always the path to survival on Central, and now her survival instinct was telling her it was the only way to survive here.

No. It couldn't be. This was Cauldwell and it was nothing like Central. Was it? The thought disturbed her and she quashed it. Instead, she started wondering if Matic was suffering from good old fashioned hubris. The plain fact was the Movement was something she worried about - something she *could* worry about - and her damn fool cousin wasn't worried. That was a problem.

She sighed as she thought about another problem. Lana. The girl was running wild. The tridio celebrity shows were full of her. "Glamorous party girl" was one of their favorite descriptions. What the hell was she doing spending all her time in the spotlight and the party circuit? Granted, most of her circle was just like her, but Clarine had tried her best to raise Lana to be better than that. What was she going to do with her?

The Narsim's worries and meditations were disturbed by a movement in the outer office and the overhead lights coming on. It was a member of the cleaning crew. Was it really that late? The cleaning woman, a short frumpy type, gave her a startled look and started to apologize. Clarine waved it away. "No, it's time I was going. You go ahead with your job."

As she left, she was still worried about Lana. The cleaning woman watched Clarine go then casually scanned the documents on the desk before she went about straightening up the office. Everything else was taken care of by the bug in the Narsim's computer terminal.

#####

Lana had finally had enough. The party was its usual glittering, noisy, actively swirling self as men and women circulated, linked up, and then went to other expensively and provocatively dressed partners. Lana looked around and realized she was probably the only one here not drunk or drugged. Looking at the whole scene with sober eyes, she felt disgusted. Ever since her mother joined Ettranty, she'd been left alone. The social whirl was fun for a while then it started to get to her.

Like tonight. She should go home.

Her mother was showing signs of strain lately and there were things she didn't talk about. Well, how could she if her daughter wasn't around to lend an ear? Lana suddenly felt guilty about that. Maybe it was time to mend fences. Jamie wasn't around for them to fight about and there really was something bothering her mother. Mother needed someone to support her. The two of them had come this far together and it looked like they still had a way to go. Go home. Try to be a daughter again instead of an air headed glamour girl.

She took a lift tube down to the ground floor and walked outside the building. Looking up, she decided it was a nice night. She felt like walking for a while. She walked a few blocks then stopped just outside a park. There was a scuffling noise in the bushes behind her, but she tactfully ignored it. Probably a couple having sex.

Thinking for a moment, she decided she'd walked far enough. She tapped her earphone and touched keys on the virtual keyboard when it appeared, dialing a robo cab. With no other thought but home and bed, she got in the cab when it arrived and was lifted up into the Beauregard traffic lanes.

Back in the bushes, a large muscular man crouched over the fallen body of another man, smaller and more raggedly dressed. The ragged man's knife was lying on the ground next to his body. The body's spine and neck were twisted at impossible angles.

A second man walked quietly out of the dark and joined the first. "What in hell did that dumass bimbo think, walking around the park after dark?"

The first man's shrug was perceptible if you had excellent night sight. Both did. "The Rhiannonithi saved her ass the first time, now it looks like the Victrix gotta keep doing it. The Lieutenant would go ripshit if we let anything happen to her. You know officers. They don't need a reason. Anyhow, she's on her way home now."

The second man grunted. "Good enough. So's her mother. That's why I went looking for LF and found you with your friend. Need help with the trash, mate?"

The first said, "Nope. I'll use one of my incendiary capsules. Put him down on the walkway inside the park so nothing shows burn marks. A few seconds and you'll need to have a molecular tracer to know he was here and I don't think anybody will ever want to know where this asshole went, anyhow. They won't miss the creep."

"Then I'm outta here," the second one said. "See you back at the house."

188

"Later," the first replied laconically then hefted the mugger's body. He had to get rid of it then he was off for the night. Just another wonderful day in the Corps.

Morning formation was over. Instead of turning her brand new platoon over to Sergeant Steel for the day's planned activities the way she normally would, Shana waited until the rest of the century was dismissed to training. Then she faced her twenty troops. Nineteen looked curious. Sergeant Steel looked like her was expecting something to happen. Well, he was right. She was going to make it happen. "All right, people, we have a little change for today. I have a surprise for you.

"Right fa-a-a-ce, ho! Forward marc-c-c-ch, ho! Quick time!"

As the pace sped up, Shana jogged to the head of the formation. "Double time, ho! Guide on me!"

The platoon sped up into a run as they matched their pace to hers and followed as she twisted and turned through corridors and down ramps until they were in one of the huge underground drill halls. This one had target dummies scattered through it at irregular intervals. Coming into the open area, Shana didn't slow her pace. Instead, she yelled, "We're going to take the blade range today. Swords!"

Every man's short sword snapped into his hand the same way her dagger flew into hers. As they ran onto the course, Shana yelled, "Combat formation... Weave!"

The platoon spread out at a dead run, breaking into three person teams, seven of them. The teams began the Gladius interlacing movement that was so confusing - and deadly - to an enemy, a constantly interweaving formation of teams that flowed onto the course. As each man passed a target, he threw his sword at a small lighted dot just below the neck of the dummy. The swords - and one dagger - drove into the target at varying small distances from the dot then flew back to their owners.

Shana took them through the course twice and looped the platoon around in some dead space at the end. "Axes," she commanded as they ran. "We'll do it again." This time her new ax was in her hand. As they flowed back through the course, the axes went out.

After the second run with axes, Shana called, "Reform... Quick time... Platoon, halt. Get the results, Sergeant First Class Steel."

He looked up at the holographic scoreboard over their heads and announced, "Ninety seven percent composite, Lieutenant."

"And mine?"

He checked the icons listed below the overall score. "Yours was ninety eight percent with the dagger, Lieutenant. Ninety six with the ax."

"Thank you, Sergeant Steel.   You may take charge of the formation and return the platoon to its assigned duties."

Instead of personally taking charge, he turned the platoon over to Staff Sergeant Amos, the senior squad leader. He waited until the men were gone then walked over to his platoon leader. "Would the Lieutenant kindly inform the Sergeant as to what this exercise was in aid of?"

Shana was happy with the way her platoon had performed, and quite proud, in fact, of her own accuracy. However, she had enough experience as a ranker to know that when a senior decurion spoke to an officer in the third person it was a sign the officer had just shot her foot completely off, with possible catastrophic consequences. That deflated her pride. "I was giving a demonstration, Sergeant. I'm the platoon leader, but I'm a woman. I wanted to show the men I could do the job as well as they could."

Sergeant First Class Steel nodded judiciously. "I see, Lieutenant. An excellent way to make your point. Perhaps it needed making. I also see you reserved the range, since we're the only ones here. May I ask if you discussed your plans with the Captain prior to this little change to the century training schedule for today?"

Shana began to get that sinking feeling that said "You just screwed up". She rallied gamely. "Sergeant, I checked the schedule and there was only weapons and equipment maintenance on it for today."

"Which we will still have to perform to standard, Lieutenant. It's also very, very necessary since we're betting our lives on that equipment. Having lost nearly two hours at this drill, the platoon will have to work several hours overtime to make it up."

By now Shana was red faced with embarrassment at the way her little gesture had backfired. Just to make things worse, Sergeant Steel added, "Can the Lieutenant think of what Captain Samson might have to say when he discovers that you've made an unauthorized change to the training schedule of one quarter of his century?"

The Lieutenant could, in fact, imagine just that. The sinking feeling hit bottom with a thud. "I'd better go see the Captain, hadn't I?"

Sergeant First Class Steel favored his brand new single pip Lieutenant with the sort of glare one gives a puppy that's just crapped on the carpet. "The Sergeant would suggest the Lieutenant do just that. As soon as possible."

Shana resisted the powerful urge to snap to attention. "I'll be on my way, Sergeant. Uh, return to the platoon. I'll be back with you as soon as the Captain's finished."

Sergeant Steel relented enough to nod grim faced approval. Then he added before his new officer could head for the Century CP at a dead run, "Two points, Lieutenant. First, keep in mind it's easier to get forgiveness than permission, so you'll probably survive what's coming. It's what you richly deserve, but I expect you'll survive it. Second, talk over any more brainstorms with your senior decurion. That last precaution might avoid your next ass chewing."

Shana nearly came to attention this time. "Aye, Sergeant First Class. Can I go?"

Sergeant Steel didn't bat an eye. "Dismissed, Lieutenant. And I'm supposed to be the one asking you." He watched her head off at top speed, smiling slightly.

#####

The smiles, grins and laughter were much more in evidence over beers in the Legion Sergeant Major's quarters later. "What did Samson do with her?" that worthy asked.

Steel grinned again. "Took a long bloody strip off her then had some real revenge. She's now the Century Training Officer. Schedules and lesson plans, among other things."

The Sergeant Major winced. "Ouch! The only job worse is weapons inventories."

"She's got that one, too. At least until Lieutenant Tobias comes back from detached duty and goes back to being Supply Officer."

The five very senior decurions sitting around the room all laughed. Taking a swig from his beer bottle, the Sergeant Major shook his head. "Well, she'll learn. Make sure the Training Decurion doesn't go all dumb with her. She still has other things to do."

Steel smiled. "Oh, she'll learn. Fast, I think. And Staff Sergeant Sheen won't dump it all on her. He'd better not. Besides, I think she'd catch on to him even if I didn't. She's good, but she needs trimming down every once in a while, like any single pip.

"Actually, running the blade combat course was a pretty good idea. The boys liked her, but they still saw her as something like a sister instead of an officer. That could have been distracting. For one thing, they might have been more concerned with protecting her in a fight than doing their jobs. I think she's succeeded in killing that notion."

The Sergeant Major nodded. "Double hit. Taught your platoon something and taught herself something at the same time. She and the boys will remember this morning."

191

Thinking about his now very chastened brand new Lieutenant, Steel nodded as he took a swig of beer. He also thought about the way the men were now a lot more normal around her, less like they were walking on eggs. "Oh, I can guarantee both parties will remember today. Better now than when we take on the Emperor. She'll be a good one by that time."

From the depths of his long experience, the Sergeant Major voiced another piece of decurion wisdom. "Lord Above, what single pips won't do."

He held up his bottle in wry salute. "Bless the children."

"Bless the children." All of them held up their bottles in reply then broke into laughter.

#####

Shana stretched out long bare legs and lay back in the pool lounger to relax. Like everyone else around the huge base pool, she was clad only in her issue khaki swimsuit. Admittedly, the one-piece suit covered more of her than the tiny bits of cloth or the body paint she used to wear at various private pools in Beauregard, but she liked the way the suit showed her figure. Chalk it up to two years with the Victrix.

She liked the short swimming trunks issued to the men even more, since they covered less. The guys were all around two measures in height, plus or minus, and in superb condition. Made for great eye candy. She reflected that the Corps considered the pool, by custom, as a rank free zone where the usual restrictions were off. A pretty good safety valve for people that led such structured lives. Like she now led.

She sighed. However, there was one problem. Eye candy or not, the guys all knew her and considered her just one of the boys, or maybe a sister. Dammit. It had been a while. Imin was her last man, and that was over two years ago. Dammit, again.

May as well lie back, drink some beer and read like she'd been doing for the last couple of hours. That was what she was here for, anyhow. After her first enervating week with her own command, she needed the break Down Days One and Two gave her - another Corps safety valve.

Still, it would be nice to spend it with a guy. Not one of the kids, but a man her own age or older, maybe. Someone with a little grown up experience.

She heard someone call her name and looked around. It was Tonya Whelk, another single pip from her OCS class, with three other

192

girls, all in their own swimsuits. "Hiya, tall and flat," Tonya said with a grin as she waltzed up and plopped on the lounger next to her.

The other three found chairs and composed themselves in a variety of comfortable postures around her. It looked like her solitary pool relaxation was over for the immediate future and she was at the center of a small crowd. Oh well.

Shana sniffed in a superior manner. "Listen you, I'll have you know your horizontal measurements are the same as mine. I was merely blessed with twenty or so more vertical centimeasures so as to put all my dimensions into proper proportion. Introduce me, short stuff."

Tonya grinned again and waved at the other three. "Julie Dass, Bett Whate, and Tana Reed. Good friends of mine."

"We all wanted to meet you," Tana popped up in chirpy tones. She leaned forward with an eager expression. "What's it like commanding all those men?"

"Tana!" Julie scolded. She shook her head and smiled at Shana in a friendly fashion. "Ignore her. She just has one thing on her mind."

"Hey!" Tana said in aggrieved tones. "You transferred here for the same reason I did. All these unattached guys."

Julie blew out a disgusted breath. "Tana, some of us can say two sentences without mentioning men. I also came here because they were rebuilding Support Command. That's a pretty good opportunity in anyone's book."

Bett smiled and piped up, "Listen to Mother and behave, Tana!" She also smiled at Shana. "I'm also happy to meet you, by the way, and no, I'm not as salacious as Tana."

Shana smiled back. "Well," she said in conspiratorial tones, "I can tell you the boys think about girls the same way girls think about boys. More so, actually."

"They do?" Tana lit up like a searchlight. Julie shook her head sadly at Tana again and favored Shana with a "What can you do?" expression.

Shana found herself enjoying the rapid fire back and forth, not to mention the laughter and occasional giggle from Tana or Bett. Girl talk like this was fun and comfortable. She joined in, shooting lines at all four and catching a few zingers in reply. "Hey," Bett finally said, "we're doing all this talking and I'm totally without a beer. Who goes?"

Julie said, "You brought it up - you go get 'em. Besides, it's your turn to buy. Canteen's on the other side of the pool, girl." Julie was apparently the group's unofficial leader, judging from the "Mother" crack. She was also a little older than the other three, nearly Shana's age. From her look, she also had a fair degree of common sense and maturity. Shana decided she'd like to know her better.

Bett was back shortly, carrying three beer bottles. Three more were carried by a young male Gladius about her age wearing a big grin. Bett distributed bottles to the four women in the chairs then waved cheerily. "So long, guys. Got a swim date. Don't wait up."

Tana pouted as the two strolled off. "Some people have all the luck. I should have gone for the beer."

"Tana," Julie said ominously, "if you don't cool down, I'm going to pour this beer on you."

"Don't waste it!" Shana and Tonya both cried then laughed at Tana and Julie's expressions. Shana continued, "We'll just toss her in the pool, I'm sure someone will rescue her."

Tana brightened. "Hey, that's an idea."

That broke everyone up again and they settled down for a good gossip/talk session. After a few minutes, Julie left Tana and Tonya to their own conversation, took a sip of beer, and asked Shana, "Seriously, girl, what in the Lord Above's Name made you want a combat command?"

Shana took a drink of her own beer and shrugged. "It was something I wanted, and I thought I could do it. It's only been a week, but things seem to be working out."

After a really painful ass chewing, she thought. She'd learned from that little goof. She wasn't ready to discuss the effect her ancestry had on wanting a combat command just yet, either. On the other hand, Julie looked like someone she could talk to once they got to know each other better.

Julie shook her head. "Must be because you're a recruit, not born to the Corps. Of course, I've noticed the boys treat you differently than the way they treat the rest of us girls. I guess that makes it easier."

Shana made a face. "That makes it easier to command a platoon, all right." She sighed. "On the other hand, I wouldn't mind it if someone not under my command happened to notice I'm a woman."

Julie nodded in an understanding fashion. "Amen. After I got over losing my first husband, I spent a while wishing someone would realize I was more than a widow. I know widowhood is something that happens to most women in the Corps, but I was ready to start over. I just couldn't find the right guy. That really was one reason I came to the Victrix. I just don't want Tana to broadcast it." She grinned. "The hunting's great here. I'll bet you find a guy soon enough."

Shana's reply was lost when Tana said in an urgent, low voice, "Hey guys, look on the other side of the pool. That's the Legate! You know, he's not half bad looking."

194

Shana looked where the girl was indicating with a nod of her chin. It was Legate Athan, all right. He was just as toned as his men, a fact made obvious by the lack of any clothing but his swim trunks. A few more scars than most, clean limbed and muscular, older than Imin, but there was a big difference between the two. The Legate had the confident, easy air of a man that was mature enough to know himself and comfortable with the fact. Imin was missing that confidence. In fact, Imin was kind of juvenile in some ways. Shana considered the Legate's confidence very sexy. Looking at him as a man for the first time, she found him extremely attractive. Tana was right, he wasn't half bad looking.

But he was the Legate! On the other hand, there wasn't any rank at the pool, was there? She also thought of what Sergeant Steel said to her. It was easier to get forgiveness than permission. Why not? Why the hell not? She had a few other thoughts in that mode as she watched him stride easily over to the canteen's poolside bar.

Suiting action to thought before she could chicken out, Shana put down her empty beer bottle and got up. "Guys," she said, "I think I need another beer."

Julie was following Shana's intent look, and apparently her thoughts. "Go for it, girl."

Then she bounced up out of her chair and grabbed Shana's arm. "If you don't tell me everything later I'll kill you," Julie whispered fiercely. Then, just as fiercely, "Good luck."

As Shana walked around the pool to the canteen on the other side, her body language underwent a subtle change. Her normal military carriage and pace shifted to become a soft swaying stroll and anyone looking at her could see that here was a sophisticated, graceful, mature woman. Sexy as hell, too.

She was certainly eye catching. The trooper detailed as canteen orderly glanced at Shana and froze for an instant. He was brought back to earth by a snarl. "Get your mind back on what you're doing, Legionnaire. Leave officers to their own business. Yours is getting the beer."

The look from the senior decurion was enough for the trooper. He went back to work with a will. Having cleared up minor distractions, the selfsame senior decurion also glanced as Shana's approach, registered mental approval, and leaned against the bar to drink his beer.

Legate Karl Athan was wondering what in hell he was doing at the pool, other than following the Sergeant Major's "suggestion". Pretty good suggestion, actually. He was working too hard lately, knew it, and coming here was a good way to clear his mind. This business about the Waltin incursion on Labatt, for instance. They were sending a whole brigade of the new Frontier Cluster troops to handle it, but that unit was unseasoned and needed a little backup for that kind of fight. Those crabs were hard to dig out once they got on the ground.

For a moment, Karl idly wondered if this was the wave of the future. The Empire was falling apart and wolves were gathering to tear into the pieces. Something had to be done about that and the SOC was doing it. Orders were on the way and he was pretty sure what they said. The Valeria was tied up supporting the exploration effort and the other three legions had subversion teams scattered damn near everywhere between the Frontier Cluster and Central. That left the Victrix, which was currently underutilized. He had some contingency planning to do.

His worries dissipated when he became aware of Shana's approach. She suddenly had his full attention, but he tried not to show it. It wouldn't do for his troops to see him goggle eyed. Grace, beauty, sensuality, and someone a little more grown up than most, single pip or not. Shana Ettranty, Karl decided, was a hell of an attractive woman. Not a girl, a woman. He turned away to face directly at the back of the bar, trying to figure out how to make an opening move and still maintain a cool detached appearance.

"A beer, please, orderly," a soft voice said at Karl's elbow. He turned to look at the voice's owner and found himself not making eye contact. Out of habit, he was looking at the usual height for a Gladius woman, but Shana was a good bit taller. Well above his chin, in fact. Very interesting. So was the sight he'd glimpsed prior to raising his eyes. Shana was very nicely constructed, if a bit tall.

"So, Lieutenant Ettranty," Karl opened the conversation as was his right, "how has your first week been with your platoon?" Keep it on professional matters for the opening moves.

She gave him the relaxed easy smile of a woman that knew precisely what she was doing. "Challenging, Legate. Fun in spots, too. I'm enjoying this assignment and looking forward to when we get the chance for a full exercise."

Karl reminded himself Shana was old enough to know how the game was played and mature enough to enjoy it. That was interesting and attractive. She was really a very exciting woman that knew exactly what was going on here... and apparently quite willing to help it along. He sipped his beer and judiciously replied, "Well, we're looking at a plan to ship a cohort at a time off planet for full field training. You'll be getting your exercise soon enough." Too late, he realized that last sentence could be taken several ways and winced, mentally.

Shana gracefully let him off the hook. "I'll be happy to get the boys out in the field, Legate," she said with just enough warmth in her smile to show she registered his slip but wasn't reading anything special into it. "It's where I'd like to be, anyway."

Karl nodded, and they both smiled at each other for a few seconds, saying nothing. He broke the silence. "Shana, I think you can call me Karl when we're both off duty. I've been around a bit too much for tap dancing and I think you're past kid games too. Shall we cut to the chase?"

Shana looked thoughtful for a moment. The offer of a first name had definite meaning among Gladii, one that meant they were headed to the next level. Then she grinned. "I've just realized I know how that expression is used, but not it's literal meaning. I'm a former journalist. I ought to know. Anyhow, Karl, I do believe you're right."

Karl snorted. "Shana, you wouldn't believe how old it is, or where it came from in the first place. We use a lot of ancient odds and ends in the Corps."

He took a sip of beer and looked at her over the bottle. "I have to get back to the office, unfortunately. A dragon's arrived and I have to slay it. Can I buy you dinner at the Club tonight?"

Her smile was pleasant and knowing. He was right, she was past kid games. "I have friends here I should get back to, if you have to leave."

She reached out and gently laid a hand on his bare arm. His skin tingled. "I think I'd like to have dinner with you. I also think I'd like to get to know you well. Meet you at twenty hours?"

He nodded. "The time sounds right to me. I'll see you there."

She nodded and strolled casually back to her new friends. Karl's eyes followed her, taking real enjoyment in her swaying walk and the flex and roll under the thin material of her swimsuit, not to mention the smooth muscle movements in bare areas like her back and legs. The whole picture was stunning and he was pretty sure Shana knew it. Finally, he had to let his breath out in a silent whoosh. That was quite a woman, single pip or not. The interesting thing, he thought as he finished his beer, was they both had a mature attitude about the world. That maturity made her damnably attractive. Of course it helped that she was a knockout, but the intangibles were really what attracted him.

He put down his empty beer and headed for the dressing room. Best get to work. He had an appointment tonight he definitely had to keep.

The senior decurion at the other end of the bar simply nodded in satisfaction as the Legate left to slay his dragon. "Get me another beer," he told the orderly.

He turned casually to look across the pool as Shana collapsed limply into her lounger with a slightly stunned look, to be besieged by the other three girls and bombarded with questions. His smile was a little sparse, but genuine. Like the Sergeant Major said, the girl's doing good.

CHAPTER 10

LEGIO IX VICTRIX
CAULDWELL

Morning formation on Duty Day One felt pretty good to Shana. Before taking command, she was always someone in the ranks. Now she was in front of her own platoon as the commander. She was a real commissioned officer, too, not a cadet appointed to lead other cadets. Great feeling. She was going into her second week with her platoon and she wondered if the thrill would ever wear off. She hoped not.

She had a typical commander's problem this morning to offset her good feeling, but it was something she could handle. Just before the formation, Sergeant Steel told her that her three youngest troopers, Kardo, Chofal, and Smythe, were in the guardhouse again. Something she'd also been told was a regular occurance. Now she had to figure out what she wanted to do with the three habitual Duty Day One headaches. Shana was determined she wouldn't be transferring any troopers for disciplinary reasons. Let someone else do that. She wanted a perfect record.

In a way, it was comforting to get back into military routine after what turned into a wonderful, if enervating, weekend - a wonderful enervating weekend spent in Karl Athan's quarters. She even made dinner on Down Day Two and her cooking was a nice surprise for Karl. So was the fact she was only wearing one of his uniform shirts while working in the little kitchen. Returning to her own quarters for Make and Mend that evening was relaxing in its own way. She was back in her own space and didn't have the usual blahs that went with Down Day Two's late afternoon and early evening. There was another date with Karl to look forward to next weekend as well. On the whole, looking at the mixture of platoon, guardhouse warriors, and new boyfriend, Shana decided she was happy.

She saluted when the Captain dismissed the formation then turned to Sergeant Steel. "Sergeant, will you get my three wayward children and bring them to the Platoon CP? I want to have a talk with them."

"You sure you don't want to have me handle the problem, Lieutenant?" His tone said it wasn't a test, simply a question.

She shook her head. "I've been told those three are ending up in the guardhouse on a regular basis. I want to know why."

Sergeant Steel had a mildly disgusted look. "That's easy, Lieutenant. They're the youngest qualified troopers in the Legion. They're transfers from the Rhiannonithi, recruits that had their Virgin Mission years too early, and Smythe's two years younger than the other two. He tries to act about five years older than he is, gets drunk and gets in fights when someone rags him. Kardo and Chofal get into it on his side and all three usually end up in front of the Captain afterwards."

Shana sighed. "I saw how young they were when I took command. Well, they're mine now. Let me see if I can stop that."

Sergeant Steel saluted smartly. "Aye, Lieutenant. I'll go get them."

As Shana turned away, the Captain stopped her. "Shana, Lieutenant Colonel Paten wants to see you this morning."

Shana said, "Aye, Captain. Have I got any time before the appointment? You know I've got three of mine coming out of the guardhouse. I want deal with that as soon as possible."

Captain Samson grimaced. "Kardo, Chofal, and Smythe. If you can keep those characters from in front of my desk, Shana, you'll be doing me a service. Take care of them first. Colonel Paten didn't say you had to be there bright and early. From what I've been told, it didn't seem urgent."

"Aye." She saluted and went off to the CP to handle her first problem children. Part of the job... and it was a job she was hugely enjoying.

#####

Shana was sitting behind her desk in the little room designated as Fourth Platoon's CP when Sergeant Steel knocked on the door frame. "Come," she said in a flat, firm voice that said she was The Boss.

"In, all of you," Sergeant Steel said to the troopers following him. "In front of the Lieutenant's desk, and smartly."

Once the three Gladii were lined up in front of her in something approaching a position of attention, Shana took the time to look them over carefully. They were dirty, disheveled, banged up, and Chofal was sporting a beautiful shiner. Sergeant Steel was holding their weapons belts, since those had been confiscated by the guardhouse detail. "You're in front of me instead of the Captain because I said I'd handle the problem," she said in a calm, even tone.

Smythe looked relieved at that announcement, but Chofal and Kardo appeared a little uneasy. All three suddenly looked very nervous when the Lieutenant rose from behind her desk and started walking down their line, examining each of them slowly up and down as she passed. Chofal began looking very worried. Shana imagined he preferred standing in front of Captain Samson and getting his ass chewed as usual.

200

Shana stopped before the oldest of the three. "Legionnaire Second Class Kardo, how many times have you made Legionnaire Third Class?" Her question was in a quiet conversational voice. Kardo also got a very worried look.

"Twice, Lieutenant," he popped, facing straight ahead at attention.

"Twice," Shana said musingly. "And I suppose you other two have had similar up and down trips."

She stopped in the middle of the line, hands behind her back, and surveyed them again with nothing more than scientific interest. "People, that stops now," she said in firm, even, professional tones. "You are members of Fourth Platoon, and I expect you to act as members of Fourth Platoon. Fourth Platoon, my platoon, is a team in the real sense of the word. Since you three don't understand teamwork, you will have to learn it from the ground up."

She reached out and popped the adhesive field on each trooper's rank numbers with a thumbnail, leaving all of them with bare collars. In essence, they were now Recruits. "You no longer have any rank, people. Not in Fourth Platoon. What you get from here on in, you will have to earn, and you will have to prove to me you deserve it. When you prove yourselves members of my platoon I will return your rank. Not before. That means your performance on duty and your conduct off duty will have to be to my standards. I don't care what you did before I took over. Your past is cleared in my book. All I care about is what you do from this day on. You perform and keep your noses clean, you can have these back and become human again. Another episode like this weekend and you're out of here with your records marked as failures. I wouldn't like that, but I'm a realist. There's always someone unable to do a combat job. You three may fall into that category."

She crossed her arms and gave them another long measuring look. "Personally, I believe you three have potential, or I'd be in the process of finding you new homes in Buildings and Grounds section... in separate legions."

Smythe looked like he was ready to cry. "Lieutenant," he popped, "permission to speak." Shana nodded. "Lieutenant, it was my fault. I started the fight."

Shana walked over and stood directly in front of him. He was still in his mid-teens and not yet at his full growth. She was almost his height, and the experience of standing at attention and looking a female officer in the eye was unnerving to him. "I don't really care, Legionnaire Smythe. You don't seem to understand, so I will make myself clear to you. You are in my platoon. Whatever we do, we do as a platoon. We all stand together. If we do something right, we all share the credit. If we make the kind of royal mistake you three made, it reflects on all of us. Not just you, Legionnaire.

She bored into his eyes. "Understand something else, Legionnaire Smythe. Being a man doesn't mean belting some jackass when he makes fun of you. It means showing the guts to take whatever the fool says, ignore it, and keep moving on. There will be times when you can't ignore something, but your response will be as part of my platoon, not as three youngsters not mature enough to understand when you're just being hazed to get a response. I expect you to grow up, Legionnaire. You've proved you can perform in combat. I expect you to perform on and off duty with that same confidence in the future. I also know full well that you can do just that if you put your mind to it. I expect you to put away small things and become a man, something you are perfectly capable of doing. Do you understand me, Legionnaire?"

Smythe replied, "Aye, Lieutenant." He looked thoughtful.

Shana nodded. "Very good. Currently, Legionnaire Smythe, you are assigned to Corporal Izzak's team as second man. You are no longer in that position. As of right now, Legionnaire Olsn will take your place and you are the third man in my team. I expect you to watch my back in the next fight. Can you do that?"

Smythe suddenly became ramrod straight. "Aye, Lieutenant. I won't let you down."

Shana stepped back. "I know you won't."

She stood and gave each of them a long measuring look. "People, I decided I was going to give you a fresh start and one chance. This is it. No punishment tours or anything else. I've started you three at the bottom again. It's up to you to work your way up. Perform like men or fall on your face like boys. Your decision.

"Whatever it is, understand that you're part of my platoon, and I'm not going to let the Captain or anyone else do whatever needs to be done in your case. You're my responsibility and I will do what's required."

She turned to Sergeant Steel. "They're yours now, Sergeant. Bring them back to me when they earn their rank again. Also, inform Izzak and Olsn of the switch then tell the First Sergeant about their missing numbers. I don't want them catching any hostile fire about bare collars."

She leaned over and spoke softly in his ear. "I also want you to have a decurion's meeting as soon as possible. This is the last time I see one of my men without every decurion in his chain along with him. I want all my decurions to understand I want problems identified and handled at the lowest level possible and that they are accountable for their men's performance. I'm not happy with Izzak right now. He should have been involved with Smythe long ago. Make sure he knows it."

They broke apart and Sergeant Steel came to attention. "Aye, Lieutenant. I'll take care of everything."

Outside the CP, Kardo spoke to the sergeant as he handed back their weapons belts. "Sergeant Steel, Lieutenant Ettranty's scary. I've never had my ass chewed that bad without someone swearing a lot. And she didn't say much, either."

Sergeant Steel eyed him with only a mild glare. He'd caught a part of that ass chewing, the part about decurion responsibility, and it smarted. The fact that he deserved it smarted worse. "She didn't have to, Legionnaire. She has your numbers in her desk, too. Right now, you three are Recruits again until you prove you can be troopers in her platoon. All I have to say is you better try hard to earn them back. Stop looking for trouble in the Club. If it finds you, well, my guess is a few of the boys will be around somewhere. They'll help you out, but not if you start it. If you start it, your asses are out of here. The Lieutenant meant that."

"No worry, Sergeant," Smythe said proudly. "I gotta stay in the platoon if I'm going to be covering the Lieutenant's back."

Sergeant Steel nodded. "Aye. Now you three go get cleaned up and report to your squads. Dismissed."

As he watched the youngsters head off, Sergeant Steel nodded in satisfaction. The Lieutenant started last week by screwing up royally. She'd made a better beginning of this week. He was pretty sure the trio had seen the last of the guardhouse. Now he had to go have a few appropriate words with the platoon's decurions regarding accountability, and that was another good move by his single pip. He should have demanded decurion accountability, particularly regarding those three, himself. It shouldn't have taken a single pip to remind him.

Despite smarting from his lapse, he smiled. The jury was still out on Lieutenant Ettranty, but it looked like she was shaping up okay.

#####

Shana knocked at Lieutenant Colonel Paten's door frame, much less apprehensive than the last few times in her office.

"Come." Colonel Paten looked at her with a reasonably welcoming glance and added. "Close the door and have a seat, Lieutenant."

Shana gave her a stricken look. "I'm not going to lose my platoon, Colonel," she blurted, "am I?"

Camille chuckled and shook her head. Everyone always assumes a closed door session is bad. "No, Lieutenant, nothing like that. In fact, we simply need to have a private discussion. No real problems, so please be at ease."

Shana nodded with a bit of residual suspicion, closed the door, and seated herself gingerly. "Aye, Colonel."

Camille leaned forward in her chair and rested her clasped hands on her desk. "Captain Samson said you would be a bit late because of a problem in your platoon that needed action. Did you get it resolved?"

Shana had to smile. "You know the egos of teenaged males?"

Camille rolled her eyes. "And male egos in general. That was the problem?"

"Not completely," Shana said, "but that was how I attacked the situation." Briefly, she explained about Kardo, Chofal, and Smythe and their latest misadventure. "The real problem was Smythe. He became combat qualified far too young and was put in a unit way too early. I understand why, but the boy still had to live with it and his two friends would back him up when he got into trouble trying to act older than he was."

"What did you do?"

"First, I pulled their rank and told them they were Recruits as far as the platoon was concerned. Then I told them they had to earn their rank back by acting as men."

Camille rubbed her chin and looked thoughtful. "You don't actually have that authority, you know."

Shana nodded. "I know, Colonel, but they didn't. I also told them I was going to transfer them to separate legions if this behavior continued, and I really can't do that either. In both cases, I know all I can really do is forward a recommendation, but I wanted them to think I could do it immediately if they screwed up again. I wanted their attention and those two moves got it. I don't expect any problems with their informal reductions within the century, and those three troopers are so closely tied that the threat to split them up is a fate worse than death to them. Sergeant Steel and the First Sergeant will make sure the decurions back up what I did and I think Captain Samson will support me if I manage to keep my three troublemakers from in front of his desk.

"Bare collars and embarrassment will keep those three out of the Club until they get their rank back, so that opportunity to screw up is gone for the moment. Then I challenged them to behave like grown men. Smythe's still in his mid-teens, so he took that particular challenge to heart.

"I transferred Smythe to my combat team and gave him the job of protecting me in a fight. Telling him to watch my back gives him his first adult responsibility and will keep him under my eye when we do have an engagement. Judging from his response, I think he'll do anything to keep that position, including stay out of trouble. He's not actually a bad trooper, just immature. The other two got into fights supporting him, so they really weren't the problem. I just had to challenge Smythe to grow up. Hopefully, ego and the challenge to show he's worthy to be called a man will do the rest."

Camille nodded judiciously. "Good job. I hope it works, and I think it will. It sounds like you're doing the right things. Keep it up and I may start to believe you actually do belong in a combat command."

Her expression got a good bit softer. "Shana, the reason I asked you here is because you don't have parents in the Legion, especially a mother."

Shana looked a bit surprised. Hadn't they already been over that? "Colonel?"

Camille waved her hand. "Oh, I'm not talking about that ancestry thing. This is about stuff you don't know and need to. The kind of information a normal Gladius learns from her family growing up." Shana looked confused.

"Specifically," Camille continued, "the fact that you are now romantically involved with the Legate."

Shana sat up rigidly and her jaw jutted out in the Gladius fighting expression. "Colonel, that will not affect my duty performance."

"If I thought it would," Camille said dryly, "we'd be having a different discussion."

Then she relaxed again. "It's just fallen my lot to explain a few things to you that you probably don't know. Please hear me out.

"You may not know this, Shana, but other militaries - like Cauldwell's - have rules and regulations that would prohibit such liaisons as you and the Legate, for what the Corps considers non-reasons. In other military organizations, those rules are designed to thwart nepotism or reluctance to place the beloved party in danger. Some military forces even prohibit members of the same family serving in the same unit.

"You know a Gladius is born and grows up in the Corps. In effect, we're all one extended family. A full strength legion has over twenty thousand men and women in it, but combat casualties progressively reduce the number of available men for a woman as she grows older. In some legions, there aren't enough available men for the women in any case. That was why we got so many enthusiastic female transfers from other legions."

Thinking of Julie, Shana nodded.

"For those and other reasons, romantic relationships aren't prohibited between differing ranks. There simply aren't enough men in the family for that luxury. The only exception is between members of the first two levels of the chain of command. If you and Captain Samson had fallen for each other, for instance, you'd be on your way to a new century in a new battalion, but that would be it. By the way, I'd regret you being moved to another platoon. From the sound of it, you have a handle on your men."

Camille took a deep breath and sat back in her chair. "Gladii don't engage in nepotism in their duty decisions, either. It's something we just don't do. I want you to understand that. A Gladius on duty sees the uniform and not the person. It's the way we are raised and conditioned."

Shana noticed the Colonel was using Unispek when she said nepotism. Why? Copio didn't have a word for it?

"I discovered what nepotism was when I was doing research for our operation to replace the current government," Camille said. "Frankly I couldn't believe what I was reading at first, but I was fascinated and really dug into the subject. I'm glad I did because that's why I'm talking to you today. With your original cultural baggage, I'm a bit worried you might not understand just what will be happening around you.

"Shana, if the Legate - man and officer - had to send your unit into a no-win situation, he'd do it as though you weren't in it. The man would mourn you if you were killed. The officer would send you again without a second thought if the situation demanded it. The Legate wouldn't take the relationship between the two of you into account in making personnel decisions, either. Nobody in the Corps would do that. Nepotism is another luxury we can't afford in the family, because we're all family. For a hereditary military to work, we can't take personal considerations into account while on duty.

"Do you understand what I'm telling you?" she asked quietly.

Shana took a moment to think. Actually, the idea of being treated like any other Gladius appealed to her. She'd never wanted anything but her professional ability and accomplishments to affect her status or future, and definitely not the fact her father was Head of the Guidance Council. That was one of the things she enjoyed about the Corps. It didn't matter to the Corps that her father was the planetary leader. She thought back to how some people in Beauregard treated her with such exquisite care as Narsima Ettranty's daughter and it always made her feel somehow dirty. The idea that nepotism didn't exist in the Corps was a relief.

She looked Camille in the eye. "Given who my father is, I've had to deal with the kind of attitude you describe, Colonel. I've hated it whenever someone thought I was using him for favors. I've also hated it when someone gave me special treatment because I was the daughter of the Head of the Guidance Council. For the record, I've never wanted preference because of birth and it makes me mad when people try.

Frankly, I'm glad the Corps is different. Being treated as a junior officer, not as Matic Ettranty's daughter or the Legate's girlfriend, is what I want."

Camille nodded with satisfaction. "I expected you'd say that. Glad to hear it, but expecting it."

Another thought hit Shana. "What about the rest of the Legion? What do they think about the Legate and me?"

Camille laughed. "Girl, you broke all kinds of hearts on Down Day One. The Legate's the most eligible bachelor in the Legion and you've caught him your own not-so-little self. Everyone knew it by the next day, too. Rumor is the only form of news that travels faster than tachyon data packet, and the whole Legion knew about you two before you left his quarters. Actually, I expect your three miscreants knew about your little affair when they were standing in front of your desk. I'm certain Sergeant First Class Steel knew. Decurions know everything.

"Other than a few dashed dreams for some women," she continued, "troops in the Legion won't treat you any differently. Like I said, relationships between differing ranks are normal. Usually the two are closer in rank, but a spread like the two of you have isn't unheard of. Don't worry about it. You've already experienced the way everyone but a few heartbroken women will react, and those girls will survive.

"Just keep on doing your duty like you have and I hope it works out between you and the Legate," Camille finished softly. "It's probably good for the both of you."

Shana was relieved. "Aye, Colonel. Truthfully, I think it is going to work out. I feel differently about him than any other man I've ever known and I'm pretty sure he feels the same way."

Camille smiled. "Good."

Then she got brisk again. "Now I suggest you get back to your collection of ruffians before they do something else to irritate your superior officers. Besides, I understand you have a training schedule and an arms inventory to do today. You probably need to get on them."

That brought Shana back to earth with a crash and a blush. Even the Support Command commander knew about her screw up! Marvelous. That meant Karl did, too. Damn! She stood up. "Aye, Colonel. With your permission?"

Camille was already looking at the hardcopy on her desk. "You have it. Dismissed."

Camille smiled a bit wistfully after Shana left. One of those broken hearts she mentioned was hers. Oh well. There were other fish in the sea. Acting as that girl's mother for a little talk had made her want to have children again. She mentally damned the Emperor for the deaths of her children and husband in the attack that destroyed the Rhiannonithi, but there was only a little heat in it. Wounds had healed in the last two years. She thought about Al Lumis for a moment. Now there was a very interesting individual. Very interesting. Yes, there certainly were other fish in the sea.

#####

When Shana got back to the Century, she found it bustling with far more activity than normal. Captain Samson told her, "We've gotten orders to renew combat certification ASAP, Shana. Get your people together as soon as possible and check all your equipment. Forget the schedule. We aren't going to need it right now. I need any of your platoon shortages and outstanding maintenance problems by COB, after you fix or replace what you can. Be prepared to run the blade range tomorrow morning and weapons range right after. We'll be running a century weave for certification in the big hall at 1700 tomorrow."

Shana nodded. "Aye, Captain. Are we going somewhere, or are there problems on Cauldwell?"

Captain Samson grinned. "Cauldwell's quiet. I expect we'll be seeing new suns very soon, Shana. I really have no idea what's up, but it must be important.

"After you get your platoon working, get over to the arms room. I need status updates on the crew served weapons after you do the inventory."

"Aye," she replied. "Anything else, Captain?"

He shook his head. "Nope. Just another wonderful day in the Corps, Shana. Get done I want done and I'll be happy. Now get going."

Shana headed off to the platoon CP. Sergeant Steel and her decurions could run the shortages and maintenance status. As soon as she started them on that, she was headed to the arms room. Wonder what was up?

#####

The same question was on the minds of the Legion's senior officers as they gathered in the conference room. Every Cohort commander was in the room, along with commanders of the combat support units, the Support Command commander, and key staff. Major Passant was being given some close looks, but he was keeping a poker face and his mouth shut.

Legate Athan was only a few moments behind his commanders. He waved everyone back into their chairs as he strode to the podium at the head of the room. "Short form, people," he began without preamble, "is that the Waltin have decided to grab Labatt from the Cluster. There are about two hundred thousand citizens on it so we're not going to let them have it. Fortunately, the citizens are scattered in enclaves too small to be worth orbital bombardment and the Waltin landing was on an unsettled continent. Makes things convenient. The situation won't remain that way and Frontier Cluster forces have to get there to stabilize it quickly. There's already a Fleet squadron on the way to reinforce the two corvettes usually assigned there on picket. The Fleet intends to keep the Waltin contained and get rid of their space support. Units from the Frontier Cluster Army and the Corps - us, in other words - are going to dig out the Crabs on the ground.

"Crab strength is in the 10K plus category, from what the corvette picket could estimate. They're backed up by a couple of destroyers and several smaller ships," the Legate continued, "and the picket is showing good sense by staying out of their way for the moment.

"This looks like an economy of force operation to see what we'll do. If they expected to really bump heads we'd be seeing a lot more of them. As it is, I think they'll leave us alone if we stamp this incursion flat. SOC has elected the Victrix to do the stamping since the other four legions are currently tied down with subversion, exploration, and other missions."

Colonel Albt Lumis of the Fifth Cohort shifted slightly in his chair. He was big, like all male Gladii, but beefy over hard muscle. Like a few, he wore a heavy beard that made him look like some kind of barbarian warrior. That reflected a lot of his personality, too. He grinned and spoke up. "Classic real estate grab. We expected that was going to start, given the dissolution of the Empire. More of the same's coming, too, until everyone realizes the Cluster can take care of itself. The whole Legion?"

Karl looked at him. "Not your boys, Al. I'm only sending one cohort, since the incursion is so small. Second, Third, and Fourth cohorts are pretty well tapped out with the subversion operation. I'm holding you here as reserve since you're still understrength." He turned and looked at First Cohort commander. "Jon, I'm sending your guys with the usual attachments, since you aren't committed too heavily on Cauldwell. Do you want any loaners from Al?"

Jon Protac snorted. "I figured that out from the warning order, Legate. We're prepping for certification now. We ought to be ready to go by tomorrow night, minus the Third Battalion. I've got parts of them out in Beauregard, and I'd rather leave them there."

He looked at Fifth Cohort commander. "Have you got a battalion to spare, Al?"

Al looked at Karl, "If a battalion and a half is okay for a reserve, Legate, I can spare the First."

The Legate nodded. "That'll work. Jon, your cohort will back up the Army brigade being sent from Niad. Those are all new troops, so I expect you'll be doing a lot of backing up, but the Army needs the experience. You're going so they don't get too much of the wrong kind of experience and I expect you'll be doing mostly battalion and century operations. Let the Army do the heavy lifting, but don't be shy if a good target shows up. Make sure every one of your units is briefed in as far as possible with the little we know before you lift. Your launch time is 1400 on Duty Day Three, so you've got some work to do. I'm glad you got a jump on certification."

Karl nodded to Major Passant. "Tom, fill in the details on the crabs would you?"

The major nodded then triggered a holographic display. "Here's a Waltin."

The being in the display did vaguely resemble one of ancient Terra's crabs or one of the analogues found throughout space. The oblong body was encased in an exoskeletal shell, with three legs on each side and two large claws projecting from the front, outside a pair of unshelled flexible tentacles that ended in branching "fingers". A mouth and two eye stalks were between the tentacles. The hologram scale overlay told everyone that the body was approximately two measures long and three across the wide part of the back.

"Corps database says they prefer mass tactics and don't mind casualties," Tom said. "Their armament is about on a par with our own, but they use kinetic projectile weapons. Roughly equivalent to bolt guns, but without the range or terminal damage. Call the effective range of their personal weapons about a quarter kilomeasure. They are most vulnerable at a weak point on the underside, just about in the middle of the shell, but it's hard to hit, given the way they move. Take out a couple of legs on one side and it's a mobility kill. A bolt in the mouth area from the front will pretty well take out the brain or proceed into key organs for a kill. They use those claws for infighting, and they're good with them. Their natural direction of movement is with one side or another forward, much like real crabs, so they won't be facing you unless they're stopped. Biologically, they're obviously descended from aquatic animals, but they only have vestigial gill slits. I doubt if they get wet any more than humans climb trees."

"Good summation," Karl said. "Anything else?"

"Aye," the Intelligence Officer responded. "The Rhiannonithi handled the last incursion about a century ago." He nodded at Camille.

210

"There was a record in the database about one of the Rhiannonithi's night attacks where they used flares and moving lights to distract the target force. Reviewing it, I'm willing to bet the crabs are easily spooked. My recommendation based on analysis is to hit them good and hard. Whenever they were smacked hard enough, they had a tendency to break and run."

"Something to think about," Jon mused aloud. "Get me a packet and I'll ensure it's in our hypno downloads for the voyage to Labatt. Meanwhile, I'll have the First ready to load out by launch time."

Karl nodded. "Good to go. I want the First to have priority on anything they need, supplies, maintenance assistance, anything. Colonel Paten, make sure your folks know that. We haven't tangled with the Predator since the Wareegan, people, but we're about to do it again. Let's get started."

LEGIO IX VICTRIX
LABATT

Shana was impressed by her second ride on a Troop Carrier. There was a little too much emotional baggage involved with her first one for it to register much. The carrier was large enough for a whole legion, including training and support requirements, so she felt like everyone in her single cohort was rattling around in a huge metal box. A huge windowless metal box. This wasn't how she envisioned her first interstellar trip, but it was still an interstellar trip. The idea of landing on Labatt had her excited. A new world!

She and her platoon were next on the load-out, waiting to board their assault shuttle for the trip down to the planet's surface. Shuttles were also carrying rations and equipment, so they only loaded a platoon at a time. The mixed loadouts actually made the operation faster. Since they were headed for an unopposed landing everyone was relaxed, just wanting to get down with a minimum of fuss. Corps SOP said full armor and weapons on any landing not totally administrative, so they were fully kitted out. Nobody expected fighting on the ground, but Shana regarded wearing armor and weapons as good training. Her boys needed a little more armor time, anyhow.

Not that they needed much else, she thought smugly. The platoon had been certified as fast as any in the cohort. That was mostly Sergeant Steel's work, but she and the Sergeant were becoming a smoothly functioning team and the platoon's performance in the training sims on the way here was like a well maintained machine because of it.

Her satisfied musing was interrupted by a call on her helmet com. //"Shana, Samson."//

What the hell? The Captain was already on the dirt with the rest of the Century. //"Go."//

//"You've got a change of orders. You'll be getting the download, but the quick take is you're going to be making a combat drop. The Army has a patrol under pressure. The Army wasn't maintaining a ready response company in case something went wrong, so it'll take them a while to get a unit loaded out to help them. With our offloading posture, we can get a platoon on the scene faster. That's you, since you're just now boarding. Cohort says to get the patrol out of trouble, and that's your mission. Let me know immediately if you need help, and don't be coy about asking. Third Century is next to move. They'll go on station with you if you need them, but you've got to develop the situation first."//

Shana stifled a gulp. From administrative landing to combat mission in thirty seconds. Another wonderful day in the Corps. She waved Sergeant Steel over. Time to get busy. They had to be ready to hit a hot LZ by the time they planeted. //"Understood, Captain. Give me a few minutes with my decurion and we'll be ready to go."//

//"One other thing, Shana. The Valeria has an advisor with that patrol, a Sergeant Koonz. He's your point of contact. Get with your POC on the way down. He'll be expecting a call. Probably praying for one if the situation's like I expect."//

//"Got it, Captain. Sergeant Steel's here with me now. We'll be lifting in about five mikes."//

//"Aye. Copy five minutes. Just get into that shuttle and on the way as fast as possible. Do good, Shana."//

#####

On the landing pad below, Captain Samson put his helmet com on standby and looked at his First Sergeant. They were both in armor with visors raised, so the only thing he saw cleanly was the First Sergeant's face. It was as concerned as his. "Am I crazy, Top? I just launched a brand new single pip that's had her - note use of the word 'her' - platoon less than a month on an independent mission to unfuck a situation for an allied force. Oh, and let's not forget we don't know just how many crabs she's facing and I'm stuck here on an entirely different continent until the Army gets its head out of its ass and scares up transport of some kind."

The First Sergeant took a deep breath then shrugged, telling himself they were doing the right thing. Yeah. Uh-huh. But he had to calm his boss down, even if the Captain's estimate of the situation was dead on the mark. "If she's what we've got, Captain, she's what we've got. Cohort gave the orders, so I guess they're sweating bullets along with you."

The Captain gave a wry smile that belied the tension eating at him. "Somehow that's not a big help."

The First Sergeant gave his commander a look of grim confidence. He knew he could believe in one person in this triple-damned mess. Well, two, hopefully. "Steel's one of the best Captain, trust me on that. Lieutenant Ettranty's good, too. She hasn't got much experience, but she's got good judgment and that'll go a long way. You can rely on Sergeant Steel to keep her straight."

Captain Samson nodded, more in acknowledgment than agreement. Then he took a deep breath of his own and let it out explosively. Top was right, but everything in him screamed to get the rest of his century out there and help Fourth platoon. One of his units was about to be dropped in the shit and he couldn't get to them.

He looked angrily around at the nearly barren permacrete landing pad. It wasn't worth triple damn to him at the moment since there wasn't transport on the ground for his century, much less anyone else's. If Fleet wasn't in control of the high orbitals, the apron wouldn't have even been in one piece, but Tanner Samson was in no mood to count his blessings. Not after some Fleet asshole had decided that an administrative landing could be done just as well by shuttling units down with "minimum necessary resources", meaning most shuttles were in ship stowage at the moment. "Let's go find that fucking so-called transportation officer," he growled. "See if she's even got a garbage scow somewhere, for Lord Above's sake!"

#####

The ride down was hectic for Shana. She reviewed the download, issued a fragmentary order then made sure all of her people had appropriate information, to include overhead imagery of the area where the patrol was trapped. The area looked like a field of boulders on a small plateau in some rough low mountains. According to the sitrep, the patrol was forted up in one of the rock jumbles and at least had their back protected. Apparently the crabs were just coming at them frontally like Intelligence said they normally did. The enemy was soaking up casualties in the process, but kept coming anyway. The crabs were going to overrun that patrol unless things changed fast. Well, she'd see if she couldn't give the bastards an entirely new tactical problem... her. She was excited, but not uncertain. She had a mission. She had good men. She had a target.

213

Her mind was working with lightning speed and her decisions were coming just as fast. Sergeant Smith's expression and minimal suggestions told her she was right.

Time to check in with the POC. She changed bands. //"Patrol advisor, 1-2-4-6 Victrix."//

//"Sergeant Koonz. Go, 1-2-4-6 Victrix."//

//"Request updated sitrep."//

Sergeant Koonz recognized a Corps platoon designation. Good enough. Just what they needed. He was a bit concerned the platoon leader's voice in his helmet was a female soprano, not the usual male baritone, but he didn't stop to ask questions. He was more interested in having that platoon on the ground. //"Aye. Sitrep follows. Patrol location WB347564. Covered position. Strength two-zero. One-five mission capable. Wounded four. KIA one, body retrieved. Ammunition yellow. Rations and support green. No indirect except five grenade launchers. Enemy positioned in a roughly 1600 mil arc to our front, at about 500 measures separation from us. Enemy has two rapid fire slug throwers, approximately thirteen millimeasures - equivalent to the Ma Deuce - located at roughly 5200 mils and 3900 mils relative to magnetic north. They're trying to come in under crossfire from the Ma Deuces. Hasn't worked so far."//

//"Aye. You didn't say enemy strength."//

//"Undetermined, 1-2-4-6 Victrix. Estimate a shitload."//

//"This is Lieutenant Ettranty. Say again more precise estimate, Sergeant."//

Sergeant Koonz's lips quirked. Must be a new lieutenant. Just wonderful. //"Terrain won't permit a count, Lieutenant. Better estimate is a shit pot load."//

//"Aye. See that you give me those kinds of precise estimates in the future. ETA approximately one zero mikes. Gladio alieyo, Sergeant."// The people on both ends of the transmission smiled.

//"Looking forward to it, Lieutenant. We'll keep 'em busy for you."//

//"Aye. On the way."//

Shana broke contact and then felt something strange. It was like the shuttle was shifting under her. The pilot's voice came over her earphones. //"We're taking evasive action due to ground fire, Lieutenant. No problem at the moment, but putting you down directly on the crabs might cost us."//

He wasn't trying to talk her out of anything, simply giving her information. If she told him to put them down right on top of the crabs he'd do it, ground fire or no. Shuttle pilots were like that. Still, there was a high risk of casualties if they gave the anti-air a better target, maybe the loss of her entire unit. There had to be a better way. She could see it, but didn't like it. It would take longer. //"Pilot. How about coming in behind the patrol's location in a clear area and making an NOE approach to the DZ? That should keep us below their anti-air envelope. We'll do a low altitude drop just behind the patrol while you cover with air-ground fire."//

//"Sounds like a plan, Lieutenant. Always liked low and fast, anyhow. More like very low and very fast in this case. Just hang on back there. I'm going to be stressing the inertial compensator a little."//

Shana grinned. Despite the situation, she was enjoying herself. This was why she'd wanted a combat command. She felt at home. //"Just go for it, pilot. We'll hang on."//

//"Aye."//

The shuttle dropped like a crazed meteor, spinning, corkscrewing, and sideslipping. The stuff the mass drivers below were tossing their way would go right through a shield but the EFO had a few tricks of his own and the pilot was crazy. Unbeatable combination.

In the back, the platoon was already in Link. Time slowed for Shana and she reveled in the sensation of knowing her troops as more than faces and voices. She felt each of them and they felt her. Again, she knew down deep that this was right for her.

Shana could feel the lateral pressure shift direction and force, even though the platoon was already braced in drop position and waiting for the green light. The pilot was right, she thought with approval. His moves were stressing the compensator, but their seats had them braced against the constantly shifting pull of inertia. Being pulled and pushed in five or so different directions at once beat getting a big hole in her transportation. She heard the pilot call red light and did a final check of her people as the air in the troop compartment glowed red. She also checked to see that Smythe was ready and was relieved to see the boy squared away, his attention already on her. It looked like she had a shadow. Good. Now to hope he lived through this.

#####

Sergeant Jame Koonz didn't waste time cursing the fact that he and the patrol were trapped in these rocks. That was just a part of doing business. Nobody's fault but the crabs, really.

The mission was to scout enemy frontage, and who'd have guessed they'd poke their heads around the side of a small hill and find what looked like a central depot, literally crawling with crabs. Lieutenant Toombs called immediate action drill when they were discovered and the patrol responded with well-trained precision that belied their inexperience, leapfrogging by fire teams and hitting the crabs hard. That gave them enough space to break off, but the triple-damned crabs were on their trail almost immediately and damn near caught them. It was pure luck this comfy little patch of boulders was right on their egress route. Now all they had to do was get out of their hole and back for pick up. Until Lieutenant Ettranty's call, that part looked like it was going to be a problem.

He eased his B-42 up between two rocks and let the sight look for a target while he watched his HUD. There. He snapped a shot into the back of a shell and put another round into the belly of the crab as it rose on its back legs. Another one down. Time to shift locations.

He took a quick scan down the line. Most of the patrol were hugging their rock cover. They'd already found out the hard way the crabs could ricochet a slug into their position. Fortunately, Champus was only hit in the foot. Lieutenant Toombs yelled, "Grenadiers, be alert for another charge!" The boy was doing the right things. Made him feel good to hear it. Toombs was going to be a good one if they just got him out of here.

Nearby, Magnificent Mouse was running through a steady stream of invective as she popped the occasional shot - and the crab she was aiming at. They'd nicknamed the girl in training because her small size and unstoppable energy reminded everyone of that children's tridio cartoon character. Now she was cool and professional, if a bit noisy. Another good one.

"Here they come!" The crabs were scuttling out of their positions again. Fortunately, they had a hard time moving through the rocks that fronted the patrol. Too much shell was showing. Sergeant Koonz wasn't going to argue with good fortune as he fired, shifted targets, and fired again. A small wave of AP grenades detonated and the charge dissolved into bloody fragments. Thirteen millimeasure slug fire swept their position, throwing rock fragments and ricochets everywhere. Someone screamed. He thought it was the Mouse, but, no, she was still shooting and cursing. He'd love to put down those two Ma Deuces, but the crabs were shifting them after every burst. Nobody said the damn crabs weren't smart.

He heard Lieutenant Toombs call out, "Jaksn, Kate, shift to grav grenades. Try to hit those gun positions." Good. Those micro black holes would just swallow up everything for five measures around their impact point. They were limited in the amount of grav heads they had, but this was the time to use them. One in the right location might nail one of the guns.

A burst of heavy caliber slugs shattered rocks just above their position and a few slugs got in among them. Looked like two centimeasure fire. His HUD said they were now down to twelve

216

effectives. Two more dead. Where the Hell had a Deuce come from? The crabs must be pulling up reinforcements.

Grav grenades went out, looking for the Deuce. A gun that size was slow to shift in these rocks and vulnerable to return fire. Apparently, they took it out. At least there was no return fire from it. That still left the crab reinforcements that had probably come with the gun. Wonderful. The party was getting bigger. The Mouse looked over and grinned at him. "Ain't we havin' fun, Sergeant?"

He popped a bolt at movement in his zone of fire. "Marvelous. Simply marvelous. Keep shootin', Mouse."

"Triple-damn it, Sarge!" she snarled back with some heat, her attention on her HUD. "I keep telling you bums my name is Elen!" She finished her comment by snapping off a couple more bolts at the crabs.

Sergeant Koonz heard a sonic boom in the distance behind them. He knew what that was. Gladio alieyo. Thank the Lord Above. Another shot, another crab down, and he mentally told the Corps to hurry and get them out of this mess while there was anyone left to get out.

The rocks hiding the crabs to his front suddenly shattered from two centimeasure bolt fire. Sergeant Koonz could hear the scream of strained thrusters and feel the heated atmosphere as the shuttle banked hard nearly over their heads and roared off at an angle designed to keep it out of the crabs' low altitude air defense envelope. That damned thing must have been just over the cliff behind them! That also meant its passengers were on the ground somewhere nearby. He resisted the urge to call the platoon leader. She'd contact him when she was ready.

#####

The platoon was indeed on the ground, moving in a relatively fast combat weave through the boulder strewn terrain. It was difficult to do, but that was what drills were for. A small portion of Shana's mind was proud of her troops' performance while the major part of it was concentrating on getting the Fourth around where the crabs' right flank looked to be. If she could do it, she wanted to hit them slightly from the rear at an angle. To that end, they were moving as fast and as silently as they could in a tactical mode.

She checked her helmet HUD for locations and did some range estimation. This looked about right. //"Heavy weapons. Locate just past those big boulders to your right front. I need rockets on the flanks of the crabs. General area of where the Ma Deuces are operating. Grav heads. On my command."//

//"Aye."// The three man weapons team found a good spot just about where the Lieutenant wanted them, set up their launchers, and dialed in their sights. //"Ready to go, Lieutenant."//

//"Aye. Stand by."//

//"Break, break. Koonz, Ettranty."//

//"Go."//

//"Put your patrol leader on this net as soon as you can. I need both of you. When I call for it, I want max fire from your people. Can you come out at them if I ask you to?"//

//"Aye. We can hit them from around our left. Haven't been crazy enough to do it before now."//

A second later. //"Lieutenant Toombs is up."//

//"Aye. Confirm crazy. Toombs, when I tell you, attack their left front. Stay on their left. I say again, stay your left, their right. The right flank will be our kill zone. Meanwhile, I'll call you for max suppressive fire on their left before I kick off. Focus their attention on your fire. We're coming in on your right. Be ready to go when I call."//

//"Lieutenant, Koonz. We won't be able to see you. Don't have your IFF. They can't link with you, either. I'm the only one that can do that."//

//"Aye. We're already Linked. Join us. Lieutenant Toombs, shift your fires left when you get a visual or my call. I don't want friendly fire casualties. The crabs will be trying hard enough as is."//

//"Toombs, aye."//

//"Aye."// Sergeant Koonz linked up with Shana's platoon. For the first time in too long, he felt a part of the Whole again. He also took note of the platoon's location. They only had a few minutes before things started happening. Tell Toombs.

Shana was closely monitoring the icons on her HUD. They were just about ready... Now. //"Weapons. Three round burst on each designated target."//

Ballistic rockets sailed overhead followed by cracks and rumbles as rocks shattered and compressed under the grav heads. //"Toombs, suppressive fire."//

She could hear bolts impacting on the crab left flank. It was time. //"Platoon."// she gave the order in combat for the first time in her life. //"Follow me. Let's hit 'em."//

The chain saw that was the Fourth bit into the crab flank and started chewing. Shana's view was multiple targets from constantly shifting directions as she and her team wove in and out of the platoon formation, firing as they went. She wasn't firing unless necessary. Most of her concentration was on her troops. The platoon's constantly shifting movements through the rocks could have been hard to follow, but they weren't, not to her. Instead, their constantly varying attack was confusing the enemy. This was what she and her men trained for and they were good at it.

She called Lieutenant Toombs. //"Patrol, come on now."//

Something whacked her helmet a glancing blow, knocking her down in a daze. She felt herself picked up and carried, headed for a space between boulders ahead.

//" L. T. 's down."//

That was Smythe, Shana realized as her senses cleared. The boy was carrying her, making pickup on his wounded leader.

//"NEGATIVE... negative. I'm good. Put me down, Smythe."// She landed abruptly on her feet and her team rejoined the weave. She'd think about her caretaker later. Right now, they had crabs in the rocks around them. Just where she wanted to be. Amid the firing, she heard loud yells and more fire from the patrol's direction. Toombs was attacking. //"Fourth. Be aware the patrol's hitting their left front and we don't have their exact locations. They don't have ours, either. Drift right to stay out of their fire."//

She paused and shot twice, killing two crabs as they were scuttling backwards towards their rear. Attacks from two different directions had the crabs running. Fine. Keep 'em moving. //"Break, break. Shuttle, land directly behind the original patrol location and be prepared for them to board with us."//

//"Ettranty. Toombs. Do you want us to pull back?"//

//"Aye. Don't get stuck into them. The shuttle will be just behind your original position. Pull back now and get all of your people aboard. We'll be right behind you."//

//"Break, break. Fourth, drift back. We want to get on that shuttle ASAP. Leave these Lord Above forsaken rocks to the crabs when they get up the guts to come back but maintain your fire. We want to keep them running for the moment. Start... now."//

#####

When everyone living and dead was aboard the shuttle, it lifted and screamed away from the crabs, still in NOE. They were headed for the Legion's landing site on the other continent now. All of them but the wounded and dead were standing, crowded into the troop compartment and

219

holding on to something to brace against the shuttle's weaving as it danced to avoid anti-air fire.

Shana was elated. Her first mission a success and no casualties! Well... except for her headache.

A figure in baggy camo uniform and refractive body paint lifted the HUD/commo visor under his soft cap and grinned at her, holding out a hand. "Lieutenant Ettranty, Lieutenant Adm Toombs. Thanks for coming to get us."

She shook hands. "Glad to see you, Adm. Shana Ettranty."

His grin got wider. "Not as glad as I am to see you, Shana."

A figure in Corps soft cammo combat uniform also lifted his visor and grinned. "Sergeant Koonz, Lieutenant. You did good. Thanks."

Shana nodded at him with another grin. It felt good to get a pat on the back from a combat veteran. Sergeant First Class Steel also smiled at her. "Good first mission, L. T. Other than forgetting to duck once, you did well."

Her grin got wider. Being awarded the title "L. T." meant she was considered a real member of the platoon and not just a new single pip. That felt better than getting a commendation from the Legate. Boyfriend or not.

Once her platoon was settled back at the forward operating base, Shana was ready to look for her quarters and a beer, in that order. Instead, Sergeant Steel flagged her down in the corridor of Officer's Quarters. "L. T., "he said, "you need to get over to the platoon CP."

"What's up, Sergeant?" she asked.

"Little something going on and you need to be involved. You'll see when you get there." Oh Lord Above, what now? With her guys, it could be anything.

When Sergeant Steel led her to the CP, she found the Fourth waiting for her. Sergeant Koonz was there as well. "L. T.," Sergeant Steel said, "we've been talking about having a platoon leader in pants. Pants aren't any sort of uniform for a good officer, so we've decided to change regs a little."

Smythe held up a kilt. The Fourth wanted her to wear a kilt! The young trooper started to stumble through what was obviously a short prepared speech. "L. T., we figured our platoon leader ought to be dressed just like the rest of the platoon so we got this kilt from supply." He blushed slightly. "We tried to guess your measurements right, so it ought to fit. We want you to wear it. You're our platoon leader."

Shana took the offered kilt from the boy and held it up to look at it, then measured it against herself. It was about the right length, just around her knees. "Thanks, people," she said. "This means a lot to me. It really does." It meant more than the world to her.

She couldn't resist ragging them a little. "It looks like it'll fit. It's a man's kilt, so it might be a little loose around the waist and tight across the butt."

Smythe blushed again. One of her squad leaders said with a completely innocent expression, "Oh, we won't mind that L. T. Just tighten your belt."

She gave him a humorous glare under beetled brows. "I'll just bet you won't."

She softened. "I'll still wear my skirt on parade. I earned that skirt, too, men. But this kilt is now my duty uniform and I'm proud you think I've earned it. Thanks, guys."

It was her turn to blush a little as her platoon cheered. The little imp in the back of her mind made her wonder what Captain Samson would say when he saw her in a kilt for the first time. For that matter, the same imp mused, what about Karl Athan?

CHAPTER 11

LEGIO IX VICTRIX
CAULDWELL
3228 I.C.E.

The First Lieutenant entering the Officer's Club was remarkable for a number of reasons. First, she was much taller than the Gladius female norm, with softly waved brown hair cut to her shoulders instead of a long straight fall of colorless blonde hair. Second, she was wearing a man's kilt instead of a woman's skirt. She had the normal female's arm dagger but also wore a weapons belt with bolt gun and ax. There was a green Strike flash behind the Legion insignia on her collar and a 30 centimeasure long Bowie knife on her right side behind her holster, both the marks of a Strike trooper. Perhaps the most remarkable thing about her was the fact that, with all of these remarkable characteristics, only one officer in the Victrix Centurion's Club so much as batted an eye on seeing her.

The lack of curiosity had to do with the fact that First Lieutenant Shana Ettranty was well known in the Corps by now, considered a very competent combat leader by the men and something of a strange duck by the women. On the other hand, the female captain waiting for her at the bar didn't consider Shana a strange duck. Captain Julie Dass considered Shana a close friend.

As Shana slid onto the next stool. Julie looked her friend up and down with exaggerated care. "So, okay," she said, "so we haven't seen each other for two weeks. What's been happening?"

Shana rolled her eyes. "Sorry. My platoon was on an anti-piracy mission as hide outs, using an armed freighter as bait. The damned pirates took forever to find us, then were dumb enough to send over a whole cutter load of their crew to board, planning to rob, pillage, rape, that sort of thing. When the 26 centimeasure guns on our decoy blew their ship to hell and gone, we appeared and explained things to the boarders. A couple lived through the explanation and we brought them back for Intel to play with. Job done."

Julie snorted. "I wasn't talking about *that*!" She shook her head woefully. "Girl, I was talking about Important Stuff! How are you and the Legate getting along? When are you two going to get married?"

Shana stifled a laugh as the bar man put a cold bottle of beer in front of her. She took a swig and grinned at Julie. "He proposed before I left."

Julie leaned over eagerly. "Now you're talking! How? When's the date?"

Shana slowly waved her left hand and its delicate gold ring with a single diamond in front of Julie's eager face. "Here. See this? That's all you need to know about the proposal, girl. Let's just say he picked a great time for it and the whole night was wonderful. With the way things are piling up for the two of us, though, I don't know when we'll get around to marriage."

Shana rolled her eyes. "By the Lord Above, sis! Just look at what's been happening! First I get back after three months on Labatt - with no casualties, I'm proud to say. Then I get approved for Strike School and *that* takes two months on Niad. Then they keep Strike jumping as soon as I get my platoon. I've been on five operations in the six months since then... and still no casualties. I'm working hard to keep that record."

Each Legion had two Strike centuries specifically to handle missions that required special capabilities. Strike platoons usually operated independently and were often found far behind enemy lines in wartime. Highly trained and uniquely equipped, they were specialists in unconventional operations requiring the application of precisely targeted force. Even in times of nominal peace, they were always active. In the situation the Frontier Cluster found itself in, there were simply not enough of them to do everything that needed doing. The operational tempo for a Strike unit was high. Thus, so were the demands on Shana's time.

Shana took another sip of her beer and her expression darkened. "We're almost ready to clean up Cauldwell and Strike will be right in the middle of the operation. I don't know how long after that Karl and I will have before we take on the Empire."

Looking at Shana's moody expression, Julie applied a little conversational medicine to snap her out of it. "Well, sis, that tells me you better make the most of what you've got. And if I'm not your maid of honor, you're dead meat, understand?

"Besides," she continued in carefully casual tones, "with all your big news, I haven't gotten around to telling you what that man-crazy Tana has gone and done now, not to mention Lieutenant Colonel Paten who is now Lieutenant Colonel Lumis."

Shana leaned over with a conspirator's grin, her previous worried mood gone, and said, "Give, sis, I'm all ears." The next hour or so was filled with happy gossip.

Across the room, a table full of lieutenants was entertaining the aide to the Legate of the 12th Ferrata, on Cauldwell for a conference. The aide, Lieutenant Rolf Sandrs, had never seen Shana before and the first sight was a bit of a shock to his system. Still a bit bemused at Shana's uniform, he looked over at Shana and Julie, commenting, "So that's the famous Shana Ettranty. Man, I just can't get used to seeing a set of curves in a kilt."

Looking around at the flat stares from his formerly jovial compatriots, Rolf got the idea he might just have committed a social blunder. "What?"

"She's one of ours, Rolf," replied Lieutenant Mik Kutlr in relaxed tones, pouring a little oil on uncertain waters. "Victrix. Shana's been ours since before the Wareegan fight. Her first platoon awarded her that kilt, so it's hers and nobody's going to argue the point."

"Some guy from the Augusta was talking about her once in the Legionnaires Club. Called her a chick. Ended up with a broken jaw courtesy of a Victrix trooper," he continued. He wasn't threatening, simply telling a story that he regarded as humorous and getting responding grins from around the table. "For that matter, I wish I'd been there when she graduated from Strike School."

Another lieutenant took up the story. "Shana always wears her skirt as dress uniform, so the SOC didn't know she had a kilt. Strike's graduation is in duty uniform, so she was in a kilt when she got called up on the stage to have SOC Garua present her knife and flash. One of the guys told me Garua's eyes got as big as saucers when she saw that kilt."

"What happened?" By now, Rolf was interested.

Mik took a swallow of beer and snorted laughter. "Word is that Garua was all set to land on Shana like a ton of bricks, but the school commandant got her aside first and explained things. No further official displeasure."

"Nice to know one of our own put one over on the brass," Rolf added, cementing his return to good grace.

"Amen, mate," Mik said, lifting his beer in salute to the last remark, followed by the rest of the table.

#####

Later that evening, Shana was applying considerable concentration to the twin tasks of brewing coffee for Karl and herbal tea for herself. "You look great with that ring on your finger," said a deep male voice from behind her.

She glanced at the engagement ring on her finger and smiled, still enjoying the warm feeling it gave her. "Considering the ring is the only thing I'm wearing," she said over her shoulder with wry humor, "I'll take that as a compliment on my looks."

"It was intended that way."

She looked back at the big bed in Karl's quarters. He was lying atop the rumpled sheets grinning at her, as comfortably nude as she was, propped up on a couple of pillows with his hands behind his head. Scars and all, she decided, he was definitely a sexy guy. "The coffee will be ready in a moment," she added.

Once they were companionably side by side on the bed, propped up with pillows and sipping their respective drinks, she decided now was a good time to discuss a few things. "We're getting close to moving on the Cauldwell government," she said.

He nodded as he sipped his coffee. "Uh-huh, and that's something you know I can't discuss with a junior officer until I issue orders for the operation."

"Other junior officers think tactically, Karl," she said with sidelong smile. "Me, I'm a former reporter, remember? I looked at the whole picture."

"Then you are one of the few that did," Karl said dryly. "Most of the ones I see on Cauldwell's tridio are as ignorant as a new born babe and can't see beyond their own agenda."

"Which is why I was one of CWNN's top rated reporters," she replied firmly. "And my reporter's instinct just told me you neatly avoided my question."

She looked at him seriously. "Karl, this isn't an idle dig for inside information. I'm worried about how long we have together before things start happening, things that will keep both of us apart. I know full well Strike's going to be in the middle of the government's overthrow and I know the government is just about ripe to fall. I also know Strike's going to be all over Central when we drop. I'm not worried about the Beauregard operation, but I'm going to be way out on the sharp end when we go into Central and I'm a big enough girl to realize I may not come home."

She took a deep breath. "I don't want to know everything, love. Nothing classified or above my level. I just want to know the big picture. Where we are. All I get is a worm's eye view as a platoon leader."

He studied her earnest face for a moment, thinking how beautiful she looked. Then he sighed. "You may not come home from Central... You realize that traditionally it's supposed to be you saying that to me."

He shook his head slightly and smiled grimly at her. "Yes, I know a Strike platoon leader hasn't got the chances of survival a Legion Legate

225

has, but Central will be different. Central will be a battle on a level that hasn't been fought in half a millennia, and it's going to be rough on leaders, no matter the grade."

He paused for a moment, thoughtfully, looking at her and not wanting to lose her like his first wife. Still, she was a combat commander and a good one. "Rougher on Strike leaders, I suppose," he said softly. "Take care of yourself, dearest."

He sipped his coffee and sighed. "If you're going to be my wife, Shana, you're entitled to know at least as much as I can tell you.

"First, you're right, the Beauregard operation is coming up quickly," he studied her eyes for a moment. "Obviously, we're going to try to take your father into custody, along with as much of the Guidance Council as we can. We've been moving slow here because your father has a direct link to the Emperor. We had to ferret out every possible conduit between your father and the Emperor before we took him down. We don't want any part of what we are doing to get back to Central. The fact that Central doesn't know what's happening out here is the key to our survival. Our whole operation here has to be totally undercover until we can move in and close the current government down as unobtrusively and quickly as possible, without the Emperor knowing what's happening. You'll be collecting Guidance Counselors, but your father will be someone else's business."

Shana was quiet for a moment. "I don't know what to feel about that, but I think I'm glad. There are a lot of things that I feel about my father... and most of them aren't good. But he's still my father. I think I should be kept far away from him."

Karl nodded. "True. So much for Cauldwell. Now for the situation here and the rest of the Empire. I'm sure you know a good bit of this, but I'm going to tell you anyhow, love, just so I'm positive you know.

"This isn't what's usually considered normal bedroom conversation," he added with a wry smile.

She looked at him over her cup's rim and shrugged. The shrug, in Karl's considered opinion, did wonderful things. "It may not be normal conversation, but it's about things that matter. That's why I wanted to have it," she replied.

"And *that's* why I fell in love with you, Shana. I'm not a big one for sweet nothings. I can have an intelligent discussion with you," he said affectionately. "That's what I need, you know. Someone I can talk to."

"And you're still avoiding the subject, love," she replied with an equally affectionate smile.

"Merciless, aren't you? Well...

"You're right, things are coming to a head here on Cauldwell," he said. "Once Cauldwell can openly join the Frontier Cluster, we'll have our bases firmly secure and be free to move on Central within a year or two at the most. Middle Empire is now pretty much of a fragmented mess thanks to us, so Central will be nearly alone by the end of next year. With Cauldwell secure, we'll also be able to get out of these caves, thank the Lord Above.

"The rest of the Frontier Cluster is coming together quite nicely. The trade alliance is becoming a Cluster wide government based on Tactine, especially with the addition of the two human populated worlds the exploration teams found. Randl Turner is already head of the trade association and calling him the defacto head of the Cluster government is only stating a fact. The initiative to form a true, not just a proposed, Cluster government will pass by the end of the year and he'll be the leader, whatever he's called. I'm sure of that."

He snorted with amusement. "You know what we have right now? We have a "proposed" government with one of the strongest military organizations outside of the Empire. The Frontier Cluster is a very real governmental entity; it simply hasn't been ratified yet. But that's going to happen soon, if it hasn't already.

"The Victrix is working on Cauldwell and the Valeria on exploration," Karl continued thoughtfully. "Exploration is something to be proud of. The Cluster will be better - humanity will be better - for that. The other three legions are busy bringing down governments all over what's left of the Empire. It's something we have to do to weaken Central, but people are already suffering because of it."

He looked Shana in the eye. "You're a Gladius, love. You know by now that sometimes there are things that have to be done to accomplish the mission that haunt your dreams later. I'm not Lane Mackinnie or Shyranne Garua, thank the Lord Above, so I don't have those people on my conscience, but any Gladius with two eyes can see we're sacrificing the well-being of billions of people so humanity as a whole will survive. We don't have to like it, but protecting humanity is our mission, and we can't protect all of it. The Corps has to protect and nurture what it can, and right now it's the Cluster. That's just a fact. We can't let what we want distract us from what we have to do - keep the human race alive. If we tried to save everything, we'd end up saving nothing."

Shana didn't say anything. She knew he was right, but she also felt the pain when she thought about the grand plan. Fortunately, she was a platoon commander. Grand plans weren't her responsibility

He took a sip of his coffee and was quiet for a few seconds, organizing his thoughts, and the ghosts slowly left his eyes as he did. "The exploration effort. The Valeria has done well there. That's our future. Humanity has to begin going out again, growing. The Empire is dying because it's too stagnant.

"Once the Empire is taken down, the Army and the Cluster Fleet will be able to handle most threats. We'll be able to slowly build down and consolidate the legions, then turn our attention to a more peaceful future."

"How long do you think it will take?" Shana asked with interest, happy to change the subject, but the idea of dissolving the Corps bothered her. Right now, she had no desire to be anything but a legionnaire - and Karl Athan's wife. "To consolidate the legions, I mean."

"A couple of centuries or more," he answered. "If we both make it through the mess Central looks like it's going to be, we might see the full realization of Garua's plan in our lifetimes. Or it may take longer. Right now, the senior officers in the Corps are thinking the Gladius will never really go away. I don't see us as hereditary soldiers forever, but there will always be some Gladii like you and me that want to be a part of a legion. We still have to give every generation a choice. The plan is that service in the Corps will be voluntary after the Central drop, with the exploration teams as one alternative for those that want to move off in a different direction. By the time Legate Garua's plan matures down the road, I see a standing strength of no more than a couple of legions to handle severe military threats, where every serving trooper is a specially trained and modified volunteer. The Corps will never really vanish, love, but it will become something a person wants to join, not something they were bred to do."

She thought for a moment. "You know, humanity is going to be different," she finally said. "There were thirty five thousand embryos in tubes in the Imperial cache, and the SOC ordered them given to parents all around the Cluster to raise. There are probably more somewhere on Central with the Emperor's Guard. They're all my genetic stock, original Gladii, and they'll add something different to the human mix. When the current Gladii breed back into the general population, there will be even more changes."

She looked pensive and shivered slightly. "I wonder what things will be like in the future."

Karl looked off into the distance, taking a different view of a future that scared her a little. "Oh, it won't be bad, Shana. We're at a turning point in human history. The Empire is decadent and dying. If it wins, the least that could happen is a Dark Age, with everything that means. With all of the competitive alien governments around us, the human race could be destroyed during that Dark Age. Humanity will certainly be attacked and every effort made to keep mankind down. If the Corona plan succeeds and we destroy the Empire, humanity will still be a going concern, just be a little different. Once the Gladius is bred back into the mix, humans will be a little stronger, faster, and have more mental abilities. They'll also be focused outward, thanks to the Valeria's exploration operation, not stagnant the way everything was just three years ago. The future's exciting, love, not scary. There's still a whole lot of the Universe out there, and humanity will be going out to see what it's like."

She thought about what he was saying. Listening to him, the future did sound exciting, but not so different as to be frightening. There was still going to be a place for her with the Victrix and her troops. That was important. Before they could build that future though, Central and the remaining Imperial government had to be destroyed. The Empire was the main threat to humanity's rebirth, and she was going to help destroy that threat. Destroying threats to humanity was the ancestral duty of the Gladius - her ancestral duty - and it felt right to have a part in fulfilling that duty. If she survived - if Karl survived - they could do their own little part to build a new future. Survival was out of her hands. Looking at the situation through a soldier's eyes, they were either going to make it or they weren't, but they had each other now. She accepted the fact and a knot inside her relaxed.

The two of them making their own future made her smile. She had this gorgeous, naked, sexy man in her bed and she was wasting time talking and drinking tea. Shana decided the future could take care of itself for a while. She gave Karl a sultry smile, and was rewarded with the look she was coming to know very well.

Karl put his cup down on a bedside table and rolled on his side, slipping an arm around her. "Care for a little more practice in making our own future?"

She did.

#####

Her platoon sergeant, Sergeant First Class Stauer, caught up with her just before morning formation. "We have three new pups, Lieutenant," he said. "They came in late yesterday while you were off. They'll be in your office just after formation."

The "pups", new Strike troopers fresh from school, weren't in the morning formation since they didn't have a team assignment yet. She and Stauer would take care of that once she'd interviewed them. "Aye. I want to see them first thing."

After the formation, Shana headed back to her little office. There was a knock on her door frame, and when she looked up from her desk and saw the three Gladii that followed Sergeant Stauer into her office, she had to stare in amazement. Not those three, surely? Yep. Legionnaires Kardo, Chofal and Smythe, her former problem children.

"Not the Three Amigos!" she said after she recovered. She'd nicknamed the trio after the mythical heroes of Old Earth legend and the name stuck. "Welcome to Second Platoon, First Strike Century, by the way. Now what are you doing here?"

Sergeant Kardo, as usual, replied for the three. "Corporal Smythe said you still needed looking after, Lieutenant, and we look after him. So here we are."

Shana shook her head in amusement and just a little pride at how the three had turned themselves around. Strike troopers were regarded as an elite among the best soldiers in history and now the Three Amigos were Strike. My, how times and pain-in-the-ass Legionnaires had changed!

"All right, you three, I'm not going to give you the usual 'Welcome to Strike, pups' speech. But I am going to give you some bad news. Strike units put pups on probation until they've proved themselves. You'll be pups until then."

Looking at their faces and gauging reactions, she continued, "The way things are going, you'll get your chance to become full grown Strike dogs soon enough. Will that suit?"

"Aye, Lieutenant, as long as I have your back," Smythe barked like an experienced veteran, which he really was - at all of about eighteen.

Shana hid a grin and put on a proper Platoon Leader face instead. When they were back in a line unit, she'd had to pull Smythe out of messes as often as he'd backed her up. On the other hand, the fact remained that Smythe had gotten damn good at watching her back before she left Fourth Platoon. She reflected that it was actually comforting to have him doing overwatch on her. "You're in my team, Smythe. I guess I can get along with you behind me.

"Go wait outside," she finished. "I need to talk with Sergeant Stauer and then he'll take you to your new teams. Dismissed."

After the three were gone, Shana broke down and grinned. "You know, Sergeant Stauer, I'm beginning to suspect I have an entourage."

Sergeant Stauer fixed her with a raised eyebrow. "Those three are from your last platoon, Lieutenant?"

She nodded. "Actually, they were reclamation cases I took in hand. I gave Smythe the job of watching my back to help him grow up and I he took it very seriously. He did while I was in Fourth Platoon, anyhow.

I had no idea he would take it seriously enough to try out for Strike and make it."

Sergeant Stauer favored her with a thin smile. "Well, motivation is what's needed to get through Strike School. If you gave him the motivation and he gave it to the other two, I suppose that's good enough. Awfully young to be pups, though."

Shana nodded. "That they are. They went on their Virgin Missions way too early, but it was a case of have-to and they did well. They're young, all right, but as good as they come. I'll leave you to juggle assignments, but make sure Smythe is in my team. He'd be worried if he wasn't at my back anyhow."

Sergeant Stauer nodded. One minor problem settled. Now for a bigger one. "Lieutenant, rumor has it we're about to hit Beauregard real soon. Know anything about that?"

Shana smile wryly. "You mean from my fiancée? Sorry, Sergeant, he doesn't give out that kind of information to junior officers. I kind of get the feeling rumor's right, but I don't know anything more than you do."

"Well," he replied, "rumor also says we'll be getting a mission brief and planning session by tomorrow. I'm betting that one's right."

"I'd take that bet too," Shana said thoughtfully. "I'd definitely take that bet."

IMPERIAL FLEET HQ, IMPERIAL PALACE CENTRAL

Commodore Ansn Jksn was a worried man, getting more worried as he studied the schematic of Imperial space. Systems and Sectors were breaking contact on an almost daily basis. The Empire was bleeding worlds, and he wasn't too sure what he could do about it. As a member of the Strategy Board, it was his job to find a fix. The problem was there was nothing he could quite put a finger on to use as a start point. Perhaps if he looked at the Tactine System. They'd lost a major force out there four years ago due to traitorous conduct of Frontier Fleet and Gladius units, but there might be a way to regain the initiative if they formed a new task force to smash in there and regain the system. Tactine was ideally placed to control that area of space and it had everything needed to build a major Fleet base.

The more he thought about the idea, the better he liked it. Move outward from Central at the same time moving inward from Tactine, and a whole string of important systems could be regained. More importantly, those were systems rich in resources and manufacturing capability. Invaluable.

Commodore Jksn was formulating a strategic concept for Tactine on a schematic, when the hologram was suddenly replaced by the figure of a slim man, richly dressed in the deep red of an Emperor's uniform with a gold circlet on his head. "Your Awesome Imperial Majesty!" Jksn gasped, and shot to his feet. Immediately, he bowed deeply. It was Emperor Shangnaman, and Jksn knew he was in deep trouble.

Nobody saw the Emperor in person anymore. Instead, his hologram stood in for his physical presence at all ceremonies and meetings. He was tapped into Central's computer system and nobody ever knew when he would suddenly appear on their terminal. It was like he was part of the system itself. There were some very strange rumors as to why, but one thing was certain: whenever Shangnaman appeared on your terminal, you were in deep, deep trouble.

The Emperor's face could have been handsome, but his heavy black eyebrows only emphasized his lavish use of eyeliner and lipstick. The effect was eerie and frightening, given Shangnaman's dangerous personality and the peculiar glint in his eyes. "You are engaged in the study of a portion of space deemed irrelevant to Our purpose, Commodore," he said. "That can be regarded as seditious."

Jksn fought hard to control the quaver in his voice, damning the fact that beads of perspiration were forming on his forehead. "I do so only to support you, Your Awesome Imperial Majesty. I'm trying to find a way to regain lost territory for the greater glory of the Empire."

"Liar!" Shangnaman squealed. "You are plotting to waste Our Fleet in useless effort in an area that has no value!"

"B-b-but," Jksn couldn't stop the stutter. He had to regain control. His life depended on it. "Your Awesome Imperial Majesty, I was attempting to find a way to regain Tactine after our defeat there. Tactine would be valuable to the Empire in the future. I was attempting to perform my duties in your service."

"We were not defeated at Tactine, Commodore," Shangnaman purred. "Any rumor of such a defeat is a lie spread by Our enemies. Tactine was never of any importance to Us, and We have forbidden any further interest in such a primitive and useless world."

Jksn bowed deeply again. "Your Awesome Imperial Majesty, I was totally unaware of Tactine's lack of importance. I have erred grievously and I place myself on your mercy." Maybe he'd get out of this with his life.

The Emperor looked at the bowing officer with a strange expression, glee glittering in his eyes. "We will consider your apology,

Commodore. Let it never be said that We do not have mercy. Remain here, Our servants will shortly arrive and take you for questioning. If you are found blameless, you will be released and no more will be said of this."

Shangnaman ignored Jksn's stammered thanks and vanished. Jksn whirled as the door to his office slammed shut in front of him, and he knew that the opening mechanism no longer worked. He collapsed into his desk chair and stared blankly at the door.

An instant later, Shangnaman's holo appeared in the office of the Chief of Investigations. "Cannon," he said peevishly, "it has once again fallen Our lot to weed out another traitor before the Office of Investigations can even find the way to the door. We will not tolerate such ineptitude much longer."

The short brown haired colorless man behind the desk immediately shot to his feet and bowed. "Your Awesome Imperial Majesty" he said in calm tones, "there are so many plots against your Imperial Person that we are working night and day. As you are aware, we have arrested over fifty among the government and populace in the last three days alone."

"Fifty, eh?" The thought seemed to cheer Shangnaman. "What did you do with them?"

"They were of course executed, Your Awesome Imperial Majesty."

"Excellent!" Shangnaman's holo was bouncing and giggling with glee. "Send people to room 218-B of the Fleet Headquarters. Kill Commodore Jksn. Keep up your good work, Cannon." The holo vanished.

Cannon breathed a silent sigh of relief. He needed to redouble his efforts to find where in the hell the Emperor was hiding. One of these days, he wouldn't survive one of these conversations if he didn't. The problem was getting past the Emperor's Guard. There had to be a way to do that, he reflected as he thumbed the intercom sensor. "Jane," he said when the acceptance light glowed, "send a team to Fleet Headquarters to kill Commodore Jksn in room 218-B. Tell them while they're at it, they may as well execute two or three other enemies of the state also. The body count will look good. Tell them to use their own judgment, but pick people that aren't doing anything apparently essential.

"And schedule a short meeting with Vice Regent Last for me," he added. He didn't need to add that the meeting would be nothing but a proud and highly loyal summation of the latest execution totals. The two of them would meet later, far away from any surveillance and very far away from any part of the Palace's computer system. Maybe between the two of them, he and Last could figure out how to get rid of Shangnaman before the insane bastard decided to kill them both.

Shangnaman's next appearance was in the terminal of the duty officer of the Emperor's Guard. The tall dark haired muscular man at the terminal didn't jump to his feet or bow. "You wish, Emperor?" he said in a flat, even voice.

Shangnaman tolerated the familiarity of the Emperor's Guard with affection. In all the Empire, theirs was the only organization truly loyal to him. Frankly, informality was a relief to him. "Have you heard from the squadron you sent to Tactine?"

"Squadron A-310. No, Emperor, we have not. Their last report was several days ago."

"Well," Shangnaman said merrily, "when you do, tell them they are on a wild goose chase. I have decided Tactine is of no importance to me or the Empire. Send a data packet drone to recall them immediately."

The big man nodded. "It will be done, Emperor. And if they have encountered some contact with traitorous forces?"

Shangnaman shrugged with the exaggerated expressiveness of a stage mime. "It's of no consequence. If they defeat the traitors, well and good. If they do not, it's irrelevant. In fact, don't waste any more time if you don't get a reply. No matter what happens to A-310, send no further units out there or waste any action on Tactine. We have more important things to occupy our time in the Middle Empire."

The big man nodded. "It will be done, Emperor. May you live forever."

"Oh," Shangnaman said in a jaunty tone, "I intend to do just that." Then he was gone back into the computer system.

VICTRIX BASE
CAULDWELL

Rumor was off by one day. Two days after talking to Sergeant Stauer, Shana was in Captain Gldblum's office with his other three platoon leaders for a planning session. The Strike mission was to capture key members of the Cauldwell government. Mission start was in three days.

"In last month's election," Gldblum said, "the Popular Movement made some heavy gains, enough to control the government. It looks like the people on Cauldwell are ready to take over their own government in seven days, when the PMGG people are seated. Once the PMGG people are in Parliament, the election of a new Guidance Council is a flat guarantee.

"Narsima Matic Ettranty doesn't like that," the captain added dryly. "He's in the process of scheduling what amounts to a coup four days from now. He's got teams of hired goons set to visit the new PMGG Members and the assessment is those that don't agree to play ball will vanish and be replaced with more compliant people or government moles."

Shana's breath caught slightly when her father was mentioned, but she put her thoughts aside and continued taking notes. Her stylus moved over the screen of her notepad automatically, but she was wondering what was coming next. What was Strike going to do?

That was Gldblum's next topic. "We're going to stage a countercoup first. The plan is for subversion teams already in place to take out the goon squads. We have them identified and located, so we don't anticipate much trouble. Strike's mission will be to take selected members of the Guidance Council - primarily Ettranty's inner circle and Ettranty himself - into custody at the same time.

"Here's one twist you need to know about," he commented as he flashed a holo pic of a tall, dark haired man on the conference table display. "One of the goons. Look familiar, folks? This guy's just like Shana, ancestral Gladius. Intel thinks he and the rest are actually Emperor's Guard, sent to Cauldwell to act as enforcers for Ettranty. Because of that, our teams are going in heavy and expecting a hard fight. We probably won't take any of them alive. If they really are Emperor's Guard, we don't want to."

He looked searchingly at Shana for a moment, noting her discomfort at the revelation about the goon squads. He could also see something more was bothering her and he was pretty sure what it was. He looked around at all four of his platoon leaders. "Okay, there are some things we all know but haven't discussed."

Captain Gldblum returned his gaze to Shana. "Shana, we all know these hard cases are from the same source as you. But they aren't you, Shana. They're Emperor's Guard, deadly enemies. You're Victrix and you are Gladius, not Emperor's Guard. Understand?"

After a few seconds, Shana nodded. The fact that the Emperor's Guard was present on Cauldwell had shaken her for a moment, but Captain Gldblum was right. She wasn't part of those people. She was Victrix. But still...

"And we all know Matic Ettranty is your father. Your platoon will not be detailed to his capture."

Shana took a deep, relieved breath. "That's okay with me, Captain. I once said I ought to be kept far away from him. I'm pretty sure he thinks I was killed by the Wareegan attack. I'd prefer he kept thinking that way."

It took a few seconds, but she finally realized what was really bothering her. "But I don't think he'll give up quietly."

The captain nodded. "Intel doesn't think so either. Shana, you need to know his capture is optional. The first priority is to take him out before he can notify the Emperor of what's happening. He's a major threat to everything we've done so far and we can't leave him free. If he has to be killed, he will. I'm sorry. I know he's your father, but it can't be helped. Do you want to sit this one out? You've got a perfect right to do it if you want to."

Shana closed her eyes and gathered her thoughts for a moment. She and her father weren't ever on the best of terms and everything she'd learned about him since joining the Corps was bad. He was nothing like she ever thought he was, but he was still her father. Could she face his death? Yes, she decided, she could take the knowledge, but the doing was something she wanted to stay away from if she could help it. Finally, she looked up and met Captain Gldblum's face squarely. "I can handle whatever happens. I'm a Strike officer, Captain. This is a Strike mission and I need to lead the Second."

The captain looked at her for a few moments longer, nodded, then continued, "Good enough. I'm assigning the Recording Secretary, Andews, to your platoon." He flashed a pic up in the display. "That's him. This guy's actually Ettranty's Imperial liaison and also has a direct line to Central.

Another holo, this one of two women, obviously mother and daughter. "You are additionally tasked to the woman, Clarine Femiam, and her daughter as secondary targets. Intel says they'll probably not offer any resistance."

"OK, back to the main brief." He checked his memo board. "There's supposed to be a big party in three days. Our targets will be easy to locate, because the current power structure is required to be there. Ettranty's order, for some reason. The trick will be to isolate them so we can pick them up sometime during that period without it becoming public knowledge. We want everyone to think the targets have dropped out of sight for a day or so. We're doing this simultaneously with the strikes on the goon squads to keep the PMGG folks safe. Once the PMGG Members are seated and we have control over the conduits Ettranty and Andews have been using to communicate with Central, we can go public with what's been happening in the Guidance Council. The PMGG will take care of what's left of the former Council and public opinion is pretty sure to demand a trial.

"Remember, people, we want to do things as legally as possible. We are part of the Cluster government and want to stay legally and peacefully on Cauldwell. For the people to allow us to stay, we need to have clean hands when the facts come out. Command says they're planning to spin everything towards the idea that we were working to free Cauldwell from secret Imperial tyranny. Leaving aside the fact that we need Cauldwell as part of the Cluster - especially because of the Imperial caches - that's actually close to the truth. Don't do anything to discredit the idea.

"Ettranty - and again I'm sorry about this, Shana - is the only exception. We simply cannot let him report on us. Logan, Ettranty's yours." He went down the list of Council members, assigning their capture to his platoons, finally returning to Shana. "Andews is the other must-have. Shana, I'm pretty sure you know him."

She nodded. "Oh, I'm quite familiar with him. I don't know Femiam, though."

"She got to Cauldwell after you dropped out of sight," Captain Gldblum replied. "I don't think she's going to be a problem. Since she showed up, Femiam's actually been playing a moderating role as far as she could, trying to reign in some of Ettranty's excesses. That might be only common sense from her standpoint, but she's looking like one of the good guys - so far as there are any in the current government. Intel thinks we might be able to work with her in the new setup. We've been monitoring her and her daughter closely and she certainly shows no signs of being overly corrupt. Actually far less so than most of the current leadership.

"At any rate, she's either at her office or her apartment and neither one is secured any more than normal. Lana used to be well known on the party circuit, but these days she sticks close to Mommy for some reason. Intel thinks they're trying to heal a rift between the two of them. Certainly, Lana is less of a wild type than she used to be. They'll be at the party, but we can be reasonably sure they'll both leave together and head back to home base. That's where I want you to plan to get them - either going to or returning from the party. If you get them before they arrive, people who miss them will just think they decided to skip the party.

"Andews is an entirely different problem and one reason why I'm assigning him to you, Shana. The guy's so security conscious, he's almost as paranoid as Shangnaman. His routes to and from his office are erratic and constantly change. His office is highly secure and so is his apartment. The only place we know he doesn't have personal guards around him is his apartment, but given the way he behaves, we're pretty sure he has secure escape routes in it. To say it again, he's a major priority because he also has with commo with Central. Andews is the other one besides Ettranty we have to isolate and take down at all costs, but we aren't really sure of his weaknesses."

"Oh, he has a weakness," Shana said with a mildly disgusted smile. "He likes high priced call girls. He takes a different one with him every time he appears at a social occasion. At least, I've never seen him with the same one twice. It's almost his trademark in upper level society.

"Where I used to be," she added with a grin. Shana thought for a moment and an idea came to her. "In fact, I think that's how we'll take him."

The captain looked at her quizzically. "Turn the call girl?"

She shook her head with a grin. "Captain, you forget I'm a woman sometimes."

#####

Inside the safe house, Victrix observation and subversion teams were getting briefed on the upcoming operation. "Strike's going to be taking down the key Council members, people," the Lieutenant said, reading the list.

"Why Strike, Lieutenant?" one of his men groused. "We've been watching these characters for years. Why not us?"

"Well, capturing key enemy personnel is a Strike mission," the Lieutenant replied reasonably. "Besides, Shana's boys are going to be collecting Andews and Femiam."

The grouser settled back. "Oh, Shana. Well, that's all right, then."

"Glad you approve Thomsn," the Lieutenant said dryly. "Shana's going to need a cover ID and clothing to match. Guess who's going to shop in the most exclusive women's store in Beauregard for what she wants?"

"Lieutenant, you don't mean..."

"Aye," he said with a nod, "and you have the thanks of a grateful Corps for volunteering. I'll download you Shana's list. Just tell the sales rep you have an expensive girlfriend."

Catching sight of a grin on one of the women at the meeting, he thoughtfully added. "Lukaanen, you go with this character. Make sure he buys the right stuff, especially with the cosmetics. You'll be his girlfriend's sister. You ought to be able to guess Shana's dress size close enough, anyway."

The two lucky Gladii just looked at each other in shared martyrdom as the meeting broke up.

#####

Totally hidden by its suppresser field, the cutter landed behind the safe house and dark figures wearing inactive body hugging stealth suits got off, moving quickly through the back door. The Lieutenant waiting to welcome his visitors knew that there were two women in the party instead of one, Shana and someone he didn't know.

He also wished the stealth suits weren't so damned complicated, power hogs, and hard to manufacture. If they were general issue instead of restricted to Strike and scouts, his people could just literally vanish. There were definite advantages to that.

After the two of them pulled the stealth hoods off their heads, Shana indicated the other woman. "I've brought Captain Dass here to help me get into costume. Do you have everything I need and a place to change?"

The Lieutenant nodded. Strange, he thought, Shana was brown haired. Now she'd done something to her hair to give it a lighter brown color, shot through with shallow gray streaks. It made her look a little older and very different. More sophisticated. "There's an unused bedroom upstairs, third door on the left," he replied. "That's yours."

Shana turned to one of her Strike troopers, obviously a senior noncom from his blocky, weathered face. "Sergeant Stauer, you and your teams move out and pick up the Femiams. I'll get going on my part."

"Aye, Lieutenant," he replied. "We'll be back soon enough. Stay out of trouble."

Shana smiled and waved towards Corporal Smythe. "I don't have to worry, Sergeant. I've got a good overwatch."

Sergeant Stauer gave Smythe a long look that plainly said he expected to get his Lieutenant back in one piece and in functioning order. Then he and his men were out the back door and part of the night.

Shana didn't watch him go. Instead, she turned to Julie and said, "Let's go so you can do your part, Captain." Both went upstairs grinning.

In the unused bedroom, Shana stripped and sat at a night stand to begin working on her makeup while Julie laid out her costume for the night. It didn't take Shana long, but the results were startlingly different from her normal appearance. Eye shadow, eye liner, makeup, and lipstick all combined to give her a different and more worldly look that was stunning and completely unlike her. She was reasonably certain that anyone she met in Cauldwell wouldn't recognize her. Once she finished her makeup, Julie helped arrange her hair in a fall over her left ear that only added to her sophisticated appearance.

Studying Shana's handiwork, Julie applied a few finishing touches to her makeup, then reached for what looked like a tube of mesh. She commented, "You know, I really couldn't wear this in public. Might be fun to wear it for a guy, but there's too little dress, too much me showing."

"Besides, it's not a uniform," Shana cracked. "Give it here."

She stepped into it, then pulled the mesh tube up. Looking on appraisingly, Julie said, "Well, it gives you plenty of cleavage, but I still say there's way too little cover in that thing. You're basically naked."

Shana grinned. "It's a smoke dress, girl. Just watch and let my body heat activate it, oh unsophisticated and innocent soldier."

After a moment, the mesh hugging Shana turned into a tightly clinging mist that thickened and faded constantly all over her body from her breasts to just above her knees, an effect that would attract and fix the male eye. The dress was erotic but not revealing, since no part of her was clearly exposed; only hinted at by a momentarily thinning patch of mist. Shana gracefully waved manicured hands with pastel painted nails at her own figure. "See? That's why it's called a smoke dress. Perfectly legal, but it'll get a guy's motor running any time. Just the thing for a high priced call girl or a woman letting it hang out at a really wild party. I had one back when I was a newscaster for the kind of parties I used to attend. They cost a mint, but I can sure tell you they're worth every little bit of the price."

Once Shana put on her high heels, diamond earrings, and diamond choker, Julie critically studied the effect. "I like it. I just can't figure out when I'd dress up like that. Makes me wish we'd get a little decadent on occasion."

Shana looked in the mirror, applied a few final touches to her makeup, and smiled as she picked up her clutch bag. Then she affixed a tiny bolt gun to the small of her back under the mist and headed for the bedroom door. "Sister," she said as she swept out of the room, "if you only knew."

The Lieutenant was talking to one of his men as he heard the click - click of a pair of high heels coming into the main room of the safe house. Wondering who had such outlandish footwear, he turned and got a good look at Shana as she sinuously strode toward him with a sensuous, knowing expression on her face. The sight stopped both his actions and his thought processes.

With a feline smile, Shana appraised his stunned expression. It looked like she was getting the right effect. She gently put a hand under his chin and pushed his open mouth closed. "Don't wait up, mate," she said in a sultry voice. "But if you do, kindly monitor my channel. I'm leaving four of my teams here with you for emergencies.

"Oh, and call us a cab," threw over her shoulder as she headed for the front door, collecting the two (also stunned) men in her team as she went.

#####

240

"Mother, do we really have to go to this thing tonight?" Lana asked.

Clarine shrugged. "Matic wants us there. The whole Guidance Council will attend. It's supposed to be a show of solidarity in the face of the election results. Certainly none of the PMGG will be there."

Lana grabbed her wrap from the hall table. "Maybe that's a good thing. Once those people get into power, they might clean this place up. I swear, Cauldwell is worse than Central."

Clarine looked grim. "Don't be too sure of that. Nobody's been arrested or assassinated yet - at least that I know of - and I'm trying to keep it that way. Matic's got some sort of plan for the PMGG, but I haven't been able to find out what, and I'm not certain I want to know. Remember, he can have us both removed simply with a word. I don't want you starting trouble, Lana. Too much rides on keeping Matic's good will."

Lana grimaced. "I'll be a good girl, Mother. But I'm not going to say I like it."

Clarine nodded, satisfied with the result if not happy with the reason. "That will have to do, dear. Let's just keep going until I can find a way to get out of this situation. I'm sure time will give us an opportunity."

The two were in the empty hall outside their apartment, headed for the waiting cab, when six big men wearing stealth suits suddenly materialized from nowhere and surrounded them. Clarine's heart stopped. To her, stealth suits meant only one thing - the Imperial Office of Investigations. How had they gotten here? Had Matic decided to remove her?

One of the men spoke in a deep harsh voice. "Narsim Femiam, Sim Femiam, you need to come with us."

"I'm - I'm - sure there's been a mistake..." Clarine started to stutter out.

"No mistake, Narsim Femiam," he interrupted. He pulled off his hood, displaying features of a type Clarine knew. "We're Corps of Gladius. We got you out of trouble once and we're not going to hurt you now."

Lana was frightened. Gladius or not, the whole situation was scary. Were they under arrest? When another of their captors spoke, she stared at him for a moment in surprise.

The speaker pulled off his hood, showing much younger features than the first man. "It's me, Lana. Jamie. Just come with us. You'll be all right. I won't let anyone hurt you."

Lana took a deep shaky breath and looked at her mother. "Let's go, Mother. It's Jamie Kardo. Jamie wouldn't hurt us."

Grimly surveying her captors, Clarine said in a low voice, "For the Lord Above's sake, Lana, I hope you're right."

#####

The expensive courtesan walking down the exclusive residential tower's hall was attractively, if not blatantly, dressed in a thin light colored ruffled blouse, dark bolero jacket, and cling pants, a discreet but sexually attractive costume suitable to her stature and tonight's appointment. Like everyone else at the top level of Cauldwell's society, she knew all about Narsima Antony Andews. She was arm candy for tonight's party and recreation afterwards, but the thought didn't bother her. It was how she made a very comfortable living, after all. This assignment was important. Andews paid well and tonight was her chance for a big bonus. She intended to earn it.

Her plans were derailed when two large men in stealth suits suddenly materialized, one on either side of her. "Sim," one of them said, "your appointment has been canceled." He made a motion with one hand and she felt a sting on the back of her neck, then everything went black.

Shana stepped out of a nearby service closet and waved her two men to put the courtesan inside it. "Leave her in here. When she wakes up tomorrow, it won't matter what she says."

"Remember," she said as they started back down the corridor, "we think Andews has detectors inside his apartment, so don't try to follow me in. Just keep monitoring. I'm trying not to get into trouble, but if I do, just take the door down."

She looked at one of the black clad figures. "Do you understand that, Smythe?" she said in command tones. "I'm a big girl and I can handle myself. Follow orders."

He replied, "Aye, Lieutenant, but I still have your back."

She smiled. "You do, but stay in the hall and stay unseen until I tell you. No telling who else is in these halls. Now fade out, you two." They disappeared as she watched. Then she calmly walked up the hall to Andews's door and pushed the door button.

When Andews opened the door he appeared quite pleased with her. He also made it vary apparent he had no idea who she was. His grand wave gestured her inside and simultaneously emphasized the opulence of his apartment. He began puttering around, preparing to leave as Shana, for her part, gazed around the luxurious room to his obvious approval.

Shana was carefully searching the somewhat overdone room with the contact lens in her left eye, looking for scanners and security alarms. She found quite a few. They could still take him here, but there would be alerts aplenty unless she could disable the control box first. She thought she found it, but didn't want to take the chance.

There was also a small device on a table near the doorway. It was a portable alert Andews carried in case he was attacked before he could get to his personal flyer. That was another problem. It was beginning to look as though grabbing this guy after the party was going to be a better bet. Maybe after she got him to bed. It would be easier to trace connections and disable the control box after he was sated and asleep.

Her plans became moot when the front door slid aside with no warning. Matic Ettranty slid the override into the pocket of his robe as he entered, a thunderous look on his face. "What's the meaning of this, Ettranty?" Andews blurted, shaken that his vaunted security could be so easily bypassed.

"I've disabled all of your silly devices," Ettranty snarled. "What we have to say to each other shouldn't be monitored. Get rid of the whore."

Andews waved Shana to a back bedroom. She nodded quietly and casually put her clutch bag on a small table as she left. "This one appears quite desirable," he told Ettranty quietly. "I will enjoy her later. She can't hear anything in the bedroom anyhow. It's quite soundproof."

Once he was sure she was in the bedroom with the door shut, Andews turned on Ettranty. "Now what in the name of hell are you doing here?"

"We have a major problem," Ettranty answered. "I cannot contact any of my men for some reason and I don't like it. Something's happening and I don't know what it is."

"You're afraid of shadows. We're firmly in control here and nothing the PMGG can do to overcome that fact," Andews shot back. "Besides, those men are the best the Emperor has, the reason they've been assigned to us for over a decade. There is nobody on Cauldwell that can stop them."

"Possibly," Ettranty rumbled, "but I don't take chances. I intend to alert our ship. We need to be gone from Cauldwell within a matter of hours if things, whatever they are, turn against us."

"That's ridiculous!" Andews said.

Ettranty glared at him. "You will not use that tone to your superior. If I say we leave, we are gone. If it becomes necessary, I will leave you here to take the fallout and the Emperor won't turn a hair."

Andews turned pale, both at the threat and the knowledge that Ettranty was right about Shangnaman's reaction. He looked down. "As you wish. What do you want me to do with the woman? Surely there's no need to be precipitous with her. Truthfully, I don't know why I haven't seen her before. She's quite spectacular."

Ettranty waved a thick hand. "Send her off now."

Suddenly, he got a thoughtful look on his face. "No! If she's not familiar to you with all your whore mongering, she may be connected to whatever is happening. At any rate, she is irrelevant. Kill her."

One of Shana's earrings was the receiver for the bug in her clutch bag. The other was her communicator, but she hadn't wanted to use it while Andews's scanners were in operation. Hearing her father casually decree her death shook her. It was time, she decided, to end this. She had no desire to confront him, but it looked as though she had no choice. She reached to the small of her back and palmed the tiny bolt gun clipped to her dress. Time to call the boys. Thank the Lord Above that her father had deactivated all the alerts and scanners! //"Lalane, Smythe, time to come on in. Be aware that there are two major targets in the room. Ettranty and Andews are together and one or both may be armed. On my command."//

She waited with her hand on the door switch until she got acknowledgment. //"Go!"//

Ettranty and Andews spun as the front door crashed open and the two troopers darted into the room, pistols out. The distraction was enough for Shana to leave the bedroom and walk into the confrontation, gun in hand. "Narsima Ettranty, Narsima Andews," she said in a cold flat voice, "you are under arrest. Do not resist."

Matic Ettranty stared at her for a moment and recognition dawned in his eyes. "Shana! You're Shana!"

She nodded without speaking. She was watching him carefully. There was something going on behind his eyes. She was warned when his expression grew more calculating.

"Sim Shana Ettranty," he said with a peculiar tone in his voice. "Listen to your father. Kill these two men." His voice didn't change as he added, "And yourself."

She felt her hand trying to move the gun towards Smythe and saw the satisfaction in her father's eyes. It was the words! They were the signal to activate the compulsion the doctor had warned her about! She was frightened for a second at the idea that she couldn't control her own will, then remembered the doctor saying he'd toned down the compulsion. It couldn't control her. That was why the gun was trying to move but going nowhere.

She let the gun drift towards her men, then stopped it and slowly swung it back to her father, watching his expression turn to shock. "You got the name wrong, Father," she said in a flat, deadly voice. "It's now

244

Lieutenant Shana Ettranty, and I'm not the puppet you own any more. I won't kill my men and I won't kill myself."

When the gun settled on her father, she fired.

#####

Legion Sergeant Major Olmeg was at the docking platform when the cutter with Shana's Strike platoon landed. He already had a backchannel report from Sergeant First Class Stauer and was dreading what was coming off that cutter. Andews was hauled off first, his head in a bag and bindings around his arms. The Femiams were next, unbound and much more politely escorted off by Sergeant Kardo. He would accompany them to their temporary quarters while Andews was headed for a detention cell and a long session with Intel's interrogators.

Shana was the last one off the cutter, just behind Captain Dass. Julie Dass had a very worried look on her face. Both were in stealth suits and had their hoods thrown back. "Mission accomplished, Sergeant Major," Shana said in a dead voice.

He looked hard at her. There was no trace of makeup and her streaked hair was pulled back in a ponytail. It was her eyes that bothered him. There was a spark missing. Captain Dass was giving him a worried look of entreaty. "You got your targets, Lieutenant," he said to Shana. "Good job."

She stared back at him with an empty expression. "I killed my father."

The Sergeant Major looked her in the eyes for a moment then growled, "Remain here, Lieutenant, if you please." He gave a toss of his head to the Captain to let her know he was now in charge of the situation and for her to leave it with him. Now he had to do something about a damaged lieutenant.

He spun on a heel and stumped over to Sergeant Stauer. "Find the Legate! He's up in the Legion CP last I heard. Tell him I said to get his ass down to your platoon bay... now! He's needed. Tell him why, and you tell him just like I said it, understand?"

Sergeant Stauer nodded, a wry smile briefly quirked his lips at the idea of quoting the Sergeant Major to the Legate, but he knew exactly what was happening. "Aye, Sergeant Major. Back in ten."

"Make it five. Go." The Sergeant Major didn't wait to watch Stauer leave. He stumped back to where Shana was standing, staring at nothing, and gently pulled her elbow around until she was facing the direction her troops were heading. "Lieutenant, with your permission, we'll both go and get your troops settled."

Once in the platoon bay, he took Shana to her little office and closed the door behind them. He sat her in one of the chairs then stood before her. "Tell me what happened, girl."

The story came out slowly, haltingly, full of pain, but she told him all of it. She once again went through the moment when she decided her father couldn't be allowed to live, when she realized he wasn't her father, just a dangerous creature that cared nothing for any other person but himself. "It was the order to kill myself that did it, Sergeant Major. I realized I was nothing but an inconvenience to him. He told me to kill myself simply to remove a problem. I had to kill him. I couldn't let him live and do the same thing over and over again.

"I had to kill him," she repeated softly, tears misting in her eyes.

"Look at me, girl," he said softly. "You did right. I would have done the same thing in your place. It's the way we are. I know he was your father, but he wasn't what you thought. He was foul. What he's done to Cauldwell was enough to earn a death sentence in any case. Girl, the man's deliberately held an entire planet isolated out here, murdered a whole city's population, and done it to serve an Emperor that personifies foulness. He did it willingly and sucked the life out of his people in the doing.

"You can mourn, girl," he continued softly, "but mourn the man he could have been. You did the right thing and nobody will ever say different. You will say it, in the dark of night. You'll always second guess yourself. Every Gladius has a thing or two we keep buried that comes out and gnaws at us at times, but we all have to put it by.

"Listen to me, Lieutenant Shana Ettranty, and listen well," he said. "You can weep for the man he could have been. Destroying the man he was is the only thing you could have done. Not a man or woman in this Legion or any other will disagree. He may have raised you, but we are your family and your family loves you. Know that."

She looked up at him, tears slowly trickling down her cheeks, but her eyes were no longer dead. "I killed my father and they still like me?" she asked in a little girl voice.

He nodded solemnly. "Not like, Lieutenant Shana Ettranty - and you have made the Ettranty name a name of pride, not a name of shame like that man made it - your family loves and respects you. Now more than ever."

He heard the door open behind him and turned his head to see the Legate quickly enter. "Some love you more than others, Lieutenant Shana Ettranty. Here's one that does."

As the two behind him fell into each other's arms, the Sergeant Major started to leave. Behind him, he heard the sound of Shana's deep, broken sobs and the Legate's soft words. He quietly closed the door to leave them alone.

#####

The Legion was released to conduct activities outside the caverns two days later. Shana's platoon assembled outside the huge camouflaged front entrance in physical training shorts, running shoes and T shirts. As Shana took over the formation from Sergeant Stauer, the whole platoon could see there was something different about her. Her streaked hair was down and held by a sweat band, not up in her habitual duty braid. Her face was different, too. There was a look in her eyes that wasn't there before, a look of maturity, of someone that understood the full price duty and life could exact.

Watching her, one of the troopers in the back muttered, "The old girl's out to get something off her chest today and us poor dogs are going to be the lucky bastards that help her do it."

Corporal Smythe started to bridle at Shana being called "old girl", but Sergeant Stauer growled from his position behind the formation, "At ease, Smythe. She was ours - and his - a long time before you adopted her. We're all original Victrix except for you and your friends. So is Lieutenant Ettranty. Ormond respects her. We all do. Just relax."

Shana looked at her platoon for a moment and said, "Boys, today we're going to celebrate our return to the sun by going for a little stroll. Right face!

"Quick time mar-r-r-ch, ho!

"Double time, ho! Link up and swing out, dogs. Sing the cadence!"

As the unit began its run she fell into the hypnotizing running chant and the rhythmic thump-thump of feet hitting the ground in cadence. She could feel the wind begin to blow her loose hair and she was again becoming part of a Whole greater than her. There was nothing in the world but herself and her twenty men, running to the chant and Linked into a single being with twenty one separate bodies and one purpose - to run for no other reason than to run. She knew They were with her still, Those Gone Before, the Legion's dead women, and she wasn't unclean, despite her father, despite what she did. She was still Their living avatar. The wind and the sun so long denied her by her duty were washing away her taint, the taint of patricide. The love of Karl, the unspoken love of the man she finally recognized as her real father - gruff Sergeant Major Olmeg - the

247

respect of her Legion, the love of the legion's women Gone Before, all were making her clean again.

"The ax song," she yelled after a running chant finished. "Sing it, boys!"

She picked up the funny little song as the men started it, joined them as they clapped to its beat, her long legs matching their pace stride for stride, feeling her sorrow and shame being washed away by the wind in her hair, the sun on her face, and the quiet love deep inside her from the dead women she represented.

"Oh, my mother was a lady, so she didn't love me,

"Hey, hanta lay ya!

"She said my father was a bastard, so a soldier I'd be,

"Hey, hanta lay yo!"

"So a soldier I'd be," she breathed to herself. She was content with that.

CHAPTER 12

THE WAHOO
IMPERIAL SPACE

The S-1024, A.K.A. the *Wahoo*, was one of the new Fleet Class S-boats. She was purpose designed, larger and far more capable than the earlier converted corvettes used to prove the concept. The S-boat had been invented over a year ago and current legend said the idea had come out of mixing a formal military dining-in, a Gladius officer with an oddball taste for ancient naval history, an admiral looking for an edge over the Imperial Fleet, and a great deal of alcohol. Whatever the source of the idea, the Frontier Cluster Fleet set out to create an analog of an ancient ocean going ship known as a "submarine".

The background idea was very simple. The ancient submarine hid by diving under water. A modern warship hid by using a suppresser field, but using suppresser heavily limited the warship's scope of maneuver and action. However, suppose a ship was designed from the keel up to be used *primarily* in suppresser? Hm.

The question of weapons became important because warships instantly revealed themselves the moment they fired their guns. Again, history came to the rescue. The primary weapon of ancient submarines was an underwater mechanically driven missile known as a "torpedo". Looking at the question, the people brainstorming the suppresser ship idea decided that a missile with an onboard suppresser generator might work. Missiles were considered obsolete because they were slow, limited in range, and easy for a warship to dodge or destroy. However... a suppressed missile with the proper penetration aids *might* just make it into contact where the antimatter warhead could kill a target.

Cluster Fleet R&D ran with the notion and converted ten corvettes to be the first S-boats. They were termed "boats" instead of "ships" because ancient submarines were always known as boats for some reason and ancient submarine tradition was already beginning to permeate the project.

The first S-boats were tested in combat when a squadron of the first Imperial frigates ever encountered attempted to enter Cluster space on a course for Tactine. The ensuing battle cost the Frontier Fleet heavily and it looked like one of the frigates was going to escape. That was the Fleet's worse nightmare because the frigate could reveal what was happening out in Cluster space. In the end, the escaping frigate was destroyed by an S-boat torpedo.

Huge sigh of relief for all concerned and the realization that something new had been added to the Cluster Fleet's arsenal.

Those converted corvettes proved successful in combat, but were not well loved by their crews. In fact, they were universally termed by their spacers with a name also dredged from ancient submarine lore, "pigboats".

Those pioneering conversions were termed pigboats with good reason. The early S-boats gave a new definition to cramped. Aboard a pigboat, for instance, the bunks for the three person crew were stacked in a niche that was slightly larger than a walk-in closet. The ten crew members of a Fleet Class boat at least had reasonable accommodations that would allow them to survive a long war patrol without going crazy.

A purpose designed Fleet Class boat was a good bit larger than the original conversions, its elongated teardrop form dictated by the characteristics of its extremely powerful suppresser field. Normal warships were optimized for combat function and the suppresser field generator was simply added equipment, making the field somewhat inefficient. Fleet Class S-boats were designed with the suppresser field in mind from the beginning and were nearly undetectable. The boats had six torpedo tubes with five reloads each, set back from the bow to allow the entire bulbous nose to be used for passive sensors, sensors far more sophisticated and capable than normal. In a nod to Fleet tradition, there was a heavy 30 centimeasure gun in a turret on the top deck, a third of the way back from the bow. The onboard compliment of recon and decoy drones was higher than a normal warship, too. A Fleet Class boat could handle itself very well in hostile space.

In all, Commander Alice Toklas, a cheerful, slightly chubby type, was quite happy to have a brand spanking new Fleet Class S-boat of her own to play with, and just simply dozens of Imperial systems in which to play. Someone looking at Alice would swear - mistakenly - she didn't have a sneaky bone in her body. Actually, she was a natural match for the supremely sneaky S-boats.

Alice was in the third system of her war patrol and they already had two kills. Now it looked like they were about to get number three. Instead of fat merchantmen like the first two, however, there was a lovely big Imperial heavy cruiser just coasting along into her attack range and begging for a torpedo or two. She was quite willing to oblige this nice gift from a beneficent Emperor.

"Make your course 4950 mils relative to current course and 1000 mils ascension, Pilot," she ordered. "Let's see if we can't get onto the six of that big bastard."

"Aye, Captain, course 4-9-5-0 relative and 1000 up."

There were 6400 military mils, known as milliradians on formal occasions, in a circle. Mils were the universal standard rather than the ancient "degrees" and "seconds" because, not only were they more precise, they were decimal based. An order to travel in the direction of 4950.551997 was quite normal, but that degree of precision was only used by navigators traveling interstellar distances.

The *Wahoo* moved upward to the left at an agonizingly slow .09C, but the crew was used to a long slow stalk by now. The watchword of S-boats was invisibility. Haste made you visible, especially if your drive was working hard enough to bleed through your suppresser field. Alice calmly watched the cruiser in her screen ever so slowly change position relative to her ship. They were nearly in position to take a shot and it had better be good, she thought. It was the only one they were going to get. You didn't get a second shot on a warship. Hell, you didn't *take* a second shot on a warship!

Two years ago, she thought, this would have been agonizing to any self-respecting Cluster Fleet crew. Everything was wham, bam, thank you ma'am for those guys. However, the S-boat service chose ruthlessly for patience and cunning. S-boat crews were volunteers, rigidly screened for compatibility, and graduates of a stiff qualification course. The qualification badge from the course was the icon of an S-boat surrounded by the dotted line indicating the icon was at a suspected, not verified, position. Every S-boat spacer was proud of what that badge implied.

S-boat operations were highly classified and even the existence of the boats themselves was closely held. Only the boat crews and Commander, S-boats, knew where a particular boat went on her war patrol until she came back bearing Imperial scalps or didn't come back at all. S-boat spacers didn't talk. They even borrowed a name from antiquity, "the Silent Service".

Full of enthusiasm for the ancient submarine crews, S-boat spacers studied every record they could find about them. The more spacers learned, the more in awe of their predecessors they got. One of Alice's favorite sources was an ancient submarine "movie" titled "*Run Silent, Run Deep*". She learned a lot about submarine lifestyle and tactics from that story, not to mention that both of the main characters were really cute. She wouldn't have minded hopping into bed with that sub skipper at all and the XO was just dreamy.

She checked her tactical screen and saw they were nearly behind the cruiser. "Weapons. Time to firing solution?"

"Solution zero one mikes from mark... Mark." One minute.

"Confirm outer doors on tubes one and six open."

"Confirm outer doors on tubes one and six open, aye." The process was automatic, but you had to check.

Alice stared at her screen, watching the attitude indicator change on the cruiser's icon then checked the time readout. It read twenty seconds. "Firing solution?"

"Firing solution confirmed."

S-boat spacers used the same formal command sequences of their submarine predecessors. No Fleet combat informality here.

The tension on the command deck was palpable, but everyone was still quietly professional, totally silent except for orders and responses. Alice had no exact analog for the feeling in the boat, but the attack scenes in that old movie conveyed the sensation exactly. No wonder she and her crew felt a kinship with those ancient submariners.

"Shoot." She gave the command quietly as the timer read zero then sensed, rather than felt, the twin rumbles as the torpedoes left their tubes. "Pilot, make your course 3150 relative and slowly bring up speed for TFD translation. Weapons, confirm outer doors closed."

"3-1-5-0 relative," the pilot repeated. "Initiating slow speed increase for TFD. Estimated time of translation in one zero mikes."

"Confirm outer doors closed, aye," added the Weapons Officer.

Alice nodded absently. "Understood, ten mikes to translation and outer doors closed. Rig boat for TFD." OPSEC, operational security, required them to leave a system after an attack, no matter what happened. They wanted the Empire to see ship losses as random for as long as possible. Hanging around an ambush site was a good way to get discovered by anyone coming to investigate, thus blowing OPSEC and the entire plan into the bargain. *Nobody* wanted that to happen.

Her attention was riveted on the main screen, just like everyone else on the control deck. The rest of the crew at their stations were probably following on repeaters. A readout in the upper right hand corner was counting down the seconds until projected torpedo impact as the blinking icons of the torpedoes crawled towards the cruiser.

"Ten seconds to impact," the Weapons Officer spoke in a flat voice that barely showed his underlying tension.

"Target has detected the torpedoes and is increasing speed." That was the sensor tech. His report was calm and professional - and just as tense underneath.

"Too late," someone else said softly. "Way too late."

The comment wasn't procedure, but Alice was concentrating too hard to care. Besides, she agreed.

"Five seconds. Four. Three. Two. One. Contact. Negative contact. Plus two. Plus three. Plus..."

The cruiser's icon turned red with terminal damage and vanished. "It took a little longer because he cranked on speed, folks," Alice announced, "but we got him. Good job, all."

There were relieved low cheers at that. Everyone felt drained after the tension of the attack, but Alice brought them back to what they still had to do. "Good job, but we've got to get out of here. Pilot, get us into TFD and make for Patrol Station Four. Let's see what's happening in the rest of the galaxy."

ARMY TRAINING CENTER
NIAD

There was a crowd in the Officers Club bar this afternoon, a bit strange for the hour. Apparently a lot of units were off cycle and their officers were trying to wind down. Others were just off duty. The whole made for a noisy, if generally amicable group. The various Army, Fleet, and Gladius uniforms also made it colorful.

Imin nervously adjusted the fit of his gray tunic. He was still getting used to the idea of wearing Cluster Fleet gray instead of his Cauldwell Planetary Guard black and light blue. The Commodore rank was new, also. That was something else that took a bit of getting used to. His rank made him senior to everyone here in the bar and provided him with some welcome privacy. He wanted it, but the reason wasn't here yet.

"The rank suits you, Commodore," said a well-remembered soft female voice behind him. Well, the reason was here now.

He turned and got a good look at Shana. He hadn't seen her since the Wareegan attack, and there were a good many changes. During his quick assessment, he got a bit of a shock. Oh, she was still very much a desirable woman, but there was an aura of physical hardness about her he hadn't seen before. That spectacular figure was wearing Gladius khakis with a kilt and sidearms, and that was another mild shock. He knew about her joining the Corps, but the seeing was much more impressive than the telling.

Being male, the last thing he took a really good look at was her face - a face wearing a mildly amused little smile at his preliminary scan. The smile said it was Shana, all right, but not the old Shana he knew. She was changed, more mature somehow, and no longer the carefree party girl he planned to marry once.

Well, he wasn't the same either. Not as changed as she was, but a bit more grown up than the old days before the Wareegan attacks. "You're looking good, Shana," he finally got out. "Different, but good."

Shana looked away for a moment after she sat down at the table and put her cap on an empty chair, looking at something only she could see. "The difference isn't the Corps, Imin. Not all of it. Most of the difference is something else."

She looked at him, and her assessment was somehow deeper than his. "Leave that in the past. How are you getting along? I heard you're now the head man for fighters in the Fleet. What's your title?"

Back before the Wareegan attack changed everything between them, she'd have made a joke or flirted. Now she was simply making conversation, like an old friend. There really was nothing more between them now. Not romantically, at any rate. That hurt, but not as much as he expected. Imin decided he'd settle for friendship. "I don't have a title yet," he said with a wry smile, "just a job and a concept. It's a job I got because I'm the only person they could find that has commanded more than two wings of fighters. Ergo, Admiral Mackinnie has me here with the rest of his staff, working on how to arrange all the separate fighter units into some sort of overall organization."

The barman put a beer - Gladius style, a bottle and no plass - down in front of her. That was different, too. The old Shana loved frou-frou mixed drinks, the more elaborate the better. She'd never drink beer straight from a bottle. "Sounds interesting," she said, returning his wry smile with one of her own. "It's also way above my pay grade. I'm here with my platoon, running a short course in unconventional operations for the Faire battalion."

"Your platoon?"

She nodded. "You can see the various cutting stuff and the pistol I'm wearing. They aren't for looks, Imin. I'm a combat commander and I've already done one campaign as a line officer and seven missions as Strike."

She took a pull of her beer and set it down. "Let's get to the heart of things, Imin. I'm not the girl you knew. I'm someone else, someone very different, and I like what I am. I'm in love with a man that understands that difference and what made me that way. We're engaged, Imin. I'm sorry to drop that on you, but it's a fact. Can we still stay friends?"

His smile was a little wistful. "If it will make you feel any better, I wouldn't make a pass at the new you. On the other hand, I wouldn't mind having you as a good friend, if you're willing."

She leaned over and hugged him, much to his surprise. "More than willing, Imin. I'm glad I haven't lost all of my old life."

There was something else in her statement, something he couldn't quite place, but it was not something he wanted to address. Better change the subject. "Did I hear you right?" he said as they settled back in their chairs. "You're working with the elves?"

The Scaanians, people from Faire, were universally tagged "elves" because of their small slim body structure, sharply defined faces, and pointed ears. Their planet, Faire, was discovered on one of the first Exploration Project missions. Back during the Empire's Expansion Period, a group of more-or-less normal humans belonging to an archaic society that played in living in the past had decided to set out from Wando. For reasons of their own, they wanted a distant world that would let them build the idealized medieval society of their fantasy.

Unfortunately, Faire had slightly higher than normal background radiation, finally producing the stable mutation that gave them an appearance out of an ancient folk tale. The die-off before that mutation stabilized was one reason Faire lost contact with the Empire. Scaanian society was still an idealized version of Old Earth's medieval period, but they'd never lost knowledge of the Empire and were quite willing to rejoin galactic society when the Frontier Cluster made an offer.

Scaanians were small, but very tough. After they joined the Frontier Cluster they insisted on becoming part of the campaign against the Empire. Lacking modern warships, they provided a battalion of troops to the Cluster Army, currently training up on Niad.

Shana nodded at Imin's question. "My boys and I just finished an unconventional warfare course for them. In a couple of days, we'll all go out to the Mossback training area and aggress against them while they run a four day raid. It's a little strange running a patrolling and dirty tricks course for guys that look like they came out of a children's story, but they're downright good fighting men. Every bit the equal of anyone outside the Corps and working hard on us."

He shook his head. "I'm a fighter pilot. I don't do mud, unless it's to shoot something in it. I still can't figure how we ended up with them anyway."

She nodded and said, "Neither can a lot of other folks, me included until recently. I've changed my tune since I came here, though."

She went on to tell the story. When the Scaanian battalion was originally offered to the Cluster Army, there was a good bit of discussion and plain old argument about what to do with them. The physical size and body structure of the elf sized men made Army commanders worry about having them in the combat line, but the King of Faire had flatly declared

255

his men were coming to fight. Political necessity made it impossible to disagree. Then someone had the thought of putting them in specially built powered armor suits. After all, the Scaanians already wore armor at home.

It turned out to be an inspired idea. The Scaanians took to powered suits like they'd invented the concept themselves and proved to be naturals as heavy troops. Not only were they used to the idea of wearing armor, but they were all former horse cavalry. Heavy armor tactics fit them like a glove. Once the army leadership saw what the Scaanians were doing with powered armor, they assigned the battalion as a strategic reserve at Army level then began negotiations with the King to raise more.

Of course, the fact that the Scaanians insisted on carrying long swords as part of their equipment was amusing to some. The Corps saw the weapons, understood, and agreed fully. At Corps recommendation, Scaanian swords were updated with the same molecular shear fields the Corps used on its fighting blades. The modified one measure long sword blade was going to be deadly in close combat and the Scaanians were both enthusiastic and skilled in its use.

Not every battle could be fought in armor and that was where Shana and her platoon came into the picture. They were giving the Scaanians a short course on how to do nasty and underhanded things to the enemy if the opportunity presented itself and her men were enjoying the respite from their hectic operational tempo. Besides, Shana told him, the little guys were enthusiastic students and hard core soldiers, elf look-a-likes or not.

#####

Later, Shana was meditating on the subjects of on her mission here and what looked like her new relationship with Imin as she walked back from the Club. The relationship issue could have gotten sticky, but Imin was taking it with good grace and he seemed to be relieved that the new Shana was more interested in friendship than romance. Given what a Gladius truly was - and she was a Gladius - Imin appeared a bit intimidated at the thought of her in his bed. That was fine with her. He really wasn't her type any longer.

That brought the warm thought of Karl to her mind and left her with a mellow glow. Karl understood her, what she'd been through, and wanted her as a life partner. That was priceless. Sex and romance were great, but the joining of two people that meshed in their personalities was far more important.

Imin, she decided, was going to make a good friend and that was also important to her. He was a link to the past she didn't want to entirely lose in her new life. Not after...

Her mind shied from the thought of her father's death and back to the incongruity of elves in modern powered armor wearing swords nearly as big as they were. Interestingly enough, Scaanian personality was closer to the Gladii than the normal run of humanity. Must have been their late medieval culture. They were a patriarchal bunch, too, but seemed perfectly willing to accept her as a combat officer. No problems there.

In fact... Shana saluted the approaching Scaanian commander. "Good afternoon, Colonel Frodi. Today's training went well, I think."

He returned her Corps salute with his own, fist to chest. Shana was familiar enough with Scaanian body structure by now to know that Frodi was a large and heavy man among his people and she was comfortable with that. It was the thick bushy beard he wore she couldn't quite get used to. Elves were supposed to be clean shaven. "Good afternoon, Lieutenant Ettranty. I agree. In fact, I'll say the whole course has gone well. Your people have done an excellent job as instructors."

The Faire dialect of Unispek was a little hard to understand at first, but she and her people were having no problem by now. Unispek was her first language in any case, so she was quite comfortable in the conversation. They fell in together and continued chatting as they walked across the parade ground towards the BOQ. "Lieutenant," Colonel Frodi said, "I've been looking at some of that marvelous recorded imagery on your Corps ground tactics, particularly the way your troops move in battle."

Shana nodded. "You mean the weave?"

"Yes," he replied, "exactly. The weave. That's fantastic! Could your people teach us how to do that? Do you have any experience with the tactic?"

"I was a line trooper before I went to Strike," Shana said. "All Strike dogs are. I've done the weave plenty of times, but it's complicated and takes a lot of training and coordination. I'm not sure we could teach your people. In fact, that's why we simplified the weave into a pulsing movement when we began to train the Army. The up, back, and around in the pulsing movement is simpler, but it still makes good use of firepower and mobility. What we taught the Army was the original combat tactic of the Corps when it was formed centuries ago. You certainly won't be facing a weave when you go up against Imperial New Forces."

"Still," Colonel Frodi said with a peculiar twinkle in his eyes, "given my men's training, I'm sure we could adapt your tactics to our experience."

He paused for a moment then asked casually, "Would you care to come to my quarters and discuss how we could do it? Perhaps over drinks?"

Shana stifled a laugh. Never good to laugh in front of a senior officer, even one that barely came to your shoulder and was making a pass at you. She could see him coming a kilomeasure away. Well, the elves were enthusiastic and motivated, all right. She had to give him points for ambition. "I'm sorry, Colonel," she said as pleasantly as possible, "but I'm betrothed. I just don't wear my ring on duty."

"Ahhh," he said philosophically, "that's a shame. Who's the lucky man?"

"Legate Karl Athan," she said with a smile, "of my legion, the Victrix."

"A very lucky man, indeed." Frodi was taking it graciously. "And he outranks me by a good bit, more the pity. However, I continue to feel we could adapt your weave to my tactics with a bit of thought. If you would still consider coming to my quarters, the discussion might be worthwhile. Perhaps with another member of your unit? An experienced one?"

Shana smiled at him. "Give me an hour to find him, and I'll bring Sergeant First Class Stauer, my platoon sergeant. Together, we might just come up with something."

Colonel Frodi sighed quietly. He knew Stauer. No chance at this big beautiful woman with him around. "Yes, well... in an hour, then."

Shana smiled again, saluted, and went off to find Sergeant Stauer. She had to admit the little guy took having his pass blown off better than most men she'd turned down. Then she got interested as she thought about his idea. You know, it just might work. Maybe if they modified the armor's IFF transponders...

OFFICES OF THE GUIDANCE COUNCIL
CAULDWELL

Nobody was more surprised than the Narsim Clarine Femiam when she found herself the new Recording Secretary for the Guidance Council after the coup. She suspected the background influence of the Corps political subversion teams, especially after her little sojourn at Victrix Base, but the PMGG Parliament Members seemed to take her with good grace as well. Apparently, she had a better reputation than she suspected.

That was a bit strange to her. She'd never before worried about a popular reputation, but her thoughts about politics and government were changing. Under Matic Ettranty - and on Central for that matter - she was more worried about political and personal survival than what was happening around her. Now, everything was different.

The revelation about Cauldwell's secret purpose as an Imperial escape hole was still causing sensational reports all over the planet. Additional release of the news about the hidden caches, not to mention what had happened with Matic Ettranty's death squads, was only adding to the furor. Everywhere Clarine looked, there was disgust at the Empire and (carefully guided by the PMGG and the political teams) a desire by ordinary citizens to stand up and fix problems.

Of course, there were contradictory views and very active political opposition to the PMGG, but that was all to the good. The opposition was in the nature of normal politics rather than any form of sinister plot. Democracy on Cauldwell was still young and messy, but it was growing and healthy.

Clarine screwed up her face into a disgusted expression at another thought. The secret concentration camp and the anonymous death squads were something to be laid squarely at her cousin's feet, and rightly so. She was never aware of them in her previous duties, thank the Lord Above. She'd thought that sort of thing was behind her when she fled Central. Had she become aware of them, she wasn't sure what she'd have done. Probably gone on the run again.

Her intercom signaled. "Narsim Femiam, you're daughter's here."

"Send her in," she told her secretary. That was another thing that had changed. Lana was no longer a party girl, nor was she the slightly aimless daughter she'd had up until the coup. She was changed, more mature now.

How changed, she realized when her office door was opened and Lana walked in. She was wearing a now very familiar gray uniform. Clarine stared at her, slightly aghast. "You've enlisted in the Cluster Fleet?"

Lana seated herself before Clarine's desk. "In Medical Service. For now." She looked mildly despondent for a moment, then determined. "I don't have any skills that would let me qualify for a Medical position yet. That's why I'm in the MS. To learn. I want to be a nurse and the Fleet will give me training for that."

A powerful rush of conflicting emotions swept through Clarine. Pride that her daughter was finally doing an adult's job. Worry that being in the Fleet could be dangerous. Sadness that she was finally losing Lana as she went her own way in life. Curiosity about... "Was it your young man that caused this?"

Lana shook her head. "Jamie? No. Well, not completely. I just felt I had to grow up sometime and had the opportunity. The Fleet needs people, Mother, and I'm a good worker when I want to be.

"And I really want to be. Finally," she said a little sadly.

Clarine stood, walked around her desk, lifted Lana to her feet, and hugged her. "You are, dear. You are a good worker. I'm certain you'll do well. It's just that..."

Still standing and holding her mother, Lana looked her in the eye grimly. "It's just that it's finally common knowledge that we're going back to Central and finish off the damned Empire. I intend to be part of that. I want to know I'm finally doing something besides getting drunk, or drugged, or waking up beside a man I barely know. I want to know I'm doing something that will help people. I've got the chance to help change human history and I'm not walking away from that chance.

"And I have someone that's worthwhile and who thinks he loves me, not just have sex. Jamie's a good man, Mother. I want to be worthy of him when we can finally be together after this is over."

Clarine stood back and studied her daughter with a mother's concern. "He's a soldier, Lana, and one in a very dangerous part of a dangerous business."

Lana's lips quirked in a grim smile. "Meaning he may not survive? We both know that, Mother. His odds aren't the best. We'll live with that. I helped keep him alive once without training. I want the training to do it right if I have to do it again. Besides, Jamie's told me he's thinking of hanging up his ax after the Empire's finished. I don't know what we'll do, but there'll be something. That exploration project, for instance. They'd love to have him and I can get qualified for one of the crews, once I get my nurse's training."

Clarine studied the very new person in front of her that was not quite the daughter she'd taken from Central. Lana in military service (as a nurse!) was something different, but her new maturity of outlook was even more different. Now there was a new and changed Lana in front of her that wanted to do something worthwhile.

Clarine was very, very proud.

She'd worry later.

THE WAHOO
JACOBS EMPIRE SPACE

The *Wahoo* was sitting in the Golden system, four AU out from the Primary, and doing an excellent imitation of pure vacuum. She had been in her position for the last 72 hours, mapping the system and evaluating Golden's potential for the Jacobs Empire. The Jacobs Empire, one of the breakaways that were so common now, was not currently classed as hostile, so the *Wahoo* wasn't hunting. On the other hand, Wltr Jacobs was an unstable megalomaniac, as beautiful an example as could be found in formerly Imperial space. That meant Niad wanted to keep a moderately beady eye on what he was doing. Ergo, the *Wahoo* quietly lying in place and watching many different things on passive sensors.

"We've about got all the intel we're going to get, Jimmy," Alice was in her tiny cabin with her Exec, Lieutenant Commander Jimmy Zand. "I'm getting to the point where I want to blow something up again. Twelve more hours and we need to set course for our next station. At least that one's in Imperial space."

Jimmy was nodding agreement when Alice's personal communicator spoke. //"Captain, Lieutenant Brk."// The third officer in their crew, he was Officer of the Deck at the moment.

She looked apology at her XO as she answered immediately. //"Go."//

//"Captain, we're getting a large ore carrier heading across our bows with a projected close approach of point zero five AU in two five mikes. Do we move?"//

Alice thought for a moment. //"No, she won't see us, but I'm coming up there after I finish talking to the Exec. Let me look at the situation. Meanwhile plot an attack profile on the merchie. It'll be good training for the watch. Out."//

Alice was on the bridge ten or so minutes later. "Captain has the conn."

"Captain has the conn, aye," replied the OD.

"Bring up visual," Alice commanded. Immediately, an image of the ore carrier was on the main screen. It was standard configuration for a merchantman, with a crew pod affixed to the front of three huge cargo globes, and a detachable drive pod fixed to the rear. It was about eleven megatonnes and slow, Alice reflected. She decided to go ahead and run an approach on the merchie, just to keep everyone in practice. "Battle stations torpedo."

Within five minutes after the gong - gong - gong of the alarm, the XO reported, "All stations closed up. We are prepared to go hot with torpedoes."

"Very good," Alice said in acknowledgment. Not bad, with the off duty watch in their bunks at the time of the alert. Meanwhile, the merchie was closer. "Commence approach, .09C. Pilot, make your course 2495 relative and 1100 declension."

"2-4-9-5 relative and down 1-1-0-0, aye."

The main screen changed to a schematic of the two ships as the *Wahoo* began to gently slide down and behind the merchie. Alice's concentration on the approach was broken when Sensors spoke up. "Captain, I have suppresser field bleed through approximately seven light minutes behind the merchie and high at a rough 3-4-0-0 mils reciprocal from its course. Designate Bogie Two. It appears to be heading for the merchie."

"Engines to 10 percent thrust. Let's slow down and see what happens. Sensors, continue to refine plot." Somebody was careless and Alice wanted to see just who it was.

The ore carrier was passing in front of them when the sensor tech spoke up again. "Captain, the bleed through is getting more definite as the bogie approaches. I now make it three sources in tight formation. If they stay on course, I ought to be able to register energy signatures at close approach."

"Understood." Curiouser and curiouser, thought Alice. The unknowns had no need for the kind of speed that generated bleed through against a merchie, if what they were doing was a hostile approach. If they weren't making a hostile approach, what in the hell were they doing? Some kind of Jacobs fleet exercise? In any case, she didn't want to be noticed, not as close as those unknowns were going to be coming. "All stop. Rig ship for silent running."

That meant no emission signature at all. Anything that could possibly radiate was shut down or minimized. Even the boat's engine was damped down.

The icons of the three bogies were solid on the screen now. Passive sensors had a firm lock. As they passed in front of the *Wahoo*, the icons were suddenly accompanied by data. "Captain, signatures on those bogies are consistent with Imperial frigates. They will do a close intercept on the merchie in less than ten mikes."

"Very good." This was the first sighting of Imperial frigates since they'd slapped around TF 16.2 near Tactine. That was the Frontier Fleet's very first contact with frigates. Possibly another boat had seen some, but she wouldn't know until they reported in on Niad. It looked like she was in a good spot to gather some data on the mysterious ships. Just sit and watch, Alice, and be sure everything was recorded. She called up the after-action report from TF 16.2 on her terminal while she was waiting for the intercept and did a little refresher reading. She had been a member of the task force during that scrap. Under orders to hide her collier, she'd worried more about detection than the fight. 16.2 had destroyed all six frigates, but at unacceptably high cost. Imperial frigates were very, very dangerous ships.

"Frigates intercepting target," Sensors announced. Alice watched the main screen as the frigates swarmed up to the merchie in a triangular formation and crash decelerated. Stupid maneuver. They could have done it a lot more smoothly. On the other hand, that might be easy for them, given the way the frigates behaved against 16.2. She wasn't prepared for what happened next.

As soon as the frigates surrounded the merchie, gunfire from all three ships destroyed the crew pod, killing all aboard. The frigates dropped their suppresser screens and simply held station on the cargo globes.

"What the hell are they up to, Skipper?" asked her Exec. "Everyone in the system will pick up those guns on light speed sensors, even the half-assed Jacobs people."

"Damned if I know, Jimmy," she replied softly, "but I think we're seeing Imperial piracy." The killing of the merchant crew bothered her in a way that destroying two previous Imperial merchantmen hadn't. They were at war with the Empire, even if Central didn't know it yet. This was simple smash and grab of an innocent bystander.

Alice was amazed at the smooth, absolutely perfect coordination the three frigates showed. No normally crewed warship in history could match that. It was like the three ships were parts of one entity. Given the firepower and the maneuverability the frigates had shown, one of those three ship formations was damn near as dangerous as a dreadnought. On the other hand, Alice thought, combat reports said the loss of one ship in a formation heavily degraded the effectiveness of the other two. A plan began to form.

"Indications of a Bogie Three approaching," Sensors reported. "Just fast enough to bleed through suppresser. It's at 3-1-3-0 mils relative to merchant ship."

The *Wahoo* was totally undetectable as Bogie Two plowed past them at a more sedate pace than the frigates. It dropped its suppresser field as it passed, turning into a collier towing a crew pod. As they watched, the collier stopped near the merchie and detached the new crew pod. Swarms of mechs emerged from the collier and began to remove the damaged pod from the merchie and affix the new pod to the front of the ore carrier.

"Piracy all right," Alice said. "One will get you ten that ore carrier's going to be headed for Middle Empire."

"No bets, Skipper," the Exec said. "What do we do?"

That was the question, Alice thought. The cautious approach would be to simply sit here and record everything. If the Empire was out grabbing cargoes with their best ships, they were already hurting. Nothing the Cluster or the S-boats had done so far was major, so they had to be already critically short of resources. This was important information. Add to that the suspicion there might be more smash and grab teams hiding in this system, and watching began to look like a good option.

On the other hand, those frigates were priority targets. The fewer of them, the more Fleet ships would survive the upcoming attack on Central. There were three right in front of her boat, and they were all preoccupied. Great chance for an ambush. But how to get the word back to Niad?

Making a decision, Alice began to issue orders. "XO, prep a tachyon data packet drone to Commander, S-boats, Niad. Download all sensor readings and my estimation that this is official piracy on the Empire's part. Include all bridge commands for the next two mikes then drop it ballistic and set it to activate in one hundred hours if no abort command received.

"Pilot, drive at 20 percent strength. Make your course 5150 mils relative and over. Put us on the six of those three frigates."

The Exec came up on his private intercom channel to her. "Sure this is wise, Skipper? We can't hide the destruction of those frigates."

"We're going to make it look like the ore carrier blew up accidentally and took the Imperial ships with it, Jimmy," Alice replied. "Then we're going to hide and see what happens. If they find us, we'll take out whoever we can then self-destruct if it looks like we can't get away. We can't afford to let the Empire know S-boats exist."

"Aye, Skipper," the Exec replied after a moment's hesitation. Every S-boat spacer knew the standing orders if detected. It went with the job, and was also why the crews were all volunteers. "Let's just keep from being detected, shall we? I'd like to get back to Niad."

"Agreed."

Alice was watching the Imperial ships and the merchie. It was going to be a while longer before that ore carrier would be ready to go. Hopefully, that would hold the attention of the frigates until the *Wahoo* got into firing range.

The approach was slow and careful. Tension on the bridge was beginning to run high again, a familiar feeling to Alice by now, but there was an extra strain to it. She was gambling her boat and all their lives on her ability to destroy all three frigates then get out of the area without being detected. Carefully, she used her terminal to go back over all the Fleet knew about the frigates. The formation in her screen tended to confirm the estimation they operated in three ship elements. Those elements were deadly, as maneuverable as any ship in space, fast as a thief, and they acted as one ship instead of three in formation. They had a weakness, however, shown in the scrap with 16.2. Kill one of the frigates and they lost coordination. Kill two and the survivor ran for it.

At least, that was the current guess at Intel. She was about to find out if that was true. In fact, she was planning on it.

With agonizing slowness, the three icons and their captive swung into her firing arc. "Designate all ships as targets. Range?"

"Range is now point oh nine light minutes, Captain," said Weapons. "Designate frigate at twelve o'clock as Target One. Target Two frigate is at seven o'clock and Target Three frigate is at five o'clock. Target Four, collier, is at eleven o'clock and close to Target Five, ore carrier."

"At point oh eight light minutes," Alice said, "launch a six tube ballistic spread set for delayed activation. Torpedoes from Tubes One and Four on Targets Five and Four, set for ten - that's one zero - mikes activation. Two and Five on Target One set for one zero point oh one mikes activation. Three and Six on Target Two same setting. Reload tubes One and Four and shoot with appropriate settings to impact Target Three at the same time we hit the first two."

"Understood," Weapons acknowledged. He was busy with his board for a few moments. All torpedoes set. The automatic reloaders on their tubes had a seven second reload time. They would be able to drop enough torpedoes to attack the whole group and move away before they activated.

"Pilot," Alice said, "once we drop, move us around in front of the group. I want to wind up as close to zero mils relative to enemy formation as possible. Weapons, set up for a down the throat snap shot in case we miss one of those frigates. Don't wait on my command, those frigates are too fast. A miss will be your signal to fire."

"Understood."

She'd set it up. Now to see if it worked.

"Point oh eight light minutes," Weapons announced. "Launching."

There was a series of six thumps, followed seven seconds later by two more. The *Wahoo* edged away from her heading and began to circle the frigates and their captured ore carrier. Alice kept her eyes on the main screen, occasionally checking the time readout as it counted down to torpedo activation.

They were nearly in position when the torpedo drives lit off. "Torpedoes are hot," Weapons announced. "All are functioning. Running hot, straight, and normal." The last sentence was unnecessary with modern missiles, simply borrowed from the ancient movies. By now, Alice was so into the attack, the thought didn't even make her smile. Besides, the phrase was just *right*.

Weapons spoke up. "Captain, we are within point zero five light minutes of the group. Request permission to fire a full spread at the frigates when the first spread is within point zero two light minutes of their targets."

Alice thought about it for a minute. It was a good idea, but it would only leave them with five torpedoes if things fell into the crapper. She snorted. If they didn't kill all three frigates and they were detected, a hundred torpedoes wouldn't be enough. "Good idea, Weapons. Do it."

They watched with breathless concentration as the icons of the torpedoes crawled towards their targets. Another spread rumbled from their tubes. Sensors said, "No active scanners detected on the frigates. Torpedoes should be within passive detector range in one zero seconds from mark... mark."

The frigates suddenly jumped forward and began firing small caliber bolts back at the torpedoes. Torpedoes aimed at the ore carrier and collier simultaneously detonated on target and the whole area was washed in antimatter backblast.

Alice could feel the nervous sweat beading on her forehead as she watched. They still hadn't killed a frigate.

There!

"Hit! Target Three destroyed," Sensors announced. "One and Two cranking on speed."

And they were fast! Those frigates had come up to speed from a dead stop faster than any ship Alice had ever seen. But...

"Hit! Two hits!" Sensors said, excitement making his voice harsh. "Both targets destroyed by second salvo."

"Pilot, make your course 3-5-5-0 relative and up," Alice commanded. "Get us the hell out of here in case there are more of them. Good job, Weapons." Hopefully, there weren't any more Impies nearby.

There were more.

"Suppresser fields dropping!" Sensors said. "Two enemy formations inbound. Confirmed as frigates."

"Drive zero," Alice snapped. "Silent running."

For the next twelve hours, the two frigate formations were all over the area, active sensors lashing in every direction. Everybody remained at their stations, tensely watching the two elements of frigates repeatedly crossing the area where their comrades had died. Several times, a triplet of frigates came close, but not close enough for them to detect the *Wahoo* coasting away on ballistic, suppressed, and drives down.

As the searchers began to work their way away from the scene, Sensors spoke up again. "Drive sources have broken orbit from Golden IV and are headed this way. Energy signature conforms to conventional destroyers. I make their strength at around twelve."

"Okay, boys," Alice breathed to the oncoming destroyers, "get those bastards off us and we'll just quietly leave." Right now, conventional destroyers seemed relatively harmless.

The two divisions of frigates did the unexpected. They joined, but instead of attacking the Jacobs destroyers, all six frigates accelerated away and translated into TFD. Alice let out her breath in a long whoosh. "Thank you, Jacobs fleet. Pilot, return to original heading, but set course for Niad. Communications, transmit self-destruct to the drone. I think it's time we went home and talked to somebody in a higher pay grade, folks."

She was leaving the bridge when the XO caught up with her. "Captain, something strange's happening with those frigates."

"Stranger, you mean, Jimmy," she cracked with a smile.

"Stranger, then," he replied with a matching smile. "They could have taken that bunch of destroyers, even at two to one. Why didn't they?"

Alice thought for a moment. "Good point, but they were sure to take damage or losses if they did."

She turned and watched the approaching Jacobs squadron in the main screen for a moment and added, "What if they didn't want to take those losses? They didn't have anything on us, and they didn't have any captured ships that we could detect. Suppose we just blew up their tidy little operation in this system as it was getting started? Running would be a pretty good option in that case."

Jimmy nodded. "I suppose so, Skipper, but that tells me they're being cautious with those frigates. I wonder if they only have a limited amount of them."

Alice nodded. That was also what she was thinking. A limited number of their best ships. Pirating resources from other systems. Was the Empire already badly stretched?

Alice went back to her cabin and thought hard as she began to mentally compose her report. She was wondering if this whole episode was bad news about the frigates or good news about the state of the Empire.

CHAPTER 13

CLUSTER MILITARY HEADQUARTERS
NIAD

"This is the take from the *Wahoo's* intercept of those frigates two months ago, edited down for time," said Commander Claude Ancel, now Intelligence Liaison Officer for the Command Staff. "The actual attack took five hours from start to finish. Once the recording is over, we can discuss these events and their implications. We think the implications are major, by the way."

His audience turned to study the holo of *Wahoo's* engagement with rapt attention. The S-boats were new and different enough that even Commander, Battleships, was willing to put up with the slow progress of the action. That told Claude quite a lot, when all was said and done. Startlingly beautiful blonde Vice Admiral Roberta Detrik was a high energy battleship spacer and not normally into slow, but she was very, very serious about the frigates of the Emperor's Guard.

While the senior officers around the conference table studied Claude's presentation, he studied them in turn. The Command Staff was originally an ad hoc grouping of previously independent commands. Now they were formally organized into an army, a corps, and a fleet, all under an overall command. Organization was necessary since the Central campaign was being planned at a level unseen for centuries.

There was plenty of rank present at the table, Claude thought. The CNO and head of the Staff was at the head of the table, Admiral Lane Mackinnie. The Corps of Gladius officers were on one side, including Senior Officer of the Corps Shyranne Garua and newly promoted Corps Legate Khev Garua. The Commanders and Legates of the Legions ran down the table from them, including the Garuas' replacements: the new Commander and Legate of the Valeria. The sole missing Legion Commander was that of the Victrix, which would not have a Commander until a senior female officer could come up through the ranks and take the position. Legate Athan had his acting Support Command Commander, Major Sharon Ariel, with him instead. The real Support Command Commander, Claude recalled, was on motherhood furlough for the next twenty months. The Corps classified pregnant women as nondeployable and extended the status for eighteen months after birth to allow a solid nurturing basis for the child.

Claude thought that was an excellent policy since his Gladius wife, Captain Carlita Ancel, was also on limited duty with headquarters Combat Information Technology due to impending motherhood and would remain so throughout the projected period of the Central attack. At least she and their child would be out of it, he thought grimly. He had no illusions about the blood the attack would spill. After their Virgin Mission, Gladius women were no longer in combat positions, but that didn't mean they were safe. Support Command went down after the main battle was over. Shit happened. For that matter, every ship in the attacking fleet was in danger on this one. That included troop carriers and supply ships.

Across the table from the Corps, the Frontier Cluster Fleet was represented by the Commanders of Battleships, S-boats, and Conventional Forces, and they'd brought along newly minted Commodore Imin Webster as the senior fighter officer. Webster was the former commander of the Cauldwell Planetary Guard, an entirely fighter force and a good one. He'd inherited the top fighter position simply because nobody else had ever commanded at least two wings of fighters within memory and word had it they were still thinking up a name for his position.

For his part, Commodore Webster seemed a bit bemused to be surrounded by an active and growing military structure he hadn't known existed a year ago. The fact he now found himself a senior officer in that structure only compounded his bemusement.

Cluster Army Chief of Staff General Jon Malcom, sitting further down the table with his seven division commanders, had his own problems. Prior to the Valeria landing on Tactine that crushed - destroyed - an occupation by Imperial New Forces, he'd been a Colonel in the not all that active Tactine militia. Fortunately, he'd also been an avid hobbyist in military strategy games and student of military history. That put him one up on any other Tactine militia senior officer and earned him the overall command of the Cluster Army. Below him were seven provisional division commanders. Every rank above platoon leader in the Army was provisional simply because nobody knew who was up to the job. The Army was organized on the basic principle of someone getting a shot at command, then being replaced if they muffed it. There had already been a few replacements after the Labatt operation. The policy brought a certain degree of uncertainty, Claude thought, but it did wonders for motivation.

As the recorded sensor imagery ceased, Claude stood up and said, "There are two glaring features of this report. First is that the Empire has apparently begun hijacking shipments in breakaway systems. None of our other S-boats reported this, but that doesn't mean it isn't happening. Our feeling is that we simply haven't caught it elsewhere yet.

"The other feature is that the frigates chose to run rather than engage what we feel was a much less capable force from the Jacobs Fleet. This could have been to maintain operational security, but we think it also reflects a marked desire to avoid risk to the frigates wherever possible. In turn, this policy implies that the frigates are regarded as a valuable but limited resource."

Vice Admiral Detrik spoke up. "I see something else here. The frigates in the report were all operating in tight divisions of three. To me, that confirms they were designed to function that way. In our original confrontation, efficiency dropped as soon as that triad was broken. Besides the TF 16.2 engagement, is there any more information about that?"

The battle between TF 16.2 and Imperial frigates was the first of its kind and the pocket battleship task force had gotten bloodied. In fact, the battleships had been unable to kill all of the frigates despite having them outnumbered, which would have meant the Cluster's existence being exposed to the Empire, but one of the first trial S boats had killed the last frigate with a torpedo. The battle rankled everyone in the battleship structure and Claude diplomatically decided to let further discussion on that subject pass. Battleship spacers regarded the battle as a failure of their beloved little ships and were very sensitive about it. Detrik hugely outranked him and she was reputed to have quite a temper. "The *Orzel* and the *U-47* ambushed frigate formations in Imperial space. In both cases, they didn't get all of them. The *Orzel* killed one and the *U-47* got two. After the attacks, the survivors immediately cracked on speed and took off on a least time course for Middle Empire. They made no attempt to fight."

"Now that's very interesting," she said softly.

"Don't make too much of it, Bobbie," Admiral Mackinnie rumbled. "Those frigates didn't have to stand and fight. Central will be different."

"It's still a weakness," she shot back. "One we can exploit. Kill one of a division and it loses major effectiveness. A single frigate isn't as effective as one of our ships. That tells me we ought to be making partial kills on frigate divisions instead of trying for all three."

Bobbie Detrik had come up through pocket battleships, so she was extremely interested in frigate vs. battleship tactics. The first confrontation between TF 16.2 and Imperial Guard frigates hadn't come off too well for the little battlewagons (the words "bloody debacle" came to mind) and she badly wanted to change the situation.

Pocket battleships were the Frontier Fleet's primary warship. They were designed fifty years ago to overcome the twin problems of manpower and material shortages that existed out on the Empire's borders. They were only possible because of the development of a new generation of AI on

271

Malthus, reducing crew requirements to three persons. They fell between a corvette and a destroyer in size, but were heavily armored and carried much more powerful protective screens, guns, and engines than any other warship its size. Their primary armament of four 35 centimeasure guns mounted in their bow was the key to battleship tactics. A 35 CM gun was actually a dreadnought weapon, which made the little ships deadly in any confrontation. Battleship spacers lived literally surrounded by their heavy guns and called the low clunk-twang noise of the guns firing "making music". The in-your-face attitude of battleship spacers turned them from deadly to savage. Bobbie fully shared the aggressive attitude of her crews. As far as she was concerned, any threat to the dominance of her beloved peewee battlewagons boded ill for that threat once she turned her attention to it.

Lane Mackinnie nodded slowly. "A point. Put your people to work on exploiting that and brief me when you have solid recommendations.

"Meanwhile," he said, turning to the group at large, "there are other points. If the Empire is hurting enough to turn to hijacking, they're already weaker than we thought. In a way, the Tactine raid was already a signal of weakness, but this program of hijacking or piracy, or whatever you want to call it, is confirmation. I think we have to discuss firming up a date to move on Central soon. I know we wanted things to get tight in Middle Empire, but they may be worse than we imagined."

Vice Admiral Fields, Commander, S-boats, commented, "Admiral, we can speculate all we want, but we don't have confirmation. I recommend that we start reconnaissance of Central and other key systems in Middle Empire. I want to assign some of my boats to go in and do just that. The S-boats were built with that capability in mind."

SOC Garua turned to Fields and asked, "Alan, could they drop our scouts? If it's time for us to start looking at Central closely, we may as well get people on the ground, too." She gave no hint of the fact that her son was one of those scouts.

Alan nodded. "I think so. Historically, submarines were used to deliver special operations teams as well as attack enemy shipping and perform reconnaissance. We'll have to run some trials, but I think the idea is solid."

"Run your trials," Lane said slowly. "If they work out, the scouts will go in with S-boats when they go. If not, we'll use other means."

Lane Mackinnie slowly scanned the room, looking each person in the eye. "We have to start moving before Central collapses completely. Letting them collapse may be the safest thing for us, but there are nine billion people on Central and trillions in what's left of Middle Empire. We've already done enough damage to innocents. We won't do any more.

"It's time to begin our campaign against Central."

THE WAHOO
ALPHA CENTAURI SPACE

She was prepared for slow and careful when she volunteered for S-boats, Alice thought, but the tension during operations was a bit of a surprise. Her previous kills had required a patient tense stalk, but that was something implied in the job. This time, they were cruising in space just off Central and the familiar nervous feeling was cranking back up again. Added to that was the additional worry that they were light on armament. No S-boat skipper was happy shipping out with only six torpedoes, but the space normally occupied by reloads was needed for the six scouts, plus equipment, the *Wahoo* was transporting.

Alice snorted. Tension or not, this was a real S-boat mission, just like in the ancient movies. Besides, she thought proudly, only an S-boat could get this close to Central without coming up on the scanners they were catching constantly on passive.

She checked the repeater screens next to her command seat. The *Wahoo* was just about in the right position, just outside Central's atmosphere. Time to go to work. "Pilot," she commanded, "put us into orbit. Engines to ten percent. I want to do a complete scan of Central before we start dropping scouts.

"Send Lieutenant Arvin to the bridge," she added. She continued to watch as the boat crept, ever so slowly and carefully, into orbit.

It was only a few moments before the Gladius officer arrived. "Use the jump seat, Lieutenant," she said. "I want you to start picking out drop points for your people."

His response was a laconic, "Aye."

Strange, Alice thought, the rest of the bridge was silent and tense, but the Gladius was simply sitting in the jump seat, watching the scans calmly, showing nothing but professional interest and occasionally making notes on his memo pad. Once again, she decided Gladii were just weird.

The information they were picking up was revealing. Imperial City, sliding into evening below, was its usual colossal self, apparently unchanged from before the Empire began to sunder. However, the troop installations on the second continent were new. She supposed that the New Forces had to be based somewhere and Shangnaman wanted them under his beady eye, but not too close to the palace complex. In fact, one of the six massive orbital defensive installations was in stationary orbit over the troop encampments. Given Shangnaman's paranoia, that was to guarantee loyalty. Be loyal, or your beloved Emperor drops a load of crap on your head. She noted there were no fleet bases on the planet any longer. Ships were too hard to catch if they decided to rebel. One of the other boats assigned to scout the system would find them, then. Her job was Central itself.

The pilot was occasionally shifting the boat's slow orbit, avoiding contact with merchant traffic or giving the orbital defense installations a wide berth. As they passed one of the defense installations, Sensors spoke up, "Captain, I'm not detecting any indication of life on those orbital defense installations."

Were they all robotic? If they were, she was willing to bet that their control points were inside the Palace itself, probably constantly within the Emperor's reach. That would fit with Shangnaman's paranoid personality. Everything that could possibly be a danger to him was either neutralized or completely in his grasp. The notion of robotic defense installations was worth verifying. "Sensors, I want a close read on each of those installations, as close as we can get on passives, anyhow. Report any life signs at all."

Things were quiet for a little longer, then Lieutenant Arvin asked quietly, "Captain, how long before we return to the terminator?"

Alice checked her status repeater then said, "About six hours. We're in an eight hour orbit."

He looked at his notepad for a moment, then up at her decisively. "If you could launch us once we cross the terminator that will work out beautifully. Given what our target is and the time I'd like for final preparation prior to launch, I'd prefer that we not be dropped on the next orbit but on the one after that, if at all possible."

Alice didn't bother to ask about the target. No need for her to know. Likewise, Lieutenant Arvin didn't know every aspect of her mission, or the fact that there were more S-boats in the system, although the latter was obvious to both of them. Neither one knew how many boats were here or their missions. Looking at the Gladius officer, Alice decided this operation was so compartmented that he probably didn't know how many scout drops were being made.

For that matter, she didn't bother to mention that every additional orbit brought more chance of discovery to the *Wahoo*. That sort of thing went with the job, and dropping scouts was one of her missions on this cruise. For a moment, she thought about what the scouts were supposed to do and decided she preferred taking her chances in her boat. More power to those guys, she thought. They can have their job. She didn't want it.

Twelve hours later, the ship's weapons techs were preparing for the launch in the forward torpedo room. The ancient method of launching special operations types out the torpedo tubes had once again proved practical, with a number of adaptations for the types involved.

The scouts' one man sleds, for instance, were now configured as long rods, with controls at one end and drives at the other. The scout would lie along the rod with the suppresser field generator under his belly, followed slightly further back by the antigravity generator and an atmosphere field to allow for launch in vacuum. A largish pod attached to the back of the sled contained all of his supplies and equipment. All of this would now fit in a torpedo tube. Carefully, the techs went over all of the sled's equipment, testing the suppresser, atmosphere field generator, and antigravity generators twice. One antigravity generator failed its second test and was immediately replaced. Finally, the equipment was ready.

At launch minus 30 minutes, the scouts appeared, fully armored, and boarded their sleds to be loaded in the tube. On the bridge, Alice was already looking at the drop points. Weapons had the locations dialed in, so there was nothing for her to do but give the word if she decided everything was good.

Tension in the *Wahoo* had settled a bit by the time the drop approached. Everyone was still on high alert, but meals and rest periods had dulled the worry a good bit. Humans could get used to anything with enough time, Alice decided, even the very real possibility of destruction at any moment. The drop points were approaching. "Weapons, confirm scouts ready to drop."

The reply was immediate. "Aye, Captain. Scouts are in the tubes and prepared for ballistic drop. All tubes ready."

Watching her repeater, Alice saw the drop point crawl towards the boat. "Initiate automatic drop sequence."

"Initiating automatic drop sequence," Weapons responded.

A few long, tense minutes later, "Sequence active, drop commencing."

They all felt the sequenced slight rumble as the tubes belched their loads of men and equipment. "Drop complete," Weapons announced. "All tubes clear. Outer doors closed."

"Understood clear and outer doors closed," Alice responded. "Pilot, begin to ease us out of orbit. We've done what we came to do. Let's go home."

#####

The scouts fell softly, slowly, and nearly invisibly towards Central's night side. The destination for this particular group was Imperial City. They were going into the tiger's den and they were very careful about their actions. The best defense for scouts was the enemy not knowing they existed in the first place. Do not attract attention. If they did, half their protection was gone.

Falling quietly and gently through Cental's atmosphere, Lieutenant Arvin worried about the drop being detected, but fatalistically decided there he was nothing he could do he wasn't already doing. He wasn't out to win a commendation. Leave that to the line troops. For scouts, getting into Imperial City just prior to daylight was enough.

CHAPTER 14

CLUSTER MILITARY HEADQUARTERS
NIAD

The room was dead quiet after the holo presentation finished. Senior Officer of the Corps Shyranne Garua wasn't sure if the silence was due to shock or horror. She'd seen the raw take from the scout data and it still disturbed her sleep.

Imperial City was no longer the rich, shining capitol of the Empire of Ten Thousand Suns. Most inhabitants were living at a poverty level never before seen in the Empire and a good portion of the city was abandoned. One of the scouts - her son - had captured an Imperial Fleet officer cowering in one of the abandoned residential towers, hiding from an insane Emperor that wandered through the Palace computer system.

The part about the Emperor being in the computer net was hard to believe, but confirmed by a passive tap Sergeant Liam Garua had managed to remotely emplace on a Palace terminal. What the Fleet officer told Liam under questioning with a hypnotic drug was disgusting... and an utter horror.

Imperial organizations including the Guard - *especially* the Guard - were now murdering people by the thousands at the express direction of the Emperor... and doing it willingly. The drugged officer admitted he'd supervised the execution of hundreds people a week, some of them simply shot down in the streets to make an arbitrary total. Then the Emperor had shown up in his computer terminal and declared he wasn't killing enough people. That was all the reason needed for Shangnaman to pronounce him an enemy and a dead man, so he ran before he could be killed.

Everyone in the conference room knew Shangnaman was a paranoid sociopath, but nobody was ready for the depth of his insanity. Imperial City was under the worst reign of terror in history and here in the Cluster they were only getting part of the story. Briefly, Shyranne wondered what they were going to find when they finally took down the crazy bastard, but she steered her mind away from that train of thought. The pictures it evoked weren't something she wanted to contemplate.

"Frankly, what we are getting from our scouts is pretty hard to take, but it's all true and consistent. With what we've found, it's no longer any wonder that we've had so few probes from the Empire since the Tactine incursion. Not only do the New Fleet officers lack the willingness to come out to us, the Emperor has expressly forbidden it! That's amazing enough, but what we've gathered about conditions in Imperial City is far worse. It's turned into something worse than the Dark Age before the Empire." Admiral Lane Mackinnie said that in his usual calm, rumbling tones, but his eyes betrayed the pain he felt at the utter corruption of an Empire to which he'd dedicated his adult life.

Chief Executive of the Frontier Cluster Randl Turner could see Lane's pain easily, Shyranne noted. General Jon Malcom couldn't, but that was because he was still a bit uncomfortable in his position as head of the Army and certainly uncomfortable in a private meeting between his civilian superior and the far more experienced heads of the other Cluster military forces.

"Shangnaman is mad," Shyranne said quietly in Unispek for Malcom's sake. "We all knew that, but we far underestimated the effects of his madness. We currently have no idea where he's bodily located, but he's loaded his persona into the palace's computer net and seems to be conducting an irrational reign of terror on the Imperial staff... and not just them.

"Imperial City has been deteriorating for years, even before this whole crash began. Now, the city is nothing but incredible slums on its lowest levels and a frantic decadence above that. Apartment towers are universally sealed off mid way up from street level to create separation between the ruling classes and the rest of the population. The upper classes are living well, but the rest are barely surviving. Constant searches for 'enemies of the state' among the poor kill hundreds every week."

"Shangnaman's purge of senior officers has gutted the Imperial forces," Lane added. "That's to the good as far as we are concerned, but the military still retains enough strength and coordination to make it a tough fight when we go in.

"The Emperor's Guard is an entirely different proposition," he continued. "Our people have only gotten flashes and hints so far, but our estimation is that they are frighteningly competent. They remain a major threat but we don't have a good handle on their strength. There are always plots against the Emperor and have been for over a century. If any of them succeeds, the thought of the Guard in competent hands isn't a pleasant one."

"Meanwhile," Shyranne commented, "billions of people on Central are suffering in Hell."

Randl looked back at Shyranne quietly for a moment. His face was deceptively mild, looking much like someone's beloved grandfather and hiding the shrewdness in his blue eyes. "Your plan was always to destroy the command ability of Central and leave Middle Empire as a broken force, incapable of attacking the Frontier Cluster.

"That's a military solution, you know," he mused. "I understand military solutions from my years in the Fleet. My years in politics tell me military solutions don't go far enough. Destroying the palace and Imperial forces won't really solve the problem, simply put it off. All your plan does is leave Central in bloody ruins. Middle Empire can rebuild and we have no idea which way it would go. Besides, there are the people on Central and other Middle Empire worlds. We have to do something about that. They are as much our responsibility as the people here in the Cluster. Shangnaman has created the problem on Central, but Central's destruction will affect all of Middle Empire."

Surprisingly, it was General Malcom that spoke up. Besides Turner, he had the most life experience as a civilian. He could see what the Chief Executive was driving at. "We've gone as far as we can militarily, Narsima Turner. What can we do beyond that?"

Lane and Shyranne both glanced at Jon then turned to Randl. They knew what they had to do, but had no plan once the Imperial command structure was in ruins. Their plan was to simply leave and let Middle Empire fend for itself however it could, as long as it was no longer a threat to the Cluster. They only wanted to mitigate the damage and give the former Empire some basis for reconstruction, not take on the task of guiding it.

Randl smiled at their looks. "The Executive Council and I have been talking a lot about the situation. The key here is what happens after the battle, not the battle itself."

"Victory still isn't certain," Lane interjected, "especially with the Emperor's Guard thrown into the mix."

Randl nodded. "No argument there. However, we also have to plan for after the battle as well as the battle itself. Your plan is basically miliary and has gone as far as it can. What happens after the battle is the Council's business and we've given it a great deal of thought. Your strategic direction is good, but it never went far enough to finish the job."

"What are you thinking about?" Shyranne asked.

"We have agencies and groups here in the Cluster," Randl replied. "A lot of them are still spread all over human occupied space, but the local heads have gone along with our request to remain incommunicado until we can come out of the shadows. The Church, the Mennonites, and other religions come to mind, but there are private organizations that are quite accustomed to circumstances like we've found on Central, if not as bad. We need to get them all into Central and let them go to work. At my suggestion, the Council's authorized the recruiting of political restructuring teams from these religions and organizations to rebuild Central's government after the battle. Given what you've told me, the original politicians and bureaucrats will be useless or worse, but we can possibly use a few after a suitable vetting process. That's what's going to be needed. With proper political guidance, we can salvage Middle Empire, Central most of all."

"Salvaging Central and Middle Empire will be a major undertaking, and one on which we hadn't planned," Shyranne said. "I'm not sure it can be done."

"You weren't sure you could salvage the Cluster," Randl shot back, "but you did it. Reconstruction after the fighting is critical if we want to spare our children and grandchildren the job of doing this all over again."

Shyranne looked at Randl thoughtfully then nodded agreement.

"We have to integrate what we're doing with what you have in mind, Narsima Turner," Lane said. "We have to get our staffs together and work out a coordinated overall plan, and soon, too. We've begun preliminary preparations for attack."

"The Fleet, the Army, the Corps, all have been given warning orders," Shyranne added.

"We're trying to save humanity's future," Randl said firmly, "but we owe it to that future to finish the job properly. We're actually further along with planning the restructure of Middle Empire than you might think. We made the decision to start creating a plan once we were brought into your military operation for the Empire. Giving those people a new life isn't your job, Shyranne, or the job of the military in general. That's mine."

IMPERIAL PALACE
CENTRAL

Tapping his finger near the hidden sensor on his terminal, Vice Regent Absolom Last contemplated the wisdom of what he was about to do. That sensor was unique to his terminal, the only one in existence unless the Guard also had one, unknown to him. Which they probably did, he thought with irritation. It enabled him to summon the Emperor, always a chancy proposition considering that Shangnaman was emotionally unstable and basically crazy - two of his good points.

Tactine was a spectacular and costly failure. Last, the commander of that misbegotten debacle, had excuses and scapegoats ready just in case, but it didn't turn out to be a problem. Shangnaman was already so far around the bend that failure of any one of his plans simply didn't exist. No repercussions for a failure that never happened. That made life a little easier for a while then Last found himself handed the job of Vice Regent.

280

Shangnaman was so busy discovering traitors and killing people that he no longer had time such distractions as running the Empire. Running the Empire was currently Last's job, and not a very desirable one.

Yet again, Last wondered why he was titled "Vice" Regent. Who in hell was designated the Regent? That was an important question and one he couldn't answer. If his plans actually succeeded, the answer was going to be very, very important. At the moment, though, it wasn't germane to the current problem - and plot - requiring him to risk his life.

You first had to identify a problem to fix it, and Shangnaman refused to admit any such thing as a problem existed. Given that his cousin - not he himself - was insane, the options weren't all that many for the Vice Regent. They weren't all that survivable, either, even if you were the only man in the universe Shangnaman relied on to run his Empire.

He often regretted setting up Shangnaman's "Perpetual Preservation" after his appointment as Vice Regent. It seemed an easy sell at the time. Suggest putting Shangnaman's body into stasis in a secure location and convince him he would live forever that way. Give his mind limited access to the palace computer net so that all he was risking during any necessary personal appearance was a hologram. That part really sold Shangnaman.

It seemed like a good idea at the time and tailor made for the paranoid son of a bitch. Get the crazy fool out of Last's hair and hide the Imperial body for disposal at the proper time. Last's personal IT section did the work, but something went wrong. Instead of Shangnaman only being able to appear when Last summoned him for an appearance, the insane bastard's mind found a hole or back door or something that let him into the palace net full time.

Shangnaman's computer existence quickly turned into something quite different and deadly. Things started badly after the crazy fool got into the palace net and were far worse now. It couldn't be stopped by killing the maniacal bastard, either. The Emperor's Guard had possession of Shangnaman's body and it was hidden away under incredibly tight security. Things were not as Last had envisioned.

Now the situation in the fragments of the Empire still controlled by Central forced him to talk to his insane cousin and any such contact was problematical, as in "will get you killed" problematical. No help for it. He tapped the sensor and waited. Shangnaman's image appeared over his terminal. The red uniform and thin circlet that confined his short curly hair actually complimented his slim, long limbed appearance, Last thought. On the other hand, the mascara, eye shadow and lipstick made the madman look like he'd been attacked by fanatical cosmeticians - or look even more insane than he already was.

"And what did you want Us for, Last?" Shangnaman's lanky body assumed a highly melodramatic pose of irritation, his pouting face conveying the idea he was interrupted while Doing Important Things. "We were investigating several suspect peons here in the palace."

"We have to talk, Cleon," Last said, using Shangnaman's boyhood nickname and the voice of someone highly irritated. It never paid to show weakness with Shangnaman. It also paid to remind him they'd grown up together. "You can order them killed later."

Mecurical as always, Shangnaman suddenly favored him with a sprightly smile and his holo curled into a lotus position as it appeared to sit in mid air above his terminal. "Oh, I can always have anyone killed later. What do you have for me, Ast?"

Boyhood nickname relationship - good. Now Last had to keep in mind the man in front of him was as unpredictable and deadly as a poisonous snake. "I just got word that the Takken Sector has split away under its governor. She's now Queen Libella, I understand. Naturally, she took the local Fleet component with her."

A brief frown flitted across Shangnaman's face. "I ordered both her and the local Fleet commander executed for incompetence last month."

Last hid a frown. Damn, how did he let that one get past him? Instead, he said dryly, "That may be why they rebelled."

Shangnaman smiled impishly and gave one of his mime-like shrugs, "Well, we can't have everything, can we? We didn't need Takken anyway."

"Except for their raw materials, food production, and two of our five remaining shipyards, I might agree with you," Last continued in the same dry voice. "However, that's not why I called you."

"Oh?" Shangnaman asked. "Then why, pray tell?"

"We're... ah... recovering raw materials, manufactured items, and food from the breakaway sectors with the help of your Guard as you ordered, but things have been happening out there," Last said carefully. This was the sensitive part.

"What?" Shangnaman was frowning now. "Just who's trying to thwart Our will?"

"I don't know, and that's what scares me," Last said frankly. Now that he had the idiot's attention, he might get something across, even if Shangnaman was back in Imperial persona again. "Your Guard is performing its usual yeoman service, but they've taken casualties. In one of the Jacobs systems, the entire recovery effort was wrecked and we don't know by whom. It might have been the Jacobs fleet, or it might have been unknowns. I've also been tracking reports of missing freighters or warships - including three more frigates to causes unknown - over the last

282

eight months. Losses are showing up more and more often, and I don't like that. That's affecting food supplies and other major imports here on Central. We're even getting maintenance problems in the Fleet, let alone the occasional missing ship which we can't afford to lose. I'm beginning to think someone out there is trying to get to us. I'm not entirely sure we're even immune here in the palace."

"WHAT??!!" Shangnaman shrieked, his holo leaping to its feet with fists clenched to each side of its head. "Are We in danger??!!"

Careful now, Absolom, careful. "It's a possibility," he said in even tones, "but I want to make sure it can't happen. We don't want someone to launch a planet buster at us. The Imperial Self could be destroyed along with the rest of us. I need to start the Fleet doing maneuvers sometime soon. Increase readiness."

"The Fleet isn't really loyal to Us," Shangnaman pouted. "They're just saying they are."

"I'll keep them well away from Central," Last said soothingly. "I just want to run some exercises. We'll know if the Fleet heads towards Central and have plenty of time to use the self destruct charges on the ships."

"Oh," Shangnaman said with an airy wave of his hand and another of his impish smiles, "feel free to tell them to play. Do 'em some good to work for a change. Tell Our commanders they have Our full trust then destroy anyone you wish."

If any of those politically appointed highbred idiots could find their ass with both hands, Last thought, Fleet exercises would be very worthwhile. Still, it wouldn't hurt.

More to the point, exercises would also give him the chance he'd been trying to create. He had two of the major commanders on his side. While pretending to to be part of an exercise, one would get close enough for precise targeting of Imperial City. One kinetic energy projectile on the Palace quarter of the City, then good-bye Shangnaman and this whole rotten lashup. Shangnaman wouldn't be able to do anything about it because his persona was restricted to the computer net. Hopefully, they'd get his body, too. If they did, the Guard would then be under his orders since he would be the only remaining pretender to the Imperial See. Vice Regent and all that.

If they didn't, well, another KE projo or two were available. Even a planet buster, although he'd personally regret it.

"Well, that's settled, Ast," Shangnaman said with satisfaction. "Quite simple, really. Now I quite must be gone. There are traitors everywhere and only I can find them. Oh, ta-ta for now." The last sentence was nearly sung.

After the holo disappeared, Last let out a breath. Still alive. That was good. Now he had to get the Fleet off its dead ass. If he could just find out where Shangnaman's body was hidden, he wouldn't need a planet buster to take over what was left of the Empire. And just incidentally stay alive.

Besides, he didn't really want to kill eight or nine billion people if it wasn't necessary. They would prove useful to his plans later. Some of them, anyhow.

He fell into a reverie where he rebuilt the mess that was now Middle Empire into something that resembled a government. All of those breakaways had to be reconquered, or simply destroyed if that was easier. He'd take whatever he needed, do whatever he wanted, outside Middle Empire. The people on those breakaway worlds didn't matter. Only Middle Empire mattered. That was going to be the new Empire. The rest could go to hell.

If he couldn't find Shangnaman's body soon... Well, maybe a planet buster wasn't such a bad idea.

FRONTIER CLUSTER MILITARY HEADQUARTERS NIAD

Nobody said a word. The group in Admiral Mackinnie's office was small, just Lane himself, Shyranne Garua, and Randl Turner. It was time for a decision on the Central attack. That was Lane's responsibility and his alone, but the other two were there to offer input. They'd reviewed all of the current intelligence as well as what Combat Information Technology wanted to do to the Emperor. The CIT plan was enthusiastically approved. Now only the final decision to launch the attack remained.

Lane looked at the quiet faces around the conference table. Randl was looking off at nothing, lost in a world of thought. Shyranne Garua was composed, simply sitting with the calmness that was the hallmark of the Gladius. Underneath, Lane knew, everyone was just as tense as he himself was. They - and he - knew what the ancient phrase "weight of command" actually meant.

Inside this room, Lane thought, was the true reality of power within the Frontier Cluster. As yet, the Fleet and the Corps were semi-independent entities that willingly submitted themselves to the civilian government they'd created - and could destroy if they thought it necessary.

Randl understood that reality. He'd made no bones about it in private conversations. He knew both Fleet and Corps had manipulated the governments of a number of worlds, including Tactine, to get the Frontier

Cluster where it was today and he wasn't blind to the fact. He knew that both Lane and Shyranned had maneuvered the situation in order for the race to survive and with the hope of building a better future. Now, however, that new Frontier Cluster government had to support the military – and the Empire's destruction – if they were going to survive and realize that better future.

That was why Randl, after very real and serious consultation with the Council, had given permission for this attack. However the Frontier Cluster government had been created, it now supported the need for the destruction of Central. The Empire was dying, but it could still kill the fragile Cluster in those death throes if they were drawn out long enough, not to mention destroy the lives of billions of others. Once this operation was exposed, the chances for the Cluster – and, by extension, humanity - to survive dropped by an order of magnitude if it didn't succeed. The Empire had to be finished off and the people in this room were gathered while one of them decided if it was time to make the kill.

Lane was glad of the Council's support. If he gave the order, hundreds of thousands of men and women under his command were going into the greatest battle in history. The one certainty of that battle was that thousands of them, probably more, possibly one or two of the people in this room - possibly he, himself - were not going to survive it. Every one of those deaths and all of the other deaths that had occurred on the way to this point, were his responsibility. He had knowingly sacrificed the peace and stability of too many Imperial worlds to get here. Now he had to give the order to take it all the way, to decapitate the Empire. And he had the full support of the new government to which he'd given his allegiance. For small favors...

Was he ready for what was going to happen? Were any of them ready? Lane felt the weight of billions of lives on Central in his hands. Once battle was joined, there was no way he could guarantee the survival of the ordinary people on that planet. Randl's political restructuring teams were ready, so the citizens on Central might have a future. Those that survived. His forces were going to do everything they could - including intentionally take more casualties - to keep civilian deaths down, but there was no way all of those ordinary people would survive. More dead. All to kill a dying Empire ruled by a madman.

Randl looked over and met his eyes. The man was now the head of the Frontier Cluster government, a government deliberately formed and fostered by abandoned Imperial forces. The Frontier Cluster was the hope of Mankind's future, but that future couldn't survive without the destruction of the greatest cancer in the human universe - the dying Empire of Ten Thousand Suns. Once Lane gave the order, they were all out of the shadows. The Empire would know about them and the threat they represented. Either the Cluster or the Empire would emerge victorious, and there was no way to guarantee which would happen in the end. It was a gamble with billions of lives - the future of humanity - on the table.

Lane looked into the eyes of Shyranne and Randl. He could see they knew his thoughts and shared his feelings. His next words would change history forever... and possibly guarantee the survival of the human race.

Pompous ass. You've got a job to do, Lane Mackinnie, so do it. He weighed the chances, took a breath, let it out, and sat straighter in his chair. His doubts were gone. In a firm, decisive voice, he said, "We will go. Begin the operation."

FRONTIER CLUSTER SPACE

The S-boats shipped out to begin infiltrating the Central system. They were the final reconnaissance before the battle and hidden snipers once the fleets made contact. Their orders were simple. Tell us what's going on then go for the heavies. Kill the Guard frigates when you can.

With the rest of her breed, the *Wahoo* translated into TFD. Destination: Central. Alice took her ship out and breathed a silent prayer to the Lord Above. It was a very simple prayer. Let us do our job well.

#####

The Cluster Army was new, untried in all but a few engagements. The men and women were well trained and ready, but nervous. They all knew their objective was the destruction of the Imperial New Forces, that the New Forces were just as inexperienced as they were and probably not as well trained, that it would be a match of more or less equals with an edge on their side. In the considered opinion of the troops that was all well and good, but this promised to be a slugging match of epic proportions. In the end, they drew confidence and courage from the fact that they weren't alone in this triple-damned mess. They looked around and drew silent comfort from their squadmates, the ones on either side when things got rough. They didn't have a reputation to uphold yet, but they were going to build one on Central.

Every one of the troopers sequestered at the embarkation points had the same thought buried in the back of their minds. It was never voiced in the gambling games, the bull sessions, and all of the other gatherings large and small that occur whenever soldiers are confined in groups, but it was there. In the end, it told of the spirit of the men and women that waited to ride into the promised hell of Central.

Lord Above help the damned Imperial sonofabitch that gets in my way.

#####

In the Corps, the feeling was different. All of them, even the newly qualified recruits, knew what they were going into and they knew it was going to be worse than anything in the past. In the end, it all came down to two things for every Gladius man and woman - millennia old tradition and the Oath.

I AM A GLADIUS.

Time to issue the "go" order to his troops. Legate Karl Athan looked over his assembled legion, a legion built from ruins and powerful once again. Out there, although he couldn't see her in the huge formation, was the woman who was his future. He couldn't distinguish Shana out there, but he knew exactly where she was. He thought a silent prayer for her survival. Nothing was guaranteed. She might survive and he might not. That was war and the fate of a soldier. Nothing he could do.

He looked at the Victrix with pride. Once, the Empire had torn the guts out of it, leaving it crippled. Now the Victrix was a living, healthy entity again, dedicated to the preservation of humanity and the destruction of the Predator. They knew who the Predator was. Oh, yes, they knew. They had a huge bloody score to settle with that Predator. Every man and woman in that formation was planning to do just that. For the other legions, this was an operation to ensure the future. For the Victrix, this operation was more than that.

It was personal.

I STAND GUARD AT THE GATES OF HELL.
NOTHING WILL PASS AND HARM
THOSE I AM SWORN TO PROTECT.

There were Corps scouts in Imperial City, simply watching and reporting, noting everything with quiet, cold, grim eyes. They watched gangs and bullies brutally take what they wanted, including lives, from citizens brutalized by Shangnaman's insane reign of terror. They watched execution squads kill people in job lots with impunity. They watched... and remembered. They had thoughts. Quiet, cold, grim thoughts.

287

With the "go" order, the scouts knew that their long time in the shadows was coming to an end. They had the freedom to do a little more than watch as long as things were done quietly and the cause was untraceable.

Execution squads, bullies, and gangs began to vanish.

MY LIFE IS NOTHING.
MY DUTY AND PURPOSE ARE EVERYTHING.
IF MY LIFE IS CALLED FOR,
*   IT WILL BE GIVEN GLADLY.*

At their various bases, the III Augusta, VII Rapax, IX Victrix, X Valeria, and XII Ferrata assembled to board their troop carriers. This operation was going to use more legions than any other in Corps history, which was no longer the history of the Empire.

The men and women in those formations had held their Rites, met Those Gone Before, and knew Their blessings. They had said their good-byes. They knew there were going to be heavy casualties, especially when they met the Emperor's Guard. The Guard was close to being their equal. Cousin was going to be fighting cousin and it would be bloody. It didn't matter. The Oath said they might have to pay the Gladius Price to do their duty and they held true to that Oath, though the demons of Hell itself came against them.

Fires danced in the colorless eyes of the men and women in those formations, but those fires were carefully banked. The Gladius knew that only the cold blooded professional had a good chance of survival in combat. In combat, the Gladius was a cold blooded professional.

The Empire had cast them out, but these veteran legions were coming back, bringing the skill, the experience, and the terrible abilities forged in a millennium of ruthless Darwinian selection in battle. They had been in hiding for years, but no longer. The Empire was going to discover the Corps still existed... and it had a new purpose.

The Corps of Gladius existed now to protect Mankind, not the Empire.

I GO NOW TO FACE MY ENEMY.

Legion Sergeant Major Olmeg watched his legion board CTC 901. He thought about what had happened in his past and what was going to happen in his future. As was standard procedure, the children of the legion, the pregnant, and the new mothers were staying behind with a guard force at Victrix Base. It would normally fall his lot as a senior

Decurion with a much damaged body to take command of that guard detachment, Legion Sergeant Major or not.

Not today, not for this operation. Shangnaman had taken his wife and son. Shangnaman was the Predator. He owed Shangnaman. Payback was coming. Legion Sergeant Major Olmeg was going to be there.

I HAVE SEEN HIM AND I KNOW HIM.

This was the true war dance of the Gladius, the one too intense to be seen outside the Corps. As commander of a fighting unit and a combat soldier in her own right, Shana was a part of it. The stamp, stamp, stamp of the dancers echoed in time to the beat of the driving music that filled the huge assembly hall on CTC 901. The fierce emotion of the war dance was a brilliant cloud shot with darkness that filled the hall and the dancers. No other thought existed but to meet the Predator as the Oath demanded and back that pledge with their skill and their lives.

Like those around her, Shana occasionally raised her arms, fists clenched, and gave vent to the unholy joy of the dance with a high shriek, whirling as she screamed. All of them were full of the spirits of Those Gone Before, but Shana had women foremost in her mind as well - the murdered women of a nearly murdered Legion. She was their avatar and they danced with her. Those women had paid the Gladius Price, but, as Shana stamped along with thousands of other dancers, she pledged a Price would be taken from the Predator - with interest.

Fire, death, and destruction were coming to the Emperor, and Lieutenant Shana Ettranty was bringing her full portion of it.

HE WILL NOT SEE THE DAWN.

Gladio alieyo.

CHAPTER 15

CLUSTER FLEET
UNDERWAY

Aboard the *Naraka*, newly minted High Admiral Lane Mackinnie sat in his chair on the Flag Bridge and pondered what they were just hours away from doing: decapitating the Empire and killing it. He had two fleets, an Army of seven divisions, and the entire remaining strength of the Corps of Gladius - five legions - under his command. There was even a troop carrier holding Randl Turner's political restructuring teams. Lane Mackinnie commanded the most powerful military force in history and it was getting ready to enter the Alpha Centauri system.

First, he had to get through the Imperial Home Fleet. That was going to be a little more difficult than originally assumed. For some reason, the Fleet was out and conducting some sort of exercise. According to S-boat recon, they'd left a good number of ships in parking orbits, assessed as probable maintenance casualties. Well, those same S-boats had worked hard enough to interrupt the vitally needed flow of materials and manufactured goods to Central, including some critical spare parts for warships. That was the good part. The bad part was the bulk of the Imperial Home Fleet was still functional, cruising, and in tactical array.

Lane took a deep breath and let it out philosophically. His staff had created operations plans for any number of conditions, including this one. However, having the Impies out and active meant this wasn't going to be easy.

Soon enough, things were going to get ugly.

TROOP CARRIER CTC 901
CLUSTER FLEET

Shana was standing in the middle of the small platoon bay with her men seated on the floor around her. As she set the little holo machine down and activated it, she took a look at their faces. The boys are going to love this one, she thought sardonically, especially since they were so close to the drop.

"Change of mission, guys," Shana said as she pointed to a highlighted area on the holo section of Imperial City. "New scout reports say there's something funny happening in those warehouses and we're going to find out what it is. Activity is tentatively ID'd as the Emperor's Guard. That's the part that's bothering Command and that's where we come in. We have to know everything about the Emperor's Guard. Third Platoon has been shifted to our original target."

"Marvelous, Lieutenant," Legionnaire Ormond said in a dry voice from the back of her seated platoon. Trust Ormond to add appropriate comments. "Speaking for those few civilized dogs you've got, we just love a hip shoot. Especially against those fanatics."

She favored her mouthy Strike dog with a grin. "You want it any other way? What's wrong with dumping a pre-briefed and rehearsed mission and going with some staff officer's hunch? You volunteered for this sort of thing, dog, in case you forgot."

A hand came up. "Lieutenant, I volunteer for a transfer to Buildings and Grounds on Cauldwell."

"I'll see what I can do after we get back, Lster," Shana replied after the snorts of laughter died down. "I don't know if they want you, but I'll put in a word with the Legate."

Lster gave a deep sigh. "So we gotta go jump into a dark hole 'cause someone's got a bad case of seeing ghosts - or Guard. Another wonderful day in the Corps, right L. T.?"

"Yup." More laughter.

Shana waited for it to die down before continuing. "One more thing," she said. "This one's more of an FYI, but you all know the bit about the Emperor's consciousness being in the Palace computer system, right? Well, Combat Information Technology has come up with something nasty. Just before the landings, they're going to upload a little gift for him into the Palace computer system, a program that will create a monster. That monster will chase Shangnaman anywhere he goes in the Palace net, but never quite catch him. He'll always be running from something that is just one step behind him as long as the net is up.

"That'll also take him out of the command chain, folks. Too busy running to make any decisions. He's crazy, guys, but he's still the final authority. Hopefully, that will cripple their response to our invasion somewhat."

The grins on her men's faces weren't pretty. Neither was hers. "Serves the bastard right," Ormond said. "If CIT wasn't so lazy, they'd do it for everybody and we wouldn't have to land."

Applause and cheers.

They were good guys, she thought. So far she hadn't lost a man from either of her platoons and wanted to continue that record. Central was going to be different, a little voice told her. She told the voice to shut

291

up and thought a silent prayer to the Lord Above. Keep my guys safe. Don't let me do something stupid and get someone killed.

That was really all she could ask.

THE NARAKA
CLUSTER FLEET

Sitting in his command chair and staring at a tactical monitor, Lane was watching Hell let out for noon. Space was literally boiling from heavy bolts crossing back and forth between *Naraka* and the dreadnought that was her foe. Heavy fire, but *Naraka* was going to win this one. The old hell ship was just too big and tough for things to be otherwise.

Lane was calm about the death fight. *Naraka* might take a hit that would penetrate her tough body all the way to the flag bridge, but there was nothing he could do about that. Combat was now in the hands of his subordinate commanders and the Lord Above.

Another tactical monitor showed him a rough schematic of a vicious battle spread out over hundreds of millions of square kilomeasures. The schematic showed him something a closer view couldn't.

The Cluster was winning. The major engagements were slowly but surely ending in the Cluster's favor and the Imperial Fleet was steadily being ground to fragments.

There was still plenty of action for the pocket battleships and fighters as they cleared near space over Central. The time was coming for the troop drop. He touched a sensor. //"Go ahead and order the troop carriers into position."//

CLUSTER FLEET
CENTRAL NEAR SPACE

Aboard Troop Carrier CTC 101, General Jon Malcom was at his post in Ground CIC thinking about his opposite number. His ground force counterpart on Central had to be working frantically and Jon fully understood the man's problems. He wished the bastard more of them. Jon wasn't looking for any kind of fair fight. The less opposition his people had to face, the more of them he was going to bring home. He expected heavy casualties because his units were new, mostly untried in combat, and with leaders yet to be proven. He had his own problems and wanted to launch his troops as soon as possible. The less time the enemy had to prepare, the better.

"Patience, Jon" Shyranne said next to him. "We can't do anything until the Fleet clears the way."

"Is it always like this?" he asked her.

Shyranne looked at him a little sadly. "Always. We have to get down fast for the best chance of survival, but without the Fleet clearing space, assault shuttles couldn't survive. So we wait. And worry. Every hour we delay costs lives on the ground, but that delay is necessary for us to survive the drop."

Jon looked at her for a moment, thinking about the dilemma, realizing deep down for the first time what it meant to command troops in combat. He also understood Shyranne's expression now. "Thanks," he said ironically. "That just makes me feel so much better."

#####

The enemy was nearly gone from Central near space.

As SOC and someone with more experience in this kind of operation than the Army, Shyranne was overall ground commander. It was her job to determine when to launch the troops. The Strike platoons were already on their way to their missions and the main force was waiting for her order. "It's time," she said softly.

Jon heard something different in her voice. It was her normal soft tones, but there was something else there. He turned to look at her curiously and was slightly shocked. She looked back at him with her jaw jutting forward and fire in her eyes. "The Emperor and his minions killed my people despite the fact they were loyal. That's when the Emperor and all of his became the Predator. We are coming to kill them. The time is now, General. Gladio alieyo."

A chill ran down Jon's spine as he heard her softly spoken words.

She reached out and touched a sensor on the board next to her. //"All troop carriers begin launch. Launch, launch, launch. Launch, launch, launch. Launch, launch, launch."//

She switched to the all hands Corps band. //"It is our time, people. The Gladius is coming to Central to kill the Predator. We have seen our enemy and we know him. He will not see the dawn."// As it had been for a millennium, a woman once again sent the Gladius to war.

#####

The troop carriers edged into launch position, with the exception of the command ship, CTC 101, and the one solely dedicated to carrying reconstruction teams, CTC 114. Twelve of the big ships swung into orbit

293

and began punching out assault shuttles. There were still heavy defenses active down there and the faster they could launch, the safer the big troop carriers and thousands of troops would be.

Shuttle pilots swiftly formed up then headed down. The assault shuttles dived towards their LZs at near maximum velocity and straight in, weaving and bobbing, to give Central's anti-air defenses minimum time to engage. It wasn't safe, but it was the safest way they could get their troop loads to their destinations.

One Corps legion and all of the Army divisions were headed for the New Forces on the second continent. The other four legions were headed for Imperial City and its surrounding area. Those four legions were wondering what they were going to find on the ground, but expecting anything.

Corps expectations were going to live down to their usual dismal level. Currently unknown to Ground CIC, five Guard legions, long lost cousins of the present day Gladius, were taking up positions to protect the Emperor and, secondarily, Imperial City. There was a vicious family fight coming.

#####

Three Guard frigates came in under full suppresser and very slowly, which meant that nobody knew they were there until they fired on CTC 106, knocking out half its launchers and killing several thousand Army troops. Killing the three frigates cost a fighter and two pocket battleships.

The frigates accomplished part of their objective. The tightly coordinated launch was disrupted, not least by CTC 106 staggering out of orbit but continuing to belch out whatever undamaged Army shuttles she had left in her launch queues. As he surveyed the damage to his carefully managed launch formation, now being interpenetrated by fighters from both sides, Commodore Aln Mson's first thought was, "What a mosh fuck!" As commander of the TCs and troop launch, he grimly started bringing order out of chaos. Fighters, pocket battleships, and defensive guns on the troop carriers were fiercely battling a swarm of determined Impie fighters still trying to get to his carriers and shuttles. It looked as though the landings were going to be even more scattered and disrupted than normally expected. Ground fire tended to spread and disrupt landings, but those triple-damned frigates had really made a hash of things. Get it fixed, Aln, and get those troops DOWN!

Shyranne was thinking much the same thing. What happened in space happened. Right now, the job of Ground CIC was to let commanders know what to expect when they hit dirt, not offer useless suggestions. Khev, as overall Corps tactical commander, was issuing rapid fire orders to his section of CIC. On the Army side, Jon Malcom was proving himself to be a good commander in the only circumstance that truly tested command - when things fell apart.

Intelligence boards lit up as scout reports began pouring into Ground CIC. Imperial troops were suddenly moving into and around Imperial City, definitely identified as the Emperor's Guard. From scout reports listing unit types, formations, and equipment, there were at least...

"Five legions!" Khev said and swore. Where in hell had that many come from? The Imperial breeding program must be far larger than expected. It made sense, seeing how many Guards were suddenly showing up in space, among other unpleasant surprises. "Notify all legions of the amount and nature of the opposition," Khev said to his communication section. "Send a digest of available information directly to Legates, details to Legion Intelligence sections."

His mouth quirked. Shit happened in battle, especially in the one this was shaping up to be. Jon's folks were going to have their hands full with the New Forces. That was why he'd assigned the Augusta as a supplement to the Army. Now it looked like the Valeria, the Victrix, the Rapax and the Ferrata were going to have just as much fun. Shit. Then he took a deep breath. Situations like this were why the Corps existed. "Transmit my complements to the Legates," he ordered. "Include my wishes that they enjoy their tour of beautiful Imperial City. Oh, and forward any responses to me except the obscene ones."

The Legions were back in a shitty situation. Just another wonderful day in the Corps.

#####

The situation on the second continent was confused. Due to the landing disruption, several Cluster divisions were scattered and three others were intermixed. Assault shuttle pilots did their best, but simple physics was against them in many cases. They could have flown NOE to their original LZs, but heavy small caliber fire was making that difficult and increasing the chances of killing a shuttle with its full load of troops. That would be a Bad Thing. Inevitably, every shuttle pilot made the same decision. Balanced against a high probability of loss, any ground was better than the right ground if it meant risking troop loads.

A number of Cluster Army units found themselves in unfamiliar terrain, with unfamiliar objectives, but they'd had excellent training and they were looking for someone to kill. Whatever New Forces units in front or around them would do nicely. Orphan units or even single troops were perfectly willing to work with any other Army unit they found to accomplish that highly desirable objective. Training began to tell.

To the Augusta, things were screwed up on the ground but there was nothing new in that. They began to get themselves organized with veteran speed. The Legate was in full control of his legion and things were progressing nicely. He wondered what unholy mess the Army was eventually going to call on him to unfuck.

#####

The other four legions were down, deployed around Imperial City and in heavy contact with the Emperor's guard. Things were going, but not smoothly. The Guard was inexperienced in major unit ground tactics, something obvious to the Corps, but they were fanatical and good fighters.

It was already apparent to Sergeant First Class Span that this wasn't going to be easy. The platoon already had two wounded and one KIA, and the Victrix was only into their second hour of the battle. He was on the far side of the platoon's weave as they swung across the area where they were in contact, but keeping a close eye on his platoon leader's icon in his HUD. New single pip, but the boy was going to be all right if he lived through this.

Span was checking the century commander's directional arrow on his HUD to ensure Fourth Platoon was in its proper position in the century weave pattern when the flood of yellow icons symbolizing Guard troops suddenly thickened and things began to get nasty. He zigged, fast. Two bolts zinged past, penetrating empty space where he used to be, and Span's two team members sent a few rounds back. Just keep moving. Speed was life in close combat.

His helmet com came to life. //"Sergeant Span, ---"// The transmission was cut off. Span's Link felt it, but the HUD confirmed his feeling. He no longer had a lieutenant. He was in command of Fourth Platoon. He was also about to be enveloped.

As he wove and ran, he contacted the century heavy weapons section. //"2-5-6, 2-4-5. Fire mission. Data sent... now. Danger close."// He was calling for supporting fire on top of his position. Not good, but they were already in the shit. Some of the boys were already using axes and he had another man down KIA.

//"4-5, 5-6. Shot."//

//"2-4, DOWN! Freeze!"// Span hit the dirt just as the ground erupted around his position. All he could do was lie there and hope his platoon made it through all right. His HUD said the Guard was catching hell. He could feel it through the Link when an antipersonnel rocket landed nearly on top of Simns, but there was nothing he could do about it. The Guards around him were catching it worse. Not many Guards left. Less, after Fourth Platoon got back up.

#####

Victrix Command Group was in a relatively stationary location, moving only when necessary. It was nearly impossible to command and coordinate a legion while on the move, as much as Karl wished he could. They were established in a partially protected area, a small crater flanked by the ruins of a building's wall. The security guard platoon had the area ringed, but, like any Gladius, each and every one of them was nervous at being in one place too long. The problem, Karl thought, was that they were now into heavily built up area on the outskirts of the City itself. Not unknown territory for a legion, but a pain in the ass tactically, none the less.

Karl put his worries aside and studied his field monitors. There was trouble building in Second Cohort's sector. It looked like the Guard was trying to push a wedge into his area. He called Second's Commander, Saml Evns. //"Sam, Karl. What's the story on that penetration in your sector?"//

//"Strong, Karl. Feels like a full legion is trying to punch through."//

//"Can you swing your weak side through the tip of that penetration just behind their lead units? Cut the point off?"//

//"Aye, but it won't stay cut. They've got too much force following that lead element."//

//"Right. Let's do this instead. Go ahead and drift back, but hold the left flank of that push. I'll bring up Al Lumis's Fifth Cohort to hold the point and right flank. We need to keep maximum force holding that penetration for a little while. I'll set up a fire sack just behind Al. When I tell you, punch over to Al's boys at the rear of the penetration and close it off. What ever gets through will be in the fire sack. That's when I'll drop in heavy artillery. Stand by for further orders because I'm going to put both you and Al right into the middle of their follow on forces as soon as we kill whatever portion of that Guard legion we catch in the sack."//

//"Aye. Do Al good to have something he can butt his head against. He's been having it too easy in the last hour or so."//

//"I'll tell him you said that when I give him his orders. Piss him off good. He'll take it out on the Guard. Out."//

Legion Sergeant Major Olmeg was leaving the battlefield to the Legate. Instead, he was in constant motion, checking the Command Group perimeter. The security platoon was doing its job, but any trooper, even a junior officer, would be more alert if he knew the Legion Sergeant Major was looking hard over his shoulder. Besides, it felt worthwhile to be back in a combat environment again. He wasn't battle happy and he didn't love fighting, but, as much body part regeneration as he'd piled up in his long life, it was good to know he was still a decent fighting soldier.

"Watch out, Lieutenant," the Sergeant Major growled as he found the security platoon commander. "There are reports of leakers and suicide teams all over the area. These Guard bastards love to hide and come out behind you. They don't care if they get their asses waxed after they hit. Just killing you is enough for them."

"Aye, Sergeant Major," the Lieutenant said absently as he watched the perimeter schematic on his helmet HUD. Was this old fart ever going to stop trying to tell him his business?

The Sergeant Major's warning suddenly took real shape as a hole opened up just behind where they were talking. Ten or so Guardsmen poured out of it and began firing in all directions. One of the security platoon's troopers died in that moment, but the others were now in action. So was the rest of the Command Group. The larger battle momentarily shrunk to just a few dozen square measures of ground as bolt fire crisscrossed and bodies dodged in every direction.

There were screams of "Ave Keesar!" everywhere, the Guard battlecry. The Gladii didn't waste their breath. The attackers were dying hard, one to a bolt from the Legate's pistol. They were causing casualties, but dying. One, larger than most, took an ax swing at a security platoon trooper that had let his combat awareness fatally lapse. The Gladius, focused on killing another Guardsman, lost part of his arm.

At least it wasn't the kid's leg, the Sergeant Major thought as he jumped towards the Guardsman. Usually, when a Gladius lost something, it was a leg. Happened to him five times. So had this situation, plenty of times.

Olmeg flipped his helmet face plate up to show his face to the enemy, seeing the Guardsman do likewise to accept the challenge. Older man, maybe senior decurion. Good. Meeting of equals. The Sergeant Major mentally chided himself because this wasn't the smart way to fight, but something deep inside him wanted this single combat to prove he was still a whole soldier, despite his banged up body. Show the children how it was done.

The lieutenant was standing over the smoking body of a Guardsman that had wandered in front of his B-42. He checked the area and it looked clear of the Guard for the moment. One of his men had already collapsed the hole with a plasma grenade. He looked up to see the Sergeant Major and the Guardsman square off. Stupid. Use your gun, you old bastard. The Sergeant Major was fighting dumb.

At least that was what he thought until the first pass the two made at each other. The action was literally too fast to follow, but the lieutenant was certain the Sergeant Major was using ax moves he'd never even seen before! The Guardsman was good, too. Both men had armor cuts, but the one on the Guardsman's chest plate was deeper and longer. It dawned on the young lieutenant that Legion Sergeant Major Olmeg was a blue ribbon soldier and the other one was damn near as good. He decided he didn't want to be between the two. Unhealthy.

After their first brush, Olmeg and the Guardsman paused for a second to measure each other. Each knew he was fighting an equal, an old master in the art of killing. There was respect, and grim resolution, between them.

"Ave Keesar." The words were spoken quietly.

"Gladio alieyo." The return was just as quiet.

Again, the Guardsman made the first cobra-quick leap. This time, as the Sergeant Major dodged to one side and crouched to avoid the Guardsman's swing, he twisted to avoid the thrown short sword that just missed his chest. The sword returned to its owner, but Olmeg was right behind it. There's a momentary distraction, even in the best, when a Gladius throws his blade. The Sergeant Major counted on that. His own short sword stabbed deep into the Guardsman's chest, followed by his ax to remove the Guardsman's arm and abort the dying ax swing that would have killed him along with his enemy.

Sergeant Major Olmeg reached down and gently closed the dead Guardsman's face plate with respect. He looked up to see the surrounding Gladii, including the Legate, frozen in place and staring at him. "Don't you people have a battle to fight?" he growled.

CHAPTER 16

IMPERIAL CITY
FIVE HOURS EARLIER

Using the massive space battles around Central as a cover, Strike platoons were inserted into Imperial City immediately before the troop landings in an operation that had been a major headache during planning. Strike was urgently needed on the ground because Imperial City held a large number of "targets of interest" requiring old fashioned eyeball investigation or someone to physically secure them before the main force arrived. Those were normal Strike missions, but the key words were "before the main force arrived". Strike dogs had to be on the ground early, and the Cluster staff didn't want to alert the Imperials that someone was creeping around their backyard with fell intent.

Inserting the Strike platoons during the main landing was discussed and rejected as both dangerous and obvious. Too much chance of catching accurate ground fire and Imperial defenses would be fully up and looking during the attack. Likewise early insertion using heavily suppressed cutters was also rejected because it held the possibility of alerting the defenses far too soon. Single scouts and occasional high priority missions could be carefully inserted, but there were 39 Strike platoons to be dropped into Imperial City. The fortieth one was already down supporting the CIT attack on the Palace computer net. Dropping 39 platoons, even under suppresser, was pushing the chance of detection further than anyone wanted to take it.

A compromise was reached. Suppressed cutters holding the Strike platoons were launched just slightly before the main landings, hiding their approach in the confusion of battle. It was risky because the Imperial defenses were fully active, but those same defenses were concentrated on the upcoming troop drop, not on sensor ghosts, even 39 of them. Or so the theory said.

Shana was praying that theory was finally going to be right. On the one hand, the plan drifted her platoon into Imperial City gently, without with the slam bang of a normal combat drop. On the other hand, that same plan only gave her limited time to accomplish her objectives before the Legions worked their way into the city. Win some, lose some, she thought philosophically. Just another wonderful day in the Corps.

The area of operations for Second Platoon, First Strike Century, Ninth Legion Victrix, was an obscure warehouse district not all that far from the palace. Recent reports from scouts had indicated an unusual amount of Guard activity in the area and the SOC wanted to know why. Second Platoon's mission was to sweep the warehouse district and find out what was so important about it.

Once dropped, the platoon quickly formed and swung into a slow stealthy version of the Corps weave as it moved quietly towards the warehouses. Strike troopers, like scouts and unlike line Gladii, always wore full body armor because their armor was intended as much as camouflage as protection. Unless someone was really looking for a Strike trooper, they were nearly undetectable. Strike liked it that way. No need for targets to get the bad news before Strike personally gave it to them.

Initially, the platoon cautiously probed warehouses that hadn't shown Guard activity. Shana wanted to get a feel for the area before getting to the more sensitive portion of her mission. Nobody really knew the full capabilities of the Emperor's Guard and dealing with the Guard was not something she wanted to rush into right after landing.

The first four warehouses were empty of people, not surprising given the battle raging above the city. Pretty much the whole civilian population was in some kind of shelter by now, for which Shana was grateful. Empty streets and empty buildings made her job much easier. Shana called a halt after the fourth warehouse and crouched for a quiet consultation with Sergeant Stauer. "Notice anything?" she asked him.

"Aye," Sergeant Stauer replied. "Every building we've checked so far has held construction materials or dry goods. Things that can sit a long time without any worries. Lieutenant, did you get the feeling that none of the warehouses have been touched in quite a while?"

She gave him a slight smile. "More than a feeling, Sergeant. There was a heavy dust overlay on everything we saw in those warehouses. That stuff has been sitting untouched for a long time, maybe years."

"So now we have a warehouse district that doesn't seem to be doing any business. That could be caused from our attacks over the last year or just Shangnaman's crazy pogroms," he replied.

Shana shook her head. "I don't think so. If these were real warehouses, I'd expect to at least see some perishable items among everything else in the buildings. None of the warehouses we've checked even has stasis capability. That isn't normal, Sergeant. Now I'm beginning to wonder if this is a warehouse area at all."

She called up her map on her HUD. "Scouts reported Guard activity around a tight cluster of five warehouses right in the middle of the district, but little to none anywhere else. Suppose the rest of the buildings were just to hide whatever those five are really used for?"

Sergeant Stauer thought for a minute. "Possible, Lieutenant. That's a lot of effort to hide something."

"Something important," Shana said decisively. "I think whatever we're here to find is in one or all of those buildings. The way the five are arranged makes me wonder, also. Check your map download. Four of those buildings closely surround the fifth. Suppose there's something key in the middle building and the other four are used as a defensive perimeter? There's really only one way to get to that middle building. Oh, there's a street leading to the back, but it's pretty constricted."

Sergeant Stauer stood up. "Then I suppose it's time for us to see just what's in them."

Shana also stood and signaled for her platoon to start moving in the general direction of the suspect warehouses. "Yep. Let's go find out."

The point found the first perimeter warning device at the next street intersection. While they were bypassing it, Shana came up on the platoon band. //"All hands, Strike 2-1-6. Remember, guys, these characters use mechanical devices as well as electronic. Don't just sweep your areas for electronic devices. Watch for trip wires and anything else that looks out of place."//

They went a street farther then a little feeling started to bother Shana. Looking around, she decided they were too exposed here on the ground. She signaled her troops and indicated a nearby roof. The warehouses were well separated, but no-weight belts would make the jumps from warehouse rooftop to rooftop easy once they were off the streets. Hopefully, their camouflaged armor would keep them from being seen during the leaps between buildings.

They found a combination of electronic and tripwire triggered warning devices scattered over the rooftops, but everything was bypassed quietly. Normal stuff for Strike. After a slow careful approach to the last warehouse outside the suspected Guard perimeter, Shana snuck a hair thin video lens over the edge of the roof's parapet. After a careful visual scan through her HUD's screen, she pulled the lens back and signaled Sergeant Stauer to approach. After he crept up and lay next to her, she raised her visor and spoke quietly, "I'm seeing guards all over the area. They don't look like guards or act like them, but they're the only human activity in the entire district and they're still in place despite the battle. That makes them guards to me. Also, those people are mostly big men with a few female counterparts built pretty much like I am. Sound like the Emperor's Guard to you, Sergeant?"

"Aye," he agreed. "I've also had reports from the guys running scans. Entire walls of some of those warehouses are rigged for perimeter alert and possibly for other things. This entire area is one huge warning device and defensive perimeter. There's something mighty important in this cluster of buildings."

"And we need to know what it is," she said. "Start mapping the guards. We need to take them down before we do any building penetration but we have to do it fast. I'm certain they're tagged to trigger a warning if something happens to any of them. We have to take out all the guards and hit the key building as close together as possible. Spread the platoon and get surveillance from every angle we can. I want to know what each guard does and if there's any pattern to their movement." She settled in place. It was going to take a while, but she was going to find out what was happening in those buildings.

"Lieutenant, look up." The low voice was Smythe.

Shana did... and was treated to one of the most fantastic sights she'd ever seen. Probably ever would see, she decided. From horizon to horizon, thousands of assault shuttles were emerging from the flame shot dark cloud of detonating air defense bolts and missiles that covered the sky, screaming down on Imperial City. Four legions were dropping.

It was too awe inspiring for her to tear her eyes away. She could do nothing but watch the incredible scene overhead. It had never happened before, she thought. The Corps had never dropped more than two legions in its history. Twice that many were coming down now, filling the skies with rapidly growing sleek shuttles that jumped and twisted in impossible directions as they evaded ground fire. The growing noise of screaming shuttle engines was beginning to overwhelm even the sound of explosions and gunfire.

She tore her eyes away for a moment and realized her men were just as awestruck and mesmerized as she was. //"Back to work, guys."//

As her platoon recovered from the incredible spectacle and returned to the tasks at hand, she snuck another look upward. Something to remember for the rest of her life, however long that was. Another thought struck her and she smiled.

Gladio alieyo.

#####

In Ground CIC, Shyranne was getting other reports. Immediately, she called Lane Mackinnie. //"Fleet, Ground. Lane, we're developing locations for the origin of those Guard legions. Probably coming from a hidden base outside the city. When it's found, request heavy kinetic strike."//

Lane listened without comment for a moment. He knew, and he was sure Shyranne knew, there were going to be noncombatants in that base, including children. Shyranne wanted that base destroyed for a reason and so did he. The Emperor's Guard had to be killed root and branch. They were so heavily conditioned from birth that literally every one of them, no matter the age, was a deadly enemy. Also, there was no telling what was going to be issuing from that base next. It had to be destroyed, no matter who was in it.

Lane wasn't afraid of the logic that forced his decision. He was afraid of the cost to his soul. They were going to be killing children. He knew perfectly well that Shyranne felt the same way, but she'd ordered the destruction of the Guard personnel in stasis on Cauldwell because it had to be done and it was her responsibility. There were still shadows in her eyes and in Khev's because they'd killed thousands of helpless people. Deadly enemies, but still helpless.

Now there would be more shadows in their eyes. And more in his. For his troops to live through this invasion - for the Cluster to have a future free of fear - every member of the Guard had to die wherever found. Every man, woman, and child had to die. If they weren't all killed, any survivors would still try to destroy the Cluster, no matter how long they had to wait.

Lord Above keep him from any more such decisions after this campaign. But that was for then and this was now. //"Ground, Fleet. I'll set it up, Shyranne."//

One of the screening battleship squadrons was already configured for heavy ground support with kinetic strike projectiles. Warning orders went out to it. Lane set one of his monitors to show the projo attacks once they happened. If he could order the death of an entire people, he could watch it. He knew Shyranne was also watching.

#####

Shana had her own problems with Guard movements around the target warehouse. There was a pattern to what they were doing, she was sure, if she studied them long enough.

A com call suddenly sounded in her ear. //"All hands, Victrix 9-6. Listen up."// It was Karl.

Briefly, Shana felt an intense wish they were together and somewhere other than this damned planet, then other feelings washed the thought away. She was a soldier. She had a worthwhile job to do and was good at it. To a Strike platoon leader, it didn't get any better than having

304

herself and her platoon stuck kilomeasures inside hostile territory. Strike was kind of strange that way.

//"We're fighting five legions of Guard, folks. They had to be hidden somewhere all of this time and we're going to find that base. Once we do, it's toast. People, that means we'll be fighting orphans soon enough. Victrix, you know how that feels and what that does to you. These guys are already sneaky and suicidal. They're going to get worse. Look alive. Stay alive. If a Guardsman loses his life killing you, he wins. We don't want him to win. Be careful, shoot straight, and take him out first. 9-6 out."//

Killing the Guard base. She knew what that meant. Noncombatants. Don't think about it, Shana. You have more than enough to pay attention to right in front of you.

For a few minutes Shana thought about what effect the landings would have on the bunch she was watching, then decided one of two things was going to happen. If the warehouses they were guarding weren't as important as stopping the Corps, she was going to see some of those people down there leave for the fighting lines. If their mission was more important, they were going to stay.

She wanted as many as possible to leave. Fewer guards, fewer problems. Activity. Something was happening. There was visible agitation from a few, but the movement patterns...

Suddenly, there was a lot of traffic around the warehouse in the center. All faint pretense of normal activity around the buildings was gone. Guardsmen were running into the center warehouse and emerging with B-42s and armor. A couple of heavy weapons positions also unmasked on rooftops. Looked like they were getting ready for some kind of desperate defense. Nice of them to show her where everything was.

//" Strike 2-1-6, Scout 9127."// It was one of the Victrix scouts.

She answered. //"Scout 9127, Strike 2-1-6. Lieutenant Ettranty. Send it."//

//"Lieutenant Ettranty, Staff Sergeant Zak Capers. Been in close contact with locals since landing. Just been advised you're investigating what people around this part of town call the Dead Zone. Reason is that anyone goes in doesn't come out. I checked that area about a week ago. Noted much traffic around central warehouse, but the only other building with observed activity was at building southwest of center warehouse. Looked into one warehouse without traffic. Contained robotic remote surveillance point."

//"Aye, Sergeant Capers. Did you make any attempt at the center warehouse?"//

//"Not that crazy, Lieutenant."//

Shana grinned. //"Confirm crazy, Sergeant. Unfortunately, we gotta check the center warehouse anyway. We *are* nuts. Anything else?"//

//"Aye. Found indications of robotic weapons scattered around the five building area. Transmitting a schematic of data. Be careful."//

Wonderful. //"Aye. Thanks for the info. If no other, Ettranty clear."//

//"Capers clear."//

Shana reviewed the schematic and waved Sergeant Stauer over. "You got that?"

"Aye, Lieutenant. Appears the southwest building has a manned remote observation position in it. It's probably a repeater for the main command post in the central building, but I'm betting it has initial control of the area surveillance and defenses. The command post will have overrides, but it might take them a few moments to get them up." He studied her expression for a moment. "You thinking what I'm thinking?"

She grinned. "If you're thinking what I'm thinking, then we're both thinking the same thing. We need to move while these guys are changing posture. Have team six demo the warehouse with the OP, five set up for AP rockets, and tell two to configure for sniping. I want the outside clear before I take one, three, four and seven inside with me. Tell the boys to get busy, Sergeant. I want to get this thing going as soon as the demo's in place.

"Here's my action sequence..."

Sergeant Stauer gave a short, sharp nod of approval once she finished outlining the plan. "Aye. I'll get everyone prepared. You call the start."

The platoon was ready in less than twenty five minutes by her HUD readout, a fact that gave Shana a little feeling of pride. Given that she'd had to issue a fragmentary order and team six had to emplace its demo charges on another building, two was configuring its B-42s for sniping, and five was readying rockets and acquiring targets, all without being discovered, that was a damn good time. Good bunch. Looking down, it appeared the Guards were getting more and more organized into an active defense. Don't let them complete it. //"All hands, 6. Initiate."//

The roof of the warehouse suspected of having the OP collapsed inward explosively, revealing the silhouette of a small blockhouse inside the building's outer shell. The OP. Multiple armor piercing rockets penetrated the blockhouse from two directions and it, too, collapsed into rubble.

Sniper teams began taking down Guardsmen, paying particular attention to those appearing to give orders. By this time, team five had retargeted their rockets. Two troopers started taking out the heavy weapons while the third began hitting the door of the warehouse, each man firing as fast as he could pick up the little rockets laid out on the roof in front of him.

Shana let the snipers and rockets do their work. The last rocket exploded deep within the warehouse, so the inner area was either clear or whoever was there was in bad shape. Good enough. //"Assault teams, let's go, Dogs!"//

Time slowed.

She led her team at a dead run off the warehouse roof, landing lightly using her no-weight belt. Her Link told her the other three teams were in motion from where they'd been deployed around the area perimeter. She verified that with her HUD anyhow. Shana's team and team seven got to the front of the warehouse just before teams four and three, the four teams smoothly meshing as they charged inside.

The interior of the warehouse was a shambles, with dead bodies and wreckage everywhere. Shana stopped momentarily as she found herself fronting another door, this one battle steel showing the effects of several glancing rocket hits. The door entered a huge heavily armored building constructed inside the shell of the warehouse. //"Kardo, demo the door."//

Shana's team split to cover left and right while Sergeant Kardo dropped out of movement long enough to slap a demo charge on the door. Shana sent four and three to circumnavigate the armored structure, checking for surprises and Guard survivors.

There were several survivors still active inside the inner building when the door blew, but the incoming Strike teams were right behind the blast. Even a Guardsman could be shaken when a battle steel hatch slammed inward into his face and the Strike dogs didn't give them time to recover.

//"Left clear."//

//"Right clear."//

//"Aye. Further in, all."// Shana replied without breaking stride and they continued into the building, running down the blank corridor hidden by the hatch. The corridor made several abrupt turns as they penetrated, and Shana was grimly certain those turns were to give defenders firing positions against a conventional assault. Well, this assault was anything but conventional. Her teams took fire several times, but the Guards were disorganized and killing them didn't slow down the attack. Shana finally called a halt when they came up against another hatch at the end. //"5,6. Set perimeter security and get the rest in here. There's another damned big hatch. We're going to have to do this again."//

//"6, 5. Aye. On the way."//

Smythe from her team took only a few moments to place his demo charge on the hatch. //" 'Ware demo! Blowing now."//

When the door went inward in fragments, Shana and her teams dashed inside, leaving Sergeant Stauer and the rest of the platoon to watch their backs. A control room containing several more Guards was immediately to the left of the hatch. The fight was brisk but short, with the advantage totally on the side of the Strike dogs.

Shana found herself facing various empty rooms and a lit staircase leading downward. She sent the halt and secure command, stopping the platoon advance. She had no desire to head down that staircase until she knew what she was going to be hitting.

One of her men was operating a life signs detector. "Lieutenant, I'm getting a lot of life signals down there, but they're funny. Could be a bunch of people in stasis. Don't detect any movement or other active signs."

Shana thought heavily. Guard troops in stasis. That fit the pattern of Cauldwell. No way did she want to wake those people up, but they were no threat right now.

Another Strike dog was scanning the security monitors in the control room. "Lieutenant, you need to see this."

Shana strode swiftly into the control room and looked at the monitor screens. Oh, Lord Above! she thought. There were around a dozen screens and all but one of them showed the same thing. There weren't Guardsmen in stasis down there, not grown ones at any rate. Those were embryo storage banks. Labels on the monitors said there were three floors beneath her. That meant there were hundreds – thousands - of embryo storage banks! This was where the Guard kept the embryos for the Emperor's breeding program!

One of the screens had a radically different picture, the interior of some kind of vault. There was a stasis cabinet in the middle of it, looking like a sarcophagus with the Imperial crest blazoned on its lid. Surrounding it were two men and two women of the Guard, each now in an alert posture with their weapons in their hand. It was clear they were in communication with the control room, and just as clear the four knew it was under new management.

It was the crest that was important to Shana. Somewhere down there was a vault with the Emperor's body. "People," Shana breathed, "we've hit pay dirt."

She spun to face Sergeant Stauer. "Sergeant, take three teams and sweep the lower floors. Two teams will act as perimeter security of the building. Last one will stay here with my team as a reserve if you need it. Try to locate that vault as soon as you can. Once you locate it, render the door lock inoperable. I don't want those four getting out. I also don't want to try to get inside until I've got orders from higher. Move!"

Shana's next task was to call the captain. She changed to the Century command band. //"Strike 1-9-6, Strike 2-1-6. We have a situation."//

//"2-1-6, 1-9-6. Say your situation."//

In quick, concise phrases, she brought Captain Gldblum up to date on her mission. //"... and that's where we are, Captain. What do we do with the Emperor, not to mention thousands of embryos? I expect visitors soon enough. This place is too important not to be under surveillance by Guard higher somewhere. We've got to have tripped an alarm."//

Captain Gldblum was thinking fast. This hot potato was way above his pay grade, too. //"Wait. I'll call higher."//

He called the Legate, who, after hearing the story and the sensational find, immediately called Corps Legate Khev Garua. Khev, in turn, got into a three way with Admiral Mackinnie and Shyranne. The discussion was short, but profound. The decision that came out of it wasn't one that made them happy, but the only one they could make under the circumstances.

Karl got Captain Gldblum on com. //"Strike 1-9-6, 9-6. Captain, bring up Lieutenant Ettranty. I'll be briefing you both at the same time."//

//"9-6, Strike 1-9-6. Strike 2-1-6 is up, this net. Send."//

//"2-1-6, 9-6. Say current situation. Strike 1-9-6 monitors."//

//"9-6, 2-1-6. We've swept building. Building clear of active Guard except for vault guards. No other threats. Suspect that Guard higher has already been notified of our activities, but no evidence shown yet. Perimeter guards report all quiet. Be advised of two key points. First, rough count of embryos indicates total of over 250,000. Say again 2-5-0 thousand. Second, vault containing possible Emperor's body has been sealed off without penetration. Be advised there appears to be no way to open the hatch from the inside. Anyone in secure area has to be let out by control room or controls exterior to chamber. Vault door controls disabled. Door controls are one way, say again, one way. Guards were locked in to guard the body and left until next shift came and got them out. Cannot leave on their own. Update complete."//

There was no hint of any personal relationship between Shana and Karl. It was simply a Legate getting an important report from one of his platoon leaders.

//"2-1-6, 9-6. Good report. Situation is as follows: Your situation reported to higher and guidance received. Be aware detectable reduction in Guard resistance throughout battle area. Reason unknown as yet. Some forces have started heading back into the City. Those may be coming after you. If so, option exists to simply blow building and get the hell out of area before the mob arrives. Comment?"//

Shana took a deep breath and looked around. All the rest of her people in the control room were doing their assigned jobs, confident in her ability to get it right. Sergeant Stauer was standing, watching her, waiting for his lieutenant to make her decision. They could blow the building and vanish into the city. Get out alive.

But there were a quarter of a million innocent babies in this same building. The Emperor didn't count as far as Shana was concerned. Oh, having his body under control would greatly help reconstruction. They would have the Emperor under Cluster control and there would be no confusion about who won this thing. Without the Emperor, there would always be questions, impersonators trying to raise rebellions, or other sham claimants.

Right now, that wasn't an issue to Shana. A quarter of a million babies were an issue, a gut issue to any Gladius. Those children were an invaluable addition to the human gene pool, uncorrupted by Shangnaman's conditioning. There was no telling what would happen if the Guard arrived, but the possibilities for those embryos were numerous and scary. Guard control of a quarter million long term reinforcements meant that there was going to be another bloodbath in a couple of decades. All the Guard had to do was recapture the Emperor and the embryos then escape. They would build their strength for a while as some kind of government in exile then come back. This time with real experience in major combat. The Guard was good enough already that giving them battlefield experience and greater numbers meant they might win the next round, especially since the Cluster wouldn't have the advantage it now enjoyed of preparing in the shadows. The Guard would already know what it was facing and they were deadly competent. A Guard strength of 300,000 or better meant they were going to win. It was as simple as that.

Stopping the next round before it happened was vitally important, but there was something else, something unspoken but present in the mind of any Gladius A Gladius existed to protect the innocent. Right in this building were a quarter million innocents and she was their only protection. Without her, the Guard would take them and warp them into their own mold. To Shana, that was the same as ordering their destruction. The Guard was the Predator as much as the Emperor. The Predator would try to take them. No Gladius, man or woman, would let that happen while blood still ran in their body.

Shana made her decision. The logic of future consequences guided her thoughts, but the real decision was based on all that was Gladius in her.

She had a quarter million innocents under her protection and the Predator was coming.

To stay here, to mount a static defense, was the worst thing that could happen to a Gladius in combat. Mobility and a fluid situation were what a Gladius exploited. Without them, he lost half of his effectiveness. To stay was to commit herself and her men to a fixed situation and Strike units weren't designed for it. A static defense against the Guard would kill all of them if the Victrix couldn't get to them soon enough. Even if they were relieved in time, most of her men could die. Including her.

Go - live. Stay - die. Stay - protect a quarter million innocents from the Predator.

Shana looked in the calm waiting eyes of Sergeant Stauer. She looked around the room and felt the presence of the rest of her men through her Link. She could feel Those Gone Before, especially the dead women of the original Victrix, killed by order of the Emperor in the vault down those stairs. They were with her now.

The Oath said it:

> Nothing will pass and harm
> those I am sworn to protect.
> My life is nothing.
> My duty and purpose are everything.
> If my life is called for,
> it will be given gladly.

Time to live up to the Oath.

Shana watched Sergeant Stauer as she answered Khev. //"9-6, 2-1-6. Negative on bug out. Intend to conduct defense of position if so ordered."//

Her platoon sergeant simply nodded as she gave her recommendation. She was doing the right thing, a Gladius thing.

//"Understood and concur, Lieutenant,"// Karl replied. He knew perfectly well he was just about to order his future wife into a near suicidal situation, but they were both Gladii. //"So ordered. Strike 9-1-6 will send more platoons to help secure perimeter. Your platoon to protect building entrance. Blow entrance if it looks like you're going to be overrun, but do not abandon position. Delay Guard forces until I can get major elements to you. Be advised Fifth Cohort plus anything I can scrounge will be enroute as fast as I can get them to you, but not before Guard arrives. Your mission to hold in place as long as possible. Understood?"//

//"9-6, 2-1-6. Understand and concur."//

//"9-6, 2-1-6, Strike 1-9-6."//

//"1-9-6, 9-6. Send it."//

//"Aye. I'm putting 4-1 on 2-1 location. They aren't too far away at the moment. No other platoons currently available. 2-1-6 will command. Projected arrival 2-0 mikes."//

//"9-6 concurs."//

Captain Gldblum was sending his 4th Strike platoon to reinforce her. She breathed a small sigh of relief. Even one more platoon, twenty one more Strike troopers, would be a big weight off her. //"1-9-6, 2-1-6. Aye. Understand, and they'll be very welcome.

//"Break, break. 9-6, 2-1-6, request."//

//"State request."//

//"Have not yet gone to Advanced Officers' School. Do not know how to conduct Die-In-Place mission. Request DIP not be made a requirement of operation. Scheduled to be at wedding in two months. Groom will be highly pissed if not present. Suggest avoidance, pissed groom."//

Karl grinned. //"Aye. Will avoid pissed groom. Reaching for sledgehammer now. 9-6 out."//

#####

On the legion major command band, Karl quickly briefed Al Lumis, his sledgehammer. //"Al, how fast can you get unstuck and start towards the warehouse?"//

//"I'm reorienting my cohort now, Karl. We ought to be able to start kicking them out of the way in about ten minutes. I'd like a little extra punch, though. Can you get me the Faire battalion? We've worked with those guys and they're good. I can use them. They can kick open a hole and we'll just keep widening the breach from that point."//

//"You'll get them if I have to personally boot Khev Garua's ass to do it."//

//"Good enough. Karl, I've already told my boys about the embryos and the Emperor. I've also told them it's Shana holding the position. That last part means something and they'll get there and get her out if there's any way."//

//"Thanks, Al."//

//"Not for you, Karl, fiancee or not. Shana means more to the guys than you do, actually."//

//"Thanks for that one, too, Al. Now get busy and stop blowing hot air out your ass. I expect you on station at the warehouse soonest or you're not invited to the wedding. Camille will be really pissed at you if that happens."//

Al laughed. This was the kind of mission he liked. Bull forward and right up the middle, taking the head of any enemy stupid enough to rear it. //"Evil, Karl. You've invoked the only force in the Universe I fear. On the way. Out."//

Legate Karl Athan momentarily allowed himself the luxury of a personal thought. Hang on, Shana; we're coming to get you.

#####

Ground CIC was busy, but Khev was watching the schematic of the Corps battle around Imperial City with quiet intensity. Something was happening, something important, but he wasn't sure what. Then he got the call from Karl Athan and things fell into place.

The Guard appeared to be doing two unrelated things. Small units were breaking contact from all over the battlefield and heading deeper into the city. Meanwhile, a much bigger portion was pulling out behind a fierce rearguard and joining a large column that looked like it was heading towards a location out of the city, probably the Guard's hidden base.

The situation at the Emperor's bunker made everything click together. The Guard realized the battle was lost and were trying to save as much as they could. They were pulling out as much fighting force as possible, but tasking units to take the bunker and recover the stasis tubes along with the Emperor's body. The second mission was the most important one. They might save enough fighting strength to come back and retake Central, but none of it would mean anything if they lost those children and the Emperor. That was one fight they had to win.

It was also one fight the Cluster had to win, too.

He waved Shyranne over. "Listen as I talk to Lane. You both need to know this."

//"Fleet, Corps. We've got something happening on the ground, Lane."//

//"Corps, Fleet. What do you mean, Khev?"//

// "Lane, one of our Strike platoons from the Victrix captured a major bunker disguised as a warehouse. It contained a quarter of a million Guard embryos and the Emperor's body. Holding the Emperor's body will be a big plus for us when things settle down, but the embryos are a major concern right now. As long as we have the embryos, they will simply become future citizens. If the Guard gets them back and escapes, we're going to be looking at a war twenty or so years down the road that will make this one look like a school yard game. We stand a good chance of losing that one, too. We *have* to keep the embryos.

//"My gut feeling is that the Guard is reacting to the capture of the Emperor and the embryos. I also get the feeling someone's not thinking too straight. We're still in heavy contact, but more Guard units are breaking away throughout the battle area. We've pretty well tagged the bulk of withdrawn units as evacuating, but a heavy contingent of mixed small units is heading back for the City."//

//"Trying for an urban terrain battle to tie you up while the rest escape?"//

//"Negative on Urban Terrain Operations - UTO. The rearguard is making things difficult enough on their own. I don't think the Guard is trying to put depth behind that rearguard. For one thing, I think they've already decided a UTO battle wouldn't give them much more time, not using the force I've seen heading back into the City. They've already figured out they can't stop us here in the suburbs and they won't be able to do it in the City itself. We're better at UTO and they know it. Once we've finished the rearguard, all the Guard can do is minor harassment, not any real delay. I think those small units are reinforcing the group attacking the warehouse. The Guard knows we're winning. They want to take the warehouse, then bug out once they get the Emperor's body and the embryos."//

//"They intend to overwhelm the platoon at the warehouse, get Shangnaman and as many embryos as possible and join with the rest. Then the Guard cuts out for parts unknown, only to come back one day much stronger this time. Is that what you're thinking?"//

Khev gave Shyranne a grim look. //"Exactly, Lane. If they come back in the kind of strength those embryos could give them, our military establishment could be twice its current size and not be enough.

//"There are only two Strike platoons at the warehouse at the moment. The Victrix has a reinforced cohort headed to pull them out of trouble, but that may not be enough, depending on how long they can hold out. We may have to put in the rest of the legion, but we need a lot more air support as well. I want everything we can throw on the bunker's attackers once we get good intelligence. Looking at the Guard situation, someone's activated a Go To Hell plan."//

Lane studied the information Khev had sent him on data link. //"I agree. Right now, there's a lot more than a couple of legions worth of Guard troops in that column heading for their base in the Momart Hills, but we can't hit them yet. We can't use kinetics while those Guard units are around Imperial City without a lot of civilian casualties. We're preparing to put a high speed mass right into that base, as soon as the retreating column gets to it. That group's bought and paid for."//

Lane was silent for a few seconds while he thought. //"Tell your people holding the Emperor's body to hang on. They've suddenly become the key to winning this triple-damned war."//

//"We'll take care of that, Lane. Just get our support. Ground out."// He looked at his wife and commander. "The Guard just made a major rookie mistake."

She knew what he meant. "They have their priorities wrong. That warehouse is the real center of gravity of this fight. The Guard should have sent a full legion. A legion could take that warehouse, soak up the casualties, and do the job in much less time. Instead they're evacuating what legions they can and sending an ad-hoc force of small units they can cut loose to attack the warehouse. Someone got it completely backward."

Khev nodded. "For small favors and major enemy blunders give thanks."

"Amen. Do you want the Augusta from the Army's fight? They're not heavily committed."

"No. Leave them there. Jon's people still have a lot to do and they may be needed. Like I told Lane, I intend to pry loose the whole Victrix if I need to. They're motivated to support those Strike troops anyhow. Lieutenant Ettranty's one of the Strike platoon leaders. She's commanding the position."

Shyranne blanked at that statement for a moment, wondering what could make a lieutenant so important to a whole legion. Then it hit her. "She was their first female recruit after Victrix Base was destroyed. The only woman I've ever seen that wears a kilt. I've met her several times, but I also noticed the entire Victrix seems to regard her as an icon of some kind."

Khev nodded. "Karl once told me that he didn't think there'd be a female commander of the Victrix until she worked her way up to the position - which he thinks she will - because the troops held her in such high esteem. She symbolizes the rebirth of the legion to them. That's important to those guys and they'll go across the floor of Hell itself to get her out of trouble."

Shyranne's face was grim. "Judging from what you've said and what I'm seeing, that's just what they'll have to do."

They looked at each other. There was something else. Shyranne spoke first. "We can't let that bunker be taken. If the Guard captures those embryos, this whole war will have been for nothing."

Khev's face was stone hard. "Understood and agree. I can get with Lane and set up a fall back in case it looks like relief can't get there in time and the bunker's going under."

His voice sounded like slate grating on rough granite. "A precision kinetic strike. No way to do that without collateral damage."

Shyranne thought for a second about the sterile words, "collateral damage". Any strike would kill hundreds, perhaps thousands of their own troops, certainly kill most of the Victrix cohort headed to relieve whoever was left in those Strike platoons. That had to be balanced against what amounted to the loss of the war, possibly the loss of the Cluster and humanity's future. The tradeoff was simple - and brutal. They simply could not take the chance of giving a quarter of a million future reinforcements to the Guard. "Do it."

As she silently watched her husband contact Lane, her thoughts turned inward. May the Lord Above have mercy. On her troops and on Khev and herself. No matter what happened, the decision was made. They'd carry that burden with them to their graves.

CHAPTER 17

IMPERIAL CITY

Shana and Sergeant Stauer were busy setting up defenses, constantly in motion checking fields of fire to ensure they interlocked and covered the right area, then explaining their defensive plan to the troops. 4th Platoon arrived to take the rear of the building and eased part of Shana's problem by drastically reducing her frontage. Lieutenant Tom Cnr, 4th Platoon commander, was junior to Shana, so there wasn't any question of her retaining command of the position.

Good and bad, she thought. She didn't have to ask Tom's permission for something, but responsibility for the position was all hers. Actually, she was okay with responsibility, she decided. She liked command.

One of Shana's teams managed to salvage some of the weapons from the destroyed emplacements on the roofs. The 2 cm guns were useless, but the recovery of five functional 12.7 mm guns was happy making. As Sergeant Stauer said when the guns were brought down, "Mark Two's. Those damn things haven't changed for a century or more. The old Ma Deuce could take a hit from a nuke and keep putting out bolts. Good guns."

Two of those went to 4th Platoon and she kept three since her platoon covered the main avenue of approach. She was going to need the extra firepower. They used one of the Ma Deuces to cut rubble from surrounding buildings, leaving piles of it all over the streets leading to the warehouse. Some channeled attackers. Others held surprises. Some of those piles were even legitimate rubble.

Working at a feverish pace, both platoons built a waist high wall of rubble around the building, but not for defense. It had another purpose. Cratering charges found in the basement's small armory had proved useful to blast deep holes forming a ditch right behind the wall. That ditch also had a variety of uses.

Even the Guard bodies were now making themselves useful. No better bolt sponge than a nice fresh dead body. The former Guard members were now an efficiently bolt absorbent layer over the outside of the defensive wall. Their no longer needed armor was used to reinforce various spots in and around the defensive perimeter.

No defensive position was ever really finished, but 2d Platoon was as close to it as they were going to get when the first alerts started to come into the control room. Shana figured that ammunition was going to be her only supply problem and that wasn't much of one given the small armory found in the building. One way or the other, they weren't going to be in the position long enough for limited food or water to have any effect. It was nearing noon, and they'd be out, or dead, before the sun went down. Her one big advantage was that the Guard had designed this building as a heavy bunker. Nice of them. Now she had to make the best use of it.

"Lieutenant, we're starting to get probes." It was Corporal Chofal in the control room, monitoring the outer perimeter sensors. She walked over and took a quick look to evaluate the situation. Guard scouts were popping up here and there. She wondered how long it would take them to find out that their booby traps were under new management and in different locations. As she watched, one of the hostile icons turned red and went out. Apparently, it didn't take them long.

//"O-Ps, be aware we're getting Guard probes,"// she sent to her two early warning teams roaming the warehouse area. //"We've started the reconnaissance battle, people. Keep them blinded. Engage whenever you can without revealing yourselves, but try to channel them."//

Keep the enemy more or less in the dark about yourself and keep them going where you wanted them to go. That was Basic Combat 101. She wanted the oncoming Guard forces fumbling around until they found the targeted corridors she'd set up. She couldn't keep them out of her outer perimeter, but she could nudge them to where she wanted them.

On the monitor, icons showing hostile troops quickly started changing color and disappearing. The boys were feeling enthusiastic today. Good. A few hostile icons were left active in the right places. Things were going according to plan and she hoped the Guard didn't notice.

Sergeant Stauer came into the control room and glanced at the monitor, where new hostile icons were appearing while others turned red and disappeared. "I see we're starting to get visitors."

Shana turned to him as he gave his report. "Lieutenant, the wall's finished and the Ma Duces are in their initial positions. We've only had time to make two alternate positions apiece for the guns, but more'll get made as we have the time. Teams are ready."

He looked thoughtfully at the monitor again. "Lieutenant, didn't the Legate say we were going to be facing forces from all over the Guard?"

Shana nodded. "Detachments from all of their legions, as a matter of fact. I don't know how many we'll be looking at, but they want this place at any cost. Protecting the Emperor is their entire mission. They want that body."

Sergeant Stauer continued to watch the monitor for a few seconds then turned to her. "I was thinking the same thing, Lieutenant. What bothers me is that I don't see the kind of reconnaissance a force like that could put out."

Shana started to answer, but stopped herself. He was right. A force the size she was expecting could just roll over her, without all this preliminary sparring. The probes outside were starting to look like a feint to attract their attention, if you thought about it. Where was the Guard? Not coming from above. The Fleet was pretty well in control of the airspace over Imperial City. When fighters could avoid ground fire. The AA was ferocious and survival of a fighter or assault shuttle in ground support mode wasn't exactly a sure thing.

The Guard wasn't coming up the streets. Not yet. Where were they? What had she forgotten?

Then it hit her. Urgently, she said, "Tunnels! The Guard likes underground stuff, Sergeant. Spider holes. Tunnels. All of the Legions are reporting that kind of encounter. Ten to one they have tunnel ingress to this building. Hell, they'd be stupid not to!"

Sergeant Stauer's eyes got big and he spun, headed for the door. "Teams Two and Six to me! We've got some walls to check! Bring all your sensor gear! Evns, grab both of the platoon's directional plasma mines! Move!"

It wasn't long before Shana got a com call. //"Got it, Lieutenant. One spot on the third level down shows an open area behind the wall. We'll have to cut through the wall to get to it; I can't find the opening mechanism."//

//"Aye, get cutting,"// Shana replied. //"Be careful. I expect there ought to be a bunch of hostiles already headed for that door and it may be booby trapped as well. Also check the floor of the bottom level. They might have a tunnel directly under the building to the Emperor's vault."//

//"Aye. Six cutting now. Two designated to check the bottom floor."//

Sergeant Stauer had team six begin cutting into the wall with their short swords. Meanwhile, team two headed for the bottom level basement floor. Soon enough there was a report of two more tunnels. Shana and Sergeant Stauer listened to the team leader's report. He replied, //"Cut into the tunnel roofs. I'm sending the second plasma charge. Set that one for command detonation in the first tunnel and place a remote so we'll know when to fire it. Cut into the other tunnel, get into it, and set some demo to collapse it as far away from the building as possible. Don't engage any

Guard force in the tunnel, just put in a few booby traps to delay them and drop the longest stretch of the tunnel you can, as far out as you can get. We don't want them digging through any time soon."//

A few moments later, //"Sergeant, Novak. We're about two hundred measures down the tunnel and starting to get distant life readings. I'm putting in demo charges here."//

//"Do it and get back as soon as possible,"// Sergeant Stauer replied. //"The ball's opening and we need you for the dance."//

Shana was monitoring but remained quiet. Sergeant Stauer had things well in hand and didn't need his Lieutenant's interference. The fact that the Guard was coming up the tunnel was enough for her to know. She walked over to stand behind Corporal Chofal, her attention on the take from the sensors in the plasma booby trapped tunnels. She wanted to take out as much of the Guard as she could with the plasma charges. The fewer that survived, the better. The survivors would be coming at her above ground and that would cause no end of bother.

It wasn't long before sensors in the tunnels started showing intruders. Novak's team was back, mission accomplished. The third tunnel was blown, leaving a dip in the basement floor along the tunnel's length. Novak believed in really plugging a tunnel when ordered to plug one. Shana had to heartily agree.

As Shana watched, scouts in the other two tunnels were followed by larger groups. This was their initial attack. Her tunnel blocking teams had carefully replaced the materials they'd cut away. When the plasma charges went off, Shana figured slag created by the backblast would reseal the breaches anyhow, but the more blockage, the better. //"5, 6. Are all of your people away from the breaches? I'm ready to detonate the plasma charges."//

//"6, 5. Aye. Blow when ready."//

//"5, a little more. I want as many of these bastards in the kill zone as possible."//

A few moments later Shana checked her sensors. The tunnels were beginning to fill. She gave the command to Corporal Chofal. "Detonate."

When he set off the charges, a large ball of superheated plasma suddenly formed in each tunnel and shot forward, collapsing walls behind it as they failed under the ball's heat, crisping anything - and anyone - in its path. Each ball slashed at light speed down its tunnel until finally impacting, one at a sharp bend, the other at the tunnel entrance, both detonating in an almost catastrophic blast.

Shana looked on with satisfaction. She could imagine the damage and hoped there had been sizable forces already in those tunnels. Her problem now was she was out of plasma charges. If the Guard came at her in mass, those charges would have been invaluable, but they had to block the tunnels. Now all she had were small arms and the Ma Deuces, which were officially small arms to anyone that had never been on the receiving end of one. Gldblum promised air support, but AA was complicating that picture. All she could do was hope she got air support in time and what she got was enough.

Chofal called out to her, "Lieutenant, we're starting to see main forces. Looks like they've given up probing."

"Aye," she replied. "Pull back those OPs. Maintain surveillance with sensors." The enemy was partially blinded, which was good, but she was going to lose her human eyes out there when the OPs came in. The sensors she'd inherited would only last until the Guard found and deactivated them. After that, she lost her electronic eyes. Cross that bridge when she came to it. Meanwhile, continue to interdict with remotely controlled booby traps. She needed those six men back here.

#####

Khev watched the tactical monitor intently as the retreating Guard column finally reached its base. The column had been tailed the whole way by a scout from the Valeria, now out of the blast area and using his recon nannies to track the retreating troops. Someone had definitely activated a Go To Hell plan and this was one part. Lieutenant Ettranty was fighting off the other part.

In a moment, a heavy kinetic strike was going to blot that column and its base from Central, hopefully obliterating the entire strength of the Guard that wasn't still engaged in Imperial City. Some might call it genocide, since the Guard was as much a people in its own right as the Corps, and Khev was honest enough to use the word. He was also honest enough to know that the Guard's death was necessary to guarantee the future of the Cluster. What he felt at the idea wasn't satisfaction, but it was close. They were going to win this one, once the Guard was destroyed. The Guard's fighting strength in Imperial City wasn't enough to stop four legions.

On the other hand, the Victrix still had to get Ettranty out of trouble.

#####

Shana got a report about the kinetic strike that killed most of the Guard, but it wasn't important to her situation. Too far away. Instead, she walked out of the control room and through the warehouse facade to the front doorway. She took a few steps outside, then stood, looking quietly up the empty street, her B-42 cradled against her chest in her right arm, her feet a comfortable distance apart, simply waiting for the Predator to arrive.

She and her troops were Strike. By definition, the best of the best. Now their prototypes as Gladii were about to come at them in force. The Guard. The ancestral Gladius. The Guard was coming up against her men, men bred from the survivors of a thousand years of battle. Led by her... and she was of the Guard's blood. There was a grim irony here, if she spent the time to think about it. Not worth it. The Guard was coming. She was going to stop them.

Shana found herself strangely calm as she contemplated the coming fight, feeling the relaxed confidence of a master craftsman about to go to work. Her troops were as ready as they were ever going to be, as ready as she and her sergeant could make them. Now all that remained was the mission. The mission. Now it was no longer a Strike mission. It was a Gladius mission - one that came from the soul of the Gladius. They were going to save a quarter million children.

She wasn't a Gladius by birth, at least in her own mind. She was a recruit. Now she was a combat officer doing a job she loved, in a life she loved. She looked back at her old life as a tridio star reporter, the parties, the glamor, the glittering surroundings, and knew all of it was time wasted. Here was where she was meant to be.

She pushed back her helmet visor and looked up at the sky. It was deep blue, but not empty. It was full of the contrails of fighters and assault shuttles as they went about their own missions and the bright lines of laser straight bolt fire from the AA guns trying to take them down. Dark clouds of smoke in all directions formed patches and haze. It was the sky of war. Still, she had to see it, one more time, even if it was crowded and polluted.

She thought about what she wanted for her future. She wanted to be Karl's wife, to be part of him and have him be part of her. Children? She was sure she wanted them, but didn't see a way as long as she was a century grade officer. How did you kiss a child then go off to kill someone or maybe have them kill you? Finally, she understood why the women of the Corps were exempt from combat. A child had to have a mother.

A child needed a father, too. Karl would be a good one and a Legate didn't go on crazy missions like a Strike officer. It would be good if both she and Karl were able to back away from this sort of thing while they raised their family.

Maybe after she made Major. Captains commanded Centuries, and she wanted her Century. Majors were staff officers. Maybe she could take a staff job in Intelligence once she made Major. Raise her family then. Buck for a battalion command once the kids were old enough.

She snorted at her thoughts. Why think about the future? She probably wasn't going to live through this afternoon. There was a short legion of mixed Guard units coming down that street to kill her and take what she protected from her. They'd try to do it properly, first. She was sure of that. They'd get their nose bloodied. She was sure of that, too. Then they'd wake up and just come at her in waves. Pick up units never worked well together, but they didn't have to. All they had to do was just come at her in mob after mob. Two platoons couldn't handle that sort of mass. They'd roll right over her.

The Sergeant Major had told her that she'd one day be asked to pay the Gladius Price when she put on the uniform. She'd already paid a part of it when she killed her father. The Price wasn't always death. Now she had twenty willing men - forty one, with Tom's platoon - and they were going to pay the Price with her.

//"Strike 4-6, Strike 2-6. Tom, patch me into your platoon band. I need to talk to everybody."//

//"Done, Shana."//

//"Listen up, guys,"// she said on both platoon bands. She didn't bother identifying herself. She was a woman. What other woman was here? //"They're coming. We know it. We are going to be here waiting for them for one and only one reason. We have the Emperor in stasis, but I don't give a shit about that asshole. If it was just him, I'd blow the building and get the hell out, but we can't do that. There are a quarter of a million innocent babies down there, and that's why we're here getting ready to kick hell out of the Guard. If we don't hold, the Guard will take them and make them into the same sort of hard core, mutated, fanatic bastard we're about to start killing. We're here to give those kids a future, people. There are forty two of us, a quarter million babies, and a couple of thousand fanatic motherfuckers trying to steal those kids. We aren't going to let that happen. We're Gladii. Our job is to hold the fucking Gates of Hell and protect innocents. We're going to do that job. We're going to kick ass and hold this place in our hands until the 5th Cohort gets here. Before the 5th arrives, the Guard will know by the Lord Above that they've been in a hell of a fight. A fight they're going to lose. We're going to pile those bastards high and deep. If there's only one of us left fighting when we're relieved, we've still done our job. We've honored the Oath."//

She shifted her B-42 into her left hand and slowly hand-drew her arm dagger. She threw it point first into the street surface at her feet. The molecular shear field of its blade let it slice into the street like butter, hilt standing above the surface. //"This far and no farther people. Here we

323

stand. We are the Gladius. We can do no other. Gladio alieyo. Ettranty out."//

Shana wondered how her men would take her declaration. She needn't have worried.

From somewhere in the defenses, a voice took up a song on the still open All Hands band.

//"Aaaay... eyn mol, eyn mol, eyn mol -
      eyn mol tu ikh zikh banayen..."//

In a moment, both platoons were singing, clapping their hands and stamping their feet in time to the jaunty music. The old, old song, sung in a language long dead except in obscure parts of the former Empire, was about a farmer getting drunk after a hard week's work. But there was an undercurrent. The undercurrent spoke of proud soldiers and a grim willingness to do unto others - with relish. It was sung on the way into a big jump, flinging the Gladius willingness to do battle straight into the teeth of an enemy. Now it was a declaration. Let the Predator come. Her men were ready.

She walked back into the warehouse with a steady tread, the song ringing in her helmet earphones, her outer mike picking up the steady thump of boots and the clapping of hands. The first trickle of attackers was down at the other end of the street. She didn't have them in line of sight, but she knew they were there. Time to go to work. She wished she could see Karl one more time.

#####

In Ground CIC, Khev was studying his monitor carefully as the situation evolved. The Guard resistance was proving stubborn, but there were cracks appearing, often caused by Guard units easing back out of the fight. Now was the time to find a pattern in the midst of the confused swirling maelstrom of the battle around and within Imperial City.

Khev finally thought he saw something forming in the monitor, but wasn't sure. //"9-6, Ground. What is the situation with your two Strike platoons?"//

//"Ground, 9-6. They've thrown back two attacks with minimal casualties. I have Scout 9127 watching Guard in vicinity of attack. He says those characters are getting more worked up by the minute. Something's pushing the Guard. Pushing hard. 5th is still enroute, but they're chopping their way through some stiff resistance. They'll get there, but it's taking time."//

//"Karl, the Guard has to have the Emperor and those fetus tubes. Shangnaman's the reason they exist. We've taken care of the evacuating units and their base, but the Guard still wants the Emperor and those fetus tubes. I expect someone feels whatever's left can still find a way to come back as long as they have that crazy bastard and those kids."//

//"I'm getting heavier resistance in the main battle, Khev, and they're trying to lock in place to try and hold us down. Delaying tactics. I'm also having a harder time keeping a corridor open between the rest of the legion and the 5th. My guess is they're trying to cut off access. Thanks for the Faire battalion, by the way. Al's going to use the elves to punch through."//

Khev studied his monitor for a moment. //"Understood. They want to keep us away from the attack on the warehouse. As soon as they can roll over the Strike platoons - and they're getting ready to try a brute force and ignorance move according to your scout's report - they'll grab the fetus tubes and the Emperor then get them to some evacuation point at all costs.

//"Go ahead and push the rest of your legion up behind the 5th Cohort. I'm going to slide the Ferrata and the Valeria in on your flanks and help you shove. We've got to get to that warehouse before the Guard does. It's the central focus of the battle.

//"Note Guard's also looking disorganized. Their operations aren't as well coordinated as they were a little while ago. Sensors detected a major explosion in the palace sometime back. Makes me wonder if something hit their main CP. In any case, keep driving a wedge towards the warehouse. Ferrata and Valeria will help you keep it open. Once we split them, we can roll these bastards up before we get completely into the city and have to do it the hard way."//

//"Understood, Khev. I've got Al Lumis and the Faire battalion kicking and slugging their way through whatever's in the way. They'll get there. We all have to hope they get there in time."//

A Gladius was the product of a thousand years of Darwinian selection through the brutal process of combat. With a life spent entirely as a soldier, the Gladius was both suited to, and trained in, every aspect of conflict from physical to political to economic. Defense of a static position was both the simplest and most dangerous form of battle. Static defense wasn't the way a Gladius preferred to fight, but the two platoons had to do it here and now. They intended to accomplish their mission.

Shana considered what was coming and how best to handle it. They'd beat back the first two attacks and done it well. Her mind skittered away from the three bodies lying in an empty niche near the control room.

Two more were badly wounded. Two dead in Tom's platoon. Her first combat losses. Her perfect record was broken. She had led her men here and committed them to this battle, a battle she was afraid she was going to lose. She was the commander. It was her responsibility.

But she still had thirty four combat capable Strike dogs defending this position. And her. Behind them were a quarter million unborn children whose future they were committed to save. That was the job of a Gladius. That was enough to keep her and her men here.

That was enough for her. It had to be. There would be sleepless nights and bad dreams in her future if she survived. That, too, was part of the Gladius Price. She was prepared to pay it, if they could only hold this position long enough.

The bunker where they'd taken their positions - there was no outer warehouse shell left - had been designed with thin firing slits for their weapons, but she'd learned fire could come in those slits as well. Two of her men were proof enough of that. So far, she'd only used one of the Ma Deuces. The enemy didn't know her full firepower. They also didn't know how heavily the approach to the building was booby trapped. She was saving both surprises for when they'd do the most good and kill the most Guards.

The weak point was the door. They'd blasted in the armored hatch taking the building and there was only a jury rigged block keeping anything out. One good push by the attackers and they'd be inside. Then it would be a matter of pistols, axes, and far more Guards than her men could handle.

She was still worrying when she got the call from the scout. //"Strike 2-6, Scout 9127. They look to be massing this time, Lieutenant, getting ready for that human wave attack you told me about. Appears to me that somebody wants in that building as fast as possible and doesn't care about casualties. Next attack will be maximum push, probably everyone they can bring. I estimate 1-0 mikes before main attack commences. "//

//"Understood, Zak. 1-0 mikes. We have air support on the way. I need you to act as air-ground control. Can do?"//

//"Can do, Lieutenant. It's going to be messy because there's still a lot of AA out here, but some of those birds will get through. When do you want it?"//

//"They'll pile up sooner or later, Zak. Hit 'em then. We'll be holding the front door. Kick the whole bunch in the ass."//

//"Understood. If nothing further, Scout 9127 out."//

Zak was out there watching what was going to happen. The Corps would know how they died, even if they all went down. That made her feel better in a way. Ten minutes. Better get busy.

It started just like the last two times, individuals drifting down the street, hugging cover and professionally dispersed. By this time, her entire platoon knew they were facing trained soldiers, but soldiers with a difference. The Guard had learned military operations from a book. The Corps was trained by battlefield survivors. Big difference.

It didn't matter, Shana thought. Those bastards could replace every Guardsman she killed with ten more. Get on the all-hands band. //"Okay, guys, they're coming at the front. We'll respond with individual weapons only. Crew serves to fire on my command. Gun Two, you'll be the sole responder, but One and Three stand by. I think this is the big one. They don't have time for another attack before the 5th Cohort gets here. Fire on my order. Break. Tom, what's your situation?"//

//"Same as yours, Shana. We get fewer than you because you have control of the only door inside. They just want to keep us busy. I've got crew serves on Weapons Tight until the major attack is identified. When you hear our Ma Deuces, you'll know we're in the shit."//

//"Understood shit,"// Shana replied. //"Just try to stay alive. The Victrix is coming, somewhere out there."//

She opened the All Hands band. //"Okay, guys, fire when you get a target. Individual Weapons Free."//

She turned to look at Sergeant Stauer standing with her in the control room. "I intend to be on the line, Sergeant. That means you have the control room. I'll call for the two booby trapped walls when I want them. Use the other booby traps to best effect. I want maximum casualties."

Sergeant Stauer nodded. He wasn't all that happy having his Lieutenant out in front of him, but, at this time and place, that was where she belonged. The men had to know she was with them, in control no matter what. "You'll get them, Lieutenant." He paused for a second and looked her squarely in the eyes. "You know booby traps aren't going to stop them. That's half a legion or better out there and they'll just soak it up and keep pushing troops at us."

She returned his look and gave him a little smile. "I know, but damned if I'm going to let these bastards think it bothers me."

She stopped and thought for a moment then her face got a slightly surprised expression. "You know, Sergeant. It really *doesn't* bother me. I feel like I was born to do this."

Sergeant Stauer snorted. "Well, Lord Above, Lieutenant, welcome to the Corps!"

He stepped closer and his voice got low. "Nobody in the Victrix ever doubted you were a Gladius, Shana. You shouldn't. You're right. This was what you were born to do. It's what we were all born to do. Now go and make us proud. Make that damned old bastard of a Sergeant Major proud. And I'm proud to have served with you, Sim. You're a damned good combat officer. Now go."

Shana's eyes widened and she felt herself blushing. Blushing! That was a hell of a thing for the commander of a besieged fortification to do! "Thanks, Sergeant. Now, someone out there is going to rue the day I joined the Corps," she said with an evil grin.

She lowered her helmet visor and headed out of the control room to the firing positions. Smythe materialized from somewhere and fell in behind her. "Got my back?" she shot over her shoulder. Old question, by now.

"Aye, Lieutenant!" Good enough.

The first trickle of Guardsmen was swelling into a stream flowing towards the warehouse. To an untrained or unaided observer, the growing mass of refractive armor camouflage in the street would create a strange shimmer that began to slowly fill the area between buildings like an invisible wave. To Shana and her men, looking out of upper level firing slits, individual Guards were obvious, as much by what wasn't there as by what was. As Shana watched, the stream became a flood. //"All right, everyone,"// she said on the All Hands band, //"this is the big one. They're coming. Break, Gun Two, commence fire."//

The stream of heavy bolts headed down range at the 600 rounds per minute cyclic rate of the M2. The gun was deliberately targeted along the right hand side of the avenue of approach, causing the oncoming Guards to drift left. That wasn't something veteran troops would do, but these guys weren't veterans. Unless they survived this day. If they did, she wouldn't. Best make sure the Guard didn't get veterans from this little meeting.

Sergeant Stauer was reading her mind. Piles of rubble in the street suddenly detonated their concealed loads of demo, further packing the attackers to the left, up against one of the booby trapped walls.

She watched carefully, trying to judge the moment. It was hard, given Guard refractive armor and the fact her position was already taking incoming fire. The Guard was starting to fill the entire street, not from tactics but simply because so many of them were using the same avenue of approach. They couldn't use other streets. Those would channel them away from her. Shana snorted in disbelief. This was something she never thought she'd see. A real honest to Heaven human wave attack. Those were supposed to be impossible with modern weapons, but that was a book the Guard had never read. She knew the logic. Lose a cohort - or two - or three - and kill two platoons worth of defenders. Guard wins. It was just that simple.

Time to make it complex. //"Blow Alpha wall, Sergeant."// Immediately, the complete wall of a warehouse behind the head of the attack wave blew outward, spreading blast, flame and shrapnel in a huge fan shaped area. Another rubble pile full of demo took out the lead group. The street was clear for a good ways back, but more were coming. The booby trapped wall was one of the Guard's defensive measures, not hers, and she only had one more like it.

The folks out there didn't seem to know about their own defenses. Possibly whatever CP did have the information wasn't available to get it to them. Or they just didn't care. Shana suspected it was both.

Suddenly, the outer wall of the bunker shook as a 4 CM bolt hit it. There was a little dust, but not much damage. The damage would start when that gun began chewing through her walls. Where was it and how the fuck did those bastards get it into firing range without being seen? Two more heavy bolts hit just to the left of her position, opening cracks, but just spreading dust and minor fragments. Ignore it. By now, the street was starting to fill. //"Gun Two, center of mass, oncoming troops."//

The M2 crew was moving from position to alternate position after every few quick bursts. That created a gap in her fire, but they had to do it. Every time they fired from one location, they'd get a 4 CM bolt back thirty or forty seconds later. It was getting noisy and dusty up here on the firing line.

The street was full again. //"Sergeant, Bravo wall."// Again, hundreds of oncoming Guards were converted to bloody flying fragments, those that weren't crisped. Another period without Guards in sight, then a whole new group filled the street. These guys were determined. Any other military force would have stopped after those losses, if only to regroup. It had to have shaken them, but they were still coming.

"Rocket!" Shana dived for the floor as the rocket hit somewhere off to one side and blew a hole in the wall. Two 4 CM bolts slammed in through the rocket hole. Missed her. A quick check and her mouth tightened in a grim expression. Another of her troops dead. Time to do something about that 4 CM.

She didn't bother to stand up.   //"Strike 1-9-6, Strike 1-2-6. Request air support. Many Guards in open. 4 CM in operation against my position. Need you to get that fuckin' gun, Captain!"//

//"Already on the way, Shana,"// Captain Gldblum answered. //"The Guard's retargeted all available AA to keep us away from the attack. They're leaving other forces uncovered to support the attack on you."//

//"Wonderful, Captain,"// she sent back.   //"Just love the idea of being important. Not all that egotistic. Wish someone else was more important, far, far away."//

Zak broke in. //"All, Scout 9127. Attacking troops are dispersed back to the jumping off point. No good targets in the attack stream unless we can hose the whole thing. Units are starting to bunch as they assemble. Will target assembly area. Notify incoming birds, will transmit target and coordinate strike."//

//"Aye, 9127."// It was Captain Gldblum. Thirty seconds later, he added, //"Alert sent to birds. They're ready for data."//

//"Target sent."//

Shana stood up and looked out the firing slit.   About a half kilomeasure away, rubble went skyward over a large area. Cluster bomb. Then she saw the flash in the sky. The fighter that had dropped the bomb was gone. AA. The 4 CM gun was quiet. They must have gotten it. For small favors...

There were starting to be more eruptions in the area around her building, and more of her air support dying. The air strike was killing Guards before they could be launched at her, but that still left the little problem of a thousand or so very active and determined Guardsmen that were out there and still coming. Coming very close, in fact.

//"Guns One and Three, Weapons Free. Open fire."//

Another rocket hit. //"The door's gone!"//

//"Keep up the fire, all,"// she said in terse, quick words as she headed to the now wide open entrance to her position. //"Team one with me. Six, back us up. Everyone take firing positions to protect entrance once you get there."//

Back from the door, Sergeant Stauer and Corporal Chofal were already in position. "The control room's pretty well useless now that we've fired everything," the Sergeant said with a wolf-like grin. "No need for surveillance, either." He fired a burst out the gaping hole where the barricaded entrance used to be. "We know where the bastards are."

#####

330

The airstrike was a fighter squadron reinforced by several shuttles that currently didn't have a job. The fighters had already dropped on targets given them by the strike coordinator and it was now the shuttles' turn. Assault shuttles weren't quite as lively as fighters. They made up for it with better armor, heavier weapons, and pilots that were certifiably insane once they touched the controls. Warrant Officer Third Class Tim Maxell was, as was tradition, certifiably insane. He'd been doing ground support all day, the alternate mission of a shuttle, and was still hot to do more. No bombs left, but there were four 4 CM guns in the nose of his shuttle that still had ammunition.

He followed the targeting data given by the strike coordinator and sailed in just over the tops of the buildings behind the main bunker, low enough to clip the odd antenna or reception dish. His EFO was busy keeping a wide variety of unfriendly attention distracted, but Tim was concentrated on his gun target line. There, range and target good. He triggered a long burst that cut a 100 measure furrow out of the street running to the warehous and the Guard troops supposed to be in it.

Tim was just coming up on the remains of the reported assembly area when he shot a glance at his ground screen and blanched. There were more troops in one place than he'd ever seen outside of a troop carrier. He dropped the nose of his shuttle slightly and depressed his trigger just as an 8.8 CM AA bolt from somewhere caught the underside of his shuttle, blasting a huge hole behind his flight deck and killing his EFO. He only had a second to realize he was also dying and shove his stick down all the way. Tim's dying command brought the shuttle slamming down just to the front of the assembly area, skidding into the crowded Guards and tumbling forward like an avalanche. The shuttle wreckage skewed as it skidded along the ground, shedding flame, sparks, pieces, and many dead Guardsmen, finally wedging itself between two heavy walls, still exploding. The shuttle killed hundreds of Guards and effectively blocked hundreds more from reaching the bunker, but there were still over five hundred Guard survivors nearly at the perimeter wall.

That should have stopped the attack cold, but it didn't. There was no longer a realistic chance the Guard could complete its mission, but they were fanatics, becoming ever more worked up and frenzied. Nothing mattered now but taking the bunker.

#####

Shana watched as the Guards were starting to clamber over the perimeter wall now, slipping on the gory bodies of their own people as they came and making perfect targets. That was the real purpose of the wall, to create a moment of helplessness for the attacker. 2d Platoon took full advantage of that moment. Two of the Ma Deuces were still firing, and their crossfire was reaping Guards like wheat in a field.

Rockets were hitting the building's face constantly. Concussion and fragmentation were having their way. There were more casualties, but her remaining troops were taking toll.

"Rocket!" Shana suddenly found herself spun to the ground and felt the rocket detonate just at the slit where she'd been. Smythe again.

"Thanks, Smythe," she said shakily and started to get up. Smythe didn't get off of her. She craned around and saw a large chunk of metal sticking out of the back of Smythe's armor. She didn't have anyone at her back anymore. She gently moved the youngster's body then grimly went back to the fight. The Guards were starting to reach the entrance and she shot the first one that appeared. There were more coming. //"Strike 1-9-6, 2-6. I'm getting visitors. Got any more air assets?"//

//"1-9-6. Hang on, Shana, help's coming."//

//"It better get here soon, triple damn it!"//

Shana shot the next Guard and Sergeant Stauer got the two followers.

Colonel Albt Lumis was fully in his element. There were better than a legion's worth of Guard units piled up in front of him. Like all random collections, the Guard units weren't fighting in coordinated fashion but they made up for it in ferocity. //"Pile on, 5th!"// he sent all hands. //"Pile on and kick ass! We're going to kick our way through this unholy mob of trash!"//

5th Cohort had absorbed the bull-like hard hitting style of its commander. They were no longer cutting their way through the Guards like a buzz saw. They were smashing like a pile driver. Albt studied his HUD with satisfaction. Just about time for his spear to drive through the sons of bitches in front of him and link up with the Strike platoons. He summoned up that spear. //"Faire 6, 5-9-6. Time to go. Crashed shuttle will inhibit your main avenue of attack, but that's it. Effect link up with those platoons, Colonel Frodi. They need you."//

//"Aye, Colonel Lumis. Don't fash yourself about the blockage. We'll go over it. Through it if we have to."//

Colonel Frodi changed bands. //"Scaanians, now is OUR time. Forward! Forward into the enemy! Teach the Guard to fear the elves!"//

The whole battalion knew how the Cluster folk looked at them. Elves. They'd all seen the illustrations and had to admit to a resemblance.

On the whole, they thought the idea funny. However, they also knew there once was an ancient belief that elves were deadly; elves were to be feared. Now was the time to prove the truth of that old belief.

The battalion started forward, their armored suits at half speed as they built momentum, using the modified weave taught them by Lieutenant Ettranty and her sergeant. When they reached the point of full contact between the 5th and the Guard they didn't break stride. Speed was safety. They simply kept going as they slammed into the Guard, firing as they went. //"Faster, men,"// Frodi commanded. //"As we did in the old days when we were mounted. Forward at a gallop."//

The suits were moving faster, firing and weaving as they ran, a spear piercing deep into the enemy's body.

//"Ready... ready... Charge! Charge! Let none survive your passing!"// The suits were at full speed.

Bolt guns mounted on their armor served for much of the battalion's killing as they thrust into the rear of the Guards massed to attack Shana's position - but their huge swords were there to be used, and the battalion used them. Swords were more satisfying than guns, anyhow. Swords they knew well.

Frodi admired the Brusharas of the Corps. He'd heard them when the legions landed and had an idea. It was no trick to have his suit's loudspeaker generate a horn sound, even if it wasn't the deafening blast of a Brushara. Frodi's sounded more like the hunting horns of Faire. Skinning his lips back over his teeth in a fierce grin, he triggered his horn again, to hear others copy the sound and cast it forth. The Faire battalion's horns sounded warm brassy tones, all singing alike. The horns of Elfland proclaimed the coming of the Scaanians, the deadly elves. Let all hear and beware.

Frodi thundered forward through dying Guardsmen, slowing as the smashed remains of the Strike defense came into view. His men split as they passed down both sides of the building. One company ran head on into the Guards attacking 4th Platoon, scattering the attackers by pure shock effect. Other companies spread out and started to clear the area, still in the weave and still at speed. There was little resistance. What Guards they found appeared demoralized and stunned... before they died. There was no quarter for the Emperor's Guard.

Frodi slowed to a walk, striding slowly through the wide breach blown into the defensive wall. There were Guard bodies piled in the ditch behind the wall, piled high enough that he could walk on them to cross the gap. He did. Slowly, he surveyed the front of the armored building, noting the many craters and gaps that now covered its exterior and the carpet of Guard bodies surrounding an entrance gaping like the maw of some huge beast. Here was a fight, he thought, a fight for poets to sing of for a hundred, no, a thousand years. There was no activity outside the building and he reached over his shoulder to sheath the bloody sword he was holding. It wasn't needed. The attackers had spent themselves trying to take the bunker.

Inside the entrance, there were more bodies, Guard and Gladius intermingled in death. Blood and rubble everywhere. One Gladius faced him, his armor scorched from near misses and covered in blood. He was standing over the armor clad body of another lying on the floor. The Gladius raised his visor and lowered his B-42 as he saw Frodi and read his identity code. When he spoke, his voice was tired, but still professionally level. He spoke in low tones, as though he was in a church. "Sergeant First Class Stauer, Colonel. Glad to see you again."

Frodi looked at the body Sergeant Stauer straddled. It was missing a right lower leg and there were scorch marks and small holes in several places on the armor. The holes weren't oozing blood. The body might have been bled out. Then Frodi remembered Gladius armor had the ability to staunch wounds. Whoever it was could still be alive. Dead Guardsmen surrounded the pair, some slashed into pieces by an ax, probably the ax lying near the still hand of the fallen figure. "Who?" he asked.

Sergeant Stauer took a deep breath and spoke with pride. "My Lieutenant. Lieutenant Shana Ettranty and one hell of a soldier. She held, Colonel. She held until relieved."

CHAPTER-18

CLUSTER FLEET
IN ORBIT AROUND CENTRAL

Legate Karl Athan, Legate of the 9th Legion Victrix and lauded as one of the conquerors of the Empire, meekly followed the slim Nurse Candidate down the hospital ship passageway. The girl was barely into her twenties, but she'd already informed him in no uncertain terms that she expected him to abide by visiting rules and not tire her patient, on pain of annihilation of cosmic proportions. Karl was sufficiently intimidated to readily agree. Besides, he'd already heard that Legion Sergeant Major Olmeg had bumped heads with this particular nurse and bounced. Very formidable young lady.

Things were anything but settled down on the planet. A few fake "Emperors" popped up, at least in the beginning, but it was becoming general knowledge that the Cluster had Shangnaman's stasis cabinet in custody. Also becoming general knowledge were the inhuman crimes that insane bastard had committed on the people of Central. Publicizing Shangnaman's "Trophy Room" with its human skins and necklaces of fingernails shook Central as much as the announcement about the death camps and murder squads.

But fake emperors were going out of fashion fast, since they had a tendency to be found dismembered if the wrong people got to them first. Being recognized as part of the old Imperial order was frequently good for a lynching. The Cluster didn't have the forces to involve itself in such free assemblies of citizenry.

Other troublemakers were also beginning to show a marked disinclination to hostile activity. Major incidents tended to bring down a Corps century or two to sort out the problem, with fatal consequences to the guilty once the entire mess was brought under control and everyone run through an Imperial lie detector.

Karl was grimly certain that low grade incidents would continue for some time, at least until Randl Turner's political teams, led by Clarine Femiam, could stabilize the situation. At that point, it would be turned over to the Army and those luckless bastards in the III Augusta until whatever Middle Empire finally turned into was on its own feet. Meanwhile it was relatively quiet, so he'd turned over his Inbox to his

Assistant Legate for Operations and told the AL(O) that he was heading out to the Fleet, to return whenever.

He had a very important visit to make, and he was just about at the door of the hospital room where he was going to make that visit. He walked meekly past the ferocious scowl on the nurse's pretty features and entered alone. The unmoving figure in the bed in front of him was patched in a variety of places and hooked up to infernal medical devices in several more. Karl knew the feeling. He'd been there himself a time or two.

Spent some time in an Intensive Care cabinet, also. Not as much time as Sergeant Major Olmeg. The crusty old decurion had the Legion record for time in an IC cabinet. Any Gladius regarded an IC cabinet as an occupational hazard, so here she was, just out of one. Just like one of the boys... again.

The figure didn't move, but the nurse told him she was awake when he arrived. Start out cheery. That was usually irritating enough to get a lively response. "Hi, darling," he said pleasantly, "I understand you're feeling better."

"Who the hell says so?" Shana growled back in a soft, fatigued voice. "Just lying here letting these nannies work on the holes in my body is exhausting, damn it. Much less regrowing my leg. That's a bitch all by itself."

"Well, you were sure shot to hell," Karl said wryly. "Shouldn't be much scarring, but it's a good thing you kept your ass down. Yours is too nice to mark up."

Shana scowled out at him through the shimmering sterile field that surrounded her hospital bed. "Thanks so much for the kind words, Legate," she said. Her voice, hell, her whole body felt weak! Thing was, she had to agree with his comments, except about her rear end. She thought it was too big. "Sergeant Major Olmeg has already been by. He said getting shot up was no big thing, so get off my butt and stop goofing off."

"I'd say we ought to name a child after him," Karl mused, "but I doubt any kid would want to go through life named Old Bastard."

She had to laugh, even if it hurt. Her body was reminding her that she'd done enough to it for a while, thank you, and it needed a little time off to heal. On the other hand, Karl was making her feel better. He always did. One of the reasons she was planning to lock him down in marriage at the first opportunity. She gave him a smile.

"You know," Karl said softly, just happy to see that treasured knowing smile after he'd come so close to losing her, "I'd hug you except that dragon of a nurse candidate threatened me with molecular disruption if I so much as put a finger inside the sterile field."

"She's Lana Femiam, the Narsim Femiam's daughter if you can believe it, and Sergeant Kardo's fiancee," Shana replied. "Kardo came through, just as shot up as I was and down the hall in another IC cabinet. Chofal survived too, just not badly wounded. Almost all of my men were wounded or killed."

She felt tears start. "Smythe had my back. And he was killed for it. More than half of them were. I led them all to it, Karl. I was in command." Damn these mood swings!

Karl's voice took on a professionally hard edge. "Yes, you did. You led them. You led them into a battle that saved a quarter million babies and took the heart out of the Guard while you did it.

"Look at me, Lieutenant," he said forcefully. "You happened to survive this one. Other officers take their men into death ground. Some of those officers don't survive. Others do and have to live with the memory of dead troops. That's you. It's a part of what we do. It's a part of what makes us soldiers. The survivors have to go on and keep doing their duty. Death, the Gladius Price, that's just part of the job. The men in your platoon were volunteers. Most of the Corps was in that meat grinder down there because they happened to be born a Gladius, but every Gladius, volunteer or not, went willingly because they were doing a mission they'd sworn to do. You can flog yourself over it if you want, but you'll let your men down if you do. The Corps lost more men in Central than at any time in our history, Shana, nearly enough to make up a full legion. Hell, I lost almost a cohort's worth of troops in addition to yours, every one of them my people. I have to live with that. You have to live with your losses. We both do. We have to keep on doing our duty because the people we lead expect us to do it. They rely on us. Don't you let them down."

She looked at him for a long moment, saying nothing. Just looking. "The Sergeant Major said much the same thing, but it sounded more like an order from him. Don't worry, I understand all of it. That doesn't take away my right to grieve over my dead.

"They were MY men, damn it!" she yelled. "I led them! I was responsible for them!"

"And when the time came, you had to use them," Karl replied softly. "That's what being an officer means at bottom, Shana. That's why we have the pretty pips and diamonds on our uniforms. By the virtue of our rank, we have to use whatever and whoever we have when the mission calls for it."

Shana took a deep breath and settled her head deeper into her pillow, calming down, ordering herself to relax. Karl was right and she knew it. "Yes," she said quietly, "and we pay the Price for it. The Price is so much more than dying. I wish it wasn't so, but that's a part of being a Gladius. It's a part of our oath and I'll never take the Oath lightly after Central.

"I'm going back on duty when I'm out of here, Karl. I'm going back and I'm going to keep on going into places where angels fear to tread because I believe deep down in my soul in what that oath means," she finished.

"Aye," Karl answered her then changed a subject that needed to be changed. "Meanwhile, when do you want to get married?"

She looked wryly down at her half leg hidden under the sheet. "When I can stand on my own two feet. Hope you don't mind a few scars next time I get naked with you."

He grinned. "As long as you don't mind mine. Besides, the doctors say you won't have any loss of leg function this time. Just don't keep getting pieces shot off or you'll end up like Sergeant Major Olmeg."

"I won't - not unless I have to," she replied firmly. "Besides... have you thought about children?"

"Yes, I have," he lied gallantly. "When do you want to have them?"

"I thought about it down there and a lot more since I woke up. I'll make Major one of these days. Too high for Strike. Staff job. We'll have one then." She continued calmly, "I've also asked that two of the fetus tubes be held for me. After those two, I want another one or two with you."

That shook him. A child was one thing, but the idea of raising a big family scared him more than finding out he had five whole legions of the Emperor's Guard to tackle. Shana had ambitious plans and, knowing her, they were going to happen. "You sure?" he asked warily.

She nodded firmly. "Yes. Five kids, at least." She took a closer look at Karl's face. "Well, maybe four." A soft smile spread across her face, a smile that got a loving response from her fiancee.

Then she got the look that marked her as ready to fight. "Karl, we both know the universe could blot us away in an instant and it's already tried to do just that. Shana Ettranty is telling the universe that it can try all the hell it wants. I'm taking on the damned universe the same way I took on the Guard. You're going to help me in that fight, Legate - you, and as many members of the next generation as I can produce. I want a big family because I want as big an impact on the universe as I can have. Every damn one of us is going to be doing just what the hell life's work we want to do, doing it with our head up, looking the universe straight in the eye and daring it to take a shot. Shana Ettranty and Karl Athan and their

338

children have a job to do, Legate, now that the Empire has fallen. There's a whole big new galaxy reorganizing out there and you and me and as many kids as you'll let me have are going to be deep in the middle of it."

"Take your best shot, asshole," Karl said with a grin. The idea behind Shana's plans appealed to him. "If I don't get you, my brother - or sister, or mother, or father - will. Gladius attitude, Shana my love."

She grinned back. "Damn right, lover. I'm Gladius and never forget it. Take a swing at me and I swing back. Harder."

She grew serious again. "Karl, when we get married I'm keeping my name. One of the boys will have the Ettranty name also. It won't die with me."

"This is about your father?"

Shana nodded with effort. She was still barely able to move. "Yes. Sergeant Major Olmeg once told me to make the Ettranty name a name of honor. I'm going to do just that, and so will our son. Whatever he does. None of our children will follow us into the Corps unless they want to do it. I don't want to be breeding hereditary soldiers."

"You don't have to worry about that," Karl said. "The SOC is going to issue a general order soon making membership in the Corps voluntary. The ones that want to leave the Corps can go to the Exploration Project or do something else. We'll be recruiting from the general population from here on in, looking for people just like you. No more hereditary soldiers unless Gladius children volunteer when they come of age."

"Good," Shana replied. "I'm glad. Let those that have had enough leave. They've done more than their part. No more recruits born into a legion, either. I'm glad about that also. You have to *want* to do the kind of job we have in front of us.

"But I'm staying," she added, "just like you. The Corps has to exist as long as there are things out there that want to prey on normal everyday people. Those everyday people have to know there's someone that will stand between them and the Predator, no matter what it costs. They have to know there's someone that scares the bloody hell out of the Predator and will come after him and keep coming until he's destroyed utterly. That's what the Corps is. That's me, too.

"I'm living the life I was born to live, Karl. That's why I held my position in Imperial City and why I'll hold another one again someday if I have to do it. I'll do it because our children deserve to grow up free of fear. I'll do it because everyone's children deserve to grow up free of fear.

"I'm a soldier and I'm proud of it."

AFTERWORD

There is a lot of music in this story, all of it old, some of it very old. Every song listed is available on YouTube. Please ignore the videos and the commentary from the usual Internet "experts" when you listen. They're irrelevant to the thoughts evoked in my mind when I heard the music. Here is a partial list of key songs:

We Don't Need Another Hero, Tina Turner (Overture. Listen to the words.)

Bury My Lovely, October Project (Chapter 1, the attack)

Le Boudin, French Foreign Legion Traditional - slow tempo (Chapter 2, end of a long march)

The Carnival is Over, The Seekers (route march)

Burning Bridges, Mike Curb Congregation (Chapter 3, Trooping the Line)

Welcome Me Love, Brooklyn Bridge (Chapter 3, Pass in Review; End of Chapter 18)

Eyn Mol, The Kelzmatics (Throughout)

Dark Time, October Project (Chapter 8, the dance)

Gimme Shelter, The Rolling Stones (Chapter 14, war dance)

Winter Born, Cruxshadows (Chapter 17, before the final battle, with thanks to John Ringo)

Citadel, Cruxshadows (same as above, especially the thanks)

The Gladio, sung to the music of Gaudete by Steeleye Span

Made in United States
Orlando, FL
04 September 2022

21986021R00205